Give the Devil His Due

PanteraPress

From **nurturing** the **NEXT** GENERATION *of best-loved* **authors** ➤ (TO) CHAMPIONING **LITERACY** *AND THE* **joys** OF **READING** we're (all about) **great storytelling**!

Give the Devil His Due

Book 7 in the Award-Winning Rowland Sinclair Mysteries

SULARI GENTILL

PanteraPress
great storytelling

PanteraPress
great storytelling

First published in 2015 by Pantera Press Pty Limited
Second edition published in 2017 by Pantera Press Pty Limited
www.PanteraPress.com

Please send all permission queries to:
Pantera Press, P.O. Box 1989 Neutral Bay, NSW 2089 Australia or info@PanteraPress.com

A Cataloguing-in-Publication entry for this book is available from the National Library
of Australia.

ISBN 978-1-921997-83-9

Cover Design: Sofya Karmazina
Typesetting by Kirby Jones
Printed and bound in Australia by McPherson's Printing Group
Author Photo by Erica Murray Photography

Pantera Press policy is to use papers that are natural, renewable and recyclable products made from wood grown
in sustainable forests. The logging and manufacturing processes are expected to conform to the environmental
regulations of the country of origin.

To my husband, Michael, who in a less fuel-injected,
power-windowed, air-bagged era,
was the undisputed king of the car yard.

1

DASHED TO DEATH

MAROUBRA SPEEDWAY SENSATION

SYDNEY, Monday

The Maroubra speedway has claimed another victim. R. G. (Phil) Garlick, well-known racing driver, dashed over the embankment, crashed into an electric light standard and was then hurled 20 feet to his death during the final of the All Powers Handicap on Saturday night.

Garlick was trying to pass Hope Bartlett and was travelling at 93 miles an hour when the car swerved and left the track. He was dead when help arrived.

The dreadful fatality is the sole topic among motorists today. There is a difference of opinion as to the safety of the track, but the view is held that it is necessary to make some alterations in order to obviate the likelihood of any further accidents of a similar nature.

The Richmond River Express and
Casino Kyogle Advertiser, 1927

Rowland Sinclair's dealings with the press were rarely so civil. To date, his appearances in the pages of Sydney's newspapers had been, at best, reluctant, and more frequently, the subject of legal proceedings for libel. On this occasion, however, Rowland's conversation with Crispin White of *Smith's Weekly* began most cordially.

The reporter was, in fact, the fourth whom Rowland had received that day. Heavily built, White's broad, lax countenance belied the wily acuity of his manner. A newshound who resembled a somewhat over-fed lap dog, but a newshound nonetheless.

Crispin White had written about the wealthy young artist before. He'd covered the various skirmishes and scandals in which the gentleman had become embroiled over the preceding years. More recently he'd reported on Rowland Sinclair's arrest for murder, though the charges had been dropped and the story conveniently buried on page twelve when the family's solicitors had contacted his editor. White might have been bitter if he were not so intrigued by the polite, unassuming man who seemed to somehow wield the might of the establishment without abiding by any of its rules.

Woodlands House, where White was calling on Sinclair, had once been among the premier homes of Sydney's better suburbs, a sandstone declaration of tradition, privilege and stately decorum. These days, however, the Woollahra mansion and its acreage were rumoured to be teeming with naked women and Communists. Regrettably, White had not been able to verify that personally, having been met at the gatehouse by a servant and escorted directly to the converted stables where his subject was waiting.

Though he could not attest to the state of the main house, the reporter had noted the nude sculptures that challenged decency throughout the grounds—urns with breasts, naked nymphs and lovers entwined in the fountain. All very fine indeed, and exquisitely improper.

White's pencil scratched quickly to capture an impression of Sinclair himself. Tall, athletic build, clean cut—good jawline despite the determination of the upper classes to breed out chins—dark hair, and blue eyes... startlingly, intensely blue. They would print a photograph with the article of course, but the writer's words would be the only thing to convey colour. Sinclair wore a dark grey three-piece suit, expensively tailored. There was a conspicuous smear of yellow paint on the sleeve, and several on the waistcoat.

Rowland offered Crispin White his hand. "Rowland Sinclair, Mr. White. How d'you do?"

If White's hand had not been in Rowland's grip, he would have duly recorded that Sinclair's handshake was both firm and single handed. His inflection was certainly refined but not excessively so, and his smile, slightly bashful.

"I am sorry to receive you out here," Rowland apologised. "It must seem a little irregular, but I thought you might like to see the old girl." He stood back to allow White to behold the gleaming yellow 1927 Mercedes S-Class.

The reporter walked around the vehicle, making the admiring noises that were clearly expected. In a few weeks, Rowland Sinclair would take his prized automobile out on the notorious Maroubra Speedway—for a charity race in aid of the Red Cross. Plainly, Sinclair believed the motorcar deserved equal billing in any media profile.

"German engineering." There was a slight reproach in White's voice, an unspecified criticism.

Those blue eyes regarded him sharply. "Yes," Rowland said. "The Germans make excellent automobiles."

"It's never bothered you then...?" White asked, identifying an angle and pursuing it now. "I believe you lost a brother in the Great War didn't you, Mr. Sinclair?"

"Aubrey, from what I remember, was not shot by a Mercedes, Mr. White."

"But how would he feel about his brother driving a German motorcar, Mr. Sinclair?"

Rowland sighed. "I think you'll find the war is over."

"I understand you were in Germany last year," White continued. "Is that when you acquired your vehicle?"

"No. I won her in a card game when I was at Oxford."

White's face lifted. This was good. "You don't say! So you're not averse to a game of chance, Mr. Sinclair?"

"I don't know that poker is a game of chance. Not if it's played well."

"But you don't object to a wager?"

Rowland paused and studied the reporter. He laughed suddenly, shaking his head. "Just what are you trying to get me to say, Mr. White?"

The reporter's smile was sly. "Something wicked would do very nicely, Mr. Sinclair."

"Why?"

"Every contest needs a villain to stir emotion and get the public involved—someone to boo and hiss. It's all part of the show."

"And you've decided the villain ought to be me?"

"Well, you are driving the German car."

Rowland couldn't quite tell whether Crispin White was in earnest.

White grinned. "Just pulling yer leg, sir, but you understand your car may upset the odd digger. I'm not prejudiced myself, but some folks don't see it that way."

"Quite." Rowland leaned back against the mudguard of his car, his arms folded as he tried to discern just how badly this interview was going.

White tapped the lead of his pencil against the notebook. "So, tell me Mr. Sinclair, how did you get involved in this charity race caper?"

"My mother," he replied, thankful the reporter was moving on. "She's a patron of the Red Cross."

White made a note. "Can't fault a man who loves his mother," he said with a breathy note of disappointment.

"Mr. White, if it is necessary to portray me as some kind of melodrama villain, I'm sure you'll need to look no further than the archives of your paper." Rowland couldn't help but be slightly amused by the reporter's approach.

"Are you asking me to leave, Mr. Sinclair?"

"Not at all. We could continue to stand here while you ask ridiculous questions, or you could join me at the house for a liquid refreshment."

White's large head bounced from side to side as he considered the proposition. "A drink you say? Inside the house?"

Rowland smiled. He could see that White had not yet given up on uncovering a scandal. One had to admire the man's commitment. "If you'd care to follow me, Mr. White?"

White did indeed care to do so, and they walked amiably to the conservatory via the meandering wisteria walk. "Good Lord, they're women!" the reporter murmured, reaching out to touch the cast posts that supported the arched iron trellis upon which the wisteria was trained. He pulled his hand back hastily when it came too close to the small pert breasts of one elongated figure.

"You can touch it," Rowland said, entertained by White's reaction. "Miss Higgins' work is designed to be handled." He ran his fingers over the curve of a sculpted hip in demonstration. "She likes to try out ideas here before she finalises a commission. You'll find a walkway strikingly similar to this one, though somewhat bigger, at the Botanical Gardens in Adelaide."

"Miss Higgins resides here, then?" White asked, puffing to keep pace with Rowland's long stride. Of course, he knew full well that Edna Higgins was a member of the hedonistic artistic set who had taken up residence at *Woodlands House* where they lived at Sinclair's expense. Some said she was his mistress, an opportunistic Communist siren with her eyes not only on Rowland Sinclair's fortune, but his political soul.

Rowland's response was brief and affirmative, his tone warned against any attempt to pursue the enquiry.

He offered White one of the wicker armchairs that furnished the conservatory through which they entered the house. The early evening was decidedly crisp but the room caught the fading light. Sunset bathed the parquetry floor in a warm glow, and patterned it with a lace of shadows thrown by fretwork brackets.

"I'm famished," Rowland said, pulling on the servants' bell. "Are you hungry, Mr. White?"

"Oh... I... Yes, I am actually," White said, surprised by the invitation. Sinclair seemed an exceedingly unaffected sort of chap, but perhaps he was trying to sway the coverage in his favour. Well, he'd find that Crispin White was not going to lose his objectivity so easily.

Rowland's summons was answered by a strong, straight woman, well into middle age, whom he called Mary. She addressed him as Master Rowly, as if he were a child, and when he told her that Mr. White would be joining him for dinner, she responded with a sigh.

"Since it's just the two of us, we might eat in here, Mary."

The housekeeper shook her head firmly. "Mr. Watson Jones telephoned to say he and Miss Higgins will be back for dinner after all, Master Rowly."

"Oh." Rowland glanced at White. He hadn't intended to give the press quite so much access to his personal life, but it was probably too late now to withdraw the invitation. "I guess we'll have to use the dining room then."

"I'm not sure when exactly they intend to come in, sir."

"I daresay they'll be back directly." Rowland responded to the unspoken complaint in Mary Brown's voice. The housekeeper believed tardiness to be a symptom of ill-breeding. "Mr. White and I might have a drink while we wait."

All this White dutifully recorded in his notebook.

A large misshapen greyhound padded into the conservatory, pausing to nuzzle Rowland's hand before turning to investigate his guest.

"Lenin's harmless," Rowland said when White pulled back.

"I've heard Lenin called many things but never harmless," White muttered as the bony one-eared dog tried to climb into his lap.

"Len, lay down," Rowland commanded, handing the reporter a glass of sherry.

The hound obeyed, settling at Rowland's feet with a distinct air of indignation.

"So, tell me, Mr. Sinclair,"—White was all business again—"have you raced before?"

"No," Rowland admitted. "But this is a charity invitational. I'm hoping at least a few of the other drivers will be equally inept."

"Well-heeled men with supercharged cars and no sense. A certain recipe for disaster, wouldn't you say?"

"It's for a jolly good cause, Mr. White."

"I don't suppose you're bothered by rumours that the Maroubra Speedway is cursed?"

"Cursed?" Rowland laughed. "My good man, you can't be serious?"

"Seven men have lost their lives on the circuit—it's been called the killer track."

"Rowly, where are you?" A woman's voice. White sat up. This was more like it.

Rowland stood and called into the vestibule adjoining the main hallway. "In here, Ed."

Despite rumours that the women at *Woodlands House* were customarily naked, the young lady who walked in was attired—a plain green frock, not drab yet certainly not the latest style. But she could well have worn a sack... indeed, the simplicity of her dress only served to accentuate the fact that she was beautiful—unusually, unforgettably so. There was a complete lack of self-consciousness in the way she moved: a natural informal grace. She'd already removed her hat, shaking out tresses of burnished copper as she greeted Sinclair with casual warmth.

White swallowed, hastily closing his notebook as he stood. Rowland introduced him to Miss Edna Higgins and Mr. Clyde Watson Jones.

It was only at that point that White even noticed Watson Jones— solid, sturdy with a face that wore the years plainly and the calloused hands of a worker. "Sorry we're so late, Rowly." Clyde helped himself to sherry. "Ed came across some bloke trying to drown a sack of kittens and their mother in the harbour. She insisted I rescue them... wanted me to thump the bloke too—"

"Oh do stop complaining, Clyde. You didn't even get wet!" Edna said, perching on the arm of Rowland's chair.

"Where are they?" Rowland asked. "These felines that Clyde liberated."

Edna directed her smile at Rowland. "Out in the tack room," she said. The old tack shed near the stables had served as Edna's studio for some years now. "Clyde thought we should give you a chance to tell Mary before we brought them into the kitchen. She's still cross about Lenin."

Rowland blanched. His housekeeper did not approve of his tendency to give refuge to what she called "ill-bred strays".

The Red Flag, sung stridently, boomed down the hallway.

"Good! Milt's back," Rowland said. "I'm ravenous."

The revolutionary anthem grew louder and a second voice became discernible, female, thin and tentative with the words. Milton Isaacs walked in laughing with an elderly woman on his arm. He was not a subtle presence, with dark hair that fell long to his purple velvet lapel, under which sat a carefully knotted gold cravat. His companion was elegantly dressed in a tweed skirt suit, her soft white hair coiffed neatly beneath a brown felt hat.

The seated gentlemen stood. "Mother," Rowland said, alarmed. He did not want White's profile on him to invade his mother's privacy.

"Aubrey, my darling, I've had the most thrilling afternoon with your Mr. Isaacs." Elisabeth Sinclair resided in her own wing of *Woodlands House*, with her own staff, including three private nurses. She had for some time been suffering from a malady of mind that often left her confused and distressed. Elisabeth had forgotten a great deal, including the existence of her youngest son, insisting instead that Rowland was his late brother, Aubrey. Some days were worse than others. Today, however, she seemed well. Her cheeks were infused with rosy colour and she beamed like an excited girl. "We've been to a splendid show at the Domain!"

"It wasn't really a show, Mrs. Sinclair—" Milton began.

"May I introduce Mr. Crispin White from *Smith's Weekly*." Rowland interrupted before Milton could reveal that he'd taken Elisabeth Sinclair to a Communist Party rally. "Mr. White will be our guest for dinner."

Milton frowned as he regarded the reporter. "Crispin?"

"Elias Isaacs… I didn't know… Hello," White pulled at the already loosened knot in his tie.

Rowland's brow rose. It appeared the reporter was well enough acquainted with Milton to know his real name. The reunion did not appear to be a fond one, but neither seemed about to elaborate.

"Will you be joining us tonight, Mother?" he asked.

"I believe I shall decline, darling. I've had such an exciting afternoon with Mr. Isaacs, I think I might need a quiet night. I'll leave you young people to it. You'll all forgive me my old age, I hope?"

"Of course," Rowland said, relieved.

"I have drunken deep of joy, and I will taste no other wine tonight," Milton proclaimed, turning his back on White to escort the old lady from the conservatory.

"Shelley," Rowland said quietly. Milton's reputation as a poet was built principally on a talent for quoting the works of the romantic bards and a practice of not actually attributing the words. He didn't seem to feel obliged to write anything himself. Rowland smiled as he heard his mother object, "I don't think a small glass of cognac before bed will do me any harm, Mr. Isaacs."

Edna glanced at Rowland. The tension between Milton and White had been unmistakable. She shrugged slightly, clearly unaware of its cause and taking White's arm, she allowed their guest to escort her to dinner.

The reporter paused as they entered the dining room, gazing at the high walls around him with undisguised awe. Stylised figures and intricate patterns were defined with white paint on a background of black—naked women, mythical beasts, peacocks given movement in the candlelight. Every square inch of the walls was rendered in this way. It was ethereally beautiful and startling.

"Is this...? Did you paint—?"

"It was a collaboration," Rowland said, pulling out a chair for Edna. "An experiment of sorts."

"I feel a little like I've stepped through the looking glass." White sat down, glancing over his shoulder. "I must say it's the first time I'll have dinner with the devil."

Edna laughed. "Oh I'm sure that's not true, Mr. White!" She patted his arm reassuringly. "You're a newspaperman after all. And that's not the devil, you know. It's a faun. Rowly was having a phase with mythology."

"I trust you're not planning to report that Rowland Sinclair has a painting of the devil in his dining room, Mr. White," Clyde said, clearly disturbed by the possibility.

"Yes, if Clyde's mother reads that in *Smith's Weekly* she'll drag him home by the ear!" Milton re-joined them. There was a note of wariness, a warning in the jest.

Clyde didn't bother to deny it. His mother would do that if she thought his soul was at risk… or if she knew he wasn't attending mass regularly. He leaned over to Rowland while White was distracted by Edna's explanation of the wall's design, or perhaps just by Edna herself.

"You invited a newspaper reporter to dinner?" he whispered accusingly.

"I didn't expect that any of you would be home," Rowland replied.

Milton threw an arm around Rowland's shoulder. "You're not ashamed of us are you, old chap?"

Rowland smiled. "I take it you and White are acquainted."

"A long time ago, Rowly."

"He knew you as Elias."

"And I knew him as Crispin Weissen. Perhaps he's reformed."

2

NEW GUARD

Opening of New Hall

More than 200 people attended on Saturday evening the opening of a new lecture hall acquired in Seaview Street, Dulwich Hill by the Dulwich Hill branch of the New Guard.

Captain Donald Walker, general president, said the event was a step forward in the consolidation of the New Guard in the ideals which gave birth to the movement three years ago. The three main tenets of the movement were: "God, King and Country." If the sacrifices of the men who served in the world war were remembered, the curse of Communism need not be feared. By carrying on the torch lit by the immortal dead, members of the New Guard were maintaining all that was Christian and British.

Mr. Ness M.L.A. said that the New Guard was a great moral force with 100 per cent loyal British men and women as members.

Presidents of other "localities" of the New Guard in the metropolitan area attended the meeting. Eighteen new members were enrolled and seven women joined the women's auxiliary.

The Sydney Morning Herald, 1934

After dinner, White and Rowland lingered at the table to finish the interview, while the others retired to the drawing room to play cards. By this time Crispin White was noticeably tipsy, though he did not seem to regard that as an impediment in any way. The reporter had a weakness for brandy and the quality of liquor served at *Woodlands House* was particularly fine. In the name of hospitality, Rowland joined him for another glass.

For his part, White was pleased with the evening's work. Sinclair was guarded and his friends rather protective, but still the shrewd reporter had managed to extract some interesting details. Of course some of them were not fit to print. The presence—or more accurately, the identity—of Elias Isaacs was a surprise. That Sinclair's set included a flamboyant Communist poet was known, he'd just not made the connection with Elias before. Even so, it had been over a decade, and Isaacs had been civil if not friendly. And surely the matter was better left alone. It was possibly this sense of satisfaction, fortified by brandy, that prompted the newspaperman to fling caution aside and put his final questions to Rowland.

"Tell me, Sinclair, this business with Eric Campbell—"

"What business with Mr. Campbell?" Rowland had assumed the subject would come up sooner or later. His infiltration of Campbell's New Guard had ended badly, and while Wilfred Sinclair had used all his power to keep the incident out of the papers, and his younger brother out of gaol, the rumours had survived.

"Word at the news desk is that you tried to assass… assass… kill the man," White said, rummaging in his jacket for his notebook.

"Well word is mistaken, I'm afraid."

"You didn't try to shoot him?"

"No."

"I like you, Sinclair," the reporter slurred, patting Rowland's shoulder vigorously. "I want to give you a chance to tell the world what really happened."

"Thank you, but the incident is best forgotten."

White sighed. "Of course, of course, what was I thinking? You're not going to admit to attempted murder."

"You'll find, Mr. White, that I was in fact the only person shot that night."

"That's right, that's right... Was it Campbell then? Were you fighting over leadership of the New Guard?"

Rowland's laugh was scornful. "I was never a member of the New Guard."

"Why?"

"Aside from the fact that the New Guard is made up of lunatics, my politics, such as they are, do not lie in that direction."

"Really?" White's manner seemed to sober somewhat. "My sources tell me that you have the Fascist cross tattooed on your chest, Mr. Sinclair."

Rowland stiffened. "That's incorrect," he said coldly.

"It's not a swastika then?"

"There is no tattoo." Strictly speaking, it was the truth. The swastika had been burned into Rowland's chest. The rumour, however inaccurate, took him by surprise. That it was being used to affiliate him with the Fascists mortified and infuriated him.

White did not miss the change in his subject's demeanour. Maybe Sinclair was not an admirer of the Nazis—there was the presence of Isaacs, after all. It was interesting, but the room was beginning to spin so perhaps the paradox of Rowland Sinclair would be more usefully pursued another day. Crispin White thanked Rowland for his time and his brandy—sincerely because he'd quite unexpectedly enjoyed the young man's company.

Realising that both he and his guest were compromised by their intemperance, Rowland suggested that White stay the night at *Woodlands* and drive home in the morning.

"Why that's most handsome of you, Sinclair."

"And unnecessary." Milton strode into the dining room. "I'll drive Crispin home. He'll be able to report that he rode in a Red Cross Invitational racecar, and it'll give us a chance to catch up."

"But my vehicle..." White began.

"I'll drop it back tomorrow, or you can pick it up... but there's no need for you to stop tonight."

White seemed unsettled, but he agreed.

Again Rowland noted the prevailing tension between them. It smouldered like dry kindling about to ignite. He was accustomed to Milton's temper which was often quick and hot. But this was different. Still, Milton declined any further company and whatever the issue between the two men, Crispin White did not appear dangerous.

And so Rowland bade the reporter good night.

Edna opened the front door for Milton as the staff had long since retired. It had been three hours since the poet had departed with Crispin White. Rowland and Clyde had passed the time with hands of poker while Edna occupied herself drafting plans for a new commission—a frieze for the Miller's Flats memorial hall. They'd all been becoming decidedly concerned about the duration of Milton's absence, and so it was with some relief that Edna admitted him.

Milton took a seat, falling wearily into the armchair with his legs outstretched. "Dropped him off at Kings Cross," he said sullenly.

"You were gone long enough to drive him to Melbourne and back," Clyde muttered.

"How do you know Crispin White?" Edna asked, leaving her drawings to interrogate him. "I don't remember him." The sculptress and the poet had known each other since they were children living on the same street in Burwood. They shared a great deal of history and most of their past acquaintances.

"His name was Weissen, not White, when I knew him. He's not a bloke I would have let near you back then, Ed."

"Why ever not?"

"I can't say."

"What did he do?"

"I can't say, Ed. Really. I have no right to say. Just trust me."

"Did you have it out with him on the way to his lodgings?" Rowland had noticed the few drops of blood on Milton's usually immaculate cravat.

"Let's say we had words and he suffers from nosebleeds. What did he ask you about, Rowly... in the dining room?"

Rowland moved to sit on the couch. Edna curled up to make room for him. She made herself comfortable against his shoulder, while he told them of his conversation with White.

"He thought it was a tattoo?" Edna asked uneasily. It did not seem right that something inflicted so brutally and violently could be mistaken for a sailor's decoration.

"Chinese whispers—clearly the details have been somewhat altered in the retelling," Rowland replied tersely.

"What did you tell him?"

"That I don't have a tattoo." He loosened his tie and released the top button of his shirt.

Milton shook his head. "At least he was using it to cast you as a villain rather than a hero, Rowly. Perhaps Weissen, or White as he now calls himself, has changed... he claims he has."

Rowland was tempted to ask from what White had changed, but they all knew Milton enough to be certain that if the poet said he couldn't say, then he wouldn't say.

"Don't worry about it, Rowly," Clyde advised. "Just focus on the race. Do you know who's on your team yet?"

"Not yet," Rowland replied. "Though I understand the teams have been drawn." The Maroubra Multicar Invitational was to be a team endurance event. To maximise public interest, the teams would run three vehicles apiece from each of three weight and engine capacity categories in a long distance relay. "We'll all be introduced to each other tomorrow at the cocktail party." Rowland had not realised the race was going to be so grand when he'd first agreed to participate. Perhaps it hadn't been then, but sponsorship, media interest and the involvement of celebrity drivers had seen the fundraiser grow into an international gala, with rumours of contestants travelling from the Continent and America.

"White's right about one thing, the speedway has a bad name— killed more than its fair share of drivers," Clyde said quietly. He rubbed the shadow of stubble on his chin. "It's probably not too late to pull out, Rowly."

"Yes it is! Far too late!" Milton said, appalled by the suggestion. "I can just see the headlines, 'Yellow Mercedes pulls out!' They'll think Rowly's the same bloody colour!"

Rowland agreed with the poet. Withdrawing now would not be sporting, even if he wanted to, which he didn't. After years of driving the Mercedes within speed limits, he was looking forward to seeing what she could do on the track.

Clyde withdrew the suggestion without anything further in the way of caution. Despite his circumspect nature, he too was eager to see the Mercedes' supercharged engine opened up. As the self-appointed chief of Rowland's pit crew, he would in any case be able to keep an eye on both the motorcar and its driver. Hopefully that would be enough to defeat the killer track.

Rowland manoeuvred past the police cars and motorbikes gathered in McLeay Street, as he drove White's rattling Ford to the bookshop above which the reporter lived. He and Edna had decided to return the vehicle on their way to see an exhibition at the National Gallery of New South Wales. They'd catch a tram back to Woollahra after a morning viewing a retrospective of Margaret Preston's woodcuts and etchings. Milton had still been asleep when they left and Clyde busy giving the Mercedes an early morning polish in preparation for that evening's event.

It was as they approached White's side-entrance door to return the keys that they were stopped by a constable who demanded to know their business.

"I am returning a vehicle to Mr. Crispin White, who I believe resides here," Rowland replied.

"A vehicle?"

"His motorcar."

The constable looked startled. He took their names and, calling out to his colleagues who were apparently inside the flat, asked Edna and Rowland to follow him.

"What appears to be the problem?" Rowland asked.

The constable refused to clarify.

McLeay Street was busy, the main thoroughfare of Kings Cross which hosted many of Sydney's teahouses and entertainment venues. A crowd had gathered outside Magdalene's House of the Macabre, a waxworks which promised "Thrills and Chills" in lurid peeling paint by the entrance. The constable stopped them just inside the threshold, handing them over to the supervision of another young policeman. "If you'll just wait here with Constable Grey, I'll inform the inspector that you're here."

Rowland tried to extract some sort of explanation from Grey, who puffed out his hollow chest and grinned excitedly. "You'll find out soon enough. Hope you've got a strong stomach."

Now a little irritated, Rowland put his question more officiously.

It was at that point the stretcher was carried past them. It seemed someone had been killed. A white sheet cloaked the identity of the body beneath it.

"Who is that?" Rowland demanded of Grey.

The constable motioned the stretcher-bearers to pause. Perhaps it was pursuant to Rowland's inquiry. More likely it was his own curiosity. He pulled back the sheet with swagger and flourish. Edna stifled a scream. Crispin White's head sat at an odd angle, the wound at his throat gaping open. The reporter's eyes stared, cold and glassy.

"What are you doing, you bloody fool?" Colin Delaney stormed into the foyer, replacing the sheet and turning to roar at Grey.

"Rowly," he said, once he'd finished dressing down and dismissing the errant constable. "What are you and Miss Higgins doing here?"

Rowland told him.

"Why were you returning the deceased's vehicle?"

"I didn't know he was deceased. He had dinner at *Woodlands* last night, and rather too much brandy. He wasn't fit to drive."

"So you drove him home?"

"Not me… Milt. God, what's happened to him, Colin?"

"That's what we're trying to determine." Delaney glanced at his watch. "I have to sort out a few matters here… organise the paperwork." He glanced at Edna who was noticeably pale. "Why don't you take Miss Higgins back to *Woodlands*. I'll come by, as soon as I'm finished to take your statements." Someone shouted from within the museum and Delaney nodded hastily and disappeared.

Rowland took Edna's hand. "Are you all right, Ed?"

"Yes… It was just a bit of shock seeing Crispin like that… We only had dinner with him a few hours ago…"

Rowland placed his arm protectively around her shoulders as they slipped into the crowd which was already abuzz with wild theories and speculation. The press had also arrived, though they were subdued and respectful. Crispin White had, after all, been one of their own.

Rowland and Edna walked around the corner, ducking into a wine bar to gather themselves before attempting to flag down a motor taxi.

The establishment was almost empty. Perhaps there was not a great demand for wine at eight in the morning, or possibly, its patrons were amongst those congregating outside the waxworks. Rowland persuaded the proprietor to bring them a pot of tea, and they sat by the grimy window watching the passing foot traffic as they contemplated the morning's events.

"Poor Crispin," Edna said wrapping both hands around the thick china cup and inhaling the fragrant steam. "What do you suppose happened, Rowly?"

"Well, I don't think it was a shaving accident," he said quietly. "Beyond that, I don't know Ed. Dreadful business though."

"It's a terrible omen for the race," Edna murmured.

"White was barely connected with the race." Rowland said firmly. "He's a journalist—probably covering a dozen stories... it seems jolly unfair to allocate your superstitions purely against the race."

Edna smiled. "Of course," she said. "One must be even-handed in the allocation of superstitions."

"It is unfortunate though," Rowland added. "It's a crying shame he didn't simply stay at *Woodlands* last night."

"Why didn't he?" Edna asked as she sipped her tea.

"Milt volunteered to drive him home... he was rather insistent."

"I thought Milt didn't like him."

"I assumed that was why he didn't want White staying overnight." He shrugged. "Perhaps White was a burglar when Milt last knew him."

Edna sighed. "Milt may now have no choice but to be a little more forthcoming."

Detective Colin Delaney arrived at *Woodlands House* only a couple of minutes after its master and the sculptress had returned. The downstairs maid admitted him without any consternation. The detective was a familiar guest, dropping by every now and then, though it was unusual for him to visit too early to be offered a drink.

Rowland received him in his studio. "Ed's just gone to check on her kittens," he said. "She shouldn't be long."

"Kittens?"

"Some strays she rescued."

"I thought that was your hobby." Delaney took the armchair and waited for Rowland to sit. "Let's start at the beginning, shall we? How do you know Crispin White, Rowly?"

"White was employed by *Smith's Weekly*. They sent him to interview me for their coverage of this charity motor race at Maroubra."

"Oh yes... I forgot you were involved in that. What time did he leave here?"

"About ten."

"And Mr. Isaacs drove him home?"

"Yes... I'd had a brandy too many. Milt dropped him off at his lodgings."

"His lodgings?" Delaney frowned. "Are you sure?"

"I believe that's what Milt said."

"You saw where he was found."

Rowland nodded. "The appropriately named House of the Macabre. Bloody hell! Why would White choose to visit a waxworks at that time of night?"

"I had hoped you might be able to shed some light on that."

Rowland shrugged. "We were barely acquainted. He called at *Woodlands* to interview me and stayed for dinner. Aside from being a journalist, he didn't seem like a bad chap."

"Did he mention anything that might—?"

"No. He seemed to be looking for a sensational angle for his story, but he didn't really reveal too much about himself."

"Colin!" Edna came into the room. She smiled at the detective. "Will you be staying for breakfast?"

Both Rowland and Delaney stood.

"I don't suppose you recall anything Mr. White might have said last night," Delaney said scratching his head wearily.

"Nothing that made me suspect he was in any danger." Edna's head tilted sideways as she tried to recall the details of their conversations. "He was rather… intrigued by the imagery on the dining room walls. I'm afraid he thought it was a little sacrilegious. Poor, poor Crispin."

Delaney didn't ask what adorned the dining room walls. He had been a guest at *Woodlands* often enough to be familiar with the room's current Bacchanalian splendour and though he could understand White's concern, he did not believe Rowland Sinclair or any of his companions were interested enough in religion to be sacrilegious by design.

"Do you know who killed him yet, Detective Delaney?" Edna asked.

"That's why I'm here, Miss Higgins. As far as we can ascertain, Mr. Isaacs might have been the last person to have seen the deceased alive."

"Aside from the person who killed him, of course," Edna corrected sharply.

"Of course… I wasn't suggesting—"

Rowland intervened. "Milt or Clyde could well remember something useful."

"They're eating breakfast," Edna said. "I haven't had a chance to tell them…"

They made their way to the dining room where, from behind *The Sydney Morning Herald*, Milton cheerily issued the detective another invitation to breakfast in a style that was characteristically erudite. "The very bacon shows its feeling, swinging from the smoky ceiling! A steaming bowl, a blazing fire, what greater good can the heart desire?"

"Wordsworth," Rowland murmured. "But yes, you should stay for breakfast, Colin."

"Unless, of course, you're here to arrest Rowly again," Clyde added in equally good humour. "That would be somewhat uncivil."

Perhaps it was the poetic eloquence of Milton's solicitation, the fact that Delaney had no thought of arresting Rowland Sinclair, or the aromas emanating from the silver warming trays upon the sideboard, but the detective decided that a cup of coffee and some eggs would not be too great a dereliction of duty. He confessed the reason for his visit, as he took a seat at the French polished table.

"They cut his throat?" Clyde said, shocked.

"Nearly took off his head," Delaney replied, wrinkling his nose as he recalled the characteristic smell of blood. "The manager mistook him for a new exhibit, initially."

"He what?"

"He was found in Magdalene's House of the Macabre at Macleay Street in Kings Cross—a waxworks specialising in ghouls and whatnot." Delaney shook his head. Clearly he could not understand the attraction.

"I've been to the House of the Macabre a few times," Milton volunteered. "It's not Madame Tussaud's but it's quite well put together for the sixpence entry fee."

"A few times? Whatever for?"

"It's a surprisingly romantic spot."

"God help us," Clyde muttered.

"Where precisely did you leave Mr. White?" Delaney asked Milton.

"Some bookshop in Mcleay Street. He lives... lived above it. It's not far from Magdalene's." Milton declared the proximity before Delaney could.

"What time was that?"

"About midnight."

Delaney flicked back a page of his notebook. "But Rowly says you left here about ten."

"Yes."

"What took you so long?"

"Traffic."

"For pity's sake, man..."

"Crispin White and I knew each other once," Milton said irritably. "We were catching up."

"And where exactly did you catch up?"

"In the car, parked outside the bookshop. After a while we were entirely caught up, he said goodnight and went into his flat."

"What were you talking about?"

"This and that... I don't remember really."

"Was this horror museum—Magdalene's—open after midnight?" Rowland interrupted in an attempt to divert Delaney's attention from the fact that Milton's answers seemed to be intentionally evasive.

"No, not according to the manager," Delaney replied, his eyes still on Milton.

"So Crispin broke in?" Edna poured the detective a cup of coffee.

"Someone must have, it seems. Either White or whomever admitted him."

"Had he been robbed?" Rowland asked.

"His purse was still in his jacket's breast pocket," Delaney said sighing.

"What about his notebook?"

"What notebook?"

"He had a notebook... wrote in it incessantly."

"Perhaps he didn't have it with him."

Rowland shook his head. "I doubt it." He, too, was in the habit of carrying a notebook, to capture moments in line and shade, to pin down ideas for later works, or simply to pass the time. The notebook sat always in his breast pocket.

"We'll look for it," Delaney assured him. He glanced once more at Milton. "It may provide a clue as to who would want to kill him."

3

PEACE PRIZE FOR HITLER?

GERMANY ACCLAIMS PACT

BERLIN, January 28

The newspapers pay glowing tributes to the pact, with Poland as a manifestation of Herr Hitler's desire for peace. They suggest that he will go down in history as the "peace-making Chancellor", and will, perhaps, receive the Nobel Peace Prize.

The "Allgemeine Zeitung" considers that the pact will create the confidence which is lacking throughout the world, despite the League of Nations, the Locarno Pact, and the Disarmament Conference.

The "Berliner Tageblatt" emphasises that the pact significantly does not mention Geneva, whose methods have been abandoned. Herr Hitler, it says, by leaving the poisonous atmosphere and international diplomacy has enabled a new European policy to win its first success.

The Courier Mail, 1934

"What on earth went on between you and Crispin White?" Edna demanded once the detective was safely away.

Milton groaned. "I can't say. I promised."

"Colin Delaney is not a fool. He knows you're hiding something."

Milton shrugged.

Rowland said nothing. He was loath to pry, though he feared Edna was right. Milton was known to the police—Rowland had never asked him for what exactly.

For several minutes the poet and sculptress argued. Edna was persistent. "Milt, whatever it is, we'll help. You know that," she said in the end.

"It's not something you can help with, Ed."

"I'm going to keep asking. So will the police."

Milton glanced at the ceiling and sighed heavily. "You're a fishwife, Edna Higgins," he said. Then, slowly, wearily, "Do you remember my cousin Miriam?"

Edna nodded. "Not very well, but yes."

"She was a brilliant girl... quiet. Her parents were very strict, traditional people. Miriam met Crispin Weissen when she was seventeen. He was about twenty then—determined to be the next Dostoyevsky. She fell in love with him." The poet shook his head.

"And her parents objected?" Edna pre-empted.

"They didn't really have a chance," Milton replied. "Miriam confided in me but she kept it from them... poor wretch was delirious about Weissen and, because he was Jewish too, she thought..." He stood, pacing now. "My aunt and uncle kept such a close eye on her, God knows how they managed it, but he got her in trouble."

Rowland flinched. It was unlikely this story was going to end well.

"Miriam came to me distraught, hysterical—God, she was terrified. She'd not heard from Weissen since she told him."

"The mongrel!" Clyde blurted in disgust.

"I hunted the swine down. At first he said he didn't want to marry a Jewish girl, work for her father and have his life decided for him. He thought he had some great literary destiny. I belted the... I wanted to kill him then, to be honest, but he talked me round..."

"Talked you round to what?" Edna asked softly.

"He broke down... cried like a child. Amongst all the blubbering he convinced me that I had convinced him. I was such a bloody fool!" Milton rubbed his face, still angry with himself. "Weissen said that he loved Miriam and that he was deeply ashamed of the way he'd behaved. He said he'd speak to her father the next day, asked me to tell Miriam that he would do right by her. I believed him. I went home and told Miriam to start organising her glory box. The following morning the police arrested me for assaulting Crispin Weissen and by the time they'd figured out he wasn't going to pursue the complaint and released me, the bastard had disappeared completely."

"But what about Miriam...?" Edna asked, horrified. Though she often seemed indifferent to the expectations and restrictions of society, Edna was perfectly aware of what its judgement could mean. "What did you do?"

"What could I do, Ed? She's my cousin, or I would have married her myself. She found a doctor who was willing to—"

"No!" Clyde interjected. "You didn't let her?"

"I was afraid she'd harm herself!" Milton flared immediately. "She was going to be condemned by moral hypocrites no matter what she did!"

Clyde bit his lip. "I'm sorry, Milt. I just..."

"I helped her keep it from her parents... from everybody," Milton continued without looking at Clyde. "For a long time, I thought it would destroy her completely. The family thought she was pining because Weissen had lost interest. They talked of committing her to a sanatorium."

"But they didn't?" Edna's voice was tentative, hopeful.

"No... now she's married, has four children. She's happy and thoroughly respectable. I don't want the fact that Weissen—or whatever he's calling himself now—has gotten himself killed to raise it all again. It just wouldn't be fair."

For a moment there was nothing as they absorbed the weight of what Milton had told them.

"If you're arrested for this, she'll find out," Edna said gently.

"And if I tell Delaney exactly why I know White, it's not going to make me any less a suspect."

"What were you and White talking about for so long?" Clyde asked.

Milton shrugged. "Miriam. And what happened. He cried again. In the end he said that he was young and he panicked and he'd been regretting it ever since. He wanted to write to her, to apologise. I said no."

"In the end? What did he say in the beginning?" Edna was adept at recognising when Milton was omitting something.

"We may have gone at it a bit first," Milton confessed. "Until I realised he was too drunk to put up a fight. Don't worry Rowly, we weren't in your motorcar at the time," Milton added, as if the fact would matter to Rowland, which it didn't.

"Oh Milt," Edna said. "This doesn't look good."

"Who else knows about this?" Rowland asked. "Other than the four of us."

"Now that Crispin is dead, just Miriam."

"Bloody oath, mate, that sounds like a motive," Clyde groaned. "I can't believe I'm saying this, but perhaps it's best that you don't tell Delaney the whole story."

"He's suspicious," Edna said. "He'll find out eventually. Presumably there's a police record of the fact that White accused you of assault."

"Hopefully the real killer will have presented himself by then," Rowland said, uneasily. He understood Milton's need to protect his cousin. He would respect it. But Edna was right. It didn't look good.

"And if he hasn't presented himself?" Clyde asked.

Rowland contemplated that inconvenient possibility. "We might have to find him ourselves," he said.

"Rowly, aren't you ready yet? Oh—" Edna screamed and ducked as the lavish stroke of Rowland's brush splattered ochre paint in her direction.

"Ed..." He grimaced as they both looked at her now speckled evening gown. "Oh blast... I'm so sorry. You have something else you can wear, haven't you?"

"Yes," she said crossly. "But I had wanted to wear this!"

Rowland apologised again. "You look smashing by the way," he added sheepishly.

Edna sighed. "I ought to know, by now, not to surprise you while you're painting, I suppose... What are you working on?" She peered around his easel at the large wet canvas. The painting was still in its very early stages but she recognised the Königplatz in Munich. Rowland had blocked in the square, somehow rendering the buildings recognisable with only a few brushed details. There was the shape of a crowd and, in the foreground, the Brownshirts against a background of flames. Edna knew immediately the scene he was painting—the book burning they'd witnessed in the square. She frowned. She had hoped that Rowland was finished with the dark images with which he had left Germany. "Why are you painting this, Rowly?"

He put down his brush and handed Edna his handkerchief, pointing to the drop of paint on her nose, before he answered her question. "I'm contemplating an exhibition. Inspired by Germany. I've been trying to tell people what we saw with no effect... it occurred to me that words are probably not my best medium. Perhaps they just need to see what we saw."

Edna studied the canvas. Already there was a menace in the composition, a kind of hard manic energy in the figures. Even now, nowhere near finished, it was disturbing. She stood back, shivering suddenly.

"Are you cold?" he asked, moving to close the windows.

"No, it isn't that," Edna said beckoning him back. She took a seat on the settee and, reaching out for his hand, she pulled him down beside her. "You've had such a beastly year, Rowly—Germany, then England, not to mention that terrible business in Yass. Would it be such a bad idea to give yourself a chance to recover?"

"Recover? I'm fighting fit, Ed. Really."

"It doesn't mean you have to fight again straight away. Even in boxing the players get to rest between sets."

"Fighters return to their corners between rounds," Rowland said smiling.

"You just seem a little lost, lately."

Rowland blinked, surprised, first by the observation, and then by the realisation that it wasn't entirely unwarranted.

"We all understand how you feel about what happened... what's happening in Germany," Edna went on gently, her eyes searching as they fixed on his.

Rowland looked down at her hand still in his own. It wasn't so much what he felt about Germany and the Nazis as what he should do about it. He tried to explain. "Clyde and Milt know what they're doing," he said. "They're Communists, they're organised—on some level, anyway. Thanks to Marx, they know exactly how they ought to be fighting. I'm not a Communist, Ed... I'm not sure what I should be doing but I can't escape the feeling that I should be doing something."

"Are you saying you want to join the Australian Communist Party?"

"No, not at all." He tried to make sense of the restlessness, to articulate the nagging disquiet. "A couple of years ago, I didn't care at all about politics… I just wanted to paint."

"Well, there isn't anything wrong with that."

"I'm not so sure that's true, anymore. What was it Burke said about evil triumphing when good men do nothing?"

"We could ask Milt," Edna suggested wryly. "He'll remember word for word, though he'll claim he said it first."

"Doubtless." Rowland paused. "I do care now, Ed. But, as much as Milt and Clyde are two of the best men I've ever known, I'm not a Communist."

"You're going to join the Country Party?" Edna asked a little fearfully.

Rowland made a face. "Good Lord, no! I'd sooner join the circus."

Edna relaxed. "I'm not a Communist either, Rowly. I really do understand… and it is a good idea—an exhibition about the horrible reality of what's happening to Germany under Hitler's Fascists."

"I'll have to make it sound like a collection of mountain landscapes painted on a walking holiday through the Pyrenees, of course."

"Whatever for?"

"I was considering putting my family connections to good use for once."

"I'm not sure I—"

"I don't need to convince the Socialists and trade unions that the Nazis are dangerous, Ed. They know. And even if they didn't, Milt and Clyde will tell them. But if I play my cards carefully, every influential conservative in New South Wales will attend the opening of Wilfred Sinclair's little brother's exhibition."

Edna's eyes widened. "That's brilliant! You're brilliant."

"I like to think so," he said gravely.

She shoved him, laughing now.

"I do wonder if I ought to put this off for the time being, though," he added pensively.

"Why?"

"Milt... this issue with White's murder. Maybe it's not the time to be preoccupied with another fight... or a car race, for that matter."

Edna shook her head. "Milt knows you'd drop everything to help him if it came to that. But he'll tell you himself that we have to do whatever we can to make sure people realise how truly dangerous the Nazis are."

"You don't think I should return to my corner after all, then?" His eyes glinted.

Poking him playfully, Edna conceded the inconsistency of her advice. "It's not polite to hold a lady to what she's said nearly an entire conversation ago!"

"Evidently. I do beg your pardon." In truth, he was comforted by her change of heart—it made his own uncertainty seem less culpable.

She continued airily. "The world doesn't stop so we can deal with one thing at a time. Life's more an all-in brawl than one of your very proper boxing matches."

"You might have to explain that," Rowland said, laughing.

"A single identifiable opponent is an unrealistic luxury," she replied with conviction. "As is an umpire to make sure everything's sporting, that you all shake hands, adjust your ties and have a cup of tea afterwards."

"Referee."

"What?"

"They're called referees. And I believe you'll find that pugilism is not quite so genteel."

Edna rolled her eyes. "Milt's already spoken about what we saw in Germany at Trades Hall and Speakers' Corner. He'll be delighted you're doing the same with an audience of toffs. This isn't just a Communist fight."

Rowland kissed the sculptress' hand. "I'd best weigh in then."

"Shall we make ourselves presentable for this party?" she asked as she stood.

Rowland glanced at his watch. "As I said, you look smashing."

"Well you look like you're wearing a drop sheet!" She ran her eyes archly over the variety of colours on his waistcoat and the streak of green in his hair. "Go and make yourself look dashing, while I round up the others."

Rowland did as she directed, returning half an hour later in a dinner suit and with his hair free of paint. Edna had also changed into a gown she had not planned to wear that night, but which, at least, was not the worse for Rowland's brush. Clyde was waiting with her.

"Milt's gone on ahead with your mother, Rowly," he said, shifting uncomfortably in his dinner jacket. Clyde had never become accustomed to what he considered polite society's obsession with dress-ups. "She was getting anxious that we were running late—Milt thought it best…"

"Yes. That's good of him," Rowland agreed. Milton seemed to bring out the best in his mother. She was almost girlish in the poet's company and Milton, having been brought up by his grandmother, was particularly kind to Elisabeth Sinclair.

Smiling, Rowland wondered what his conservative brother would think of their mother's friendship with the disreputable Communist. Still, Wilfred was no longer quite as censorious of his brother's set as he once had been.

The venue for the evening's event was the Maroubra Speedway itself. A grand marquee had been erected on the grassed area at the centre of the concave track, the acoustics of the graded cement bowl proving ideal for a twenty-piece orchestra. Rowland parked the Mercedes within the cordonned area reserved for vehicles taking part in the invitational. Running slightly late, theirs was the last car to arrive and so the gaggle of newspaper photographers had no other distraction.

"What the devil!" Rowland blanched under the onslaught of flashing cameras as he made his way around to open Edna's door. Her emergence seemed to only intensify the explosions of light. When Clyde alighted there was a little confusion as the pack moved their focus.

"They're not sure which one of you is Rowland Sinclair," Edna whispered.

Rowland grabbed her hand. "Let's go before they realise."

The strategy might have worked if Clyde had not called out, "Hey Rowly, where are you going, mate?"

Edna laughed as Rowland groaned. Unable, within the bounds of decorum, to do anything else, they posed for photographs by the Mercedes. Edna sparkled in the spotlight, Rowland looked, at best, bemused, and Clyde tried to hide behind the car. The photographers made requests: Edna on Rowland's arm, Clyde and Rowland leaning on the grille, Edna kissing Rowland's cheek. With all this they complied relatively amicably, until Rowland was asked to raise his arm in a Fascist salute. He said nothing, glaring at the offending photographer, his face suddenly dark, his anger undisguised. The cameraman took a photograph of that instead, and Rowland's temper flashed in return. The exchange may have escalated if Milton had not appeared.

"Rowly, there you are!" The poet pushed his way through the media huddle. "Are you aware the prime minister's here? He's dancing with that American actress. Frisky old blighter!"

The photographers instantly lost interest in Rowland Sinclair and his Mercedes.

"Thank heavens for Lyons," Rowland murmured, as they were finally able to make their way unmolested towards the marquee.

Milton grinned. "It might not have been the prime minister," he said, winking. "Could have just been some short bloke with white hair dancing with his wife. I'm not really sure…"

"A perfectly understandable mistake," Rowland assured him.

4

"JACKO—THE BROADCASTING KOOKABURRA"

Who has not heard Jacko, the broadcasting Kookaburra. Surely no picture fan has missed his merry chuckle, which acts as introduction to so many Australian films. Now we have the story of his life narrated interestingly by his owner, Dr. Brooke Nicholls, and charmingly illustrated by Miss Dorothy Wall. We find it a little hard to make up our minds as to whether this story is meant for children or grown-ups. We certainly think it will be read as eagerly by the one as by the other.

Jacko must be easily the most famous bird in existence, for he has broadcast, he has appeared in more films than has any human star, his laugh has been recorded for the gramophone, and he has made a 4,000 miles caravan tour of Victoria, New South Wales and Queensland, laughing heartily to illustrate his master's lectures on nature. His master's is hardly the word, for Jacko is such a valuable bird that his owner is very much his servant. His value lies particularly in his intelligence, for Jacko has learned to laugh by request, and no wild Kookaburra ever laughs except when he feels like it.

Albany Advertiser, 1933

The marquee had been decorated with paper lanterns and great sheaves of blue gum leaves, which surrounded the golden banksia flowers wired onto supporting poles, and scented the air with the fragrance of eucalypt. Advertising billboards for various fuel and tyre companies were tastefully displayed beside Red Cross banners. Fondant automobiles raced around the five tiers of a massive cake displayed on a linen-draped table at the centre of the marquee. In dinner suits and evening gowns, the racers were indistinguishable from the motor enthusiasts, philanthropists and dilettantes who made up the crowd.

"Aubrey, finally!" Elisabeth Sinclair greeted her son with relief and mild disapprobation. "I sent Mr. Isaacs to look for you."

"He'd been waylaid by photographers, Mrs. Sinclair," Milton said in Rowland's defence. "Your boy's a celebrity now."

Elisabeth smoothed Rowland's lapel. "I would prefer he be uncelebrated and punctual."

Rowland laughed, pleased with how well his mother seemed. This was the most assured he'd seen her in years. A nurse stood within arm's reach as always. This evening it was Sister Kathleen O'Hara, a stout sensible woman of Irish stock who had, in light of the occasion, swapped her uniform for an elaborately frilled gown from an era thankfully past.

The formalities began with a welcome address by the President of the New South Wales Light Car Club, who outlined the rules of the endurance event. The contestants would compete in teams of three cars, one from each of three weight divisions, completing two hundred laps of the track apiece. All this Rowland knew. He was more curious to see who else had been conscripted for the race. He had heard rumours of international racers.

The radio station 2GB was broadcasting live from the marquee and Australian Cinesound was recording the event on film.

Various sponsors took their turn at the microphone and the race trophy was unveiled with abundant fanfare. The extravagant gold cup had been fashioned, in a nod to the speedway's heyday, as a replica of the "Lucky Devil" Cup which had been awarded in the past. The new trophy was rather unimaginatively dubbed the "Lucky Devil II" to somewhat subdued commendation.

"The last bloke to win the Lucky Devil crashed and died on the speedway soon after," Milton informed them under his breath. "Let's hope the Lucky Devil II is less of an exercise in irony."

To assist in the task of announcing the contestants, the star power of an international luminary had been enlisted. Jacko the Broadcasting Kookaburra, whose distinctive laugh heralded Radio Australia's programs, was introduced to applause and cheers as the honorary patron of the Maroubra Invitational. Perched securely upon a steering wheel inside his cage, he oversaw the proceedings quite silently. Indeed, Jacko appeared to be asleep.

The announcements were made nonetheless.

The teams had supposedly been drawn in lots, and yet there was a surprising even-handedness in their composition. Celebrities, experienced racers, locals and women seemed to be equitably distributed.

"Flynn?" Clyde murmured when the name was read out with that of Rowland Sinclair and Miss Joan Richmond.

"Ed says he's a film actor of some sort," Milton whispered in reply, having just made the same enquiry of Edna.

"I met him at the Cinesound studio last year," the sculptress said quietly. "He's very handsome."

"Well that'll be useful on the racetrack," Rowland muttered.

After catching the eye of Cinesound filmmaker Ken Hall, Edna had, over the last couple of years, secured a number of minor parts on screen. As the men she lived with had never considered films art, they treated her forays into the form, and the actors who inevitably accompanied her home, with a kind of amused indifference.

With Joan Richmond, Rowland was himself acquainted, through the social networks of the establishment. Having won the

British 1000 miles race in 1932, her abilities as a driver were beyond reproach.

"Rowly, give me your notebook." Milton held out his hand.

"My what?"

"Don't pretend you don't have it. I need a notebook."

Rowland handed over the slim leather-bound artist's journal, wondering what on earth Milton wished to draw.

The poet set to work making a list.

"What are you doing?"

"Just jotting down the names of your competition," Milton replied. "You'll need to know what you're up against. There are a couple of Honourables in here, you know."

"As long as I'm not racing the Kookaburra."

The list, as it turned out, contained the names of actor Roy Rene, racing identities Hope Bartlett and Murray Maxwell, as well as a couple of English aristocrats—a brother and sister team—the Honourables that Milton mentioned. Glasses were charged and the gathering drank to the good health of all the contestants before putting down their drinks and raising their voices for "God Save the King". The formalities thus concluded, the orchestra struck up again and the crowd mingled with purpose.

Rowland spotted Joan Richmond. Years ago they'd been attendants in the same wedding party. Tall and slim, there was a practical sophistication about the young racing driver. Dark hair bobbed and parted cleanly in the middle, she was clearly at home at events of this kind.

"I say, Rowly Sinclair! Long time no see," she said warmly. "I didn't know you raced."

"I don't generally," Rowland confessed. "You've been saddled with at least one novice I'm afraid."

"You can drive can't you?"

"Of course I can drive—"

"Well the rest is just experience. We'll have a jolly time!"

"I must say, I'm very pleasantly surprised to find you here. Aunt Mildred told me you were racing around Europe."

Joan nodded. "I'm due back for the Alpine Rally, but I thought it would be rather fun to come home and see my brother, Alan, for a bit," she explained. "This came up—thumping good cause and all that. Victor Riley's been kind enough to lend me a car. Now where's this chap Flynn? We'd better check he can drive."

Rowland was relieved that Joan seemed to be taking charge. "I haven't had the pleasure as yet."

"What does this fellow look like?" she said, scanning the marquee.

"An actor, I presume."

The problem was solved by Edna, who found Errol Flynn and brought him to meet his teammates.

"Rowland Sinclair, Mr. Flynn. How d'you do?"

Flynn shook Rowland's hand enthusiastically. "Very well, Mr. Sinclair. Delighted, Miss Richmond. I say, shall we have our picture taken with Jacko?"

"Jacko?" Rowland asked.

"The bird," Clyde reminded him.

"Come on! It'll be a lark… or at least a kingfisher!" Flynn signalled a photographer and bustled them towards the kookaburra. He then attempted to engage the bird in conversation.

"Come on fella, do you want a cracker? Give us a laugh."

Jacko ignored him.

Rowland could see Milton and Clyde laughing as they watched, even Edna seemed amused, but the bird was clearly not. It remained sombre indeed. Mercifully, the photographer took a picture anyway and they could leave Jacko in peace.

"What do you drive, Mr. Flynn?" Rowland asked, trying to distract him from the beleaguered bird.

"I believe it's a Triumph," Flynn replied.

"You believe?" Joan said curtly. "Surely you know?"

Flynn smiled, a charming disarming smile. "I'm really more of a sailor, you know."

Joan Richmond exhaled impatiently. "We may well need to do some practice runs," she said. "I'll arrange for some time on the speedway and be in touch."

"I say, she seems a trifle put out," Flynn whispered as the motorist walked away.

"Miss Richmond is competitive," Rowland conceded. "But she's an excellent driver and on the whole, a rather good egg."

"Mr. Sinclair!" A young woman interrupted before Flynn could reply. She was somewhat extraordinary to look at. Small and slight, she wore a black silk scarf with one end tied around her neck and the other about her waist as a blouse of sorts. It only barely served that function.

"I don't believe we've been introduced, Miss…?"

"Norton. Rosaleen Norton from *Smith's Weekly*," she said, lifting her chin to meet his eye with a dark intense gaze accentuated by brows carefully groomed to sweep upwards. Her features lent themselves to line drawing, he thought, contemplating the sharp planes of her face.

"I've already spoken with *Smith Weekly's* Mr. White—" Rowland began.

"Oh, didn't you know?" she said enthusiastically. "Mr. White's dead. Murdered! I've been assigned to replace him. He didn't write up your interview before he died so we'll have to do it again." She beamed at him, revealing crooked teeth behind scarlet painted lips. "You don't have a cigarette do you, Mr. Sinclair?"

"I'm afraid I don't smoke, Miss Norton."

Flynn, who, up until this point, the reporter had ignored, extracted a silver case from his breast pocket. He offered her a cigarette as Rowland introduced him.

Beyond his cigarettes and a light, Rosaleen seemed to have no interest in Errol Flynn at all. She directed her conversation at Rowland, explaining that she was a cadet with *Smith's*, engaged as writer and artist. She had heard he too was an artist. Rosaleen's movements were gangly, loose, those of an adolescent still becoming accustomed to the length of her limbs.

Rowland handed her his card. "Why don't you call by the house tomorrow, Miss Norton. I can tell you what I told Mr. White before his untimely passing."

"Certainly, Mr. Sinclair. But I won't be asking the same questions Crispy did. You'll find that he and I are very different on that score. I am first and foremost an artist, after all."

"I have no doubt, Miss Norton." Rowland paused before he asked, "I don't suppose you've heard anything about what happened to Mr. White?"

"His throat was cut at Magdalene's I heard—ear to ear." She pressed her lips together and studied him. "You know Mr. Sinclair, I think I may have had a premonition about what happened to Crispy."

"A premonition?"

Rosaleen glanced at her watch, and sighed. "It's nearly midnight. I really must go! We can discuss premonitions and art and death tomorrow." She backed away, blowing him a kiss as she went.

Rowland stared after her.

"I suppose she'll want to interview me as well," Flynn murmured. "Excuse me," he said suddenly, as he caught sight of Edna again. "I must ask that glorious damsel to dance. You don't mind, do you Sinclair?"

Rowland did mind, but he said, "I don't own Miss Higgins, Flynn."

"Good to know!" The actor straightened his bowtie as he strode away.

Rowland had been watching Flynn and Edna dancing for a few minutes when Clyde joined him. "I wouldn't worry about Flynn," Clyde said, handing Rowland a glass of champagne. "He's too much of a show pony."

"Ed's not averse to show ponies," Rowland murmured recalling the actors and artists with whom Edna had been enamoured in the past.

Clyde shook his head. "You can't be a star with Ed on your arm, mate. It's like trying to shine next to the sun. Flynn's not going to like that."

Rowland looked back at the dance floor. Clyde had a point—the eye was drawn to Edna. She was mesmerising, and unsuited to men who wanted the spotlight for themselves.

Clyde's presence was wordlessly sympathetic. Once he would have tried to dissuade Rowland's devotion, to reason with him, for they all knew that Edna's loves were intense and joyful and frivolous. They came and went. And the sculptress cared too much about Rowland Sinclair to love him, to risk his heart. Unfortunately, Rowland cared too much to do anything else. Both Clyde and Milton had decided some time ago to let it be, and to simply hope that whatever happened, it wouldn't all end in disaster.

Still, Clyde almost cheered when Rowland left him to cut in.

The morning light was still soft and new when Rowland emerged from the stables with a mewling kitten in each hand. The tiny creatures had somehow scrambled under the bonnet of the Mercedes and fallen asleep on the warmth of the engine block. Luckily, Clyde was now constantly fine-tuning the engine in preparation for the race, and they were discovered.

Rowland stopped, startled to see Rosaleen Norton on his lawn. She was wrapped around a statue of Pan, her gaze focussed intently on the figure's horned face. He had not forgotten that he'd invited her; it was just her current position, and the hour, that were odd. Rowland doubted the statue had ever been so ardently admired—certainly not at seven in the morning.

He cleared his throat loudly. "Good morning, Miss Norton."

"Hello, Mr. Sinclair." The reporter reluctantly released the statue. "He's beautiful, don't you think? Is he a Lindsay?"

"No, but Miss Higgins did study with Lindsay for a time," he replied, impressed that she could recognise the influence. While similar in its mythological inspiration, Edna's work was more avant-garde than Norman Lindsay's, the lines of her Pan with its swirling horns owed more to the Art Deco movement than the Nouveau.

"I've always admired him."

"Norman's an extraordinary artist."

"Yes, I suppose he is," she said. Her dark eyes glistened. "But I was talking about Pan. There's an ancient, knowing power about him that makes one think of dancing naked in the moonlight."

"I can't say that's occurred to me," Rowland replied quite honestly.

"What are their names... your companions?" Rosaleen stepped forward to take the kittens from him. She dropped on to the lawn crooning and purring and rubbing her face against the creatures.

"They haven't been here long enough to be named..." The journalist obviously wasn't listening, so preoccupied was she with the kittens. "I'll just fetch my jacket and we might go up to the house," he said, unrolling his shirtsleeves. He left her on the lawn with the cats and ducked back into the stables to retrieve his jacket.

"What took you so long?" Clyde asked, raising his head from the engine. They'd been working on the Mercedes since first light.

"Miss Norton—White's replacement—is here."

"Poor White," Clyde said, shaking his head. "He's probably not even cold. It seems indecent."

Rowland slipped on his jacket. "I shouldn't be long. She seems much more interested in Ed's statues and the blessed kittens than the race. With any luck, she'll write about them and leave me in peace."

Rosaleen Norton walked with him to the house, skipping occasionally and bubbling with enthusiasm about the array of wanton sculptures that adorned the grounds. He had intended to speak with her in the conservatory as he had done with White, but she asked to see his studio the moment they stepped into the house.

"Don't we need to talk about the Red Cross race?" Rowland asked.

"I'll have Crispy's notes for that," she said waving away his suggestion. "I was given to understand that Mr. White's notebook wasn't found with his body."

"Really? How do you know?" Rosaleen's upswept brows sharpened into an acute V.

"The police mentioned—"

"Of course! The police. It's fascinating, don't you think? How he was killed and where. I must say I find it all quite lusciously exciting."

"Did you know Crispin White very well?" Rowland asked, disconcerted by the young woman's guileless admission.

"Oh, not particularly. I'm more an artist than a writer. He seemed nice enough but I did think he was boring… Not anymore, naturally. I would never have expected he had connections at Magdalene's."

"The waxworks?"

"Yes, I used it as inspiration for a story once. There's a coven that meets there you know."

"A coven?" Rowland smiled. "As in witches?"

Rosaleen nodded emphatically. "I wouldn't laugh if I were you. I've met some of them. They are not people to be laughed at."

"Have you mentioned this coven to the police?" Rowland asked trying to distract himself from the ludicrousness of the notion.

"Why on earth would I do that?"

"To help determine who killed Crispin White."

"Well that's obvious." Rosaleen shrugged. "Crispy must have been after a story. He violated the secrets of the coven and he was punished by dark forces summoned to take vengeance."

"Summoned by whom?"

"The coven, of course. They protect their magic as vehemently as any church."

"You're suggesting a ghost cut White's throat?" Rowland said slowly.

Rosaleen looked at him as if he were a particularly stupid man. "There's no such thing as ghosts."

"I see." Rowland was a little confused now.

"It might have been the track, I suppose," Rosaleen said thoughtfully.

Rowland gave up pretending to follow. "I'm sorry... you might have to explain."

"The speedway is cursed. It's only killed drivers before, but perhaps Crispy got caught in the curse."

Rowland recalled that White had said something about the track being cursed. He was no more convinced of its veracity. His scepticism must have shown, for Rosaleen seemed annoyed.

"I'd like to see your studio now," she huffed, pulling out a notebook and a pencil from her pocket.

Rowland wasn't sure he wanted the reporter in his studio but there was no way he could politely refuse. He took her into what had, in his father's time, been the opulent drawing room of the Sinclairs' Sydney residence. The room afforded views of the grounds through generous bay windows. It was the light in this part of the house that had moved Rowland to select it as his workspace. The room faced north-east. It caught the first clean light of morning and remained well lit throughout the day. There were large studio easels in each of the bays and another behind the couch. They were all splattered with paint, the largest almost entirely red—the result of an accident with dilute vermillion. A wing-backed armchair faced the wall on which was hung a daunting full-length portrait of Rowland's late father, Henry Sinclair.

They found Milton ensconced there with a novel.

"Rowly, did you—oh hello." Milton stood as he noticed Rosaleen. Rowland introduced the poet.

"I should leave you alone so you can talk," Milton said, preparing to depart.

"No," Rowland said hastily. "You carry on. Miss Norton is interviewing me for the paper. We won't be speaking in confidence."

Rosaleen Norton's attention was, however, elsewhere. She rummaged carefully through the canvasses stacked against the wall with an eye that was appraising. "Do you always paint from life, Mr. Sinclair?"

"Wherever possible. Sometimes, by necessity, I work from sketches or memory."

"But those sketches and memories are of actual things?"

"Yes, of course."

"But don't you think it's far more interesting to paint those things that other people can't see?"

"Like what?"

"Like whom," she said sweetly.

5

INTIMATE JOTTINGS

Did You Know That—
TRAVELLERS RETURN

AMONG those at Warwick Farm on Saturday were Major and Mrs. George Cossington Smythe. The Cossington Smythes are just back from a trip to China, and are settling into a new home in Point Piper. Their son has been packed off to Tudor House.

The Australian Women's Weekly, 1934

Milton was telling Edna and Clyde about the interview when Rowland joined them in the billiards room after seeing Rosaleen off. The poet had remained uncharacteristically silent throughout the conversation between Rowland and the reporter, occasionally lowering his book to grin, but refraining from any input.

"She told Rowly he should paint spirits?" Edna's legs swung as she perched on the edge of the billiards table.

Clyde poked her with a cue. "Get off, Ed, you're interfering with my shot."

"She was of the opinion that your spirit would be far more interesting than your body," Milton said as he watched Clyde take his turn.

Edna shrugged. "I do wonder what my spirit looks like."

"Fangs. You would definitely have fangs," Milton replied.

"A decent portrait is always more than visible features, I suppose," Rowland offered in a gallant attempt to be fair.

Milton snorted. "That's not what she meant Rowly and you know it!"

"I don't suppose Miss Norton's a Theosophist?" Clyde asked.

"Doubt it." Rowland slipped off his jacket and took a cue. "She's just a girl—couldn't be much more than eighteen. I suspect she simply says the most shocking thing that comes to mind."

"Young people these days." Milton shook his head.

"Did you talk about the car, Rowly?" Clyde asked.

"No. She says she has White's notes."

"But his notebook wasn't with the body."

"Perhaps it was discovered at his lodgings," Rowland said, frowning. He paused for a moment. "Miss Norton seems to believe that he was working on a story about a coven at Magdalene's Waxworks. She thinks that might explain why White was there."

"A coven? That's ridiculous!" Edna said. "Are you sure she wasn't joking, Rowly?"

"No, I don't believe so."

"If White were at Magdalene's researching a story, why didn't he take his notebook?" Milton said, leaning his cue against the table.

"My thinking exactly," Rowland agreed.

"He was pretty sloshed when you drove him home, Milt," Clyde pointed out. "Perhaps he just forgot."

"And yet he was sober enough to get into a locked building to follow a news story," Rowland murmured.

"Perhaps you should mention this to Detective Delaney," Edna suggested.

Clyde agreed. "We need to feed Delaney everything we can, so he doesn't feel the need to look too closely at Milt."

"You do know I didn't kill him, don't you?" Milton said irately.

"Of course I do," Clyde replied. "But that might not be enough to keep you out of prison. They arrested Rowly last year despite his impeccable connections. Your connections, old mate, are not impeccable and you have a habit of falling out with the authorities."

Rowland had to concur on that count. Milton's politics and his nature had seen him arrested on a number of occasions— misdemeanours, as far as Rowland knew, aside from the time the poet had assaulted a police officer so he could accompany Rowland to gaol. That police officer had been Colin Delaney. Rowland suspected that the detective was avoiding looking at Milton, but he would have to do so if no other candidate presented. "I'll telephone Delaney," he promised, though he wished he could do so with more than a young girl's claim that there were witches at the end of the garden.

Milton changed the subject. "When are you trying out the speedway, Rowly?"

"Joan Richmond's arranged for our team to practise laps at Maroubra tomorrow," Rowland replied. He was looking forward to testing the Mercedes on the bowl. He glanced at his watch. It was nearly nine o'clock. "I'm taking Ernie out today. Would you all care to join us?"

Ernest Sinclair, Rowland's nephew, was seven years old. He had that year started at Tudor House near Moss Vale, where his father and uncles had attended before him. Like most boarders, Ernest would go home to the Sinclair estate in Yass at the end of each term, but rarely a weekend went by where he didn't see his uncle. Ernest would catch the train up to Sydney or Rowland would collect him from the school to take him on some outing or other. Often the other residents of *Woodlands House* would come along, and together they would give Ernest a time that made him the envy of his school chums.

"Rosie's parents are in town," Clyde said miserably. "She wants me to come to dinner at her cousin's house so I can spend some time with her father."

Rosalina Martinelli had once found gainful employment as Rowland's model; a job for which she proved temperamentally unsuited. Now she was Clyde's sweetheart; a role that suited her much more and which she was determined to convert into something more permanent.

"I thought her father didn't like you…" Edna began. They'd all heard Clyde's accounts of the man he swore was a retired Fascisti.

"The man loathes me," Clyde groaned. "But Rosie's convinced he'll get used to me."

"Well, you don't want that." Milton's warning was in earnest. "Once Martinelli gives you his blessing, it's all over, mate."

"Luckily, he hates the very idea of me." Clyde's mood lifted a little. "He'll never let Rosie marry someone like me."

"Perhaps you should ask for her hand before he changes his mind," Milton suggested.

Rowland offered no advice, he had none to give. His friend's love life had become inexplicably complex of late. It was not that Clyde wasn't devoted to Rosalina, but that he was not in a position to get married. Certainly not as an artist. And he was not ready to not be an artist, even for Rosalina. Rowland could have helped, would gladly have helped, if Clyde would allow him. But for reasons that were probably more than simple pride, Clyde would not hear of it.

Milton was less circumspect than Rowland. "Be sure to tell them you're not hungry."

"What?" Clyde demanded wearily.

Milton leaned in and outlined a plan. "At dinner, claim you're not hungry. Pick at a couple of things, but eat nothing. And screw up your face a lot." He nodded confidently. "Then her mother will hate you as well. My granny cried once because I wouldn't have a second helping. They take it very personally."

"I don't want to make Rosie's mother cry."

"It's self-defence, comrade, just in case the old man has a change of heart."

Clyde called the poet an idiot.

"Poor darling," Edna said, rubbing Clyde's arm. "I'm afraid I have another engagement as well, Rowly."

"Where are you off to?" Milton asked.

"I'm not really sure. Errol's collecting me."

"Flynn?" Clyde said. "You're stepping out with Flynn?"

"Well, yes?"

"You realise he's on Rowly's team?" Clyde threw his arms in the air. "If we lose because you break the poor blighter's heart, Ed…"

"Oh for heaven's sake, don't be absurd. I don't care about the race!"

They were still arguing when Milton and Rowland rose to leave.

Ernest Sinclair was ready when his uncle's flamboyant motorcar pulled up. Half a dozen boys waiting to be collected for weekend visits stood in an orderly line at the designated collection point, just outside Central Station, after catching the train from Moss Vale. Ernest paused only to have his name signed off by an older boy before running to the yellow Mercedes.

Rowland stepped out and shook Ernest's hand. "How are you, Ernie?"

"I'm very well, thank you, Uncle Rowly. Oh hallo, Mr. Isaacs." Ernest peered in through the window. "Aren't you getting out of the car?"

"Should I?"

"Nobody can see you in there, Mr. Isaacs."

Slowly, Milton alighted, glancing questioningly at Rowland who was equally bewildered. The poet shook hands with Ernest and then they all climbed back into the car and set off.

"Righto, Ernie, why did Mr. Isaacs need to get out of the car?" Rowland asked when it became clear that Ernest was not about to volunteer the information.

"Digby Cossington Smythe's never seen a real Communist up close. He gave me two shillings."

Rowland smiled.

"I believe you'd best give me one of those shillings, Ernie," Milton said looking back at the boy. "Since it seems that I am the means of production!"

Ernest fished a coin out of his pocket.

"I'm not sure you ought to be taking your classmate's pocket money, Ernie," Rowland said, trying to sound stern.

"I'd call it an equitable redistribution of wealth!" Milton laughed, handing back the shilling. "Keep it, Ernie mate, but you remember you made your first shilling off the back of a worker!"

Ernest nodded solemnly, committing the poet's words to memory. "Where are we going, Uncle Rowly?"

"I thought perhaps we might catch the ferry across to Manly."

"Can we go to the Fun Pier?"

"I don't see why not."

Ernest beamed. "That's so very kind of you, Uncle Rowly!"

They left the Mercedes at Circular Quay and boarded the ferry to Manly, standing on the deck and taking in the glorious blue of the harbour on a clear day. Ernest pointed out landmarks and described them with potted histories as if Rowland and Milton were first-time visitors to the city. He told them of the day the Sydney Harbour Bridge had been opened, forgetting entirely that he'd seen it all from Rowland's shoulders. Being a Saturday, the ferry was full with weekend trippers to the state's premier seaside venue. The sea air seemed festive, a cheerful anticipation of sand and sunshine.

The Fun Pier itself was a crush of families and sweethearts strolling arm in arm.

"Keep your eyes peeled for pickpockets," Milton warned as he glanced sideways at a band of youths moving through the crowd. Rowland grabbed Ernest's hand and kept him close. They rode the Ferris wheel first, and then watched as Ernest took a turn on the carousel. They split up to race through the mirror maze, accepting the tin medals awarded at completion with gravitas and acceptance speeches. Once they'd been through every exhibit and entertainment at least twice, they left the Fun Pier for the Shark Aquarium next door. That done, the party of three found a table at Burt's Milk Bar which stretched across the wharf frontage.

"May I have a milkshake, Uncle Rowly?" Ernest asked, having seen the American fad drink advertised on sandwich boards outside the milk bar.

"If it's not a cocktail," Rowland said, signalling a waitress. She assured him there was nothing stronger than flavouring in a milkshake and recommended the Girvana Sling for him and Milton. Apparently it was a specialty of the house.

"So what part of the Fun Pier did you like best, Ernie?" Milton asked as they enjoyed their respective beverages.

"The Ferris wheel, I suppose. The mirror maze was smashing too!" He pursed his lips thoughtfully. "The wax museum was appalling, don't you think?"

"It wasn't that bad, surely," Rowland protested, defending the handful of wax fairytale characters out of some vague inexplicable sense that it would be impolite not to do so.

"It was pretty poor," Milton confirmed.

"The statues weren't frightening at all, and nothing looked real," Ernest complained.

"I do believe Madame Tussaud's has made your standards a little high," Rowland said wryly. He had taken Ernest to the iconic waxworks when they were in London the previous year. Expecting Tussaud's at Manly Beach was probably optimistic.

The boy's deep blue eyes brightened on mention of the London wax museum. "Remember the werewolf? He was my favourite!"

"I thought you were frightened?"

"I'm seven years old now, Uncle Rowly," Ernest replied fiercely. "You'll find I've grown up quite a lot. And I do like being scared."

"It's a shame Magdalene's is closed," Milton sighed. "Plenty of ghouls and monsters there. Guaranteed to frighten even men of Ernie's advanced years."

"Is it closed?" Rowland asked, forgetting about his nephew for a moment.

"I expect so... after White."

Rowland frowned. "That was a couple of days ago. They probably wouldn't close down the entire waxworks."

"We could drop in on the way home."

Rowland winced. "I can't take Ernie to—"

"Oh yes you can!" Ernest interjected. "I'm seven!"

Milton pulled on the goatee he was currently sporting. "We could just drive past and have a gander. Ernie won't be out of our sights."

"I don't know." Rowland hesitated. "It seems a little macabre."

"It's a House of Horrors, Rowly. It's supposed to be macabre."

"Please Uncle Rowly. Please, please, please!"

Rowland made a valiant attempt to resist Ernest's pleas despite his own curiosity about the scene of White's grisly end. Eventually, however, he was defeated by the fact that his nephew and the poet joined forces to make the case for Magdalene's.

"Very well, if it's open we might stop in for a bit," Rowland conceded. Ernest was, after all, completely unaware of the murder, so there was no danger that he would be unduly disturbed, and anything they could learn about Magdalene's could well prove useful.

They finished their drinks and a plate of chipped potatoes before catching the next ferry back to Circular Quay. From there it was barely ten minutes' drive to Kings Cross and Magdalene's House of the Macabre. The waxworks was open and, indeed, busy.

They parked the Mercedes and joined the queue at the door which spilled out onto Macleay Street.

"Eternity." Ernest read out the word inscribed in chalk on the concrete as they waited for the line to move. "It's spelled wrong."

Rowland looked. Eternity had indeed been spelled with a "u" in place of the second "e".

"What's it mean, Uncle Rowly?"

"I'm not sure," Rowland admitted. He'd seen the word chalked in the same copperplate hand, with the same spelling mistake, a couple of times on pavements in the city. He'd never given it a great deal of thought.

The elderly cashier who took their money and passed out tickets from a narrow booth window at the hall's entrance was, to Rowland's mind, ideally suited to employment in an establishment like Magdalene's. Her face was more crumpled than wrinkled, her hair a wild mane of frizzled grey. She wore a patch over one eye and glared at them with the other while she puffed on a chipped black pipe. Rowland noticed that Ernest's eyes had widened already.

They shuffled into the first exhibit room, which had been designed to resemble a crypt. Some of the sarcophagi were open to reveal wax corpses inside. One contained a mummy. Ghouls and vampires inhabited the shadows. On closer examination, Rowland could see that the statues consigned to the gloomy corners were damaged or unfinished in some way. Count Dracula was little more than a vampire scarecrow with a wax head. The cobwebs, while fitting, were real. Still, Ernest seemed impressed.

The second hall housed a fearsome collection of historical figures: Genghis Khan, Napoleon Bonaparte, unnamed Vikings and a caveman. Skeletons hung from wires in the internal courtyard. Rowland stopped, surprised, as they happened upon a young woman sobbing inconsolably as she perched on the edge of a rocking chair.

Rowland offered her his handkerchief, which she took though she didn't stop crying.

"She's an exhibit, Rowly," Milton whispered as he hoisted Ernest onto his shoulders, so the boy could get a closer look at the tusked boar's head mounted above the door.

"Oh, I see." Rowland laughed, but did not attempt to retrieve his handkerchief. Instead, he observed the other visitors to Magdalene's. Several families, as one would expect, quite a few young courting couples as well as a surprising number of single men. Nobody who looked like they might belong to a coven. The attendants, however, all looked like they dabbled in black magic, but he presumed that was a requirement of employment. A narrow stairwell leading to the second floor was cordoned off. Intrigued, Rowland peered up in the hope of catching a glimpse of what was up there.

"I'm sorry, sir, the second floor is not open to the public." The young woman who had accepted his handkerchief tapped him on the shoulder. It seemed she had been relieved by another girl in a similar white dress, who wailed in her stead while she partook of a cigarette.

"Oh, pardon me." Rowland smiled contritely as he removed his hat. "I don't suppose that's where that poor chap was killed?"

"No, the second floor is always private. The gent passed over in the Greek Room." She pointed towards a closed door. "It's all cleaned up now, but Mr. Magdalene thought we oughta close it to the public for a week outa respect."

"Quite properly. But it is a shame. I've always had an utter fascination for Greek mythology. I expect it's an impressive exhibit."

"Oh, it isn't that great. A couple of men in sheets, a woman with snakes in her hair and the devil."

"The devil? Really? I'm pretty sure he wasn't Greek."

"Well he's always been there. Cloven hooves, evil little horns…"

Rowland nodded. "That's probably meant to be Pan. It'd make a little more sense in a Greek exhibit."

The young woman in white laughed. "This is a House of Horrors. I wouldn't be expecting much in the way of rhyme and reason!"

"I suppose not." Rowland glanced back up the staircase. "Why is the second floor closed off? Is it a residence?"

The young woman shrugged. "Staff ain't allowed up there neither. Mr. Magdalene uses it for his meetings. Why are you so interested, Mr…?"

"Sinclair." Rowland introduced himself. She giggled at the formality of his manners, told him her name was Daisy Forster, and promised she would return his handkerchief once she'd laundered it. Her mother took in laundry, she said, so it would be no bother. By the time Daisy finished talking, she appeared to have forgotten whatever suspicions she might have held about his interest.

"I wonder who'd meet in a House of Horrors," Rowland mused aloud.

"The Magdalenes are a little odd," Daisy confided. "I do this circus act for my wages, but the Magdalenes, they like this sort of thing. Their friends too."

"What friends?"

"The men who come to their meetings… skulking upstairs in their capes and masks." She shuddered. "Still, they're not mean or nasty to work for. Just strange." She took one final long drag of her cigarette and then crushed it under her heel. "I'd best get back, Emily sounds a little hoarse."

6

BRIDES FROM ITALY

Included among the passengers on the Orsova, which reached Brisbane last week from London, were a number of Italian Immigrants who are about to seek their fortunes in Queensland. Some of the menfolk, however, were not making the trip for the first time. They had been settled in the North before, and had amassed sufficient money to visit their homeland and marry, and they have brought their brides back with them.

Daily Mercury, 1934

"Easy, Rowly," Milton cautioned. Rowland hadn't said anything, but his fury was plain. Ernest silently took his uncle's hand.

Quite heroically, Rowland managed not to curse.

"What happened to your car, Uncle Rowly?" Ernest whispered.

"Some… scoundrel's slashed the tyres, mate," Rowland replied, editing out his more profane sentiments.

"Who?"

Rowland glanced at Milton. This was not the first time the Mercedes had attracted unwelcome attention, though it had been some time since anyone had attacked the car herself. He was annoyed with himself for having become complacent about where he parked the automobile. "It's only the tyres," he sighed. "They're replaceable." He shook his head. "We had better see about getting her home."

Rowland left Milton and Ernest with the Mercedes and went back into the waxworks in the hope of using their telephone.

The old woman with the patch and pipe was initially reluctant, but she was eventually persuaded by the gentleman's willingness to pay compensation. The ticketing booth was so small she had to step out in order for him to use the wall-mounted telephone. Rowland rang through to *Woodlands House*, looking curiously around the inside of the booth while he waited for connection. All manner of objects had been pinned to the walls: the usual pamphlets and notes as well as medallions and a large poster on which columns of numbers had been written within the triangles of a pentagram. A large jar of dead spiders sat on a shelf and a dagger lay on a pile of opened envelopes.

When *Woodlands House* came on the line, he spoke to Johnston, the chauffeur, explaining what had happened and asking him to arrange for a lorry to collect the Mercedes.

"I'll be out to fetch you directly, sir," Johnston declared when Rowland told him of his intention to call a motor taxi.

Rowland conceded. He did not want to offend the old chauffeur, and he was aware that Johnston felt slighted by the fact that the current master of *Woodlands* generally preferred to drive himself.

And so it was in one of the family's Rolls Royces that Ernest Sinclair was driven back to Tudor House. There were no tears, just a fleeting sadness as they said a manly goodbye. The first time Rowland had returned his nephew after a weekend outing, Ernest had only been at school a couple of weeks. He'd sobbed bitterly and pleaded with Rowland to take him home.

Despite the protests of the housemaster, Rowland had taken Ernest back to *Woodlands* and, determined to rescue the boy, telephoned his brother in Yass. Wilfred had told him not to be an idiot. "Of course he'd rather live with you and have every whim indulged, Rowly. He's seven years old. If you're going to take him out on weekends, you're going to have to learn to deal with this sort of thing."

Even so, Wilfred had come up to Sydney the following week, to check that Ernest was settling in at boarding school.

Over the weekends that had followed, both Ernest and Rowland had become accustomed to the parting, so that now it was conducted with a simple and dignified handshake.

When the Rolls Royce finally pulled into the stables behind the house, the Mercedes had been returned and was jacked up on blocks.

Clyde popped up from under the bonnet. "What the hell happened?" he demanded.

"Someone slashed the tyres," Rowland murmured as he greeted Lenin who had woken from his slumber in a shaft of fading sunlight when he heard his master's voice.

"Well, I can see that! Bloody oath Rowly, did you park her next to the Cenotaph?"

"Can we get another set of tyres before tomorrow?" Rowland asked, a little surprised. Clyde was the most even-tempered of them. He occasionally found cause to call Milton the odd name, but that was probably understandable.

"I got in some extra tyres and wheels because of the race, but I didn't expect to have to use them already," Clyde growled, kicking one of the ruined tyres.

Rowland remembered then that Clyde should have been dining with Rosalina Martinelli's family. "I say, what are you still doing here, Clyde?"

"What did you do?" Milton said, glancing over his shoulder to see that Johnston had discreetly retired.

Clyde swore. They let him do that for a while and they asked again. "What happened, mate?"

"The Martinellis didn't just come to Sydney to see Rosie. They were meeting a ship." He shook his head and groaned. "They've brought some bloke over from Italy."

"So?"

"They brought him over so he could marry Rosie."

"That's medieval!" Milton scoffed. "Rosalina won't agree to that!"

"I'm afraid that's not how her family works." Clyde slammed down the bonnet. Rowland winced, as much for his car as for Clyde. "I'm such a bloody fool. I had my chance and I blew it!" He turned away, his shoulders slumped.

Milton climbed into the Rolls Royce and opened the walnut cabinet fitted into the back of the front seat. He grabbed a half-sized bottle of sherry, another of gin, and three crystal tumblers. With no regard for the duco, he poured drinks on the Rolls Royce's bonnet.

"Clyde," Rowland said gently, "she hasn't married him yet, mate."

"Rowly, you don't understand Rosie. She wouldn't do that to her parents."

"She wanted to marry you, remember?"

Milton handed Clyde a drink. "Where is she?" he asked.

"Why?"

"We'll put new tyres on the car and go get her. You can marry her tomorrow, before the other bloke's had time to unpack."

Clyde laughed bitterly. "You want me to abduct her?"

"You say abduct, I say rescue."

"Whatever you want to do, Clyde," Rowland said calmly, "we'll help you. Are you sure Rosie won't defy her parents? She was my model once… I'm sure her parents wouldn't have approved of that either."

Clyde rubbed his face. "You're right. Maybe I'm underestimating Rosie."

"Perhaps if you talk to her?" Rowland suggested. "Before you abduct her, at least."

Clyde nodded.

"We could take the Rolls if you'd like to go now."

"No." Clyde picked up a tyre lever. "We'll fix your vehicle while I try to work out what I'm going to say."

Rowland and Milton removed their jackets and rolled up their sleeves. With Clyde directing the process, they replaced the Mercedes' wheels with the four already prepared for the race. Clyde refitted the tyres on the four they took off. "Just don't get a flat tomorrow," he warned Rowland. "I can't put any of these on until they're balanced and weighted."

"Have you decided what you're going to say, comrade?" Milton asked.

Clyde shrugged. "Thought I might beg."

Milton nodded. "Nothing as attractive as a desperate man."

Rowland swatted the poet. Poor Clyde was not in the mood for jest. "It might be an idea to get cleaned up first," he said.

Clyde looked down at his grease-covered hands. "Yes, I suppose I should." He sounded quite forlorn.

"Chin up, old mate." Milton gripped his friend's shoulder. "Rowly and I will be there. You'll seem eminently marriageable by contrast."

Rowland was the first to come downstairs after showering. Milton had always taken greater time and care with his personal presentation and, on this occasion, perhaps Clyde was doing so too. Rowland, however, maintained an indifference to his appearance, possibly born of the knowledge that his suits were impeccably tailored and generally the best that money could buy.

He spoke to Mary Brown, requesting the housekeeper arrange for a posy of flowers to be sourced from the gardens, before ducking into his mother's part of the house. Elisabeth Sinclair had spent most of the day with her sister-in-law, Rowland's Aunt Mildred. They'd taken luncheon at the Queen's Club and then played euchre for the afternoon.

"We might be quite late home, Mother, if you'd like to join us for supper?"

"No, no, Aubrey darling. I'm rather tired this evening. I don't have the same vitality now that I'm fifty." She shook her head. "We all get older, I suppose."

Rowland smiled faintly. His mother was sixty-five. It was one of the facts she'd forgotten. The consequence was that she behaved as if she were fifty, taking up the pastimes and amusements and vigour she'd had back then, which he did not consider a bad thing. To be honest, Rowland had been as surprised as anybody when Elisabeth Sinclair had resettled so well to life at *Woodlands*. Indeed, she seemed a lot less perturbed by the unconventional manner in which he ran his house than Wilfred had always been—for now at least—and Rowland was not a man to borrow trouble from tomorrow.

He kissed his mother goodnight and left her to the kindly, watchful eye of Nurse Samuels, who was on duty that evening.

"Your mama seems very well, sir," she whispered before he departed. "She's talking of taking up golf again."

"Well as long as it's not tap dancing," he murmured, taking his leave and returning to the main part of the house to wait for his friends.

"Why are you wearing a dinner suit?" Milton demanded when Clyde finally came down.

"I thought..." Clyde began uncertainly. "Ed always said..."

Rowland bit his lip. It was Edna's oft-declared opinion that every man looked his best in formal wear. Clearly sensible, practical Clyde had been paying more attention than any of them realised.

"Oh mate..." Milton groaned.

"Clyde's right," Rowland said. "Dinner suits are the appropriate attire for proposals."

"No, I look daft." What small confidence Clyde had was dissipating quickly.

"Ten minutes," Rowland said. "Milt and I will change. We'll look like we're all on our way to dinner somewhere."

Milton glared at Rowland, but he agreed and they too donned dinner suits.

"So what exactly are we doing?" Milton asked from the back seat as they pulled out of the drive.

Rowland glanced at Clyde who sat rigidly beside him with a bouquet of flowers in his hands. "Clyde?"

Clyde stared at his friends for a moment. "I'm going to speak to her father. Ask him for Rosie's hand."

Neither Rowland nor Milton said anything. Clyde seemed to be choosing the most dangerous possible course of action.

The Martinellis were staying at Sorrentino's Guesthouse in Leichhardt, a respectable but modest establishment that catered to families and commercial travellers.

Upon enquiry at the reception desk, they were informed the Martinellis were in the communal dining room. "Will you be dining here, sir?" the manager asked eyeing their dinner suits.

"Umm… yes, we will," Rowland replied.

"Will anyone be joining you, sir?"

"No."

The manager's gaze lingered on the bouquet in Clyde's hand before he invited them to make their way into the dining room.

"Right," Clyde exhaled. Milton and Rowland fell in behind him.

Rowland wasn't sure what he'd expected to be the reaction to Clyde's appearance, but he wasn't surprised that Rosalina burst into tears. In his experience, she did that a lot. When Miss Martinelli had been his model, he'd resorted to painting her weeping because she seemed to hold no other pose for long. It was also not a shock that Rosalina's father seemed angered by the intrusion. They had, after all, been hearing for some time how much he disliked Clyde. It was the other men that he had not anticipated: seven of them, who stood when Clyde entered.

Guesthouse patrons at other tables looked on with interest at what was clearly a drama about to unfold.

Clyde continued nonetheless, addressing the patriarch at the head of the table. "Mr. Martinelli, sir, I'd like to speak with you if that's possible."

Martinelli's moustache bristled. He glanced at his daughter who was sobbing into her mother's ample breast. Mrs. Martinelli shouted in Italian, as indeed did almost everybody else at the table. Only Rowland understood the language but they all gathered that their presence was not welcome.

Finally Martinelli spoke. His English was slow but clear. "My wife and daughter are upset. We'll speak outside." He nodded towards a door that led out to a courtyard garden.

Clyde nodded. "Thank you, sir." Awkwardly, he left his bouquet of flowers on the table, and stepped out. Martinelli did likewise.

Rowland and Milton hesitated. It was only when the other gentlemen at the table moved to follow Martinelli that they realised the meeting was not going to be private and they, too, stepped into the courtyard.

"So speak!" Martinelli demanded.

7

AUSTRALIAN GIRL WINS ENGLISH CLASSIC

JOAN RICHMOND'S UNIQUE SUCCESS

AUSTRALIA'S greatest success in classic motor racing for years past, was secured during the weekend by Joan Richmond, a Melbourne girl.

WITH Mrs. Wisdom, an English driver, she won the 1000 miles race at Brooklands—most important of the British long distance races. It was the first time women had won the race, which is a two-day handicap event.

The winners used a Riley: averaged 84.4 m.p.h. and in a vicious skid at a spot where one of the drivers fatally crashed, had a perilously close escape.

Referee, 1932

Clyde cleared his throat. "Mr. Martinelli, I'd very much like to ask for your daughter's hand—"

"No, no, no... No hand, no finger, no toes!" Rosalina Martinelli's father poked the man who would be her husband in the chest. "You go! Speak never to Rosalina again!" Clyde was oblivious to the string of Italian insults that followed but he did recognise, "Comunista!"

Valiantly, he stood his ground. He seemed more confident now. "Rosie cares for me, Mr. Martinelli. I promise you, I'll look after her."

"No! She is for Antonio, not you."

"She doesn't know Antonio. Just ask her what she wants." Clyde turned back towards the dining room. "Rosie!" Three men charged, dragging him back as he tried to get Rosalina's attention.

"Hey!" Rowland and Milton stepped in, as did the other four men who'd followed Martinelli outside. The first punch was swung by the Martinelli camp, but it was returned unequivocally. Waiters from the dining room came out to join the fray, their allegiances clearly with the Martinellis.

"Clyde!" Rowland dragged off the man who'd had his friend pinned, as he tried to get Clyde to his feet before the next blow descended.

"Time to retreat, comrades," Milton shouted, defending a blow and delivering one of his own.

Rowland doubted they would be given a chance to retreat. He was right. Outnumbered, they were, in the end, subdued and thrown out, unceremoniously with no regard whatsoever for their dinner suits.

Rowland was the first to rise gingerly to his feet. "Milt, Clyde, are you chaps all right?"

Milton cursed. Clyde grabbed Rowland's hand and pulled himself up.

"Bloody hell!" Rowland murmured as he looked at Clyde's bruised face.

Clyde took out a handkerchief and mopped his bloody nose. Milton moved his jaw tentatively, wincing as he did so. "That went well."

Rowland reached inside his jacket and extracted his notebook. He handed it to Clyde. "Write her a note," he said. "We'll get it to Rosie."

"Her father isn't going to allow—"

"Leave that to me. Just write."

Clyde stared at the open page. "I don't know how to start."

"How about, Dear Rosie?" Rowland suggested.

"My beloved Rosalina," Milton amended.

Clyde wrote.

"You could compose a sonnet in her honour," Milton suggested. "What about, O! I shall soon despair, when I shall see, that thou lovest mankind well, yet wilt not choose me."

"Sadly, John Donne's already composed that one," Rowland cautioned. "And I believe it's a religious exaltation, not a romantic one."

Clyde cursed and crossed out the words, "O! I shall soon despair".

Over the next ten minutes Clyde wrote his heart onto several pages of Rowland's notebook. Milton and Rowland both tried to help when words eluded him. Clyde made his admiration and devotion plain and asked only that Rosalina let him know, somehow, if she welcomed it. If so, he promised he would press his case and marry her. He tore the pages from the notebook and handed them to Rowland who slipped the missive into his pocket.

"Righto, just give me a few minutes." Dusting off his trousers, Rowland slipped around to the rear of the guesthouse. The back door was open and he could see the kitchen. A couple of children stood outside with empty cooking pots, which a waiter soon came out to collect. Rowland waited until he reappeared with the pots filled and had returned them to the children.

"Excuse me," he said quietly, stepping out of the shadows to catch the man's attention. He spoke in Italian, quickly offering the waiter a pound note if he would slip Clyde's note to Rosalina Martinelli.

The man shook his head, alarmed.

Rowland doubled the incentive, emptying his pocket book.

Still the waiter resisted.

"Please," Rowland said. "My friend is in love with Miss Martinelli. She ought to know that before she marries someone else."

"*Amore?*" The waiter waivered and then relented. Perhaps he was a romantic. Even so, he took the money as well as the note.

"So what do we do now?" Milton asked when Rowland returned with the news that the letter would be delivered.

"We go home and wait for Miss Martinelli to reply."

"If she replies," Clyde said miserably.

"Did you work out which one the imported husband was, Clyde?" Milton asked.

"I believe he was sitting next to Rosie. The other blokes are her brothers and cousins. I've met them all at some time or other."

Rowland glanced back at the restaurant. "Come on, let's go, before the Martinellis come out and find us still here."

Mary Brown sighed as she directed a late supper be prepared. She had not asked what had happened to cause Rowland Sinclair and his companions to return in such a state. She assumed that Mr. Isaacs had taken them to some disreputable premises, where at some point he'd involved them in a common brawl. It wasn't the first time. The housekeeper had never understood why a young man of Rowland Sinclair's breeding would insist upon consorting with men who were beneath him in every way. She had hoped he might see sense and settle down once Mrs. Sinclair had come to live at *Woodlands*, but it appeared that hope had been in vain.

She delivered a cold supper of venison pie and new potatoes to the drawing room. One of the maids could have done it, of course, but Mary Brown would not allow young girls into the desecrated parlour lest they be distressed, or worse, corrupted by what the master of the house did in there.

"Let me help you with that, Miss Brown," Clyde said, attempting to take the laden tray from her.

The housekeeper's glare was so hostile that Clyde stepped back. Mary Brown sniffed, and very purposefully placed the tray on the sideboard before she picked up the dinner jackets which had been hung over the back of the couch.

"I shall send these to be repaired," she said tightly.

"Yes, thank you, Mary," Rowland replied, trying not to smile. His housekeeper's ability to strike terror into the hearts of his companions amused him. He was not entirely inured to Mary Brown's ire himself.

For some minutes they said nothing.

Then Milton suggested they drink. Surely Clyde had good reason, and it would be churlish to allow him to drink alone. Rowland was not unwilling, but Clyde would not hear of it.

"Rowly's got to drive tomorrow," he said firmly.

"It's just a practice run," Rowland argued.

"Do you know how many men have been killed practising on that track?" Clyde replied. "It's got a bad name, Rowly, you'll need your wits about you."

Rowland grimaced. "You and Milt can drink."

"I need to keep an eye on your motorcar." Clyde was resolute.

Milton rolled his eyes and poured himself a glass of whisky.

Rowland pushed up his sleeves and studied the work on his easel. He squeezed a tube of burnt umber onto a clean palette and selected a palette knife.

Clyde considered the painting from his armchair. "That's Germany again," he said, recognising the scene—the cowering prisoner under the brutal shadow of the Stürm Arbeitslung. He scowled. Rowland was not a man to speak of what was troubling him, and the last time he'd painted like this, he'd been in a bad way. "Is there anything wrong, Rowly?"

"Wrong?"

"Yes. Are you sleeping all right?"

"Me? Yes, of course." He realised suddenly why his friend was concerned. "I'm not painting to expel demons this time." Rowland looked back at the scene on the canvas. "My head's not here, not all the time anyway." He told them about his plans for an exhibition.

"So you want to trick people into coming?" Milton asked.

"Yes, I suppose so."

"You're going to need some landscapes," Clyde said.

"Why?"

"Decoys… for publicity, programs, that sort of rigmarole. You don't want anyone to guess what you're up to until they're actually at the exhibition."

"Rowly doesn't paint scenery," Milton pointed out. "What's more, he's not particularly good at painting scenery."

"That's true, his landscapes border on horrible," Clyde agreed. He pointed to a full-length portrait of Edna, a frontal nude that managed to be gentle and wistful despite the starkness of the pose. There was a softness in Rowland's brushwork that seemed to caress his subject as much as define her. Clyde shook his head. "I've never understood how you could paint something like that and not be able to draw a tree."

Rowland couldn't offer anything in his own artistic defence. He'd given up painting landscapes for good reason.

"I could paint something for you, Rowly," Clyde offered. "I have some sketches I did at the Starnberger See as well as Ed's photos I could work from. You could just sign the finished product."

Rowland hesitated. "You wouldn't mind?"

Clyde laughed. "There are some very fine portraits with my name on them thanks to that caper you pulled on the New Guard, so let's call it even." He paused. "Actually, I'd like to help. Doing nothing after what we saw in Germany doesn't sit well with me either."

"You and Milt haven't done nothing…"

"Addressing the crowds at Trades Hall is preaching to the converted and a few surveillance officers, mate." Milton considered the painting of the book burning which sat on one of the other easels. "What you're planning could change the minds and attitudes that matter. I can't paint, Rowly, but count me in too." He glanced at Clyde. "If nothing else it'll be a relief to think about something other than our current troubles."

Joan Richmond was already at the speedway when they arrived. Clyde and Rowland watched her taking the Riley around the track. The day was cool and clear. Dark-suited men with notebooks and briefcases stood alongside cheering children and looked down over the bowl from the outer perimeter fence.

"Sydney's SP bookies are taking an interest, I see," Clyde muttered, glancing up at the onlookers.

"Are they taking bets?" Rowland asked, looking for the characteristic boards.

"No. I'd say they're sizing up the runners before they set the odds."

Joan brought the little Riley to a stop.

"Hallo there," she called, climbing out of the car.

"Miss Richmond," Rowland said, tipping his hat.

"For pity's sake, Rowly, it's Joan!"

"Of course. May I introduce my friend and the chief of my pit crew, Mr. Clyde Watson Jones?"

"Charmed," Joan said, pumping Clyde's hand. "Let's not waste any time, Clyde. You must call me Joan, too. By the end of all this we'll be well acquainted enough to warrant it." She beckoned to the man checking over her engine and introduced him as Bucky Oldfield, her mechanic.

"Righto, Rowly, are you ready? We've already cleared the track of snakes."

"Snakes?"

"Oh yes. The cement holds the heat, you see. You don't want a blessed snake getting caught up in your axle."

"Indeed."

"I might drive in front of you for a while, till you get used to the bowl." She pointed out the parts of the speedway where the cement track was crumbling. "Just jolly well try to avoid those patches if you can, especially if you're at speed."

Clyde handed Rowland his driving helmet and goggles. "Good luck, mate."

Joan Richmond slid in behind the wheel of her Riley and waved. "Try and keep up, Rowly."

Over the next hour Rowland followed the Riley, becoming accustomed to driving in the bowl by staying in Joan Richmond's tracks. He learned not to fight his Mercedes, allowing it to take its natural position on the banking. It became much easier to control despite the ever-increasing speed at which he took each circuit. Even so, he did not have the need or opportunity to engage the supercharger. In time, the Riley pulled out so he could give his larger engine its head. He did so, being careful to remember where the cement bowl had deteriorated since its construction just over a decade earlier. Eventually, Rowland pulled back allowing the Mercedes to slow, lapping lower and lower on the bank until he eased her to a gradual stop.

Joan met him as he got out of the vehicle. "Good show, Rowly! You probably don't have to give her so many laps to slow down, though."

"Oh, I was just following your lead."

"No need. The Riley's never had much in the way of brakes, but Clyde tells me that your braking system is top drawer. Might as well use it, there's a good chap."

"I see," Rowland said, impressed that Joan seemed to regard brakes an unnecessary luxury.

He spotted Errol Flynn's silver Triumph. "I see Flynn's arrived," he said. "Good Lord, what is he doing?" Flynn was standing on the bonnet addressing a small gathering.

"Talking to the press," Joan said, clearly exasperated. "I say, Rowly, I don't suppose you could distract the journalists long enough for me to teach him to drive?"

"Distract them? How am I supposed to do that?"

"Perhaps if you just give the reporters someone else to talk to. We only have the jolly track for another hour."

"I'll try," Rowland said uncertainly.

He and Joan walked over to the Triumph. Flynn greeted them cheerily. "And here, gentlemen, is my crewmate and our intrepid captain." Flynn saluted and then introduced them to Mr. Murray from *The Sydney Morning Herald*, Mr. Caletti from *The Guardian*, Mr. Bergin from *The Times* and their respective photographers.

"I'm sure you gentlemen are as eager as I am to see Mr. Flynn behind a wheel," Rowland said.

"There's plenty of time for that!" Flynn replied. "I was just telling these gentlemen about my time aboard *The Bounty*."

"Oh, I thought that was a film set?"

"Yes, yes it was, but I'm from seafaring stock, Sinclair. Just show me a horizon towards which to point my prow—"

Joan Richmond reached the end of her tether. "Get in the car, Mr. Flynn!" Her tone invited no further discussion.

Flynn was plainly startled.

Joan reached into the driver's seat of the Triumph and tossed Flynn his helmet and goggles, and fixed the actor with such a glare that he meekly put them on.

"Right," she said. "Follow my car."

"She's bloody fearsome," Flynn whispered to Rowland as Joan returned to the Riley. "I find it rather fetching myself. If I hadn't just spent the evening with Miss Higgins, I'd be tempted…"

"I suggest you get into your car, Flynn," Rowland said tersely.

"Oh yes, right. Don't want to upset the captain. Heave-ho, then!"

When the time came to hand the raceway over to another team, Errol Flynn somehow invited himself back to *Woodlands* for a late luncheon. "Nothing like a meal and few drinks to get the crew pulling together," he declared.

Joan Richmond declined to join them despite, or perhaps because of, Flynn's appeals that it was her duty as captain to "come ashore with the crew".

Flynn's Triumph had been blowing light grey smoke. Joan and Bucky Oldfield volunteered to have a look at it and adjust the carburettor, refusing hastily when the other gentlemen offered to stay and assist. "Just take Errol," Joan whispered to Rowland. "Please."

And so Errol Flynn was in the back seat of the Mercedes when they approached the underpass that led in and out of the Maroubra Bowl. The motorcar's canopy, having been removed for racing, was still down. The gentleman who flagged them was just outside the underpass.

Assuming that the man was in need of assistance of some sort, Rowland pulled over and stepped out. It was only then that he noticed the half-dozen other men who exchanged cigarettes in a haphazard contingent behind the first. Flynn and Clyde had also alighted, so it was too late to reconsider stopping.

"Wombat Newgate! What are you doing here?" Clyde singled out a fat man with a large flat nose who did, in brutal truth, look rather like a wombat.

"Good day to you, Mr. Watson Jones," Newgate said nervously.

Clyde introduced Rowland Sinclair and Errol Flynn to Milton's SP bookie.

Newgate said nothing. Instead, the man who had flagged them down spoke on the group's behalf, introducing himself as Redmond Barry, a businessman, entrepreneur and motor racing enthusiast. "So are we all," he said, waving a hand towards his companions, "all motor racing enthusiasts."

"Indeed," Rowland said. "What can we do for you, gentlemen?"

Barry grinned, exposing a gold tooth which caught the light in a manner that was almost dazzling. "Nothing at all, Mr. Sinclair. We just wanted to tell you of our interest, and wish you the best of luck."

Rowland glanced briefly at Clyde. "That's very civil of you, sir."

"How do you rate your chances, Sinclair?"

"Chances of what?"

"Of taking home the Lucky Devil, naturally."

"Why, excellent!" Flynn interjected. "I'd say we're the team to beat, wouldn't you, Rowly?"

Rowland's face was inscrutable. "We'll do our best, but you should understand that Mr. Flynn and I are complete novices to the sport. I expect the competition will be rather fierce."

The gathered men regarded them solemnly for a moment. "You're being modest, Mr. Sinclair," Barry said suddenly. "I'm willing to wager that Mr. Flynn here is dead on. You'll be leaving with the Devil."

"You're most kind," Rowland replied. "Thank you for your good wishes, gentlemen, but we'd best be on our way."

"We'd hoped you gentlemen might join us for a spot of luncheon," Barry said a little too pleasantly. "As our guests, of course—a show of our esteem."

"Thank you, Mr. Barry, but we are expected elsewhere," Rowland said calmly.

For the most fleeting moment Barry's face became hard, and then he was beaming again. "Well, we're disappointed, but rest assured we'll ask again. Good day, gentlemen. And drive carefully."

"I say, very decent of them to want to treat us to lunch," Flynn said as they got back into the Mercedes.

Rowland pulled back onto the road before he said, "They were bookies, Flynn. They are at best trying to get some kind of inside information before they set their odds."

"And at worst?"

"Well, that would also be about setting odds," Clyde replied. "Just not so sporting."

8

IN THE WAKE OF THE BOUNTY
NEW AUSTRALIAN PRODUCTION

Travelogues and dramas have drenched the screen with the spray of South Sea beaches until the filmgoer imagines that he knows every angle from which a palm can be photographed. Then an Australian, Mr. Charles Chauvel, makes "In the Wake of the Bounty," and presents the Pacific under a strange and cloudy beauty such as has never before been filmed...

...the first part of the film is a glamorous reconstruction of history, with young Errol Flynn playing the part of Fletcher Christian, Mayne Lynton that of Bligh, and Victor Gouriet that of the blind fiddler, who tells the tale.

The West Australian, 1933

There was a kitten asleep on the greyhound's head, and four more snuggled into the crevices of his bony body as he lay on the hearth. The sight might have been alarming if it weren't apparent that the felines were in charge. Lenin did not greet his master with more than a martyred glance. Rowland bent to scratch the hound's single ear. He had been worried that Lenin would eat Edna's rescued litter, but it seemed the small fluffy creatures had elicited a misplaced maternal instinct in the dog. Lenin was as besotted as a child by his kittens, tending them like a fussy hen and even poking his long sharp nose in when their mother was nursing. Milton called it embarrassing. Edna told the hound he had a better heart than most men.

Errol Flynn was delighted to find Edna at home when he arrived at *Woodlands* with Rowland and Clyde. But her presence did make proceedings somewhat awkward. Rowland was rarely hostile to the men who pursued Edna—after all, being so would have put him at odds with half of Sydney. But he did try to avoid anything more prolonged than the occasional handshake. Flynn, however, seemed eager to not only woo Edna, but also Rowland, who he'd taken to calling "the first mate". Milton, who clearly found it all amusing, encouraged the familiarity.

"Wombat Newgate!" Edna exclaimed, when Flynn finished recounting a somewhat more confrontational version of their encounter.

"Be careful," Milton warned. "Wombat's slow and harmless on his own, but he does have a tendency to mix with some nasty types."

"What do you know about Barry?" Rowland asked. Milton's connections within the criminal classes were extensive.

"Not much, but I'll find out. Just watch your back, Rowly. They may well be trying to fix the race."

"Well, they'd best reconsider that idea!" Flynn declared. "The first mate and I will send that notion to the bottom of the sea."

"Does he think he's a pirate?" Clyde whispered.

"Shhh!" Edna replied, giggling.

"I gather you're a sailor, Flynn," Rowland asked, keeping his face straight.

"Indeed, I am, mate!" Flynn replied. "Nothing like the roll of a deck on the waves, the taste of salt on your lips and a fair wind at your back…" He put his arm around Edna's waist and pulled her towards him. "A beautiful woman in every port!"

Clyde and Milton both waited for Rowland's cue, but he said nothing.

Edna laughed at Flynn, quite openly, and Rowland was heartened by the fact that she did not seem to care in the least that the man was a cad.

They sat down to luncheon in the conservatory as the day had become warm. Flynn was garrulous company, and though he was only twenty-five had already had quite the adventurous life. A Tasmanian by birth, he'd been educated in England and then at the Shore School in Sydney, from which he'd been expelled.

Having himself been expelled from Kings, Rowland was not particularly shocked by Flynn's almost boastful admission.

But the actor seemed keen to offer details.

"A youthful indiscretion with the school's obliging laundress." Flynn grinned, observably pleased with the story. "She was a very understanding lady. Shore was less so."

After his expulsion young Errol Flynn had gone to Papua New Guinea, seeking his fortune in tobacco plantations and mining. Sadly, fortune proved elusive, though he did do a lot of sailing.

Only the previous year had Flynn discovered his talent for acting, and now he'd set his sights on a career in films, where he expected his success with the ladies would be less of a problem. All this he recounted with such little malice that it was difficult to hold his cockiness against him.

If anything, Rowland was relieved. Flynn would not hold Edna's attention for long, however handsome he was supposed to be. Rowland had become accustomed to the sculptress' loves, and as long as they remained fleeting he could bear it.

When luncheon was concluded, Edna and Flynn decided to take a stroll. Clyde and Rowland retreated to their respective studios. Milton went with Clyde, and Lenin, having reluctantly relinquished the kittens to their mother, kept Rowland company. The artists were painting with purpose: Rowland images of oppression and violence and Clyde the pretty landscapes behind which they would hide.

Rowland had always worked quickly. Already a number of paintings were complete. There was one image, however, with which he struggled—a likeness of Ernst Röhm, whom he had first met in the Königplatz in Munich. His second encounter with the Nazi had ended badly. It was not that he'd forgotten the scarred, flaccid contours of Röhm's face. He had not forgotten any of it. Perhaps that was the problem. Whatever the reason, the painting of the book burning was still unfinished.

He worked intensely for the next few days. That was not unusual and, in a household of artists, perfectly acceptable. It had always been Rowland's way to paint feverishly when the muse was with him, late into the night and again at first light. He'd eat by his easel and come away from it only to shower or visit with his mother. She'd scold him for the state of his suit and send him on his way.

His houseguests came in and out of his studio: Milton read and intermittently poured drinks; Clyde borrowed pigments and commented collegially on the progress and the challenges of whatever piece was on his easel at the time; and Edna visited to chat about all manner of subjects and left him feeling somehow lighter. Occasionally all three would come at once and play cards, but he would paint.

It was Thursday when Mary Brown came in to inform him that Miss Rosaleen Norton of *Smith's Weekly* had called to see him. Rowland frowned, a little irritated to be interrupted. He'd thought he'd finished with the decidedly strange Miss Norton.

Still, it would not do to be discourteous.

"Ask her to come in, Mary. Don't worry, she's already seen the studio."

The housekeeper sighed fiercely, but she showed the reporter in.

Rosaleen Norton was once again wearing a scarf as a blouse. Rowland couldn't help but think it was a distinctly precarious way to dress with rather too much reliance being placed on corners remaining tucked. She carried a large cardboard folio awkwardly under her arm.

Rowland put down his brush and wiped his hands on his waistcoat. "Miss Norton. Hello, again. What brings you back to *Woodlands*?"

"I felt a need to share my drawings with you, Mr. Sinclair. I thought you might like to see them."

"Oh, yes, of course," Rowland said, though he could not remember expressing interest in the reporter's drawings.

She glanced at the canvas on his easel—the book burning. "Weren't you working on that last Sunday?"

"I have been painting other pieces since," Rowland replied. "I'm just now resuming work on it." This was not strictly true. While Rowland had worked on other pieces he had also tried several times to complete the painting.

"I do like it," she said. "There's a sense of ominous ghastliness about it… as though there's something monstrous lurking behind the canvas."

Rowland glanced at the space in the composition waiting for Ernst Röhm. Perhaps there was.

He cleared the brushes and palettes off the card table so that Rosaleen could lay out her folio. The first drawings were those she'd drafted for *Smith's Weekly*. Visual jokes really… Two fat ladies with cigarettes captioned "heavy smokers", two cats dressed as women making catty comments about the attire of a third. They were well drawn. Rosaleen's line work was competent if unremarkable. But she seemed young, so Rowland expected that she would, in time, develop a more individualistic style. Then, as he leafed through, the drawings became more confronting. A circle of young mothers devouring their babies and laughing hysterically, and esoteric pieces of fantastic and explicit figures.

"As you can see, I too have been influenced by the works of Norman Lindsay, and am also a great admirer of Pan," she said, pulling out a detailed pencil sketch that depicted the god on his cloven haunches, a rearing snake in place of a phallus.

"Do you mind if I ask how old you are, Miss Norton?"

Her chin pulled back as she smiled. "I see you've read my story in *Smith's Weekly*. I know it states I'm fifteen, but that was just when I wrote the story. I'm seventeen now."

"Actually, I'm afraid I haven't come across your work."

"Oh." She rummaged through the folio. "Never mind. I do believe I have a copy of it here. It was published in January." She handed him a newspaper cutting. "You can keep that if you like." She rolled her eyes. "My mother bought about sixty copies, so I have plenty."

"Thank you, that's most kind," Rowland murmured, not quite sure what to do with the cutting.

"Mr. Marien—Frank—employed me on the basis of my writing, but I'm an artist really. I'm sure the paper will publish my drawings soon, but it's peculiar that they're so much more conservative about drawings than stories." Rosaleen walked about the room studying the paintings on its walls, commenting occasionally in a manner designed to demonstrate her knowledge of technique. She stopped before the portrait of Henry Sinclair which glowered over his son's studio. "I do like this. There's a delicious rage in his face, don't you think? And the hint of wickedness and danger. It's exciting."

"I didn't paint that one. It's a McInnes," Rowland informed her.

"Oh, pity." Rosaleen moved onto the nude of Edna. "This is one of yours?" she asked tentatively.

"Yes."

She considered it thoughtfully. "I model, you know… if you need someone new."

"Thank you, I'm well accommodated in terms of models… but I'll pass your details on to Norman Lindsay next time I see him, if you like."

Rosaleen beamed. "Oh, would you? That would be splendid!"

"Consider it done."

"Perhaps Mr. Lindsay would like to look at my drawings."

"Perhaps." Rowland was beginning to feel sorry for the young reporter. She seemed to be quite desperate for attention. He'd have to warn Lindsay to be kind. The artist could be brutally blunt and he wasn't sure how well Rosaleen would take criticism.

"I'm going to leave these with you," she announced, putting the drawings back into the folio and leaving it on the card table. "Perhaps you could show them to Miss Higgins or even Norman Lindsay if he calls on you."

"I'm not sure Mr. Lindsay will call by anytime soon, but I'm certain Miss Higgins will be interested to see your work," Rowland replied.

Rosaleen nodded enthusiastically. "I'll pick the folio up next week."

"I could return it to you at the paper, if that's more convenient?"

"Oh, yes! I could show you where Crispy used to sit. They won't let anyone use his desk, but you can feel his presence in the office."

Rowland struggled for an appropriate response. He opted for simple courtesy in the end. "Yes. Thank you."

"Well, I'd best get on and let you get back to your monster," she said, nodding at the unfinished canvas.

He walked her out to a waiting motor taxi.

Rowland's houseguests all barged into the studio the moment he returned, making no secret of the fact they'd been waiting for Rosaleen Norton to leave before showing themselves. Milton and Clyde had decided she was odd, and Edna, who had not yet met the reporter, was trying to be considerate of any burgeoning attachment.

"For pity's sake, Ed, she's seventeen!" Rowland said horrified, though he had only just discovered that fact himself. "And Milt and Clyde are right. She's quite odd."

Edna laughed. "We were all a little odd when we were seventeen."

"Not this odd," Clyde murmured, leafing through her folio. "These drawings are rather macabre, aren't they? Come and have a look, Ed."

Edna did so, spreading the drawings out on the table.

"What do you think?" Rowland asked. "Miss Norton was particularly interested in your assessment."

"Mine? Why?"

"Because of the sculptures of Pan in the garden, I expect. I told her in passing that they were yours. I suspect she's concluded the two of you have a common obsession."

At this the sculptress smiled. "I sculpted Pan for the gardens because he's the Greek god of the woodlands... as in *Woodlands House*. It was a play on words, not a religious homage!"

"Really?" Rowland was genuinely surprised. "I thought you just liked Pan."

"I do," Edna said. "But no more than you do. Pan's curious, interesting to work with but—" She looked back at the drawings. "I expect Miss Norton admires him for *other* reasons."

"These works are quite explicit and violent for a nice girl from Lindfield, don't you think?" Milton observed.

Rowland shrugged. "Perhaps Lindfield is not quite as respectable as we've come to believe."

"What's this, Rowly?" Edna asked, picking up the newspaper cutting from the table.

"It's some story Miss Norton wrote when she was fifteen. Apparently *Smith's Weekly* published it earlier this year and employed her on its strength."

"What's it about?"

"I don't know, I haven't read it yet."

Milton took the cutting from Edna. "We'd best hear it then," he decided, clearing his throat as he prepared to read the piece aloud. "The Story of the Waxworks..."

"Waxworks?" Rowland said, startled. The others, too, had not missed the coincidence.

Rosaleen Norton's tale was that of a young Sydney musician with a particular and maudlin passion for wax figures. Late one evening he happens upon a waxworks museum and pays the sixpence entry fee. The exhibits were not the usual kind—of celebrities and statesmen—but grotesques of the sort found in a House of Horrors. Among them, described in detail, a demonic satyr with "twisted horns and splayed goat's feet". With Rosaleen's drawing fresh in their minds, the image was too easily conjured. The musician in her tale is locked in the museum overnight. The next morning, two policemen enter an abandoned house after hearing screams and manic laughter from within, and find the musician, his hair completely white, sitting pitifully in an empty room playing a discordant tune on a violin. He screeches, "Call it the 'Dance of the Waxworks'" before falling dead at their feet.

Nobody said anything for a few moments after Milton finished.

Clyde broke the silence. "Well, that was creepy."

"Quite well written in spots, though," Milton added. "Considering she was only fifteen."

"Disturbing parallels with how White died." Clyde went to the sideboard and poured each of them a drink.

"Miss Norton did say that the story might have been a premonition when I first met her," Rowland offered uneasily.

"You're all being utterly silly!" Edna said. "Mr. White was not a musician and he did not go mysteriously insane before falling inexplicably dead. The only common thread is a waxworks and that could easily be a coincidence!"

"Didn't White die in the Greek Room, Rowly?" Milton asked. "Pan's a Greek god—a satyr with twisted horns and splayed cloven hooves."

Rowland recalled his candid conversation with the girl employed to cry and wail at Magdalene's. She'd said there was a devil in the Greek Room. He had to admit the coincidences were uncomfortably uncanny.

"You don't suppose Miss Norton is behind White's murder, Rowly?" Milton suggested. "She did end up with his job."

"Did she want it, though?" Rowland mused. "She seems committed to becoming an artist rather than a journalist."

"She's only seventeen!" Edna protested.

Milton shook his head. "The murderers I know all started their apprenticeships young."

Edna rolled her eyes. "Just how many murderers do you know?" she challenged.

Milton chose to ignore her.

"Miss Norton does seem to find White's death strangely exciting," Rowland said quietly.

Clyde scowled, clearly conflicted. His natural instinct was to warn his interfering companions to stay out of police investigations, but he also suspected that Milton's involvement with White would become more problematic as time went on. "I wonder if Delaney has come across Miss Norton yet."

Rowland returned to his canvas, dragging a hand through his hair as he stared at the frustrated progress of his painting. He'd not advanced any further than a tonal underpainting of Ernst Röhm, and it was clear he was not going to finish it before the day's end. "Perhaps we ought to invite Colin round for a social drink."

9

THE STORY OF THE WAXWORKS

by Rosaleen Norton

…Then the full horror of the position burst upon him. Locked in with those grinning monstrosities for the night. Commonsense strove to reassert itself. It must be a mistake of course. The old woman would, no doubt, come early in the morning, to let him out, and in the meantime—well, there were worse places to spend the night than in a warm room, and the waxworks were only life-sized toys, after all.

Smith's Weekly, 1934

Colin Delaney perused Rosaleen Norton's story carefully, grimacing and grunting every now and then. "She's seventeen, you say?" He angled his head to one side as he considered the scenario. "It's possible, I suppose. She told you Crispin White was working on a story at Magdalene's?"

Rowland nodded. "She's adamant that a coven meets there—that its members unleashed some kind of demonic retribution upon White to protect their secrets."

"Sounds more like a Masonic Lodge than a coven, Rowly."

Rowland laughed. "We'd have disposed of the body more effectively."

"What else did Miss Norton tell you?" Delaney asked, chuckling.

"That the Maroubra Speedway was cursed, and that she had premonitions."

"I don't know, Rowly. She just sounds like your stock-standard nut."

"Maybe... probably."

"Why did she leave her folio with you anyway?"

"An excellent question. I'm not entirely sure. She's determined to be an artist. I suppose she's seeking like minds."

"I'll look into it, but I wouldn't be too concerned. A lot of youngsters these days seem to be dabbling in the occult... Ouija boards... séance parties." He lit a cigarette, sighing as he drew. "Some kind of fashionable rebellion, I expect. I have no doubt that Miss Norton will settle down and take up embroidery once she meets a nice respectable bloke."

"Why, Detective Delaney!" Edna came into the room having overheard the last. "Who would have thought you were such an old conservative!" She put her hands on her hips. "I do hope you don't wish such a terrible fate on me!"

Delaney stuttered, flustered.

Rowland winced. "I've seen Ed embroider, Colin. It's a blood sport when she does it."

Edna sighed. "Needlework is not for the fainthearted, Rowly."

"Are you going out?" Rowland asked as he noticed the sculptress' gloves and bag.

"Errol's taking me to a tea dance in the city," Edna replied, twirling to demonstrate the subtle flare of her skirt. "It's been an age since I've been dancing in the afternoon! It feels quite decadent. Why don't you come too, Rowly?"

Rowland smiled, charmed as he always had been by Edna's way of finding delight in the most inconsequential things. "It would be exceedingly impolite to cut in before the first dance, Ed."

"You don't have to dance with me."

"Then what would be the point?"

Edna rolled her eyes. "Very well, I'd best leave you gentlemen to it. It's lovely to see you again, Detective Delaney."

"Likewise, Miss Higgins."

Rowland waited until Edna had gone before he asked Delaney about the crime scene—not because he thought the conversation would upset her but because he knew the detective might be reluctant to discuss any grisly details in the presence of a lady.

"As you saw, his throat had been quite savagely slashed," Delaney said. "The killer used a knife or a razor. Poor bastard would have bled to death very quickly."

"What else was in the room, Colin?"

"No murder weapon, if that's what you mean. We still haven't found it."

"Where was he in relation to the wax figures?"

"You're not buying into all this black magic nonsense, are you?"

"Not at all. I was just wondering if his throat was cut from behind while he was looking at a figure… whether he saw his assailant."

Delaney shook his head. "He'd fallen forward, away from the statues. His back would have been to them. An assailant would have had to go around White to get behind him."

"Unless he was hiding in the room when White came in, I suppose."

Delaney considered the idea, nodding slowly. "Look, Rowly, we'll need to speak to Milton… officially."

"I see. He's out, but if you were to call in—"

"It won't be me. Superintendent Mackay feels I'm too close to,"—Delaney adopted his superior's manner and accent, "—'Sinclair and his bloody band of criminal circus performers'."

"Who then?"

"John Hartley. He's just been promoted to detective." Delaney's concern was unmistakeable. "He lacks imagination, I'm afraid."

"I'm not sure I understand."

"Let's just say he sees Mr. Isaacs as a likely candidate."

"Because he drove White home?"

"That, among other things."

"What other things?"

"It has come to light that Mr. Isaacs was arrested some years ago for assaulting the deceased, and that the deceased moved away and changed his name soon after." Delaney grimaced. "That, in addition to a witness who saw two men fighting by a yellow Mercedes automobile in Kings Cross, and the fact that Mr. Isaacs is known to the police and is being decidedly evasive."

Rowland groaned. "All those things have perfectly rational explanations, Colin."

"I'm listening."

"It's not my place to say, but I give you my word as a gentleman—"

"We're not living in the eighteenth century, Rowly!" the detective said laughing. "Look, I'm sure Milt has his reasons, but this doesn't look good and Hartley will be less interested in his explanations."

Rowland cursed. "What if we find out who really killed White?"

Delaney blew out his cheeks. "It would be entirely unprofessional of me to recommend you do anything of the kind. But if the identity of the real killer was revealed to you somehow, yes of course, it would help Mr. Isaacs."

"I see."

"Just watch yourself," Delaney warned. He paused, his eyes brightened suddenly. "I seem to have retained a set of the crime scene photographs—must have forgotten to return them in the handover. I don't suppose you'd care to see them, Rowly? Off the record, of course," he added when Rowland looked at him quizzically. "You saw White last—you might notice something I'm... we're missing."

"Yes, of course," Rowland accepted, though he was not really sure he wanted to see images of the murdered reporter. Clearly Delaney was unhappy with the reassignment of the case to Hartley. Working together was possibly in both their interests.

"Good, I was hoping you might say that." Delaney reached into his inside breast pocket and took out a large envelope. He handed it to Rowland, glancing at his watch as he did so. "I must go. These are copies. Have a look at them and telephone me if you come up with anything." He stood and shook Rowland's hand. "I'll call by tomorrow for the photographs. For God's sake don't lose them in the meantime or the commissioner will have me drawn and quartered."

Rowland took the photographs into the sunroom Clyde used as a studio.

"Clyde... Oh, Miss Martinelli, I do beg your pardon."

Rosalina Martinelli stood in the centre of the room, clutching her handbag with gloved hands. Her shoulders were square and determined and there was something about the crisp pleat of her skirt, or perhaps her manner, that told Rowland she'd refused to sit down. While he'd sworn, for reasons other than the fact that she was Clyde's sweetheart, that he would never again use Rosalina as a model, Rowland could not deny she was strikingly beautiful. She looked more composed than he'd ever seen her. Clyde looked horribly broken. "I'm so sorry... I'll leave," Rowland said into the grave silence of the moment.

"No, Mr. Sinclair." Rosalina's voice trembled. "I am engaged to be married. It is no longer appropriate for me to be alone with

Mr. Watson Jones. So stay. I'll leave." She turned back to Clyde. "Goodbye, Clyde. I wish you a good life."

With nothing more, she left.

Rowland closed the door to the sunroom after her and waited. Clyde sat down, dropping his face into his hands. He did not lift his head for some time. Rowland said nothing, simply sitting down on the settee beside his friend.

Eventually Clyde handed over the letter he'd written to Rosalina, scribed in pencil on leaves of Rowland's notebook. "She returned it," he said. "She's marrying that bloke, Antonio. She wants to."

Rowland had never been particularly fond of Rosalina, but he was shocked that she could be so inconstant. For the past several months, she'd seemed utterly determined to become Mrs. Clyde Watson Jones.

"Rosie doesn't want to lose her family," Clyde said wretchedly. "She says she sees now that she doesn't want a life with me, that I'll never give up 'my ways'."

"Bloody hell, mate, I'm sorry." Rowland could hear the hoarse agony in Clyde's voice. He would have done anything to help.

"Oh God, Rowly, what am I going to do? I didn't realise... I would have, you know. I'd have given up everything... settled down, worked for her father. I just needed a little time. I thought I had time."

"We'll change her mind, Clyde," Rowland said despite his misgivings about what Rosalina had asked.

"I suspect it's hopeless. I've always known Rosie just wants to be married and settled. I had my chance."

Rowland gripped his friend's shoulder. "What can I do, Clyde? Just say."

"The painting you did of Rosie, can you get it back?"

Rowland had painted Rosalina Martinelli as Psyche weeping on the banks of the River Styx. The work had been acquired by a gallery.

"You want a painting of Miss Martinelli?"

"I want you to destroy it."

"I'm not sure I understand."

"Rosalina always worried that someone would recognise her from that painting, that her modelling would come out and she'd be disgraced."

"I didn't realise. You've never mentioned—"

"Of course not. It's a bloody good painting. I thought Rosie was being hysterical. I dismissed it, like I dismissed how much she wanted to be married." Clyde pressed the heels of his palms into his eyes. "It's the one thing I can do for her now."

"I'll buy the painting back," Rowland said.

"What if the gallery won't sell it?"

"Then I'll buy the gallery. Don't worry, Clyde. I'll get the painting back even if I have to steal it, and then you can destroy it in front of her if you like. I'm so sorry if my work is what—"

"No, it isn't your work, mate. This is my fault. I was trying to have everything, and now I've lost Rosie."

"I'm sorry, anyway." Rowland paused, desperate to offer his friend some sort of solace. "Would you like a drink?"

"Yes, I would. In fact I'd like several."

"Rowly... Rowly..." Edna whispered, shaking him. He was aware of her rose scent before he opened his eyes.

"Ed?" Clyde's studio came into focus and then spun a little.

"Shhh." Edna looked over at Clyde and Milton who lolled unconscious in their armchairs. "What are you all doing out here?" she whispered.

Rowland squinted at his watch. It was well past midnight. "We might have had a little too much to drink," he said, rubbing his face.

"Come on," she said. "I'll make you a cup of coffee and then we can do something about these two."

Mary Brown and the rest of the staff had long since retired so they had the kitchen to themselves. Edna placed a glass of water on the table at which she seated Rowland. "Drink this while I make coffee. It'll help with the hangover."

"I don't have a hangover."

"Not yet. Whatever were you all celebrating?"

"Not celebrating." Rowland told her about Rosalina Martinelli's visit.

"She did what?" Edna was furious. She raged for a time about Rosalina's disloyalty. "Poor darling Clyde," she said, pouring the coffee she'd made while ranting. "He's not like you and Milt and me, Rowly. Clyde believes in love and marriage."

"Don't you believe in love, Ed?" Rowland asked, trying to pour milk into his coffee without spilling it. The task was proving strangely difficult.

Edna's eyes softened. She took the milk jug from his hand and poured it for him. "Yes, of course I do. But you know what I mean."

Rowland nodded. "Yes, I think so." Clyde had always been the most orthodox of them. "How was your tea dance?"

"Perfectly lovely," she replied. "But we're not talking about me, we're talking about Clyde."

"Oh yes, Clyde. Did I tell you about Rosalina jilting him?"

"Just how much did you drink?"

"Quite a lot, I suppose."

"So there's no point trying to talk to you tonight, I expect."

"Marry me, Ed. I'll take you dancing every afternoon. Mornings, too, if you like."

She laughed. He laughed too because he loved the way she did, and he'd had too much to drink.

"And what about Clyde?" she said.

"We'll adopt him. Milt too."

"Errol might be a bit surprised."

"We can give Flynn a very nice burial at sea."

Edna pressed his hand to her cheek. "You shouldn't propose when you're drunk, Rowly. It's more dangerous than driving." She pushed the hair out of his face.

"Why don't you want to get married, Ed? Almost every other girl I meet seems to be intent upon it."

"That might have something to do with how charming you are." She paused, her voice became wistful. "My parents weren't very happy, Rowly. At least my mother wasn't, and it made her hate my father in the end, no matter how much he loved her." She kissed his forehead. "I really couldn't bear to hate you."

"We could have a mad wanton affair instead, I suppose," he murmured.

Her laugh was warm, entirely unoffended by the impropriety of the proposition. "If we did that, I'm afraid you'd finish up hating me."

"I couldn't," he said with iron certainty. "Ed, I—"

"Do you think you can remember where your bedroom is?" Edna brought the conversation to a gentle end.

"I'm really not that pickled."

"Well, you go up and sleep it off. I'd best throw blankets over Milt and Clyde."

10

SMUGGLING OF DRUGS

The report from Canberra that, with the gradual lifting of the economic depression and the release of more money, the use of illicit drugs in Australia is increasing is disturbing. In the trail of the drug seller has always stalked the criminal, and in both Sydney and Melbourne, the drug trade has been blamed for the outbreak of the gang warfare which, until scarcity of money restricted trade, was such an unsavoury feature of the daily lives of these cities.

Thus on top of the harm done to young men and young women who fall victims to the drug habit is piled a growth in criminality. The "razor gangs" which terrorised a central part of Sydney for so long came into being in this way, their original purpose being the holding up of drug pedlars for the purpose of demanding a share in the profits. Where the pedlar showed reluctance to pay up a razor slashed. It did not stop at that; feuds sprang up, "razor gangs" grew in size, and Sydney for a long time had its weekly razor victim, a victim who would not speak to the police, but relied on his pals to avenge him.

Examiner, 1934

Rowland woke early the next morning despite the previous evening's consumption. He had a thumping headache and a vague memory that he'd asked Edna to marry him. He assumed she'd declined but he couldn't quite recollect anything other than that she'd laughed.

A shower did little to alleviate the pounding in his head and he was reminded that it was not a sensible idea to allow Milton to set the pace when drinking. Unfortunately he and Clyde had been already compromised when the poet joined them, and so they had not been in any state to mount a cautionary resistance.

They had discussed Rosalina and Crispin White and Rosalina again… none of it had been particularly useful or coherent.

Milton sauntered into the breakfast room while Rowland was having toast and coffee. The poet was, in his custom, unconventionally but meticulously attired in a candy-striped jacket and crimson cravat. It was very bright for the hour and Rowland's current disposition.

Milton grinned, sitting across from him. "And how are you on this fine morning, my friend?"

"Stop shouting," Rowland muttered.

"I wasn't shouting."

"Your clothes are."

Milton sniggered, thoroughly unrepentant and annoyingly unaffected, though he had imbibed far more than had Rowland. "Man, being reasonable, must get drunk; the best of life is but intoxication."

"Yes, Byron would know, I suppose. How's Clyde pulled up?" Rowland asked.

"Still asleep on the couch. Someone very kindly brought us pillows and blankets last night."

"That was Ed."

"Of course. She's a good egg." Milton stood and helped himself from the warming trays on the sideboard. "Have you seen the papers?" he asked, pointing to the neat stack at the centre of the table.

"No, I haven't had a chance to peruse them yet." Rowland reached for *The Sydney Morning Herald*, which sat on the top of the pile. The Red Cross Charity Race was featured extensively on pages two and three—profiles of each of the racers, a social pages account of the opening event and a passing reference to the chequered histories of the Maroubra Speedway and the original Lucky Devil Cup.

Milton pulled out *Smith's Weekly* and *The Sun* and passed them to Rowland. "You're bound to find the coverage in these rags more interesting."

Rowland winced. Clearly by "interesting" Milton did not mean reasoned and well researched. But then, that was not the reputation of either paper.

The Sun ran the headline, "Race on the Killer Track". It carried pictures of all the racers. The image of Rowland was that taken just after he'd been asked to give the Nazi salute. He looked murderous. The caption read, "Rowland Sinclair Esq. of Woollahra, determined to eradicate the competition in his German automobile."

Rowland groaned and moved on to *Smith's Weekly*, choking on his coffee as he read its version of a racer profile. *Smith's* had used a photograph quite artfully taken with the Mercedes' mascot in the foreground, to which they had referred as the "Mercedes swastika". The article carried details of Aubrey Sinclair's death fighting in France during the Great War, and made a point to mention that Rowland had not served before quoting him as follows: "Aubrey, from what I remember, was not shot by a Mercedes. I think you'll find the war is over."

Rowland swore. "Bloody hell, that makes me sound like… What the devil are they doing?"

"*Smith's* is the diggers' bible, Rowly," Milton reminded him.

Rowland rubbed the back of his neck. His headache was getting worse. "I knew they were going to cast me as the villain because of the car. I just didn't think they'd bring Aubrey into it."

"It's bloody unsporting," Milton agreed. "Who wrote it?"

"It doesn't seem to have a by-line," Rowland said on inspection.

The telephone rang in the hallway.

"That'll be Wilfred," Rowland said, knowing his brother read *Smith's*. He glanced at his watch. "Milt, would you mind checking on Mother? I don't want her to see this, if she hasn't already." Although his mother seemed to read all references to Rowland as "Aubrey", he was unsure of what a direct mention of his brother's death would mean for the fantasy to which she was so devoted.

Milton nodded. "I'll speak to the nurses and make sure she only sees *The Sydney Morning Herald*."

"She's going to want to see what the other papers say about the race," Rowland warned.

"Leave it to me, mate."

Wilfred Sinclair was, not unexpectedly, furious with *Smith's Weekly's* coverage. While he had already telephoned Frank Marien to make his displeasure known, he did save a small measure of his ire for his brother's errant car.

"If you didn't insist on driving that bloody Fritz contraption people wouldn't get the wrong idea!"

"What idea, Wil?" Rowland demanded. "It wasn't so long ago that *Smith's* bloody *Weekly* was branding me a Communist. The blithering idiots don't seem to know the difference!"

"We're coming up to Sydney next week."

"For God's sake, I'm not ten years old!"

"This isn't about you, Rowly. The Royal Easter Show opens in a week, in case you'd forgotten."

Rowland had forgotten but he was not about to admit it. Like most pastoralists and graziers, Wilfred Sinclair took the Royal Easter Show very seriously.

"Kate's rather missing Ernie, so we thought we'd all come up for a couple of weeks. And naturally we'll stay for your race."

"Yes, of course."

"We'll stop at *Roburvale*," Wilfred instructed. "It'll save you having to reorganise *Woodlands* or your… houseguests."

Roburvale had been the Woollahra home of Rowland's late uncle and namesake. Although the old man had been gone for more than two years, the elderly staff had been retained and the mansion kept ready as a second Sydney residence for the family's use. As Rowland and Wilfred Sinclair ran their houses very differently, the extravagance was proving fortuitous.

"I'll speak to Mrs. Donnelly," Rowland promised, frowning. His uncle's housekeeper was ancient and quite deaf. He hoped she was still able to cope with the demands of a young family.

"How is Mother coping with all this nonsense?" Wilfred asked.

"She's perfectly well," Rowland replied, hoping that was in fact the case. Wilfred was still very dubious about the idea of their mother living at *Woodlands*.

Wilfred sighed. "Very well. Try not to let this get out of hand, Rowly. There's only so much I can do."

Rowland paused at the door to Clyde's studio. Edna sat on one of the plinths Clyde used for still life, talking softly while he sipped a cup of tea with his eyes closed. Rowland waited, not wanting to interrupt. As different as steady, country-born Clyde was from the free-spirited sculptress, Rowland knew that they had their own special relationship. It was Edna who had taught Clyde to dance, who teased him out of his more stuffy moods, and told him fiercely that "any girl would be proud to step out with him" on those occasions when he needed to hear it.

"Ed has ordered me to go upstairs and shower," Clyde complained, when Rowland finally came in.

"That mightn't be a bad idea," Rowland replied. "It was a long night."

"Yes." Clyde was a little unsteady as he stood. "I'm not sure I'm sober yet." He glanced around the converted sunroom. "Who made this mess?"

Rowland blinked. Aside from a clutter of empty bottles and tumblers, and the bedding Edna had brought in the night before, the room was in fairly good order. But Clyde was fastidious. His studio usually looked as though it had been organised by a middle-aged librarian, every brush in its place arranged by type and size, only one canvass in progress at a time. It bore a stark contrast to the manner in which Rowland worked.

"Go shower, mate," Rowland said, collecting bottles. "Ed and I will have it cleaned up by the time you come back down."

Clyde snorted, but he was eventually bullied into going. He didn't mention Rosalina and neither did they.

"What's this?" Edna asked, picking up a large envelope with Rowland's name scrawled upon it as she gathered up the empty tumblers.

It was only then that Rowland remembered the crime scene photos that had been in his hand when he'd come upon Clyde's disappointment.

"Colin wanted us to have a look at them?" Edna said when he told her what the envelope contained.

"I don't know that he meant all of us—" Rowland started.

"Of course he did. He knows what you're like." She extracted the photographs and spread them on the bench Clyde used to stretch canvasses.

"Oh poor, poor Crispin," Edna whispered as she studied the images. The chamber in which Crispin White had died was windowless.

The walls were lined with wax figures all facing into the centre, so he appeared surrounded. The scene was strangely reminiscent of a gathering about a grave. The waxen statues included Spartan warriors, the Minotaur, Medusa, an out-of-place Egyptian and Pan. White's eyes were open, his mouth parted in a final scream. A dark pool of blood formed a grim halo about his head and shoulders.

"Are you all right, Ed?" Rowland asked, taking her hand.

She leaned her head against his shoulder. "I wish his eyes had been closed, Rowly. The last things he ever saw were monsters. It's so very sad."

Rowland nodded. Edna was probably correct, though he wasn't sure the monster was wax. From the photograph of the body, it did seem likely that Crispin White had been facing his attacker. Other photographs clearly showed the blood splatter on the walls as well as the waxen figures.

"What's that?" Edna pointed to lines in the plasterwork.

Rowland held the photograph to the light. "It's just electrical cabling, I think."

They were still poring over the images when Milton joined them. The poet carried several newspapers under his arm, which he dropped onto the settee.

Rowland told them both of his conversation with Delaney.

Milton cursed. "Miriam's husband knows nothing about what happened," he said. "If I tell this bloke Hartley the first thing he'll do is pull her in to verify it."

"You may not have a choice, Milt. This is a murder inquest."

"Telling them is not going to exonerate me. It'll make me look more guilty if anything."

"I think Hartley might have guessed that, which is why he wants to interview you," Rowland said. "We may just have to hurry up and find the perpetrator ourselves."

"Yes, let's do that." Milton took the sheaf of photographs from Edna and leafed through them. "One helluva way to go..." He stopped and brought the photograph of the body closer to his eye. "Where's his tiepin?"

"What tiepin?"

"He was wearing a tiepin when he came here—flash gaudy thing with a diamond. Shaped like a couple of gold horseshoes. I noticed it because it seemed so inconsistent with the complete lack of panache in his suit."

The fashion of White's suit aside, Rowland did now hazily recall a tiepin.

"It was a gift from a lover," Edna said, quite definitely.

"He told you that?" Rowland asked, though he was not surprised. The sculptress was the kind of person in whom even strangers often found themselves confiding.

"No," she said. "But look at him. His suit is plain, his tie is plain, his hat didn't even have a feather in the band. A man like that would never buy a diamond tiepin, and he'd never wear it unless it was a special gift. The kind of gift a lover would give."

"Exactly!" Milton agreed. "We already know that he wasn't a gentleman. Perhaps he had a liaison with this woman at Magdalene's... they fell out or she already hated him. She slashed his throat and, in a fit of spite, took back the tiepin!"

"A woman who carries a razor?" Rowland asked sceptically.

"Have you not met Tilly Devine or Kate Leigh?" Milton replied.

Rowland had, in fact, made the acquaintance of both women through no orchestration of his own. The reigning queens of Sydney's criminal underworld, he expected they would indeed carry blades of some sort on their persons, as would, he supposed, many women who lived their kind of life. It was possible White was involved with a less than lady-like character, but it was rather a lot to conclude from a missing tiepin.

"I'll mention it to Delaney. He might still have enough involvement in the case to establish if the tiepin is among White's personal effects."

"Why don't you ask Miss Norton if Crispin was seeing anyone?" Edna suggested. "Or," she added tentatively as a thought occurred, "if she were stepping out with him herself."

Rowland glanced at the photographs again. Rosaleen Norton was only seventeen but some of her artwork revealed violent sensibilities. Perhaps they were more than artistic. His face darkened somewhat as his mind moved to the profile in *Smith's Weekly*. "How did you find Mother?" he asked Milton.

"I can report that the Dowager Sinclair was in excellent spirits," Milton replied. "Excited to finally see the coverage of the Red Cross invitational. She loved the picture of you in the *Herald*, though she thinks you might need a haircut. I read her the coverage in *Smith's Weekly* and *The Sun*, personally." He winked. "I don't think their writers have ever been so eloquent. Poetic even! I took *Smith's* and *The Sun* with me," he added, nodding at the papers on the settee.

Rowland picked up the offending newspapers and handed them to Edna. Milton pointed out the articles.

"Hopefully this will blow over in a couple of days," Rowland murmured without much in the way of optimism.

"It's a good picture of you, albeit a little cross," Edna said as she began reading. She gasped. "Why, this is ridiculous!"

"I wonder who wrote the article, Rowly. Was it Miss Norton?" Milton asked.

"I expect so, though the quotes are cobbled from what I said to White." He frowned. "I'm sure she said he hadn't written anything up. When would he have had time?"

"Perhaps his notebook was found and duly returned to the paper," Milton mused.

Rowland put the crime scene photographs back in their envelope. "I might just ask Miss Norton when I return her folio."

11

NOT GUILTY

FRANK GREEN ACQUITTED
DEVINE'S TIEPIN
Shooting Affray Recalled

SYDNEY, Monday

Charged at the Central Criminal Court to-day with having assaulted James Devine on June 16, 1931, and stolen a diamond tiepin while armed, Francis Donald Green, 28, a clerk, known as Frank Green, was found not guilty and discharged. Green failed to answer when the case was called on last year, and was arrested at Moore Park a few weeks ago.

The Senior Crown Prosecutor (Mr. McKean, K.C.) said that the case rested on the evidence of James Devine. There was no doubt that Green was present at the time of the robbery.

James Devine, a fruiterer, said he met Green at the Sir Walter Raleigh Hotel, and Green asked for money. He was driven to his home in Maroubra, and Green arrived later with a man and a woman. Green again asked for money and seized witness's tiepin, at the same time pressing a revolver against him. Green then backed to the door, and the witness went to get a gun. Shots were exchanged, and the taxi driver, named Moffitt was shot dead.

Devine said he fired three shots at Green who told him that Moffitt had been hit. He denied having gone through Moffitt's pockets that night.

Mr. MacMahon (for accused): I put it to you that you robbed that unfortunate man of his money the night he was dead?

Devine: I deny it. It is not my job to rob the dead.

GREEN DENIES CHARGE

Green denied having fired at Devine. He said he did not have a gun, and did not have his hands in Devine's pockets. Devine invited him to attend a party at his home at Maroubra. When he got there he found Moffitt inside and also a man named Jordan. Some liquor was consumed and a fight began. He and Moffitt went out to the taxi, and were followed by Devine, who fired at them.

"We crouched in the bottom of the taxi and he fired again," said accused. "I called out, 'Turn it up, Jim; you have shot the driver.' Devine replied. '—the driver, and you, too.'" Green said he ran away with Hourigan.

Concluding his evidence, accused said: "Devine's evidence is manufactured to save himself from the charge of murder. I never fired the shots, or held Devine up, or took his tiepin."

Newcastle Morning Herald and Miners' Advocate, 1932

John Hartley did things according to the rules. Unlike his predecessor, he would not pander to the whims of the entitled and privileged classes—cosy chats over a drink, invitations to breakfast. Rowland Sinclair and his mates would be treated just like every other potential criminal. Certainly Elias "Milton" Isaacs had a file as dubious as most petty thugs, regardless of where he now resided. Hartley did not consider himself a difficult man, simply one who had respect for the due process of the law, applied with all its force and rigour against every man.

And so it was under Hartley's insistence that Milton was brought into the station for questioning.

Thanks to Delaney's warning, Rowland was ready and they were met at Central Police Station by the gentlemen of Kent Beswick & Associates. It was possibly that fact, and that fact alone, that prevented

John Hartley from arresting Elias Isaacs for the murder of Crispin White then and there. The presence of the solicitors cautioned the detective against moving too soon, lest Isaacs' representation find a technicality on which to overturn the arrest. The case he'd built was significant but it was circumstantial. Hartley recalled that Rowland Sinclair had been arrested for murder and incarcerated the previous year, only to be released when the case fell apart. Isaacs had been arrested with him for assaulting a police officer and that charge had been conveniently dropped at the same time. Sinclair and his mates were a slippery crew, and John Hartley was determined that Elias Isaacs, at least, would not escape justice.

Hartley sighed. Kent Beswick and associated barmaids would also make it difficult to beat the truth out of the Commie mongrel.

Rowland waited for Milton to raise what had happened in the interview room. He hadn't been privy to the interview, of course, waiting outside for over two hours. Milton thanked the solicitors for their able and learned assistance. Matthew Beswick gave the poet his card and they walked out of the station with Hartley glowering after them.

Milton's grin didn't quite reach his eyes. "Glad your fancy lawyers were there, Rowly. Hartley is an attack dog. He seemed committed to the idea that I killed Crispin whatever-he-called-himself."

Rowland cursed. It was as Delaney warned. Hartley would not bother to look anywhere else for the murderer with Milton in his sights.

"I didn't tell him anything about Miriam," Milton continued. "It won't help me and it would hurt her."

Rowland accepted that. It was probably true. "Did you say anything about the tiepin?"

"He didn't show me the crime scene photos, so I couldn't really say I'd seen them. We'll just have to tell Delaney and let him present it, somehow, as his own brilliant deduction."

They made their way on foot to the Lion Rampant which was a good three blocks and four pubs away from the Central Police Station—a fact which kept it from being a watering hole of the constabulary. The public bar was always quite crowded in the middle of the day—patrons ducking in for a lunch-break fortification, and the hardened bar flies who'd been there since opening. Still, the atmosphere was more relaxed than it would be later, the drinking less determined. After all, there would be time to duck in again at the end of the day.

Contented, Milton sighed as he wiped froth from his upper lip. It was with plain derision that he regarded the glass of lemonade in front of Rowland. "That isn't going to do anything to numb the pain, comrade."

Rowland ignored him. There was very little Milton would not treat with a stiff drink.

Colin Delaney made his way over with a schooner of beer in each hand.

"Is someone joining us?" Rowland asked when he sat.

"No, I just didn't want to have to get up again," Delaney replied, lining up his drinks. He tapped the side of his nose. "Planning ahead."

They briefed Delaney on their morning with John Hartley. Delaney commiserated. "Miserable upstart is under the impression detective work is just some kind of mechanical procedure, like plumbing. But Mackay seems to think he's a chip off the old block. We'll all need to be careful."

Rowland pulled the envelope of photographs out of his jacket and handed it to the detective. Delaney slipped it into his breast pocket as Milton informed him of the missing tiepin.

"Not another bloody tiepin!" Delaney grumbled. "Who would've thought a tiepin was worth killing a man for?" He pointed at Rowland. "Your friend Green stole Big Jim Devine's tiepin if I recall. Got at least one man killed over it."

"Green's hardly a friend, Colin." Rowland had encountered Frank Green in Long Bay Gaol a few months earlier, where the man had threatened to kill him and tried quite earnestly to do so.

Delaney sighed. "Green's still locked up, else I'd bring him in." Even so he was pleased. "It's something at least. Rather clever of me to risk my job to leave the photographs with you chaps. I'll tell Hartley that I just happened to notice a discrepancy between the photographs and your statements."

"Did any of us mention the pin in our statements?"

"No, but Hartley doesn't know that."

"Do you know whether White had a sweetheart?" Rowland asked.

"He had a wife," Delaney said. "She might have been his sweetheart once, but they've been estranged for the last five years."

Rowland noticed Milton tense. That White had married soon after abandoning Miriam must have rankled. "Ed's certain it must be someone on whom he's currently keen," he said.

"Is she indeed? It's good to know Miss Higgins is running CIB now," Delaney snorted.

Rowland explained Edna's reasoning. "She does have a rather good point," he added.

"Yes, I suppose she does." The detective sighed. "I'll make the necessary enquiries."

"You'll let us know?" Milton prompted.

Delaney eyed them both sternly. "I suppose you chaps have been promoted above me now that Miss Higgins is in charge," he muttered good-naturedly.

"Good man," Milton replied. "You'll go far."

Delaney laughed and drank deeply from his first glass. He questioned Rowland about the race then, and listened thoughtfully.

"Is there something untoward about the race?" Rowland asked, alert to the detective's sudden interest.

"According to the tabloids you're driving for Germany."

"Apparently one should never let the facts get in the way of a good story," Rowland replied.

"Yeah, well just you be careful. You have a distinctive car and we're coming up to Anzac Day. War wounds take a long time to heal."

Rowland nodded. It was not the first time that the Mercedes had been a victim of patriotic animosity. Over the years he'd often found himself defending his automobile, both philosophically and physically. He was not entirely unsympathetic to the hostility she evoked, but despite having lost a brother in the war, he didn't share the sentiment and was quite fond of his car. Recalling the *Smith's Weekly* article, he asked, "Was Crispin White's notebook ever found, Colin?"

"Not by our people. Why?"

"The profile piece *Smith's* ran on me contained quotes, details of my conversation with White."

Delaney took out his own notebook. "What quotes exactly?"

Rowland shifted uncomfortably. "Something about the war being over and that my brother was not shot by a Mercedes."

"You said that?" Delaney asked surprised.

"Not in the context in which it was printed."

"But you did say it?"

"To White. Which is why I don't see how it got into the article unless White wrote it up or they found his notebook." Rowland rubbed his chin. "I don't suppose White has any family other than this estranged wife?" he asked.

Delaney shook his head. "The coroner will have to eventually release the poor bastard's body to his editor—some bloke called Frank Marien. The paper's taking care of the funeral, apparently."

"I'll speak to Mr. Marien this afternoon," Rowland decided.

"Steady on, Rowly," Delaney said, alarmed. "You're not actually a member of the force. You can't interrogate the public."

"Of course," Rowland said, his eyes widening innocently. "I'm simply enquiring about the funeral arrangements."

The female artists at *Smith's Weekly* were accommodated in the "Keep Out" room, an area set aside with the best of intentions so that the ladies could work unmolested by their male colleagues. In this sanctuary from the presumably simmering lust beyond the door, Rosaleen Norton had been assigned a desk and drawing materials.

She was attired in one of the peculiar garments of her own making, fashioned from a long knotted scarf. When she was seated, the design exposed more than Rosaleen's sense of style in a manner that bordered on the indecent. That fact did not worry Rowland as much as a suspicion that Milton might feel challenged to outdo the reporter's fashion eccentricities. The poet was not accustomed to being mundane by comparison.

"Did you show Norman Lindsay my work?" she demanded as Rowland attempted to return her portfolio.

"I'm afraid I didn't have the opportunity."

She thrust the folder back at him. "Well then, you must keep these until you have!"

"I don't know that—"

"I insist. You promised you would!" Rosaleen now sounded like the adolescent she was.

"Yes, of course." Rowland took back the folder. He had said he would show Lindsay, and however irritated he presently was with the reporter, he was a man of his word. In any case, he was not there to talk about Rosaleen Norton's artistic ambitions.

"Miss Norton, I did want to speak to you about the piece on me that appeared in this morning's edition."

"Oh, I didn't write that," Rosaleen said, evidently disgruntled about the fact. "Frank didn't like the angle I was working on and had Ken Slessor put it together from my notes and Crispy's."

"I see. Do you suppose I might speak with Mr. Slessor?"

"You'd have to ask him."

"Well how about you introduce us?" Milton snapped, losing patience now.

Fleetingly, Rosaleen's eyes narrowed into angry slits, and then perhaps she thought better of antagonising the gentlemen any further. She stood, and flicking her head imperiously, walked out of the room. "Follow me."

Kenneth Slessor's desk was positioned closest to the newspaper editor's office. Rowland assumed it indicated some sort of seniority. The journalist stood when Rosaleen introduced Rowland Sinclair and the friend whose name she had forgotten. Rowland introduced Milton Isaacs.

"Mr. Sinclair wants to talk about your profile piece, Ken," Rosaleen said smugly. "He didn't like it." Clearly there was some professional territoriality at play.

Rowland watched Slessor. There was a precise neatness about the man, his collar crisp, his thin moustache trimmed and waxed. He regarded Norton with a kind of martyred indulgence. "Shall we use the office?" he suggested. "Frank's not in and I'm sure he wouldn't mind."

He opened a door labelled "Frank Marien, Editor in Chief" and waited till they'd walked through. He stepped in himself and closed the door before Rosaleen could join them.

"So, Mr. Sinclair, what can I do for you?" he asked, motioning them to seats while he took the one behind the desk.

"We have a few questions about the profile piece you did on Mr. Sinclair, in this morning's paper," Milton informed him.

"I presume you are Mr. Sinclair's solicitor?" Slessor said with an air of resignation.

"Solicitor? No. I'm a poet."

Slessor's brow rose. "I see. Isaacs you say. I'm afraid I don't know your work."

Milton responded sympathetically. "Don't worry about it, comrade. Poetry's not for everyone."

Slessor paused. "Am I to understand, Mr. Sinclair, that you and your… poet are unhappy with this morning's profile?"

It was Rowland's turn to pause. "You may understand that, sir," he said. "However, it's not my unhappiness about which we are here."

"I see. What exactly brings you to this garden by the dark Lane Cove?"

"Garden by the dark Lane Cove…" Milton repeated thoughtfully. "Is that Henry Lawson?"

"No." Slessor's reply was frosty.

"Are you sure? It sounds like him."

"I'm sure."

"We were wondering, Mr. Slessor, from where precisely you sourced the information upon which you based your profile of me." Rowland brought the conversation back to the topic at hand.

Slessor shrugged. "Roie—Miss Norton—had made rudimentary notes though they were for the most part unintelligible. Some nonsense about a second story coming to pass. Most of the story, in fact, came from poor Crispin White's notes."

"Where exactly were these notes, Mr. Slessor?"

"In his notebook, of course."

"Can I ask how you got hold of Mr. White's notebook, Mr. Slessor?"

"I'm not sure I understand, Mr. Sinclair."

"Mr. White was in possession of his notebook when he left my home in Woollahra, but the police could not find the notebook on his body or among his possessions a couple of hours later. How did it come to be in your hands, Mr. Slessor?"

Slessor reared. "You're not suggesting I—"

"I'm simply enquiring where you got the notebook." Rowland's voice was even, his eyes piercing on the journalist's face.

"On what authority do you question me, Mr. Sinclair?"

"On the same authority that *Smith's Weekly* makes its enquiries, I suppose—public interest."

Slessor was clearly rattled. Milton's admiration was undisguised. Rowland was for the most part easy-going, and, to the poet's mind, unnecessarily civil. But just occasionally the Sinclairs' black sheep channelled the steely power that his brother Wilfred used to rule the world. If Milton had not known Rowland so well, it might have worried him.

"The notebook was found and returned to the paper," Slessor said, taking a handkerchief from his pocket and pressing it to his brow.

"Who returned it?"

"Some vagabond, I believe. We gave him a guinea for his trouble."

Rowland leaned forward in his seat. "Do you know this fellow's name, Mr. Slessor?"

Slessor scowled. "Perhaps these questions are better directed to Mr. Marien. I suggest you telephone to make an appointment when he returns."

For a moment there was silence as Rowland considered pressing on regardless. He decided against it. "Very well, Mr. Slessor. I'll do that." He stood. "In the meantime, I would appreciate it if you would keep references to my late brother out of any fiction you care to publish about me. As you can imagine, it's something that my mother would find particularly distressing."

At that Slessor seemed a little surprised. He nodded curtly, whether in concession or merely to get Rowland Sinclair out of the office was debatable.

Rosaleen Norton was leaning against the wall opposite, smoking, when they emerged.

"May I have a word before you go, Mr. Sinclair?" she purred.

Rowland and Milton followed her back to the "Keep Out" room where, this time, she shut Slessor out.

"What can I do for you, Miss Norton?"

"It's what I can do for you, Mr. Sinclair." The reporter lit another cigarette from the stub of the first and continued to smoke. "I have a warning from the psychic sphere."

"I beg your pardon?" Rowland glanced aside at Milton who was already grinning.

"I did tell you when first we met that I had seen Crispy's death in one of my stories."

"Yes, I recall that."

"There was a clipping of its publication in my folio."

Rowland nodded to indicate he had read the piece.

She walked around her desk, opened the drawer and extracted another cutting. "I wrote a second story. It was published a few weeks after the first." She gave him the page of newsprint. "It wasn't until I came to your studio to show you my folio that I realised that you are the artist in my story."

"I see."

"Go on, read it!"

Milton took the cutting from Rowland. "Allow me," he said clearing his throat. He read then, giving the work its due in his characteristically theatrical style.

The Painted Horror was the story of a young artist called Peter Raynham, who, inspired to paint a life-sized demon, becomes consumed by the task and the evil that surrounds his subject. Despite advice that he should stop, Raynham continues to paint until the demon is painted into life and devours him. Milton finished the recitation screaming the final line, "I know what killed him!"

The ensuing silence stretched uncomfortably. Rosaleen smoked and Rowland fought the impulse to smile. The story reminded him of the kind that passed about the dormitory when he was in boarding school. Inevitably one of the younger boys would go to the housemaster in terror and they'd all be in for it.

"Do you see?" Rosaleen said finally, her dark eyes gleaming. "You are Peter Raynham. That painting is going to kill you."

"Which painting?"

"The one with the hellfire in the background. The one you can't seem to finish."

"I'm not painting a demon, Miss Norton."

"Are you sure, Mr. Sinclair?" She came around the desk and looked up to meet his eye. "I foresaw Crispy's death. Do not dismiss me."

Rowland took the story from Milton. "May I keep this for a little while, Miss Norton?"

Rosaleen's narrow shoulders relaxed. "Yes, of course. Mummy bought dozens of this edition too."

"Thank you. And thank you for your concern about my welfare."

"You'll be in touch once you speak to Mr. Lindsay?" Rosaleen asked, nodding as she did so.

"Most certainly."

They took their leave of the reporter soon after.

"You're not starting to believe she can see the future through short stories, are you, Rowly?" Milton asked as they walked out onto Phillip Street.

"Lord no!"

"You asked for the cutting."

"It's not a bad tale, and she seemed so desperate to be taken seriously. To be honest, I couldn't think of any other way to get out of there politely."

"Oh yes, manners," Milton muttered. He glanced at his watch. "What now, Rowly?"

"We ought to go back and check on Clyde."

"Do you suppose one of your paintings has devoured him by mistake?"

Rowland laughed. "I'll telephone Delaney from *Woodlands* and tell him that Crispin White's notebook has turned up."

12

THE PAINTED HORROR
by Rosaleen Norton

..."Queer thing the way the police hushed it up—a sensational murder like that! Most of the public never heard of it at all. My brother (he's connected with the police) told me that Raynham, poor devil, was literally torn to pieces, and chewed! As if by a wild beast. Seems to me as if no man could have done it.

"Funny, too, the way a big canvas (he was found in his studio you know) had a great hole in it, as though something had jumped right through it...

Smith's Weekly, 1934

Clyde and Edna were in the conservatory poring over her photographs from Germany when Rowland and Milton returned. Edna had progressively posted prints and films back to Sydney, and so, despite having fled Munich, her record of their time had, for the most part, been saved.

Clyde compared the snapshots to sketches he'd made, trying to gather enough recollection to inspire a painting. Edna's photographs gave him composition, shape and detail, his own sketches gave him movement and in his memory there was colour.

"Good," Clyde said, looking Rowland up and down. "You seem to have recovered after last night's lapse."

"Lapse?" Rowland asked, bemused. He had not been drinking alone.

"You're driving again tomorrow, Rowly. You've got to be alert, your reflexes must be in top form."

"Oh, I see."

"Motor racing is a sport like any other, mate. You'll need some sort of training regimen to get you race ready."

"I expect you're right," Rowland conceded, without any real conviction. Clyde seemed to be taking the race a little too seriously, but Rowland was not of a mind to argue with anything that took his friend's thoughts from Rosalina Martinelli. Rowland had already made enquiries about the painting that had caused the young model so much regret. But that was something they could talk about later. For now the issue of White's murder pressed.

Rowland excused himself to telephone Delaney.

"They have his actual notebook?" The detective was furious.

"It seems someone handed it in."

"Who?"

"A vagabond, apparently. They didn't have a name."

"Did you see the notebook?"

"No. I wasn't really in a position to demand they show it to me."

"Don't worry, I'll speak to Detective Hartley and if he's not interested, I'll fetch it myself."

"Why wouldn't he be interested?"

"As I said, Rowly, he's got his gun trained on Milton. Anyway, thank you."

"Pleasure, Colin. You will keep me informed, won't you?"

"You know I can't do that, Mr. Sinclair, but the odd classified snippet has been known to slip out over a social drink now and then."

When Rowland walked back into the conservatory Milton was reading *The Painted Horror* to Clyde and Edna.

"So Miss Norton believes Rowly is this Peter Raynham character?" Clyde asked, shaking his head.

"She seems to," Rowland replied, taking a seat beside Edna.

"And you're going to be murdered by something in your painting?" Edna said smiling.

"To be fair, I was very nearly murdered by the man I'm trying to paint, but that was before I had any thought of painting him. Perhaps Miss Norton's psychic sphere is a little confused as to chronology."

"Still, it is a bit of a coincidence," Milton mused.

Rowland sighed. "I'll keep the turpentine on hand in case any of my paintings come to life. I'm more interested in this nameless 'vagabond' who returned White's notebook."

Milton agreed. "But I don't know how we'll find him. Slessor didn't seem to have the vaguest clue who he was."

"Perhaps the notebook wasn't returned to him personally. Who gave this vagabond the guinea?"

"I expect it was the editor, Frank Marien."

"Well then he might have a name… or at least a description."

"Hopefully Delaney will be able to extract that information," Rowland said. As much as it seemed incumbent on them to offer an alternative to Milton, he was well aware that they were not policemen and had no real right to demand answers of anyone.

Rowland pulled on his driving helmet and leather driving gloves. He depressed the starter button and brought the six cylinders to life. Revving the motor, he checked the gauges.

Clyde ran around the Mercedes in a last visual check before signalling that all was well. The British Racing Green Vauxhall with the Honourable Charles Linklater at the wheel was also ready.

Joan Richmond and Hope Bartlett had arranged the practice races to give the less qualified members of their teams some experience driving against another car of similar engine capacity and horse power.

Linklater had been less than pleased that he was being relegated to what he called the "dunces' class" but had eventually conceded to the practice race for "young Sinclair's sake". He was at pains to make it known that he had accrued extensive touring experience in the British Isles and on the Continent. Consequently Rowland was determined to win. Milton and Edna watched the proceedings with Flynn and Joan Richmond.

A whistle sounded, the flag was dropped, and they were away.

Both cars went out hard and for the first ten laps the lead changed regularly. Then the yellow Mercedes extended the gap, pulling ahead as the supercharged motor engaged. Rowland allowed the vehicle to settle into the bank, pleased. She still had plenty in her and he suspected that Linklater was on the ropes. He moved the car higher on the wall of the bowl to avoid the worst area of deterioration, as he did each lap. Later, he could only assume that Linklater had, in the heat of the moment, forgotten about the danger.

The Vauxhall surged to come through. The motorcars were abreast when the Vauxhall lost control and spun. Rowland pulled the Mercedes hard to the left to avoid a collision and she skidded as he fought to bring her safely out of the path of his careering competitor. A jolt as the Vauxhall clipped his rear bumper. Rowland was thrown hard against the steering wheel and the windshield. Dazed he fought to correct the steering and keep his car upright. It was only when he'd finally stopped that he saw that Linklater had hit the outer wall. The Vauxhall was on fire.

Rowland kicked open the door of his own car in an effort to lend aid but found himself unsteady. The track seemed to be spinning. Men were jumping the fence to get to the Vauxhall in which it appeared Linklater was trapped.

Rowland staggered towards the flames. Milton grabbed him. "Whoa, Rowly, there's nothing you can do, mate. They'll get him out."

The poet sat Rowland down on the track as the crowd began to build around him. "Rowly, can you hear me? Rowly?"

"I'm all right, Milt... just a little dizzy. Linklater..."

Milton craned his neck. "They've got him out of the car."

Frantic, Edna broke through the concerned circle of onlookers.

"I'm fine," Rowland said, seeing the panic on her face.

"You're bleeding, Rowly," she said, kneeling to get a closer look at his face.

Rowland touched the abrasion on his brow gingerly. "Must have hit the windscreen," he said. "But I'm not hurt." He stood to prove it, being careful not to grimace as the bruising impact of the steering wheel on his chest asserted its presence.

By then an ambulance had arrived for Linklater. Rowland flatly refused any attempt to take him to the hospital, insisting he was perfectly well. Joan Richmond might have pressed the issue if not for the fact that they were all preoccupied with Charles Linklater, who it appeared was quite dangerously injured. The Vauxhall was beyond repair.

The track was a bedlam of police, race officials, the media and inquisitive locals.

Clyde drove the Mercedes off the incline of the track so he could properly inspect her. Edna poured Rowland a cup of sweet black tea from the picnic thermos that Mary Brown had packed for them, and, worried that he still seemed too quiet, watched while he drank it.

"There's a dent on the rear mudguard and bumper and a crack on the windscreen to match the one on your head, but otherwise she seems in good shape, Rowly." Clyde flinched as he glanced at the mangled remains of Linklater's motorcar. "You're bloody lucky, mate!"

Rowland nodded slowly, playing the accident over in his mind.

"You!" The woman who stamped up to Rowland was nearly as tall as he. Pearls and the Peter Pan collar of a pink blouse were visible at the open neck of her racing suit, which bore a crest of some sort. "What the hell did you think you were doing out there?"

Rowland stepped back startled. She turned around and kicked the grille of the Mercedes.

"I beg your pardon, Miss..."

"Linklater, Charlotte Linklater!" She turned back to him, shaking. "That was my dear brother you nearly killed out there."

Rowland faltered, wounded by the accusation. "Miss Linklater, I'm—"

"I saw what you did. You, sir, drove him into that wall! You cheating blaggard! You won't get away with this!" Charlotte Linklater pulled back her fist and swung. Not expecting fisticuffs from someone called Charlotte, Rowland failed to duck and took the full and considerable force of the blow. He fell back and she went after him again.

"Steady on!" Clyde leapt between the two before the enraged young woman could have a second go.

The press photographers missed the punch but they swarmed now, and Charlotte Linklater repeated her accusations, breaking down in the midst of her tirade against the man who'd raced her brother. Hope Bartlett and Joan Richmond tried to restore calm, to reason with Charlotte.

In the end, Joan pulled Clyde aside and told him to take Rowland home. "And for pity's sake make sure he's seen by a doctor," she instructed. "I'll call with any news about Charlie Linklater."

Edna tapped and poked her head around the door. "Rowly, are you decent?"

"Decent enough," Rowland said as he pulled on a fresh shirt. The doctor, upon whom Edna had insisted, had just left. "I'm fit and well, nothing broken," he added, before she could ask.

"I met Dr. Yates in the hallway," Edna said, staring at the impression of the steering wheel turning blue on his chest. "That's not quite what he said."

Rowland smiled. "It's the gist."

Edna hesitated. "Joan just telephoned."

"Oh yes?" Rowland buttoned his shirt.

"Rowly, Charles Linklater has died."

"What?"

"He died. They couldn't save him."

Rowland swallowed, his throat suddenly dry. He sat down on the bed, horrified, shaken. For the hundredth time the accident replayed in his mind. Had he made a mistake? Had he somehow forced Linklater onto the dangerous part of the track?

Edna sat beside him and held his hand in both of hers. "Rowly, this wasn't your fault. Mr. Linklater lost control of his car and there was a terrible accident. It's a wonder you weren't more badly hurt, but if you had been it would have been his fault, not yours."

"Miss Linklater—" he began.

"—Has one heck of a right hook," Edna finished, reaching up to touch the swelling around his eye. "She was distraught, Rowly. She knows it wasn't your fault… she was just angry and scared."

"God," Rowland squeezed her hand, "what a flaming mess!"

"It is rather," Edna said. "Come on, finish getting dressed. Joan will be here soon."

Joan Richmond sat down and addressed Rowland in her no-nonsense way. "Now Rowly, regardless of what Miss Linklater said, you are not responsible for the tragic passing of her brother. I say this without equivocation or reservation. The fool was so determined to pass you that he took the worst part of the track at quite ridiculous speed. I could see that, so could Hope. And once Charlotte is calm enough to be reasonable, she will see that too."

Rowland nodded. He was grateful that Joan had called simply to reassure him. "Would you tell Miss Linklater that if there's anything at all I can do…?"

"Of course, of course. But what I need to know, Rowly, is how soon you'll be ready to drive again."

"Drive? They're still running the race?"

"Motor racing is a dangerous sport, Rowly. These mishaps, accidents, acts of God—call them what you may—they happen. And there's a great deal invested in the Maroubra Invitational. The Red Cross is relying on us."

"It just seems…"

"I don't mean to sound callous, but if we cancelled events every time a driver was injured or hurt, motor racing would not exist."

"But Charlotte Linklater… Surely she wants the race cancelled?"

"Charlotte is an Englishwoman. Her upper lip is admirably stiff and she's keen to race in her late brother's memory."

Rowland exhaled. "What do you want me to do?"

"We have to get you back on the horse as soon as possible, old boy. Your man, Clyde, tells me that your car is in good shape aside from a dent or two. We shan't be able to use the speedway for a couple of days but I'd like you to get behind the wheel as soon as possible." She looked critically at the damage to his brow, now cleaned and dressed. "Tonight, if you're able."

Rowland shrugged. "I'm quite able to drive, Joan. I do have a short errand to run—will that do?"

Joan nodded. "Yes, I just want you in the saddle before you begin to doubt yourself or anything equally daft. This sort of mishap can make you quite shaky." She reached over and patted his hand. "Hope is terribly cross with Charles Linklater, if you must know. Charles knew the issues with the speedway as well as you did and he tried to pass anyway. He might have killed you, too. As it is, he's left us all with a dog's breakfast."

13

GREAT ART

...Given the conditions I have tried to explain as constituting good art; —then, if it be devoted further to the increase of men's happiness, to the redemption of the oppressed, or the enlargement of our sympathies with each other, or to such presentment of new or old truth about ourselves, and our relation to the world, as may ennoble and fortify us in our sojourn here, or, immediately, as with Dante, to the glory of God, it will be also great art...

From "Style," by Walter Pater
Advocate, 1934

The white-washed corridor was hung with smaller works—lino prints and etchings for the most part. Rowland and Clyde followed the prim young woman who led them from the reception area. It was after opening hours and so the gallery was almost entirely empty of people.

The main exhibition room was not particularly large but interestingly shaped, with multiple alcoves and nooks which lent themselves to displaying sculpture as well as paintings. It was here that Rowland's painting, *Psyche by the Styx,* had hung for nearly a year.

A diminutive man in a fine suit and white gloves stood before the canvas, studying it with his arms folded. His cologne was noticeable from about six feet away.

"Mr. Frasier," Rowland said. "How do you do, sir?" He spoke loudly because the gallery's proprietor was partially deaf.

Frasier turned and enclosed Rowland's hand in both of his. "Very well, Mr. Sinclair, very well indeed." He peered at the gauze dressing on Rowland's brow. "My dear fellow, what have you done to yourself?"

"An accident," Rowland said tersely, not wanting to go into the incident. He introduced Clyde, lowering his voice a little now, as Frasier could see his lips.

"I have seen your work, I believe, Mr. Watson Jones," Frasier said regarding Clyde over the top of his half-moon glasses. "In fact, I'd be very interested in acquiring a piece for the gallery."

"Oh, yes. Thank you," Clyde said, wrong-footed. They had not come to sell paintings.

"Actually, Mr. Frasier, we're here to acquire a painting," Rowland said.

"Georgina did mention something of the sort." Frasier nodded at the corridor down which the young woman who'd let them in had long since disappeared. "What piece are you interested in, Mr. Sinclair?"

"The one you're looking at actually."

"But that painting is yours, Mr. Sinclair. I acquired it from you."

"I've decided I want it back, Mr. Frasier."

The generous space between Frasier's two front teeth was exposed as he smiled. He clicked his tongue against the gap. "I'm afraid I've become rather fond of this painting," Frasier said sweetly. "I'd be loath to let it go, even to you."

"I'm not expecting you to gift it to me, Mr. Frasier. I ask only that you name your price."

"Rowly..." Clyde said, alarmed.

Rowland placed a reassuring hand on Clyde's shoulder.

Frasier beamed. "I don't think I could possibly part with it for less than, say, three hundred pounds..."

"Are you out of your mind?" Clyde exploded. "Why, that's got to be fraud. That's what it is—fraud!"

"Done." Rowland reached into his breast pocket for his chequebook.

"Rowly, this is ridiculous. He's taking you for a fool!"

"It's all right, Clyde, really." Rowland turned back to Frasier. "I do have a condition."

"Oh yes?" Frasier eyed him suspiciously.

"I would like you to let it be widely known that you sold this painting for three hundred pounds, but you are not to let anyone know who bought it. I do expect the strictest confidentiality in that respect."

"You want me to publicise the sale price, but the purchaser, he is to be anonymous?"

"That's correct."

The gallery proprietor played with the edges of his moustache as he considered the proposition. "I'll want to sell your next work," he countered.

"That can be arranged, Mr. Frasier. In fact, I'll need a gallery for an exhibition I'm planning. I believe this fine establishment will do nicely."

Frasier beamed. "I think we can do business, Mr. Sinclair."

And so the transaction was done. Rowland and Clyde removed *Psyche by the Styx* from the wall themselves and carried it out to the back seat of the Mercedes. Rowland negotiated a date for his exhibition, in late April, some weeks after the race.

"Right then," Rowland said as they turned the Mercedes back towards *Woodlands House*. "Miss Martinelli's modesty is saved!"

Clyde shook his head. He looked unwell. "Jesus, Mary and Joseph; Rowly, you paid three hundred bloody pounds for it. How the hell am I going to burn it now?"

Rowland laughed. "Consider it an investment."

"In what?"

"What do you suppose is going to happen to the asking price of my work when it gets around that Frasier just sold a piece for three hundred pounds?"

"Mate, that would comfort me if I didn't know for a fact that you've never cared what people pay for your work. You give most of it away, for pity's sake."

"The rumour of this sale won't hurt the exhibition, Clyde."

"But three hundred pounds, Rowly."

"I don't particularly mind being fleeced by Randolph Frasier, to be honest," Rowland confessed. "He knows full well that I can afford it. He would never have charged you that for a painting."

"That makes it worse! How the devil did you get involved with such a crook?"

"The usual way. Milt introduced us." Rowland could see that the sum involved was causing his friend considerable distress, so he tried to explain. "Frasier has, for the last twenty years, brought the homeless and the destitute into his gallery with the promise of a meal and a couple of shillings. All he asks in return is that they look at what's on the walls. He's determined that art has some kind of redemptive, transformative effect, and that it ought to be for everyone. He hands out pencils and chalk and drawing paper to street children. In order to do that, he takes advantage of people like me. Milt would call it an equitable redistribution of wealth. On the whole it seems fair."

"You're saying he's some kind of artistic Robin Hood?"

"Except that his victims are usually complicit, I suppose."

"I can't burn it now."

"It is still the same painting, Clyde."

Clyde's face dropped into his hands. "I know. What was I thinking? I can't burn it. It would make me as bad as the Nazis."

"You're not burning it to stifle ideas and oppress minds, Clyde. You're doing it for Miss Martinelli."

Clyde clenched fistfuls of his thinning hair. "I can't—not even for Rosie. I love her but I won't be turned into a vandal… I won't."

"What say you just give her the painting, then," Rowland suggested. "She can do with it what she wants."

"But what if she—"

"Look, Clyde, it's not my only or last painting, or even my best work." It was not a convenient depreciation. While Rowland had in the end been happy with *Psyche by the Styx*, they all knew that there was no one he painted quite like he painted Edna Higgins. There was a certain elusive quality to his work when she was his model which elevated it into the realm of greatness. Critics and commentators saw it as a subtle variation in technique, or a change of palette, or light; Clyde and Milton could see that it was because the artist was in love with his model.

The argument continued back and forth for most of the journey back to *Woodlands*, but by the time they drove through the wrought-iron gates, Rowland had persuaded Clyde to gift the painting to Rosalina.

"How'd he go?" Milton addressed the question to Clyde, who'd accompanied Rowland to the gallery primarily to see for himself that Rowland's driving had not been affected by the accident.

"He was fine. We'll just have to see how he does on the actual track." Clyde set down the painting, facing it against the wall.

"Randolph sold it back to you then?" Milton asked.

"Yes, and he's agreed to host my exhibition there," Rowland said before Clyde could bemoan the cost of the exercise yet again.

"Splendid!" Edna said. "We'll have to start thinking about invitations, framing, that sort of thing. How many paintings have you finished, Rowly?"

Rowland frowned. "Not enough. All this blessed racing nonsense... I'll be pushing it to have enough pieces by the middle of April."

"I had a thought about that," the sculptress said, going to the shelves on which were stacked his old notebooks. She rummaged through to find the sketchbooks he'd used in Germany. "We could take this apart, frame the sketches you made in Munich. There's a wonderful sense of immediacy about them. I expect they'll work as their own collection of sorts."

Rowland took the notebook from her and flicked through the pages. There were at least twenty sketches of Brownshirts, rallies, citizens going about their business past vandalised shops on which the word "Jude" had been scrawled. There were occasional notes in the margins made to remind himself of what exactly was happening. Some of the sketches had been made the day after, so he would not lose the image of what went before. "Yes," he said quietly. "This might work."

Rowland moved to the bookshelf and found a second notebook. He'd used it in London after they'd escaped Munich... once he found himself able to draw again. The sketches had been made with his left hand as his right arm had been broken. Rowland was ambidextrous— if anything, the use of his left hand made his line work more fluid if a little less detailed. The drawings in the second book were starker than those in the first. He'd been drawing to exorcise images of torture and violence from his head.

"Yes, these will shock the caviar out of them," Milton murmured looking over his shoulder.

Clyde agreed. "They'll make an interesting retrospective."

The four of them spent some time planning how the exhibition would be hung, descriptive plaques, publicity. It was decided that Clyde's landscapes would hang in the corridors leaving the main exhibit room for Rowland's more confronting work.

"Let's lull them with pretty pictures until they're in the heart of the exhibition," Clyde said.

"Perhaps we could construct a display of the books they burned at the Königplatz," Edna said, excited now.

Rowland nodded. It was an excellent idea. "I've a list of the books the Nazis banned somewhere."

They discussed lighting and grouping and bit by bit the exhibition was built.

"We'll have to make sure no one gets wind of what exactly you're planning to exhibit," Milton warned.

Edna agreed. "We might have to stop letting every man and his dog into your studio."

"Speaking of which, where's Len?" Rowland asked, looking around for his greyhound.

"He's in the kitchen with Ed's kittens," Milton said clearly unimpressed. "I fear he's had some kind of breakdown... Seems to think he's a cat."

Rowland was determined to return to his easel that evening, but Edna would not have it. "Don't be an idiot Rowly. You were involved in a serious car accident this morning! Go to bed!"

Rowland resisted. After the horror and mayhem of the day he felt a need to paint, simply to clear his mind. "I'm not sure I'd get much sleep tonight, Ed," he said, as he faced off against the painting of the book burning.

"I wonder why this image in particular is giving you so much trouble," Edna mused, studying the canvas as she stopped beside him.

"Perhaps I'm afraid something will burst out of the canvas and eat me." Rowland laughed as he placed an arm around Edna.

The sculptress sighed. "As much as I suspect Rosaleen Norton is a little mad, her story did give me the creeps."

"You're not—"

"Of course not." She broke away from him and grabbed the slim volume of poetry Milton had left on the sideboard before curling up in the wing-backed armchair. "You paint. I'm just going to read for a bit."

Rowland smiled. "I'm perfectly safe, Ed."

"I'll stay anyway… keep a weather eye on the back of your canvas."

"Weather eye?" Rowland winced. "You're spending too much time with Flynn."

Edna laughed. "It's rather like a having a shipboard romance on solid ground. But he is handsome and very charming."

Rowland retreated behind his easel where it would be less difficult to feign indifference. He painted till late. Edna kept him company, though she fell asleep, at which point Rowland was distracted by the exquisite shadow of the sculptress' lashes on the curve of her cheek. He began painting her sleeping figure onto a clean canvas.

14

NO APOLOGY

FROM FASCIST BLACKSHIRTS
"PROUD OF RECORD"

LONDON, June 12

The Black shirts offer no apology, declared Sir Edward Moseley, at a Fascist meeting in Shrewsbury, regarding the allegations of brutality by eye-witnesses attending the British Fascists meeting at Olympia. Moseley declares that the allegations are evidently of corrupt alliance and are the frame up of a case against the new movement, threatening them with political destruction. Moseley adds: "We are proud of our record in restoring free speech in the face of red terror." He continued: "I challenge half a dozen Cabinet Ministers who attacked me to debate with me on a public platform instead of running about carefully picketing our meetings and lying about Fascism."

Albany Advertiser, 1934

By morning there was a bevy of reporters at the gates of *Woodlands House*. The daily papers carried lurid accounts of the accident. Both *The Sun* and *Smith's Weekly* made much of the involvement of Rowland Sinclair and his German car in the accident.

The Honourable Charlotte Linklater, youngest daughter of Lord Chancy, champion horsewoman and game hunter, spoke to the

Herald, and although she refrained from accusing Rowland Sinclair directly, she did address the aggressive driving which she felt caused her brother's death.

"Hold on," Milton said, looking closely at the article. "The Honourable Charles Linklater was a Blackshirt."

"It doesn't say that!" Clyde muttered, taking the paper from the poet.

Milton pointed. "Miss Linklater says she's received a telegram from Oswald Mosley, who was deeply saddened to hear of the passing of his old friend and compatriot."

"Well, the papers might have to decide whether Rowly's a Nazi or a Communist if they want to accuse him of something," Clyde muttered. He was wearing his best suit—one of those purchased on Rowland Sinclair's account before they last went abroad masquerading as well-to-do art dealers. *Psyche by the Styx* had been carefully wrapped in brown paper.

"Where is Rowly?" Edna asked, pouring tea. Rowland was usually the first of them to come down to breakfast.

"He took Lenin for a walk to get him away from your cats," Milton replied.

"Rowly doesn't mind the kittens," Edna declared, poking the poet.

"He's concerned that Len has started to purr," Milton replied.

Clyde looked at his watch. The anxiety was plain on his weathered face. "I'd better go get this over with."

"Are you taking Rowly's car?"

"Struth, no, I've booked a taxi. I don't want to announce my arrival until it's necessary, and the Mercedes is not a subtle automobile."

"Would you like some company, mate?" Milton offered. "Considering what happened last time, you might need a second."

Clyde shook his head. "I'm just going to leave the painting and a note with her landlady."

"Enclose the receipt or they might fear it's stolen," Milton advised.

Clyde nodded glumly.

Edna embraced him. "Poor darling, Clyde. I'm so sorry it worked out this way."

Clyde sighed. "It's probably for the best. Rosie seemed quite impressed with this Antonio chap."

"Did she indeed?" Edna's words were terse. As much as the sculptress' own loves were fleeting she had never promised anyone anything else. She could not bear the thought of Clyde alone and heartbroken as he called on Rosalina this one last time. "I'm going with you," she said.

"Ed, I don't—"

"I'm coming." Edna put down her tea and began looking for her bag and gloves. "Milt, would you tell Errol when he calls that I've stepped out with Clyde for a moment and won't be able to go sailing with him today?" She paused and turned back to the poet. "You should go if he still wants company."

"Me?"

"Yes, I rather think you and Errol would rub along beautifully."

"I can't swim, remember."

"That won't matter unless he's a particularly bad sailor which I'm sure he isn't," she said sweetly.

Milton groaned. "Go," he said. "I'll keep Errol occupied."

Woodlands House was almost empty when Rowland and Lenin returned. Mary Brown was visiting family in Burwood, leaving Bessie, as the most senior downstairs maid, to attend to the running of the house in her absence.

"Mrs. Bainbridge collected Mrs. Sinclair for luncheon and matinée, sir," she said, when Rowland enquired after his mother.

"Thank you, Bessie." Rowland removed his jacket and loosened his tie. His Aunt Mildred, Mrs. Bainbridge, was his father's sister. Rowland had always thought her an old dragon, but she was fond of his mother and had been kind since Elisabeth Sinclair had moved back to Sydney.

Lenin followed Bessie back to the kitchen in search of his kittens, and Rowland proceeded into his studio, shutting the door behind him before discarding his jacket on the couch.

His easel held a completed painting of Edna asleep in the armchair, curled up like a child with her head pillowed by her hands. Her lashes were dark against the natural rose of her cheek. He stared at it for a while and then removed the painting, replacing it with the canvas he should have been working on the night before.

The sun had risen high enough that the light in the bay window was neither direct nor harsh. Rowland set out his palette and began. The painting was finally finding a rhythm with each brushstroke inviting the next, making sense with the next. He painted Röhm as a portly grinning figure, strutting proudly as his men burned books and declared ideas enemies of the state. Somehow the banality of the image was more chilling than any traditional monster. In the background, the silhouettes of Brownshirts going about their thuggish work as men cowered on the ground.

Engrossed in the detail of Röhm's bloated, scarred face, Rowland teased out the shadows cast by the firelight. He needed a finer brush and he turned away to find one.

An explosion of glass.

A solitary bullet shattered a pane of the bay window and pierced the canvas from behind. A second earlier, the shot might have proved fatal. As it was, Rowland felt the breeze it created as he dropped to the floor. He waited, his heart pounding, his ears ringing.

The door to the studio moved.

"No!" Rowland shouted, still expecting a second shot. "Don't come in!"

He crept away from the window, and sat pressed against the wall. Still nothing. Carefully he stood and peered out the window. The grounds were, as far as he could tell, empty.

A knocking at the studio door. "Mr. Sinclair, are you all right sir?"

"I'm fine, Bessie, but don't come in. I'll come out."

Rowland moved to the door doing his level best to stay out of any line of sight from the garden. He closed the door behind him as he stepped into the entrance hall.

Bessie gaped at him, a pudgy hand clasped over what Rowland presumed was an open mouth. "What happened, sir?"

"I'm afraid someone's fired a shot through the studio window."

"Oh my Lord, oh my Lord, oh my Lord," the maid chanted, turning in an erratic circle while Rowland tried to calm her.

"I'm sure he's gone now, Bessie."

"How do you know, sir? Perhaps he was trying to get into the house." She stared at the studio door. "Lord, he might just walk through the broken window."

"Do you have Mary Brown's keys?" Rowland asked.

She pulled a large ring of keys from the chatelaine around her waist. Rowland found the key to his studio quickly and locked the door.

"There," he told the distressed maid. "I might just telephone the police now."

Rowland made the call with Bessie hovering anxiously beside him.

"Come into the library and I'll pour you a medicinal brandy, Bessie," Rowland said as he re-cradled the receiver. The maid looked as though she could do with a stiff drink.

Bessie shook her head so hard that her cap came loose. "There're windows in the library, Mr. Sinclair, and he could still be out there."

"Oh... I see." Rowland tried to recall a part of the house not made vulnerable by windows. "Why don't you stay here for just a moment?" he suggested. "I'll duck into the library and bring you a glass of brandy."

"What if you get shot and killed, Mr. Sinclair?"

"You have the keys, Bessie. Go upstairs and lock yourself in somewhere. The police will be here soon."

Bessie nodded, sniffling tearfully.

"Is there anybody else in the house?" Rowland asked.

The maid shook her head. "No, sir, we all usually have a half day off today. I'm only here because Miss Brown wanted to visit her sister."

"Good, I won't be a moment." Rowland walked into the library and grabbed the decanter of brandy and two tumblers from the silver tray on the mantel.

When the police knocked on the front door, Rowland and the maid were seated on one of the lower steps of the grand staircase which swept up from the tiled foyer. Lenin had padded out of the kitchen to investigate briefly and then returned to his kittens.

Rowland answered the knock. He was a little surprised to see Delaney at the head of the small force on his doorstep. "Colin... what are you doing here?" He shook the detective's hand.

"I have the desk sergeant call me whenever you get into trouble. It saves time."

"I see."

Delaney winked as he signalled his constables to make a search of the grounds. "I'm no longer investigating the White case as you know, but there's no reason to believe this is related. It's not the first time someone's tried to shoot you, after all." Delaney removed his hat and stepped into the house. "We'd best have a look at where the bullet came in."

The decanter crashed onto the tiles as Bessie stood. She cried out in dismay before descending into frantic apologies.

"Excuse me a moment." Rowland diverted momentarily to the staircase to reassure the servant and suggest she make herself a cup of tea while he spoke to the detective.

Bessie sobbed and apologised again about the decanter. "Miss Brown will take it out of my wages, sir," she lamented.

"It was my fault entirely for leaving it on the step," Rowland said, handing her his handkerchief. "We'll clean it up before Miss Brown gets back, and she need never know."

At this suggestion poor Bessie gasped, for fear Rowland intended to participate in the cleaning somehow. The horror shook her out of her anxiety. She made it clear that she would see to the broken decanter directly and under no circumstances must he touch a broom.

So chastised, Rowland returned to Delaney, opening the door to the studio and observing the damage. The floor below the bay window was strewn with shattered glass. The easel hadn't moved and the canvas he'd been painting was still clamped in place. The bullet had come through what should have been Ernst Röhm's mouth. Rowland considered the result while Delaney searched for the bullet.

"So, Rowly, did you see anyone… anything?" Delaney asked, as he delicately pried the bullet out of the wood panelling on the opposite wall.

"No," Rowland said, poking a finger through the hole in his canvas. "But I was painting. I wasn't really watching anything else."

Delaney came round to peer at the canvas. He cursed. "How he missed you beggars belief."

"I suspect I turned away at an opportune time," Rowland said uncertainly.

"You might just be the luckiest man alive, Rowly."

"That's one way of looking at it."

"Who wants to kill you at the moment?"

"No one, as far as I know."

"Where is everybody?"

"I'm not entirely sure. Bessie might know."

Delaney sent a constable to fetch the maid. Bessie rattled off the whereabouts of the household as best she could. "Miss Higgins went with Mr. Watson Jones to deliver a painting, sir, and Mr. Isaacs has stepped out with Mr. Flynn."

"Milt left with Flynn?" Rowland asked, surprised.

"I believe they went sailing, Mr. Sinclair."

"Who's this Flynn?" Delaney asked.

"An actor, I'm told. He's driving for my team in the Maroubra Invitational."

"It's not been cancelled?" Delaney asked. "I thought with the crash and all…"

Rowland shrugged. "Apparently not."

"Where was your mother this morning, Rowly?" Delaney tried to sound casual.

"My mother did not try to shoot me," Rowland said, bristling. "Whatever may have happened in the past… What happened to my father was…"

"I have to ask."

"She's out with my Aunt Mildred."

"Good." Delaney looked out the now glassless window to the grounds.

"What are you looking for?" Rowland asked.

"Places where our mystery shooter might have stood so that he would have a clear line of sight and not be easily seen."

"As I said, I wouldn't have noticed anyone."

Delaney held up a finger. "Yes, that's right. But he would only have known that if he knew you." He paced, pleased with the revelation. "If we can establish where the shooter actually stood, we'll at least be able to ascertain whether he was likely to have known you well or not."

Rowland conceded. There was an undeniable logic to Delaney's reasoning. "Will we be able to work out where he stood?"

"Could you place your easel in the exact position in which it stood before the shooting?"

Rowland gingerly cleared the shattered glass with his shoe and manoeuvred the H-frame easel so that it was parallel with the outer wall of the bay, using the paint splatters on the polished floorboards to guide him. "This would be about right," he said, standing back for perspective. "So how will this help?"

Delaney pointed to the oak panelling from which he had just dug out the bullet. "Bullets fly in a straight line, more or less. We know where it ended up and where it went through your painting. If we simply follow that trajectory, it should give us an idea of where the bullet originated."

"Good Lord, you've been reading Conan Doyle."

"Hand me your longest paintbrush, Rowly," Delaney said, ignoring the jibe.

Rowland did so. Delaney poked the brush through the hole in the painting from behind, lining the wooden end up with where the bullet had embedded. He signalled Rowland to grab the brush from the other side of the canvas and hold it absolutely motionless, before he stepped away. "Right, it's a bit rough and ready, but the brush should point to the general area from where the bullet came."

The paintbrush directed them towards the shaded driveway, lined with claret ash.

"Perhaps he used the trees as cover," Delaney mused. "I'll have the area searched in case he left anything behind."

15

Night Tin Hares
ARE TO
Be Abolished!

DAY COURSING AND NEW CONTROL

NIGHT tin hare coursing is to be changed to day coursing. And the dogs will race under different and clean non-proprietary control, or else a strict and impartial board of control.

That is the Intention of the majority of the Cabinet, which has deputed the Chief Secretary (Mr. Chaffey) to inquire into all the factors and interests involved in the "poor man's sport."...

EXPERIENCED PATRON

One of the syndicates which wishes to race at Wentworth Park on nonproprietary lines is headed by Dr. R. Stuart Jones, of Canterbury, who claims a considerable experience of tin-hare racing in England, where it has been established on a much more desirable basis than here. His organisation is called the Australian Greyhound Club, and it includes Ald. A. C. Samuels, ex-Mayor of Manly; Dr. Roy Croft, of Balmain, a follower of Plumpton coursing: Mr. L. J. Lager, a chemist of Balmain; Mr. Gordon McKay, a well-known courser and one-time owner of the champion, Fearless Buttons; Dr. Caleb Goode, of Vaucluse; Mr. J. J. Salkeld, master butcher of Darling Point; Mr. G. Harvison, a dentist of Campsie: Mr. W. C. B. Fahey, retired grazier of Waverton; and Mr. J. Collier, an executive member of the National Coursing Association and secretary of the Greyhound Owners and Trainers' Association.

> Dr. Stuart Jones states that an option has been obtained
> over Wentworth Park oval, and plans and specifications and
> also an application for a licence has been in the hands of
> the Government since July. Increased prize money, better
> accommodation, and catering on a large scale for the social side
> of the sport, to elevate the game to the high plane it at present
> enjoys in other countries, are objects.
>
> *Truth, 1932*

The absent members of the *Woodlands* household all seemed to return within the same fifteen minute period. The result was somewhat chaotic. Without actually lying, Rowland somehow managed to leave his mother with the impression that he'd not been in the studio when the shot was fired. He was careful to tell Mary Brown that Bessie had responded to the crisis in an admirable manner which reflected well on the thorough training she'd received under the housekeeper. Between them, Delaney and Rowland managed to tell the others what little they knew. Edna volunteered to walk Errol Flynn to his car.

"Oh, I couldn't leave now." He put his arm around Edna. "Don't worry sailor, you're safe with me."

"That's very sweet, Errol." Edna squeezed the actor's hand warmly. "But I'm perfectly well protected. And the police are here now. We really just have to clean up, so unless you're proficient with a broom?"

Flynn laughed, throwing his head back as he did. "I've scrubbed more decks than I care to remember, so I might leave you to it!"

Rowland noticed the fleeting upward movement of Edna's bright eyes. Was it relief? He hoped it was.

The broken glass had been swept up and the services of a glazier engaged by the time Delaney's men had finished their search.

"Any luck?" Clyde asked the detective.

Delaney shook his head. "Nothing." He turned to Milton and Clyde. "I don't suppose you blokes saw anyone loitering about the place this morning?"

"Only reporters," Milton replied.

"Reporters?" Delaney took out his notebook. "I thought that they arrived after the gunshot."

Milton shrugged. "Some may have, but there were some here this morning. To interview Rowly about the crash at Maroubra, I expect."

"We'll follow that up," Delaney assured them. "Perhaps the shooter entered the grounds under the guise of a reporter, or perhaps one of them saw something." He pointed at Rowland. "There's no point having gates if they're not secured, Rowly. Do something about it!"

Rowland grimaced. The gates at *Woodlands House* were rarely locked, but given recent events, it was probably time to improve security—at least for the moment.

"I'll station some constables here for the moment," Delaney went on, "but I'll need them back in a day or two. Until we find out why the shot was fired, we must assume someone is trying to kill you."

Rowland protested. The assumption seemed to him somewhat hysterical.

Delaney pulled him aside to press his point.

"Rowly, your mother lives here now, not to mention your less genteel companions. You don't want to be too cavalier about danger."

"You're right, of course," Rowland said, chastened. "I'll see to it, Colin. You have my word."

"Good man." Delaney offered him something in return. "White's tiepin might have been stolen," he said.

"Yes, I gathered that from the fact it wasn't on the body."

"No, I mean it was stolen before it fell into White's hands." Delaney flipped back a page or two in his notebook. "A twenty-four carat gold tiepin, a bar with two interlocking horseshoes in the middle and set with a half carat diamond was reported stolen by a Mr. Lesley Bocquet, from his premises in Lindfield a couple of weeks ago."

"That does sound like it," Rowland replied thoughtfully. "I don't suppose there might have been two?"

"Possible… but unlikely, I would think. My instincts tell me it's too much of a coincidence that the first is stolen just before the second turns up on the soon-to-be victim of murder."

"Have you spoken to Mr. Bocquet?"

"Yes, briefly. He's never heard of White." Delaney shook his head. "To be honest, I'm not sure the tiepin will lead anywhere. A flashy piece like that would probably have been difficult for any murderer to resist."

"I suppose. But one does wonder how the tiepin came to be on White's tie. He was rather too portly to be a cat burglar."

"We're making enquiries at all the local pawn shops," Delaney said. "My guess is that he, or perhaps this unknown woman that Miss Higgins is convinced he's been seeing, came by it after it had been fenced. Of course, getting a pawnbroker to admit he'd accepted stolen goods might be a trifle challenging."

"No doubt." Rowland hesitated. "I don't suppose you'd consider allowing me to have a chat with Bocquet?"

"Out of the question!" Delaney said as he wrote a note and then tore the page from his notebook. "You are not a policeman, Rowly. You cannot go about questioning suspects!" He slipped the folded page into Rowland's hand. "It would be highly improper!"

Rowland opened the page: an address in Lindfield in Delaney's loose scrawl.

"So, did you leave the painting?" Milton whispered to Edna once Delaney had departed.

Edna nodded. "Rosalina was out, so we left it with her aunt. I think it was easier for Clyde that way, and hopefully she'll appreciate the gesture."

"What charm can soothe her melancholy?" Milton said shaking his head. "What art can wash her guilt away?"

"Goldsmith," Rowland made the attribution reflexively. The verse was apt. He hoped possession of the evidence that she had modelled nude would assuage whatever shame Rosalina Martinelli felt. "How is Clyde, do you think, Ed?" Rowland asked quietly.

Edna wrinkled her nose as she contemplated the question. "He's sad, but I sense some part of him is relieved it's over."

"As are we all," Milton muttered.

"Milt!" Edna said, appalled.

Rowland did not wholly disagree with Milton, though it was not a sentiment he was willing to voice. As a sweetheart, Rosalina Martinelli had required an extraordinary amount of maintenance. She had made no secret of the fact that she did not like Clyde's friends in general and Rowland Sinclair in particular. It seemed the reformed model had never forgiven him for the manner in which he'd painted her.

Rowland decided to take Lenin for another walk around the grounds. However, having already been taken for his customary constitutional, the hound was noticeably reluctant.

"Leave Len be." Edna tucked her hair under her hat. "I'll come for a stroll with you."

"Where are you going?" Milton asked.

"To see if the police missed anything," Edna replied.

"You're searching for clues?" Milton rose from the armchair.

"Well, not exactly." Rowland tried to moderate the poet's enthusiasm.

"I'd better assist. Come on then Sherlock and Watson."

"Where?" Clyde asked striding into the conservatory wiping the grease from his hands with a towel. He'd been working on Rowland's car, practising timely wheel changes, windscreen cleaning and the like.

"To search for clues of the bloke who tried to shoot Rowly." Milton grabbed a magnifying glass from the secretaire and held it to his eye.

"Haven't the police already searched the grounds?"

"I suspect the constables were paying more attention to Ed's statues," Milton replied, slipping the magnifying glass into his pocket. "I heard Delaney bellowing at them to keep their eyes on the ground and off the garden ornaments. I'm afraid Colin has the sensual understanding of a Methodist preacher."

"Why don't we all go, then?" Clyde suggested. "It's a shame Len is a greyhound rather than a bloodhound."

"I think the jury's still out on greyhound," Milton muttered, bending to pat the ugly misshapen dog.

"Len's all right," Rowland laughed. He liked dogs. He loved Lenin in spite of, or perhaps because of, the hound's obvious lack of breeding.

Delaney had stationed two hard-chested constables at the gate to the property, who watched the four as they strolled through the trees and over the expansive lawns in search of anything out of place. It was more a ramble in the gentle warmth of the autumn sun, not quite a lark, but not an earnest investigation either.

Rowland stood behind the claret ash which grew closest to the house and surveyed the bay windows of his studio. A glazier and his young apprentice were already at work installing a new pane of glass, but Rowland could see easily into the room. Still, the shooter must have been a reasonable marksman. The ground at the base of the tree was hard enough to preclude footprints.

He found himself becoming increasingly angry as he contemplated the attempt on his life. While it was not the first time someone had tried to kill him, this attack had taken place at his studio, his sanctuary. From where he stood, he could also see the wing-backed armchair in which Edna often posed for him. The possibilities did nothing to placate him.

"And watching with eternal lids apart, like nature's patient, sleepless Eremite. You're reckon he stood here?" Milton stopped beside him.

Rowland nodded. "Keats. It seems likely." He looked back towards the gate. "I'm just not sure how he could have slipped in without one of the reporters seeing him."

"Perhaps one did," Milton mused. "Delaney hasn't questioned them yet."

"Or perhaps he slipped in before the reporters arrived, and waited." Clyde shaded his eyes as he followed Rowland's line of vision.

"The reporters were here at dawn." Edna pushed back an auburn tress which had escaped the confines of her hat.

"How do you know that?" Milton asked.

"I'm working on a sculpture of Eos, the goddess of dawn, so I got up to watch daybreak from the verandah. I saw the reporters arrive."

Clyde scratched his head. "He may have waited all night for all we know."

Milton pulled at his goatee as he walked around the claret ash. "He must have come after Rowly went to bed last night, or he could have shot him then. When did you finish in the studio last night, comrade?"

"About one in the morning," Rowland replied.

"So, maybe he slipped in between one o'clock and dawn and waited." Milton sighed. "It's not much but it's something."

Edna rubbed her bare arms. "It's a little unnerving to think of him out here, just waiting."

Rowland removed his jacket and placed it around her shoulders. "Yes, it is," he said, his face darkening as he thought of Edna alone on the verandah with a gunman in the garden.

"Where did you take Lenin for a walk this morning?" Clyde asked, wondering why Rowland had not spotted the intruder.

"I didn't walk him on the grounds," Rowland replied. "I had Johnston drive us to Watson's Bay in the Rolls Royce and walked him there. The reporters were watching for the Mercedes, they didn't pay a great deal of attention to the Rolls Royce. I expect they assumed it was Mother, off somewhere."

"Well, it's a good thing you didn't walk Lenin here." Edna entwined her arm in his. "He might have shot you then."

Clyde sighed. "Perhaps that was his plan all along. Rowly, who would know you'd be walking Len this morning?"

Rowland shook his head. "No one, Clyde. It's not like I do it every morning."

"But you do walk him often, and usually in the morning. Who'd know that?"

"You, Ed, Milt... the staff, I suppose."

Milton grinned wickedly. "It was Mary Brown. All this nonsense about visiting her sister... she finally figured that shooting you was the only way to get undesirables out of the house!"

"My housekeeper is not trying to kill me," Rowland said calmly.

Milton sighed. "You're right. Why would she shoot at you when she could so easily poison you instead? Still, perhaps you should have Clyde taste your food."

The attempted shooting at *Woodlands House* was reported widely. The fact that the gunman was still at large, having mysteriously disappeared from the scene of the crime, was almost as newsworthy as if he had not missed.

In any case, the near thing was enough to rekindle rumours that Maroubra's "Killer Track" was cursed. Rowland refused to talk to the media on the basis that they had become ridiculous. He was most frustrated by the fact that the constant presence of reporters in his wake made it impossible to visit the address that Delaney had given him with any semblance of discretion. The note remained in his pocket and the question of White's murderer in his thoughts.

The Honourable Charlotte Linklater publicly vowed that she would beat Rowland Sinclair on the track, to avenge her late brother. The controversy was a marketing boon for the Red Cross with interest in the race increasing in all quarters.

When the speedway was reopened a couple of days later, Joan Richmond was careful to ensure Rowland's practice schedule did not coincide with Charlotte's. She rode with him when he first resumed the track, ensuring he would not flinch.

"Don't worry," she said quietly, as they lined up against Bartlett. "Hope is a better driver than Linklater was. He won't cock things up so royally."

Rowland regarded his captain warmly. It was the seventh time that day that Joan had not so subtly pointed out that the accident had been Linklater's fault and not his. He appreciated the effort, and while Rowland still felt sick when he thought of what had happened to the Englishman, he had more or less accepted that he had done nothing to force the disaster that followed.

He and Clyde were preparing to head home after the session on the track when they were approached by a gentleman clad in a fashionable double-breasted suit. His hair was slicked back, with a sheen which rivalled the duco of the lovingly polished Mercedes. It had been a couple of years since Rowland had last seen him. Their association had been brief and not one Rowland would seek to revive.

"Dr. Stuart Jones," Rowland said.

"For pity's sake, it's Reg!" He held out his hand and pumped Rowland's enthusiastically.

Rowland introduced Clyde, who had not been present when last he'd encountered the dubious gynaecologist at one of Sydney's seediest nightclubs.

"Phil Jeffs sends his regards and salutations, incidentally," Stuart Jones said opening his cigarette case and offering its contents to both men.

Rowland declined the cigarette, nodding politely in response to the conveyance of good wishes. Phil "the Jew" Jeffs' regards were not something for which he cared, but they were preferable to the gangster's presence. Not that Dr. Reginald Stuart Jones was much of an improvement. Stuart Jones' medical title, at least, was not an affectation. He had married his fortune but had made his name as a gynaecologist by assisting unmarried women in trouble. He catered particularly to those parts of society who could afford to pay him well for the service. They all knew that Stuart Jones' purpose was not social, but the doctor insisted upon a preliminary charade of niceties and chitchat.

It wasn't until Rowland said, "I'm afraid we really must be going", that Stuart Jones came to the point.

"You know your team is the favourite, don't you, Sinclair?"

"No, I can't say I am aware of that."

"Oh yes, especially now that Charles Linklater is dead. Hope Bartlett's team was the favourite till that happened. It's understandable, of course." He patted the Mercedes' bonnet. "You looked good on the track just now, and Joanie Richmond is very well regarded. Even Flynn isn't driving too badly."

"Yes... well... thank you." Rowland's eyes narrowed. He was aware of Stuart Jones' connections with greyhound racing. In fact, Milton had acquired Lenin as a reject from the doctor's stable of dogs. He was, however, fairly sure that the notorious punter was not a devotee of motor sports. But perhaps Stuart Jones did not care what form his dogs took.

"Not at all, old chap, not at all. How do you think you'll go? Are you confident?"

Rowland didn't reply.

Stuart Jones continued regardless. "You be careful out there, Sinclair. You wouldn't want to end like Linklater, you know."

"I beg your pardon?" Rowland stepped towards Stuart Jones.

"Just friendly concern, old bean. Good luck, break a leg and all that." Stuart Jones patted Rowland's shoulder cheerfully before departing quite hastily.

Rowland stared after him, and then turned to Clyde. "What the hell was that about?"

"Bookies don't make any money when a favourite wins, Rowly. The bastard's just trying to unnerve you."

Rowland glanced up at the crowd gathered on the fence at the top of the bowl. It had been growing each day. "I just hope that's all it was, Clyde."

16

THE LETTER OF LETTY

Norman Lindsay and Mae West

Dear Cynthia,—

...I must tell you a story about a work of art that was not disclosed to the public's gaze on the opening night. This was a huge picture by Norman Lindsay, which arrived some time before. It was unwrapped in the upstairs foyer before several of the "Heads," not to mention interested workmen. Like most pictures by this artist, its subject was several rather startling feminine figures—one even more striking than the rest. So much so, in fact, that it drew from one of the open-mouthed workmen the comment, "Look, Bill! Mae West's come up to see us!"

Table Talk, 1934

Rowland slipped his own notebook into the inside breast pocket of his jacket before taking the folio from its place of last discard on the sideboard. He glanced out the window. Wilfred had organised a private security detail of half a dozen men to replace Delaney's two constables. One was stationed permanently at the gate, which was locked, another at the stables-cum-garage. The other four patrolled the grounds ensuring the tall hedges hid nothing more sinister than a cloistered garden bench.

Where Wilfred had found these men, Rowland did not ask. His brother was a powerful man, he had his own enemies and he'd always had his own security, too. The men had a bearing and collective manner that evoked the military. Whether that was because they had known Wilfred in service or because they were associated with some clandestine army of the establishment, Rowland did not know. He assumed he would be rid of the intrusion, however discreet, once the gunman was caught or a sufficient time without incident had passed.

"Are you going somewhere, Aubrey?"

Rowland glanced up to see his mother at the door. She looked well. Always elegant, Elisabeth Sinclair had decided today to wear a jaunty feather in her cloche. The embellishment was bright red—not a colour Rowland had seen his mother wear in many years. "I had planned to call on a friend, Mother, but I could leave that till later if you require me for something."

"No, I don't require you, but I had hoped you might have some time for me... But no, you go. Enjoy the morning calling on your friend and don't worry about me."

Smiling, Rowland offered a compromise. "Why don't you come with me, Mother? You might find Norman's studio interesting and we could take tea in town somewhere afterwards if you fancy it."

"Tea? Heavens, Aubrey, when did you become so stuffy? We're not Presbyterians! Couldn't we go for a drink? Where is it young people go these days?"

Amused, Rowland regarded his mother, her eyes sparkling now with rebellious enthusiasm. "We'll find somewhere, I'm sure. Would you like to accompany me then?"

"Only if you comb your hair. I'm not stepping out with a vagrant."

Rowland gave the nurse on duty the morning off, assuring her that he would look after his mother. They took the Rolls Royce and the elderly chauffeur, Johnston, because Elisabeth Sinclair had never thought it entirely gentlemanly to drive oneself. In any case Rowland was becoming increasingly cautious about his all too conspicuous vehicle. The Mercedes had been vandalised once and Stuart Jones' interest made him wary.

Norman Lindsay had moved from Springwood to the Bridge Street studio earlier that year. Rowland was aware that the artist had felt creatively exhausted for some time and unable to paint or write. For an artist of Lindsay's prolific, frenetic nature the inability to make art had been torturous. He had left his wife and children in Springwood to chase a muse who had turned her face away. She had led him, it seemed, to Bridge Street, where he now resided in a studio convenient to the offices of *The Bulletin* which had first made him a household name.

Interestingly, Rowland quite intentionally saw him less often now that they inhabited the same city. Lindsay had always been unconventional, outrageous and prejudiced in his outlook, but it seemed to Rowland that his mentor had adopted much darker views of late.

"Would you prefer to wait, Mother?" Rowland asked hopefully, as they pulled up outside the studio. Three young women whom he recognised as models were walking out. They waved when they saw him and suddenly Rowland realised that bringing his mother to the studio of Norman Lindsay might not have been the most sensible idea. "I shouldn't be long."

"Absolutely not! I used to sketch a little as a girl, you know. My governess declared my watercolours quite accomplished. Perhaps I shall take it up again."

Rowland grimaced. "Mr. Lindsay is what is called a life artist, Mother. You might find some of his work—"

"For pity's sake, Aubrey, my education was not so neglected that I am unaware of, or offended by, the classical nude! You young people seem to believe you invented the risqué!"

Appropriately chastised, Rowland got out of the car while Johnston opened the door properly for Elisabeth Sinclair. The pace of the elderly chauffeur was such that Rowland had time to straighten his tie, adjust his cuffs, walk around the car and still offer Elisabeth his hand as she alighted.

Lindsay's studio was on the second floor, an ample space with a residence attached. It was in the chaotic studio that they were received. Elisabeth Sinclair held onto Rowland's arm as they picked their way through sculptures in progress and laden easels. The artist was at work on a large oil painting while he chatted with a gentleman who watched his progress.

"Rowland!" Norman Lindsay said as he stood back from his canvas, regarding the image with one eye closed. "What do you think? I fear it's a little overworked but I'm still becoming accustomed to oils. Even so, it's not entirely incompetent."

Rowland studied the Ruebenesque nude. The painting did not have the lightness of touch that was characteristic of Lindsay's etchings and watercolours.

"I can't tell you how much I have been renewed by oils," Lindsay continued. "I viewed the work of the classical masters in Europe you know, the beautiful reality of the human form. It reinvigorated my faith, reinspired me despite the perverse obsession of the masses with modernism—Oh, I say! You've brought a friend!" Lindsay seemed to notice Elisabeth Sinclair for the first time.

Rowland introduced Norman Lindsay to his mother.

"Mrs. Sinclair, you are most welcome in my humble studio," Lindsay said graciously. "Allow me to introduce my friend and one time publisher, Mr. Inky Stephensen."

Rowland shook hands with Stephensen whom he'd known for some years, having first met the man at Oxford. The publisher had been a Rhodes scholar and though they had not moved in the same circles, their paths had crossed on occasion.

Stephensen shared a political affiliation with Milton and Clyde, and while they too were acquainted with him, Rowland knew his friends had little time for the publisher. Milton maintained that Stephensen simply liked to wave his fist, that his commitment to Communism was more to do with an oppositional nature than philosophy.

"I take it you are no longer with Endeavour Press?" Rowland asked for the sake of making conversation.

"Regrettably, Endeavour Press and I had an irreconcilable difference of opinion. I've struck out in my own right, now—P. R. Stephensen & Co." Stephensen handed Rowland a business card.

"What brings you here, dear boy?" Lindsay asked.

Rowland handed him Rosaleen's folio. "I promised the young lady who made these drawings that I'd show them to you. She's an ardent admirer of your work."

Lindsay preened, gratified, and took the folio. He spread the sheets of paper on an oak table along the wall, studying each work in turn. "This friend of yours, did she train at the East Sydney Technical College?"

"Yes. How did you—"

"Because the Tech produces artists with technique and, alas, no spirit. The drawings are unsophisticated and rough. I doubt she has a great future."

"She's only seventeen, Norman." Rowland found himself speaking in Rosaleen's defence. "I'm sure her technique will mature as she does."

Lindsay shrugged and seemed to lose interest. "Perhaps." He glanced at Elisabeth Sinclair, who was studying a sculpture a few steps away and lowered his voice and winked. "I take it this girl, Norton, has replaced Miss Higgins as your muse?"

"Great Caesar's, no! She's just rather insistent that I show you her work, and inform you that she models. As I said, Miss Norton is an admirer of your work."

"Of course, of course." He shook his head. "Pity. I had hoped you'd send Edna back to me if you're finished with her."

Rowland laughed. "I don't send Ed anywhere, Norman, she goes where she pleases. If you want her to model for you, ask her, by all means. But I won't ever be finished with Ed."

Lindsay sighed. "I once believed that about Rose, but creativity and desire are linked, Rowland. Your paintings of Edna are extraordinary but what will happen to them, I wonder, when your lust for her has been sated."

Rowland was well accustomed to the intimate bluntness of Lindsay's philosophies but the sating of lust was not something he wished to discuss with his mother in the room.

Inky Stephensen rescued him from the uncomfortable direction of the conversation by showing an interest in Rosaleen's drawings. "Rowland, this is fascinating," he said holding up one of the surrealist depictions of Pan. "More black magic than Bacchanalian. I published Aleister Crowley when I was with Mandrake, you know. He might have liked this."

"You don't say." Rowland was unsure of what endorsement the favour of the legendary Satanist held.

"I do."

Lindsay snorted. "If this girl is after advice, tell her to study the masters, not to be swayed by the modernist rubbish that Jewish dealers are trying to pass off as art!"

Rowland stiffened. "For pity's sake, Norman. I'm not telling her that."

"Why?"

"Because it's idiotic!"

"What! You've become a modernist, have you?"

"Whether or not I'm a modernist has nothing to do with any imagined Jewish conspiracy!" Rowland said hotly.

Stephensen intervened. "Jews are at the heart of the capitalist oppression of the worker, Rowland," he said, placing a conciliatory hand on Rowland's shoulder. "The greed-driven money lenders have Europe in a vice-like grip."

Rowland shook off Stephensen's hand. "Aren't you supposed to be a Communist, Inky?"

"It's because I'm a Communist that I understand how damaging the cooperation of Jewish interests has been to the rights of the worker."

"I spoke of this at the Royal Academy of Arts," Lindsay said. "I'll never forget. Afterwards Sir Edwin Lutyens kissed me on both cheeks and cried, 'At last, an honest man'!"

"He could have kissed you on the mouth and proposed marriage for all I care!" Rowland replied angrily. "What you're saying is detestable, Norman, and aside from being codswallop it's dangerous."

Lindsay's sharp eyes were piercing. "Why are you surprised Rowland? I have never made any secret about what I know. I admit, I am truly fond of Milton Isaacs, and I am not saying that Jews as people are necessarily bad, but as a race you cannot deny that they are responsible for a great deal of the world's troubles. You can't blame people for finally taking a stand."

Rowland was white. Disappointment and fury left him momentarily speechless. How could this be the case? Lindsay had taught him so much as an artist. Rowland had looked upon him as a friend and a mentor, a man of letters and wit. He felt like Norman Lindsay was dying before his eyes and he was staggered by grief and anger.

Rowland gathered up Rosaleen Norton's folio. "We'd best be off."

"Nonsense," Lindsay said. "Stay, let's have a drink and talk of how we will resist the modernist movement. I can show you papers, essays which prove the extent of the problem."

If it were possible to curse without saying a word, Rowland was doing so.

"We won't discuss the Jews if that upsets you, comrade," Stephensen offered.

Rowland's voice was controlled, but the strain of keeping it so was audible. "What I wish to say to you gentlemen, cannot be said in the presence of a lady, let alone my mother, so I think that we shall leave."

Elisabeth Sinclair returned to her son's side, and bade Lindsay and Stephensen farewell, before allowing Rowland to escort her from the studio.

Elisabeth patted Rowland's hand as they sat in the back of the Rolls Royce, much as she had done when he was a child beset with emotions he needed to control.

"I am sorry about that, Mother," he said, furious with himself for so many reasons.

Elisabeth sighed. "You mustn't worry about me, Aubrey. I gather you and Mr. Lindsay had a falling out?"

"Yes, I expect we have."

"I heard Mr. Lindsay mention Mr. Isaacs. Does he not have a good regard for Mr. Isaacs?"

"No, I don't think he does."

"Well, that won't do. Mr. Isaacs is a thorough gentleman."

Rowland rubbed his face. He leaned forward and gave Johnston an address in Woolloomooloo.

"Where are we going Aubrey?"

"Dancing," Rowland replied. "I'm taking you dancing."

"Don't be silly. It's two in the afternoon!"

Rowland nodded gravely. "It is decidedly scandalous, but I believe dancing in the afternoon is all the rage now."

17

EXPANSION OF PUBLISHING

A PROGRESSIVE MOVE

According to "Newspaper News" of 18th instant, Mr. P. R Stephensen, who visited Melbourne last month, says the objective of P. R. Stephensen and Company Ltd., is the publishing of one book a week. He has come with his partner, Mr. E. C. Lemont, to establish a Melbourne branch of the business. The Commonwealth he considers is happily placed for the book industry. The South African market is as accessible to Australia as it is to Great Britain, in Japan, the second language spoken is English, and elsewhere throughout the East there are communities of English people whose interest could be attracted to novels and other works by Australian writers. The exchange rate, too, is an advantage in marketing books to that public. "Australian authors in England," said Mr. Stephensen, "are asked to write about some other country more acceptable to English readers than Australia. We can put a stop to such effrontery only by developing our own literature on our own soil, as the Americans have done."

Mr. Stephensen hopes to reprint many worthwhile Australian books which have been allowed to go out of print by the original publishers.

The Central Queensland Herald, 1934

Elisabeth Sinclair bubbled excitedly as she told her son's houseguests about her day out. Already, the specific memories of where she had been, and their sequence were a little muddled, but the fact that she had willingly participated in something quite outrageous had not. "Heavens, who would have thought a woman in her forties would suddenly take up dancing in the afternoon!" she said blithely.

Rowland smiled at his mother's diminishing age and the manner in which his friends accepted her frailty without question. The tea dance had for the most part been attended by fresh-faced couples and hopeful, unchaperoned singles. For their five pence entry, there had been tea and scones as well as punch on a linen-draped trestle, a six-piece band and a bunting-decorated hall. A cheeky young man had asked Elisabeth to dance and hinted that Rowland should request the same of his sister, who stood nearby in mortified expectation. Rowland had done so, as declining seemed impolite and possibly unkind. Plump and pale, the young lady was unsure of her steps and painfully shy. She appeared to blush with all of her body, her rounded arms suffusing pink with her cheeks. Rowland spoke gently to her while they danced and by the end of the bracket elicited that her name was Jane, but that was all. Now, he sketched her into his notebook from memory while he listened to his mother explain the nuances of foxtrotting as if the dance were some new fad. He would have liked to paint Jane, to capture her shyness and uncertainty on canvas, but that disposition in itself would probably ensure she would never pose.

Exhilarated and exhausted by an afternoon of dancing, Elisabeth Sinclair elected to retire early.

"Right, Rowly, what's bothering you?" Edna asked when it was just the four of them again. She peered sternly into his face as if she could read the truth in the dark blue of his eyes. "You're brooding, my darling."

Rowland told them of his conversation with Norman Lindsay and Inky Stephensen.

"He said that?" Edna said, unconsciously grabbing Milton's hand.

Rowland shook his head, too furious to speak.

"I've always said Stephensen was an idiot," Milton said calmly.

"But Norman?"

"I did wonder sometimes, you know, but you want to believe a man like him is not... I guess we all wanted to believe it was just his cracked sense of humour."

Rowland groaned. In hindsight he could see that Lindsay's anti-Semitism was not new found. He had dismissed it because he wanted to believe in the artist. And now he was as appalled with himself as he was with Lindsay, ashamed that his principles had been so conveniently forgotten in his esteem of Lindsay.

"Look, Rowly." Clyde was philosophical. "Norman is rude to just about everyone. He doesn't like Catholics, or Freemasons, hates Europeans and regards modernists as a scourge on the earth. Is it any wonder we assumed that he was just being characteristically offensive on this matter, too?"

"It's unnerving," Rowland murmured. "Norman is one of the cleverest people I have ever known. That someone like him could possibly think that way..." He shook his head. "I don't understand it."

"Probably a good thing, comrade," Milton said coldly. "Far too many people understand hating Jews." He stood. "Can I borrow your dog, Rowly?"

"Len? He's in the kitchen with Ed's kittens, I expect."

"I'm going to take him for a walk," he said, declining offers of company.

Rowland let him go, recognising the poet's need to be alone with his anger. For Milton Isaacs this was all the more personal.

Once Milton had gone, Edna embraced Rowland gently. "I'm sorry you've lost Norman, Rowly. I know how much you admired him."

Rowland shook his head. "Not anymore." For some reason, he felt personally betrayed by Lindsay, and by his own naive assumption that men of art and literature were above ridiculous prejudice.

Edna perched on the arm of Rowland's chair. She had modelled for Lindsay often and learned much from him as an artist. It was under his guidance that she'd begun to sculpt. But Rowland Sinclair had been Lindsay's particular protégé. Edna combed Rowland's dark hair back from his face with her fingers, sensing the self-recrimination in his thoughts. "We were mistaken about him, darling, that's all. When we visited Springwood we were distracted by art and poetry and Norman's wild soirées."

"I daresay we won't be invited to any of those again."

"Well, perhaps you should invite Norman to your exhibition," Edna suggested. "You may be able to reach him with your work."

Rowland closed his eyes. "I sincerely doubt it, but I will invite him."

"Are you going to repaint this?" Clyde asked, standing before the painting the bullet had pierced.

"Actually, I thought not," Rowland replied, sitting forward. "The bullet hole is fitting somehow."

Edna nodded. "I agree. There's a quite portentous violence in the painting, and Mr. Röhm did, after all, attempt to have you shot."

"I was contemplating patching the painting from behind with black canvas... a bullet hole through which to glimpse Röhm's soul." He glanced at the work. "I'm tempted to shoot it a few times, myself."

Clyde smiled slightly. "Sounds dangerously modernist."

Edna laughed. "I took the pages of your notebook in to be framed today," she informed Rowland, making sure the conversation did not return to Norman Lindsay.

"Thank you, Ed." He stood. "I ought to telephone Wil while I think of it... make sure he brings his Old Guard chums."

"Are you going to tell him what you're doing?"

"I'll tell him I'm having an exhibition."

"Won't he think it odd? He knows what happened in Germany."

Rowland frowned. That was true. How was he going to explain a sudden desire to exhibit? He didn't want to make his brother complicit, but Wilfred was not a fool.

As it happened, Wilfred was not at home when Rowland telephoned and he spoke instead to his sister-in-law. Kate Sinclair was delighted to learn of his upcoming exhibition.

"Why Rowly, how exciting. I'll write to everyone I know in Sydney, and all the families who'll be in town for the Royal Easter Show to tell them they simply must come!"

And then it occurred to Rowland that the powerful men in Wilfred's acquaintance had wives in Kate's. In this respect, she probably had more influence than Wilfred. His brother's young wife did not even think to ask about the motivation behind the exhibition. "That would be very kind of you, Kate. I'm afraid I haven't exhibited in so long that nobody may come otherwise."

"Of course they'll come, Rowly," Kate said determinedly. "Once I tell them what a talented artist you are…" She trailed off. "Rowly will you be exhibiting paintings of… of models?" she asked hesitantly. She had seen some of Rowland's portraits of Edna when she'd visited *Woodlands* the year before.

Rowland chuckled. He had not been home when Kate Sinclair, and her chum Lucy Bennett, had entered his studio, but Clyde and Edna had given him lurid accounts of the shock and horror and fainting spells which ensued. "There's not one naked person in the exhibition, Kate. I promise."

"Oh, that's wonderful!" The words were breathy with relief. "Leave it with me, Rowly. As soon as Wil returns, we'll get in touch with everyone we know." Her voice rose in pitch as she became excited again. "I know Premier Stevens and Mr. Bruxner will come. Perhaps Wil could persuade Prime Minister Lyons to attend."

"You're a brick, Kate."

It was late when Milton came in behind the greyhound Rowland had loaned him. His long hair was damp with perspiration and his usually pristine attire askew. Lenin went immediately to the water bowl Rowland kept by the hearth and drank noisily before he collapsed.

Milton fell onto the couch and loosened his cravat, pointing at Rowland as he tried to catch the breath to speak.

Rowland and Clyde put down their playing cards and Edna stood to make the poet a drink.

"What happened?" Rowland asked. "Why have you been running?"

"To... get... away." Milton paused to swig the drink Edna handed him, choking when he realised it was whisky.

Rowland and Clyde slapped him on the back while Edna poured him a glass of soda water.

"Who were you running from?" Rowland asked when it looked as though Milton might be able to speak coherently.

The poet shook his head and reclaimed the whisky. "I don't know... I just know Len and I were being followed. We tried to lose him... Must have run at least two miles back."

"Did you lose him?" Clyde asked.

"No idea." Milton removed his cravat completely and used it to mop his brow. "At first I thought I was imagining things... getting jumpy because of the attempt on Rowly, you know. And then it struck me that I had left Rowly's house with Rowly's dog."

Clyde remained sceptical. "You figured someone thought you were stealing Lenin and gave chase?"

"No, you idiot. I thought someone may have mistaken me for Rowly and be looking to finish the job!"

Clyde glanced at Rowland.

"It's possible, I guess," Rowland said uncertainly. "Are you certain you were being followed?"

"Yes, definitely. He came after me when I bolted."

"We should notify Detective Delaney," Edna said. "Perhaps the police have a suspect by now."

"We'll call him in the morning," Rowland decided. "In the meantime, I'll have a word to Armstrong."

Percy Armstrong was in charge of the security force Wilfred had retained. He insisted on questioning Milton in private and did so for more than thirty minutes, before stepping out to inform Rowland that the matter was in hand.

"I suspect Mr. Isaacs overreacted to a simple passer-by who happened to be taking the same route. I would recommend, however, that you in particular do take every precaution until the police identify and locate the assassin."

"Are you sure?" Rowland said. In his experience, Milton was not prone to panic.

"I'm quite certain," Armstrong replied. "These… well, highly strung chaps, you know, sir."

"What makes you think Mr. Isaacs is, as you say, highly strung, Armstrong?"

"It's obvious, sir. Just look at his hair."

"I see. Thank you, Armstrong. Would you have your people check the grounds, just in case?"

"Of course, sir."

Milton was understandably unhappy that his story was being dismissed as hysteria.

"Armstrong's an old soldier," Rowland said apologetically. "He thinks everybody under thirty-five is hysterical by definition."

Milton cursed under his breath. The great divide between those who'd served and those who had not, had often been used against the latter regardless of whether they'd been old enough to enlist.

"Mr. Armstrong doesn't know you," Edna said, clutching Milton's lapel. "If he understood just how fearless you are, he would never have suggested such a thing!"

Clyde laughed.

Milton called Edna an ill-mannered harridan.

"I'll telephone Delaney first chance tomorrow," Rowland said, trying not to smile as Edna mocked Milton, distracting the poet from whatever damage Armstrong might have done to his ego by inflicting some of her own.

They played poker until midnight, at which time Clyde insisted that Rowland retire.

"You'll need to be up at five tomorrow."

Rowland groaned. He'd hoped Clyde would forget this nonsense about a training regimen.

"Five!" Edna exclaimed. "What on earth do you plan to do in the middle of the night?"

Clyde responded with the laboured patience of a parent to an errant child. "Rowly's about to take part in an endurance race."

"But he's driving not running."

Clyde cleared his throat. "My dear Edna, driving in an endurance event is as physically demanding as running a marathon. When you are behind the wheel of a motorcar you cannot let your attention falter for a moment. If Rowly is not prepared he'll get himself killed."

Edna made a face, but she let it be. Over the years, she'd become inured to the peculiar enthusiasms of the men with whom she lived. Clyde Watson Jones had always been excessively diligent… and perhaps there was more to driving a car in circles than she could see.

18

The MODERN Fighter has lost his PHYSICAL Fitness!
| By JIM DONALD. |

IT is the opinion of veteran ringsiders that Australian pugilists of to-day are less tough, hardy, resolute and enduring than those of the olden time.

The Mick and Charlie Dunns, Jim Barrons and Chiddy Ryans, of old Sydney town, are emphatic in their septuagenarian scorning of the pluck, condition and capabilities of the modern mitt-slinger, and his man Friday, the 'la-de-da trainer,' as grim old Charlie Dunn expresses it.

There's a large slab of truth in the old 'uns' contention that there is a certain slackness and softening in the timbre of Thumpia. A stiff old-time preparation would prostrate the majority of present-day pugs, and conditioners. Let us go back to the dawn of things and swings. The great days of the prize ring. In the late eighteenth and early nineteenth centuries, the days of the "Bloods" and the "Whips," "Tom Cribb's Parlour," and the yellow "Belcher," and "Blue Birdseye"; when a "pet-of-the-Fancy" rode to the ringside on the box seat of a noble man's coach and four—and the windy echoes of the tootling horn awakened the sleeping villagers in the dark hour before the dawn. The majority of the pugilists were publicans and ginners—ardent followers of the great god Lush. In all bar the actual training and fighting was a spacious, leisurely attitude towards the job in hand…

ONLY AN IRON FRAME COULD STAND IT!

Spartan treatment brought the warrior lean and hard and phenomenally fit, to the ringside for the fray... The trainer was king, and he was a hard taskmaster. He took his man to a camp on the outskirts of the city, and never left him day or night until he stepped into the ring. He talked, walked, ate, and slept with the boxer in training. Ten miles on the road, walk, jog, trot, and sprint, and a solid hour and a half in the gym was the order of the daily grind...

Until the boxers get back to the old regime of genuine old-fashioned roadwork and stiff, sturdy application in the sparring rooms, and favour the conditioners who insist on this procedure, the boxing game so far as the production of dyed-in-the-wool champions is concerned, will remain on the wane in Australia. Fisticuffs is a hard game, and its rotarys must accustom themselves to hard usage in preparation for the fray—as it is, the proper conditioning of pugilists is almost a forgotten art in Australia.

Referee, 1933

The heavy leather bag creaked on its chain, groaning under the assault as Rowland rained blow after blow. Clyde stood by, one eye on his watch as he counted the minutes, assessed his charge's progress and kept his thoughts from Rosalina Martinelli. That Rowland had boxed at Oxford was clear, as was the fact that he'd not forgotten the technique. Clyde was a little surprised with the ferocity with which his friend was want to punch, regularly cautioning Rowland to pace himself.

They had been at it for nearly an hour, though the sun was barely free of the horizon. Rowland's dark hair was wet with his exertions, but his breath was still relatively even and he was not flagging. Clyde was, if truth be told, astounded that Rowland's lifestyle had not taken more of a toll on his fitness. One would not have thought that painting, dancing and the occasional brawl was enough to counteract the effects of luxury. Clyde pushed Rowland further than was probably fair in the search for some evidence that the indolent lifestyle of the upper classes had some deleterious effect.

"Rightio, take a break." Clyde glanced again at his watch. "Gotta say, mate, you've surprised me. I expected you to be softer than this."

Rowland stopped punching and accepted the canteen of water Clyde held out. He took a mouthful and then poured water over his head and neck. "I haven't gone completely to seed," he said grinning.

"I can't understand why, to be honest."

Rowland was actually in more pain than he would admit and he was pretty sure his muscles would protest for days. As his breathing had become more laboured, he was made uncomfortably aware of the bruising to his ribcage, sustained in the accident that killed Charles Linklater. But he reasoned that if he managed somehow to convince Clyde that he was in peak physical condition, he could go back to sleeping until a more civilised hour. Still, the time at the boxing bag had been therapeutic in many ways.

"Right," Clyde said as he helped Rowland remove his gloves. "We'll just run a few miles and call it a day."

"What?" Rowland groaned. "I thought we were done."

His protests were to no avail. Clyde, it seemed, was determined to ensure that not only the Mercedes, but Rowland Sinclair himself, would be in perfect working order for the race. To that end, he had enlisted the advice contained in an array of training manuals published by various American strongmen. While Rowland thought that a brisk walk would more than suffice and be a great deal more dignified than pounding the streets half-dressed, he conceded in the hope that Clyde's enthusiasm would wane in a couple of days.

They did attract the odd second glance from early-rising servants and the occasional milk cart driver, but for the most part the residents of Woollahra were asleep. The streets were quiet and the rhythm of their own footfalls and breathing became the dominant sound. Initially, Rowland noticed the vehicle only because there were no others about—a black and maroon Singer which appeared at the end of the first street, and then the second and the third. It kept its distance but he spied it every now and then. The fourth street and then the fifth and sixth.

Rowland stopped suddenly and looked back.

"'Struth, Rowly… Don't tell me… you're knackered… already…" Clyde wheezed as he braced his hands on his knees.

Rowland was, but he shook his head anyway. "I believe that car is following us."

"Then why did you stop?"

"To find out what it wants. No point trying to outrun a car."

Clyde straightened, clutching at the stitch in his side. "You're right. No point. But what if it's whoever tried to shoot you?"

"There is that."

Clyde squinted at the car. It was too far away to see who was behind the wheel. "They're not coming any closer."

Rowland frowned. The Singer seemed to be waiting for its quarry's next move. "I wonder what they're playing at."

"Perhaps they're hoping we'll separate so they can shoot you without witnesses," Clyde folded his arms. "What do you want to do?"

Rowland glanced about the street. Daily life was starting; gardeners were out tending front lawns and rose beds, bakers' and butchers' carts had commenced their daily deliveries and curtains were being drawn open. The Singer seemed a great deal less threatening than it had in the long quiet shadows of daybreak.

Rowland started towards it at a run.

"Rowly! What the hell—" Clyde stumbled after him.

For a moment the Singer didn't move and then gears screeched as it tried to reverse and turn. A passing milkman's cart blocked its path. It reversed once more, scraping the gutter.

Rowland jumped onto the running board before the car could pull away and reached in through the window to grab the driver by the collar. Startled, the man swore and attempted to shake him off. Clyde caught up, flung open the passenger door and climbed into the car. He reached across and reefed on the handbrake.

"Right! Who the devil are you, sunshine?" Clyde demanded.

Rowland pulled the man out of the car. "Why are you following us, sir?" he demanded as Clyde cut the Singer's engine.

"My name's Beejling, Robert Beejling." He cursed some more. "I'm with your security detail."

"My what?"

"We've been retained to follow you when you leave the premises."

"Why?"

"To ensure your safety."

"Why wasn't I informed?"

Beejling shrugged. "We were instructed to not approach or make you aware of our presence unless it was necessary."

"We?" Rowland looked around quickly. "How many of you are there?"

"We work in shifts."

"Who retained you?"

Beejling's face became rigid, immovable. He stood at attention and would say nothing more.

"Right," Rowland said angrily. "Get into the car—the back seat." Once Beejling had complied he climbed in beside him. Clyde slipped in behind the steering wheel. "We might just see what Percy Armstrong has to say."

Percy Armstrong was, in fact, as unforthcoming as Robert Beejling.

"I'll have to get instructions, sir."

"I'm giving you instructions, Mr. Armstrong."

"I'm afraid that in this respect I answer to your brother, Mr. Wilfred Sinclair."

"For crying out loud!" Rowland stalked furiously into the house and booked a call through to *Oaklea* in Yass. He caught his brother at home. The conversation was terse and heated.

"If I had told you that I'd hired bodyguards you would not have cooperated, Rowly."

"So you just went ahead and had me followed secretly? Bloody hell, Wil! What's wrong with you?"

"I know you too well, Rowly! You're reckless and you have more enemies than any man in New South Wales. I also have our mother's safety to consider. What in the name of God were thinking taking her to a nightclub? Have you lost all sense of propriety?"

"It was a tea dance, not a nightclub. She wanted to go dancing."

"For Pete's sake, Rowly, don't be ridiculous. Mother is nearly seventy!"

"She seems to have forgotten that."

"Well, remind her!"

"Why on earth would I do that? She's having a lovely time! It might do you good to forget you're so old from time to time."

"How very droll." Wilfred's tone conveyed the roll of his eyes.

"Your bodyguards, Wil, call them off."

"Certainly, as soon as the police arrest and incarcerate the wretch who tried to shoot you."

"Dammit, Wil—"

"I have neither the time nor the inclination to argue with you, Rowly. You won't change my mind." Ignoring Rowland's continued protest, Wilfred said, "Kate tells me you're staging an exhibition."

"Er... yes." Rowland was caught by the sudden change in subject.

Wilfred sighed. "Well, I suppose if you must paint, this sort of thing is unavoidable. Kate's rather taken it as a personal mission to ensure your show is well patronised by the right sort of people from the right circles."

"That's very kind."

"Yes, she is. She's under the impression that this exhibition will not contain any lewdness or nudity."

"Not in the paintings."

"What do you mean by that?" Wilfred's voice became sharp and suspicious.

Rowland laughed. "A jest, Wil. No one will be naked."

"Very well. I'll make some enquiries. Perhaps the prime minister will be available to open it."

When Rowland telephoned, Detective Delaney seemed awkward and specifically requested he not call into the station. "Mackay finds my consorting with potential suspects somewhat unseemly, Rowly."

"I'm a suspect? For what?" Rowland demanded, surprised.

"Milton was the last man to see White alive. I'm afraid that places you all in it, old boy."

"You're not in earnest?"

"No, not really. I'd be surprised if Mackay actually believes you lot have been murdering reporters either, but he doesn't like how it looks. He'd have me flogged in the street and permanently assigned to some backwater station if he knew I'd shown you the crime scene photographs."

"I see. Where would you suggest we meet then?"

Delaney gave him the address of Pretty Mabel's Tea Emporium in Darlinghurst and they agreed upon a time. Rowland grabbed Rosaleen Norton's folio on the way out the door. He would return it to the *Smith's Weekly* offices after meeting with Delaney. With any luck he would catch Frank Marien on this occasion.

Rowland found the optimistically named Tea Emporium housed in dilapidated premises. The interior was dim and quite opaque with cigarette smoke, the counter top invisible beneath glass domes containing sticky buns and cakes. A narrow stairwell led to the upper floor and, presumably, a residence.

Spying Detective Delaney at a table in the back, Rowland joined him. Delaney summoned the harried proprietor, a heavy, ruddy-cheeked gentleman with naval tattoos on his thick arms, who responded good-naturedly when the detective addressed him as "Pretty Mabel". Delaney ordered an entire sponge cake and a pot of tea.

"Is anyone joining us?" Rowland asked as a six-inch sponge sandwiched with strawberry jam and mock cream was placed before them alongside a silver teapot.

"You wait till you taste this Rowly—you'll declare I'm a saint for splitting it with you!" Delaney replied, his eyes gleaming as he contemplated the cake. "Shall I be mother?"

"Why not?"

Delaney splashed tea into thick china cups, before cutting the sponge in two and pulling the larger portion onto his plate. He grinned like a naughty child, forked a massive chunk into his mouth and closed his eyes in appreciation. For some moments he was unable to speak and patently uninterested in doing so.

Rowland partook nodding his own approval. The sponge cake was superb. "So what did you need to tell me that you couldn't say at the station?" Rowland asked between mouthfuls.

"Detective Hartley is pushing for the immediate arrest of Elias Isaacs for White's murder," Delaney said, washing down a large mouthful of cake with tea. "It's only your fancy lawyers that have made the bastard hesitate, but they won't hold him back forever. Hartley's like a rabid dog with a bone." The detective sighed. "It may be time for Milton to come forward with whatever he's not telling us."

"It's not anything that will help him, Colin."

"He didn't—"

"No, he didn't." Rowland spoke with absolute certainty.

Delaney removed his hat to scratch his head. "Hartley's narrowed his investigation to Milton. The evidence is circumstantial but unless someone else comes up with an alternative…"

Rowland nodded, grateful for the detective's efforts. It would be up to them now.

"Of course, I'm not investigating the White murder anymore," Delaney murmured. "And I'm afraid I haven't had any luck locating the chap who fired that shot through your window. Sadly a couple of ocean liners were due at the harbour so, by the time the shot was fired, the reporters camped at your gate had left in search of something more newsworthy." Delaney returned to his notebook to check the facts. "None of them recalls seeing a chap enter the property."

Rowland groaned. He'd hoped that at least one thing would resolve easily.

"Considering the light in which the newspapers are portraying you, Rowly, I wouldn't be surprised if it was some outraged veteran acting on impulse and a few too many beers."

"Capital." Inwardly, Rowland cursed *Smith's Weekly*.

Delaney regarded him sympathetically. "Hopefully this will all blow over quickly. In the meantime, you should be careful."

Rowland indicated the gentleman drinking coffee at a table by the front window. Beejling nodded. "Don't worry, Colin, Wil's ensuring that I'm careful whether I like it or not."

The detective chuckled. "One way of keeping an eye on you, I suppose."

Rowland sighed. He did indeed suspect that Wilfred was using the shooting as an excuse to check on the conduct of his brother. "I'm afraid Wil is still unsure that *Woodlands* is the most respectable place for our mother."

"How is that arrangement working out?" Delaney asked. The detective was aware of Elisabeth Sinclair's frailty of mind and more particularly the crime her sons suspected she'd committed years before. As a friend, Colin Delaney was sympathetic; as a policeman, he monitored the situation lest that violence recur.

Rowland knew what the detective was asking and why he asked it. For that he could not blame Delaney. It was a difficult situation, but he was convinced his mother was not dangerous—if she had ever been. Certainly, Elisabeth Sinclair had not done anything that Rowland could confidently say he would not have done himself given the chance. "Very well, I believe. Mother seems settled and happy. She's getting out quite a bit and has become rather fond of Milt—seems to think he's some nephew of the Governor-General."

Delaney laughed.

"Mother relocated to Yass—to *Oaklea*—when Aubrey was killed and when my father became... hard," Rowland said, even now struggling to verbalise his father's violence. "Perhaps Sydney only has happy memories for her. In any case, she seems better than I've seen her since the war."

Delaney nodded, satisfied for now. "I'm bloody glad to hear it, Rowly. I just want you to be careful—you've taken on one hell of a responsibility."

"With Wil's private army following me around, what could go wrong?"

Delaney glanced at his watch and wiped his mouth. "I'm going to see Frank Marien now. I don't suppose you'd like to come along?"

"I thought you weren't on the investigation into White's murder anymore—"

"I'm not." Delaney winked. "I'm just looking into the theft of his notebook. Do you want to come?"

"Yes, I do actually. I have to return Miss Norton's folio to her anyway."

"Oh, we're not going to the office," Delaney said, dusting the crumbs from his tie as Rowland took care of the account. "Marien's in the hospital here."

"The hospital? Why?"

Delaney shrugged. "He's poorly. Something quite grave, apparently. He's been running *Smith's Weekly* from his hospital bed."

19

SOME DAY IT'LL DO THE RIGHT THING!

DO you remember the time when "Smith's Weekly" had a front page to say that Alan Kippax was through as a batsman, and ought to be dropped from the State side? And the same day Kippax made a double century, and has been making centuries ever since!

Last Wednesday "Smith's Weekly" published a wild screed attacking the "Sun" for its heat wave stories. Wednesday was the hottest day for two years; Wednesday night the hottest for 19 years, and Thursday hotter and hotter. It's a shame the way "Smith's" points out the errors of others, and always misses the bull's eye itself. Someday "Smith's Weekly" will do something right, and someone will get the sack. "Smith's" bosses will think it's wrong!

Truth, 1934

Frank Marien's hospital room was crowded with journalists and artists. So much so that if it were not for the hospital bed at its centre and the occasional nursing nun, one might have been excused for thinking it a gentlemen's club of some sort. The antiseptic smell of the corridor was replaced with that of cigarettes and pipe smoke as one entered the room. Deep-voiced conversations were broken intermittently with resounding laughter.

Rowland recognised Kenneth Slessor standing by the doors that opened out on to a small private balcony and provided the room with a view of the St Vincent's lawns and gardens.

Marien was propped up with pillows, smoking a pipe and issuing instructions about how to strip down a linotype printer while he inspected the artworks spread out on his bed coverings. The newspaperman was generously built with shoulders that spoke of a past athleticism. Indeed, he appeared so strong and vital that his status as a patient was unsettling.

Delaney introduced himself and Rowland Sinclair.

"Come in, come in!" Marien instructed, choosing three drawings for the next edition. "What can I do for you, Detective Delaney?"

"I was hoping you might be able to answer a few questions, Mr. Marien?"

"Is this about Crispin White?"

Delaney nodded.

"Then yes, of course. You won't mind if my reporters observe, will you? Just say when you want the conversation to be off the record."

Delaney looked around at the men in the room who watched with hungry interest. He hesitated and then thought better of it. "Don't mind at all, Mr. Marien."

"What's Sinclair doing here? He's not joined the police force, has he?"

"He's observing," Delaney said, smiling faintly.

Marien grinned. "Touché, Detective. We'll all stay then. What can I do to help?"

Delaney asked the routine questions about Crispin White. Marien spoke fondly of the reporter and soon the other men in the room offered stories about their colleague, warm accounts of past larks and scoops. The exchange began to resemble a dry wake as they painted a picture of a congenial, experienced newspaperman, who had a nose for a story and an eye for the ladies.

"And was Mr. White involved with any person in particular?" Delaney asked.

"You mean a woman? God no. Crispy was too bloody ugly. He wouldn't know what to do if a woman actually said yes!" Marien declared to the general approbation of the room.

"Did any of you notice the diamond tiepin he was wearing the day he died?" Rowland asked suddenly.

"Oh yes." It was Kenneth Slessor who volunteered the information. "Gaudy piece... paste, I expect. Unless Frank paid him much better than he does me."

A roar of jest and jibe, and a protest from Marien that Slessor was paid more than he was worth.

"Had you seen him wear it before that day?"

"Once or twice, possibly..."

"Did you speak to him about it?" Delaney asked.

"About his tiepin? Whatever for?"

"Well, it was an unusual item—weren't you curious where he got it?"

Slessor shook his head. "I assumed someone had given it to him. I quite assiduously avoided mention of the ghastly thing in case he asked me what I thought of it."

"When are you going to return White's notebook?" Marien demanded of Delaney. "It's the property of the paper now, you know."

"Once the investigation is finished," Delaney said. "Can you tell me a little bit more about this chap who brought it back to you—the gentleman you paid a guinea for his trouble?"

"Oh, I didn't form the impression he was a gentleman, Detective. Looked and positively smelled like he might have been living rough. Skinny bloke with one of those weaselly faces, only about half his allotment of teeth. Didn't say much... wished me well and asked me if I knew how I was going to spend eternity." Marien's eyes became distant. "He couldn't have known, of course..."

For a few breaths the room was silent, uneasy. Then the stocky man leaning against the iron foot of Marien's bed growled, "Just make sure the devil gives you an exclusive."

A blast of laughter as unsympathetic humour was restored.

"Did the gentleman tell you his name, Mr. Marien?" Delaney asked when the mirth lapsed into conversation again.

"No. He was very particular about that. Wanted to remain anonymous."

"Could I ask you about Miss Rosaleen Norton?" Rowland ventured tentatively.

"Oh God, what's Roie done now?"

"Nothing. But I was curious about her stories. She believes the first—the one about the waxworks—was a premonition of Mr. White's death."

Marien's lower lip protruded, his mouth curved downwards as he considered it. "There's a coincidence there, I suppose, but White had his throat cut. He didn't die of fright." He shrugged and shook his head. "Roie is talented, but like many great writers, she's eccentric."

"Would you say Miss Norton was particularly ambitious?" Delaney asked, following Rowland's lead.

"As an artist, more than a writer, but yes, she's a very driven young lady."

"And how did she get on with Crispin White?"

Marien's brow furrowed into the bridge of his nose. "I'm not aware of any difficulty."

"Roie is passionate and admittedly a little odd, Detective Delaney." Slessor spoke up with a chorus of assent behind him. "But there's a lot of that in this game. She's harmless really."

Delaney jotted a few lines in his notebook but made no comment about the perceived harmlessness of Rosaleen Norton. Rowland recalled the unnerving relish with which Rosaleen had told him of how White's throat had been cut. Still, that might well have been adolescent immaturity as opposed to a true delight in violence. He found it hard to believe that a seventeen-year-old girl could be so cold-blooded.

"What was it that Mr. White was investigating at the waxworks, Mr. Marien?" Rowland asked on the off chance that the reporter had been at Magdalene's on business.

"Blowed if I know!" Marien was adamant. "He was covering the car race—the Maroubra Invitational—as you know. I expected him to cover all major sporting events, but otherwise he was free to pursue whatever newsworthy stories took his fancy. An experienced journo like Crispy had his own sources, spotters and leads." He looked round at his journalists. "Any of you fellows know what he was up to?"

A general murmur claiming ignorance but Rowland noticed one man, short and round with a hefty distinctive head. He said nothing, but a line appeared in his expansive forehead that had not been there before.

"Tell me, Detective," Marien said, blowing billows of sweet smoke from his pipe. "When are you going to give White back so we can give the poor chap an appropriate send-off?"

"The coroner will release the body as soon as his findings are finalised, Mr. Marien. Soon, I expect."

"Good, good. We must do the right thing by Crispy."

"Great Scott!" Slessor jumped as a pebble skipped through the open French doors.

"That'll be Brian," Marien said excitedly. "Mo, quickly, keep an eye out for Mother Superior will you? George, send down the rope."

The rotund gentleman with the large head moved to stand watch in the corridor. Rowland followed him out.

"Rowland Sinclair, Mr...?" Rowland said, offering the cockatoo his hand.

"Moses, Reg Moses. Most people call me Mo." Moses' handshake was firm. "I'm the *Weekly's* literary editor."

Unsure how much time he had, Rowland came straight to the point. "I couldn't help but notice that you were perhaps not as ignorant of Mr. White's activities as your colleagues."

"You noticed that, did you?"

"I believe so."

"Well bully for you, Sinclair!"

Rowland persevered. "Do you know what White was working on?"

Moses regarded him disdainfully, and then he sighed. "I don't know anything really. Crispin was looking into the occult. At first I thought he was just trying to impress Frank."

"Mr. Marien is interested in the occult?"

"No, no. He's Catholic. But he did like Roie's stories, was convinced she'd be the next Edgar Allan Poe. I suspected Crispin was put out and I assumed he was trying to write his own story to show Roie up."

"But you don't think that now?" Rowland asked, reading Moses' face.

"No. I don't. Crispin was probably too long in the tooth to be rattled by Frank's infatuation with Miss Norton's scary fairy tales. It must have been something else... a piece he was working on."

Cheering and applause from inside the hospital room.

"I think we can go back in now," Moses said opening the door. Clearly the conversation was over.

Within the room, a large tin pail had been pulled up via the balcony. Marien beamed, regarding the bucket as if it were filled with gold.

Rowland leaned over to Delaney. "What's in the—"

"Baked rabbit. Forbidden by his doctors and some killjoy called Mother Patrick, and all the more delicious for that reason."

Rowland laughed quietly. "Of course."

As the conversation fell again to linotype and advertising space, they took their leave of Marien and his staff and departed. On the steps of St. Vincent's, Rowland told Delaney of his conversation with Reg Moses.

The detective was impressed. "You sure you don't want to join the force, Rowly?" He winked. "Earn an honest living. There's a pension, you know, and you'd make the height requirements easily."

"A pension you say?" Rowland accepted the compliment hidden in the joke. Sinclairs did not get jobs, with or without pensions. "I'll give it some thought." He decided to push his luck a little. "I don't suppose I could look through White's notebook?"

Delaney pushed his hat back and scratched the top of his head. "I'll see what I can do." He exhaled heavily. "Is your interest in White just about clearing Mr. Isaacs, Rowly?"

Rowland shrugged. "White had dinner with me just before he died. Milt drove him back to his lodgings because I'd had too much to drink. A little part of me wonders if we dropped him off into the hands of his murderer."

"Even if you did, Rowly, you weren't to know."

"Yes, I realise that, but I can't help feeling… responsible is not the right word." He shifted, struggling for an explanation that did not sound silly. "I feel like I ought to care what happened to a man who left my table just two hours before being brutally slain."

"Care?" Delaney shook his head. "I take it back. You'd be a bloody dreadful policeman. A good priest maybe."

Only the female staff of *Smith's Weekly* were in the Phillip Street offices as it seemed all the men had decamped to St Vincent's, and when Rowland called in, two of those three had stepped out.

"Rowly Sinclair!" the tall willowy blonde who opened the door to the "Keep Out" room greeted him warmly. "They told me you stopped by the other day. I'm so sorry I missed you."

"Miss Horseman, hello." Rowland responded to Mollie Horseman with pleasure. He had known her years ago as one of Norman Lindsay's models. "I wasn't aware that you worked here."

"Clearly you're not a reader of *Smith's Weekly* or you'd have seen my work!" she said sternly.

"I have been remiss," he apologised. "I shall henceforth read it from cover to cover."

"Oh, you needn't bother with the articles. Come and see what I'm working on."

Mollie took him to her drafting table upon which lay a black and white drawing in progress, a rollicking depiction of a party which she told him would be captioned: "What was the party at Darlinghurst like last night?… They sang God Save the Furniture."

For a while Rowland forgot the reason for which he had come, as he discussed line and ink, and generally became reacquainted with Mollie Horseman. The now established black and white artist had, like most of her colleagues, trained at the East Sydney Technical College. Married to a William Power, she still illustrated under her maiden name. Rowland found her the effervescent young woman he remembered.

"I have actually come to return Miss Norton's folio," he admitted after a time.

"She's out following a story, I expect, though between you and me, Rowly, I'm not sure she's cut out to be a newshound."

"Why do you say that?" Rowland asked.

"She's a little odd, and the poor girl wants to be an artist not a writer. Unfortunately, Frank is convinced she's a literary genius."

"I have read her horror stories." Rowland was non-committal.

"She's refusing to write any more until Frank publishes her drawings. I'm not sure why he lets her get away with ultimatums like that, but then, he's not been well." Mollie frowned. "Roie has a way of getting her own way."

"I've noticed."

Mollie laughed. "You poor dear! What did she bully you into?"

"Nothing particularly unthinkable." Rowland took the stool the artist offered him. "She wanted me to show her drawings to Norman."

Mollie Horseman rolled her eyes. "Oh, that. I didn't mention I knew Norman, so I escaped. Roie has rather a fearsome temper, you really can't say 'no' to her without dire consequences." She handed Rowland an ink pen. "Why don't you help me finish this?"

"I beg your pardon?"

"Come on, it'll be a lark. Joan Morrison and I often draw together. It's jolly good fun to be honest."

"I'm not—"

"If the result is terrible, I can start again. If it's not, maybe Frank will give you a job."

Rowland removed his jacket and rolled up his sleeves, wondering fleetingly if there was some conspiracy afoot to find him gainful employment.

"I think we need a couple of louche characters here." Mollie Horseman pulled up a stool beside him.

They worked in companionable silence for a time. Rowland tried to match the style of Mollie's linework, carefully drafting straight onto the heavy cartridge paper in ink. He drew a couple dancing a wild Charleston with beads and limbs flying askew. The woman was elderly and conservatively dressed despite her actions. He drew a second gentleman swinging from a chandelier, a cliché perhaps but not something he hadn't seen. Mollie approved, adding tiny stylistic tweaks to integrate the figures with the rest of the drawing.

"Good heavens, you've ink all over your shirt!" she exclaimed. "I really ought to have given you a smock."

Rowland looked down and buttoned his waistcoat over the ink stain. "There, fixed."

Mollie shook her head. "I'm not sure Mrs. Sinclair is going to think so."

"Mrs...? Oh, I'm not married."

"A nicely turned out gentleman like you? Why ever not?"

"Ink stains, I expect. I say, Mollie, did you know Crispin White well?"

"Depends what you consider well, I suppose. He was sweet, ruthless in pursuit of a story—a real old-fashioned honest-to-goodness newshound. He liked the odd drink and the odd flutter. A perfectly ordinary, decent bloke really."

"Do you know what story he was pursuing that might have led him to the Magdalene's House of the Macabre?"

"Roie loaned him some books about the occult. She was most put out because they were library books and Crispy had not returned them when he died. If she gets fined, not even death will excuse Crispy!"

Rowland glanced at his watch. "I really ought to let you get back to work. I don't suppose I could impose upon you to see that Miss Norton gets her folio?"

"Of course." Mollie swung her long legs around and stood to walk Rowland out. "It's been a real treat seeing you again, Rowly. You let me know if you want to think seriously about becoming a black and white artist. It's not a bad way to earn a crust."

Rowland handed her his card as he kissed her on the cheek. "It's been grand, Mollie. Would you let me know if you discover anything about what Crispin White was doing at the Magdalene's?"

"If I discover anything you'll be able to read about it in the paper," Mollie replied. She smiled. "But I'll telephone you, too."

20

CENTRE PARTY

ERIC CAMPBELL DEFINES
UNIFICATION PROPOSALS
REPRESENTATION ON FASCIST LINES

SYDNEY, Tuesday

The policy and aims of the Centre Party, a newly-formed political party, were explained by Colonel Eric Campbell at a largely attended meeting tonight.

Col. Campbell told his audience that the middle section of the community was at the moment without adequate representation in the affairs of the country and the aim of the new party was to endeavour to remedy that defect. He added that they had no confidence in professional politicians and party politics.

"Australia is grossly over-governed and there are too many laws," declared Col. Campbell, "and we are out to simplify matters.

"The present organisation is of only a preliminary nature and none of us is after jobs, and we will leave them to better men if they will come along."

Referring to constitutional reforms, Mr. Campbell said the first plank on the platform of the Centre Party is the abolition of State Parliaments and the redistribution of Australia into provincial areas, administered by provincial councils with powers of taxation strictly limited. There would also be a Federal Government which would direct the major issues which faced the nation. All governing bodies would be elected by a system of vocational representation, giving the employer and the employee equal strength in the Legislatures.

Col. Campbell suggested that one method of unifying the continent would be to petition the King to appoint one of the Royal Princes as a permanent Governor-General of Australia.

"The dole and relief work are only making proud citizens descend to the coolie levels," added the speaker.

He suggested that the only method whereby the unemployment problems would be solved would be by the settlement of the unemployed on abundant surplus land. He had it on the best authority that given the opportunity, a million families could be transferred from Great Britain over a period of years for settlement on land and each family would have a capital of £1,000...

...Replying to a question, Col. Campbell said that he did not think that the system of Government obtaining in England was better than it was in Italy. He added that he was satisfied that the system of Italian representation would be in force in Great Britain within five years.

The Canberra Times, 1934

"Rowly, thank goodness you're here!" Edna met him at the portico before he reached the door of *Woodlands House*. "We have to go!"

"Where?"

"Central Police Station. Milt and Clyde have been arrested."

"Arrested?" Rowland turned on his heel. "Whatever for?"

"Disturbing the peace, apparently."

"Were they at a rally?" Rowland asked. Gatherings of the Communist Party were routinely invaded by the New Guard or like-minded militant groups. When this happened, it was not uncommon for skirmishes to get out of hand. Of course, Milton—ever the crusader—had been arrested on a number of occasions, but sensible Clyde usually managed to avoid police detention. The fact that both his friends had been arrested struck Rowland as unusual.

"No," Edna said. "As far as I know, Clyde was calling in at the soup kitchen in George Street to see that friend of his, and Milt was just tagging along as Milt does."

Rowland frowned. This was odd.

They took the Rolls Royce again. Rowland apologised to the chauffeur whose workload had risen sharply with Rowland's newfound reluctance to use the Mercedes, not to mention the resumption of social order brought about by the residence of Elisabeth Sinclair. "I'm afraid Clyde's adjusting the tappets again. I'm sure things will go back to normal after the race."

"Not at all, Mr. Sinclair," Johnston said as they pulled out of the driveway. "In your late father's day the bell rang every quarter hour." He sniffed. "You'll find I'm quite able to do my job."

"Of course, Johnston," Rowland said hastily, realising the chauffeur had read an unintended slight in his words.

"Do you prefer driving motorcars to carriages, Mr. Johnston?" Edna asked, knowing the chauffeur had started work at *Woodlands* in the stables.

"Well, I don't know, Miss. They both have 'vantages and problems. Some folks believe there's less work in motorcars, but they take a darn sight more polishing than any horse."

Rowland listened, as his normally tight-lipped chauffeur chatted to Edna about the pros and cons of carriages and automobiles. Though he'd known Johnston all his life, the chauffeur rarely spoke so freely to him. Indeed, Johnston seemed always to have regarded him with a vague air of profound disappointment.

"Shall I wait, sir?" Johnston asked as he pulled up outside the station.

"No, thank you. We'll find our own way home once we get this nonsense sorted." He stepped out of the Rolls Royce, pausing at the chauffeur's window as he walked around the vehicle. "Don't worry, Johnston, I'll attend Miss Higgins' door."

Johnston's lips pressed into a disapproving line, resigned to the lax conduct of his employer. The younger Mr. Sinclair had never observed protocol. "Very good, sir."

Rowland offered Edna his hand as she alighted. "Come on, we'd best see what trouble Milt's got them both into."

Although it had been less than three months since Rowland had been taken to Central Police Station in handcuffs and under arrest for murder, he showed no sign of hesitation or embarrassment. He approached the desk sergeant as a Sinclair. Polite and unfailingly courteous, his manner was nevertheless that of a man who understood the power behind his family name.

The drowsy desk sergeant was decidedly flustered, but within minutes a more senior officer was called. From him, Rowland ascertained that Clyde and Milton had been arrested at a public event at the Town Hall where Mr. Eric Campbell was launching his new book.

Rowland's face was unreadable, his tone calm and reasonable. Surely this kerfuffle could be sorted out between gentlemen? Perhaps Mr. Isaacs and Mr. Watson Jones had been a little strident in their literary criticism—Mr. Isaacs was a poet, after all. Rowland would be happy to personally pay any fine to settle what was, on balance, a misdemeanour at most.

The chief inspector had only recently been assigned to Central Police Station and so he did not recognise Rowland Sinclair as a past prisoner. He assessed on face value the man who spoke for the two he had in the holding cells. Sinclair was clearly a man of means and well bred. He could tell that not only by the superior cut and fabric of his suit, but by the fact that his waistcoat was buttoned, not left to hang loose as was the style with the supposedly fashionable young larrikins of the day. No, this was a man who valued order and had a respect for authority. Perhaps it hadn't been necessary to arrest his friends… Eric Campbell did have a tendency to overreact and demand the incarceration of all and sundry who criticised him. It was quite possible that whatever penny dreadful Campbell had written, was just that. The state of New South Wales was not in the business of locking up people for hurting Campbell's feelings.

In the end, the fine was paid and Elias Isaacs and Clyde Watson Jones were released without further action.

Edna waited until they were out of the station before she slapped Milton on the shoulder. "What did you do?"

"Me?" Milton said indignantly. And then, "All right, it was me. Clyde was just trying to stop Campbell's goons from killing me."

"What were you trying to do?" Edna asked again.

Milton groaned. He looked quite despondent. "I don't know, Ed. We noticed there was something going on at the Town Hall so we went in to have a look and found ourselves at some kind of Boo Guard event. Bloody Campbell was on the stage talking about his time in Germany and spruiking his book, *The New Road*... some kind of manifesto for Australia under Fascism. When he started talking about how the Jews he met in Germany were fat and rich, I lost my rag... started shouting... Not even sure what I said."

"He called Campbell a bloated, Nazi-loving, sycophantic Fascist fool," Clyde said by way of clarification. "Then he grabbed one of Campbell's books from the display and threw it at him."

"Only just missed him," Milton added. "Would have got him with the second book if the police hadn't arrested us."

Clyde sighed. "Was the fine huge, Rowly?"

"No," Rowland said quickly, if not entirely truthfully. "I don't suppose the chief inspector holds a particularly high opinion of Campbell." He swallowed a curse. "I'd hoped Eric Campbell was a spent force. Were there many people at the Town Hall?"

Milton nodded. "All the seats were taken. There were stands and sign-up sheets for his new Centre Party and every man and his dog there seemed to have a copy of the colonel's bloody book under his arm."

Rowland cursed. He had no doubt that Campbell had written *The New Road* in imitation of Adolf Hitler's path to political domination. The leader of the New Guard obviously hoped it would become for Australian Fascists what *Mein Kämpf* was for the German counterparts. A good part of Rowland wanted to laugh at the idea, to ridicule the notion that something so absurd could find adherents in Australia, among Australians, but he was no longer as sure of his fellow man as he once had been. Germany had been the centre of culture and art and Berlin its vibrant, progressive heart. But no more. The Nazis had put an end to that.

Milton suggested a drink. Rowland agreed, realising suddenly that he was famished. They elected to eat in town, rather than incurring Mary Brown's reproval by requesting luncheon so late in the day. And so they made their way to Romano's on York Street. The restaurant had been Sydney's premier dining venue since its opening, and so it was crowded even at three in the afternoon. They enjoyed a drink in the lounge as they waited for a table to become available in the extravagant dining room. Milton and Clyde recounted in more detail the events that led to their arrest.

"Rowly, Charlotte Linklater was there… sitting on the stage beside Campbell."

"That shouldn't be surprising, I suppose," Rowland said after a moment's pause. "The Linklaters are friends of Oswald Mosley. They're quite possibly members of the British Union of Fascists, which would, of course, endear them to our Mr. Campbell."

"Perhaps, but it does give you more reason to be careful of Miss Linklater on the track," Clyde warned.

The tail-coated maître d' came out to inform them that their table was ready and seated them on the edge of the dance floor. It seemed that dancing in the afternoon was catching on, as a dozen or more couples moved to the subdued strains of a string quartet.

A gentleman in white tie and tails and a fez stopped by their table. A pencil-thin moustache defined a smiling lip beneath an aquiline nose. He greeted them each by name, kissing Edna's hand and complimenting her so lavishly that Milton threatened to leave if he did not desist.

"Milt's just jealous, Mr. Romano," Edna said. "You must tell him he's pretty too, or he'll sulk."

Azzalin Romano laughed. "It has been too long since you beautiful people were last here. We have been bereft."

Rowland glanced around the crowded dining room. "I don't think you've been too bereft, Mr. Romano." Despite the economic stringency of the times, the restaurant was doing well, offering a low-cost menu that was within the reach of sparser purses, in spite of its reputation as the bon ton. Of course cost was not an issue for Rowland Sinclair, it was the easy atmosphere of Romano's he liked, the reckless ostentatious furnishings that contrasted with the quiet refined elegance of fine dining to which he was accustomed.

They all ordered the specialty of the house—steak Diane prepared at the table by the maître d'—and a couple of bottles of Romano's sparkling wine. Over the meal they discussed Campbell's new push.

"Hopefully your exhibition will head Campbell's account of the glories of Germany off at the pass," Clyde said thoughtfully. "Perhaps we should just let him wax lyrical about his Nazi mates and the wonders of the fatherland for a couple of months. Surely he'll look like a fool or worse when your exhibition opens."

"Possibly," Rowland said pensively. "It might be a bit ambitious to expect my exhibition will have wide coverage. Campbell could well just ignore it."

"What if you invite him to the opening?" Clyde suggested.

202 — **SULARI GENTILL**

"He's hardly likely to accept an invitation from me."

Clyde conceded regretfully. "You're right, of course. Still, it would have been interesting to see him explain what we saw, and what happened to you."

"I'm not sure I could explain it," Rowland murmured. Their experiences in Munich had taken a strangely vibrant, loud place in his memory. It seemed too real and unreal at the same time... like a nightmare from which he'd just woken, remembered in snatches that still moistened his brow with cold sweat.

"There'll be a way to get him there," Edna said quietly.

"Rowland Sinclair! Fancy seeing you here."

Rowland winced visibly before he turned to acknowledge Reginald Stuart Jones. The good doctor was not alone. Redmond Barry and Wombat Newgate stood with him. "Well, well," Stuart Jones said rubbing his hands together. "What a happy accident. You don't mind if we join you, do you?"

"I'm afraid we've just finished," Rowland replied quite civilly.

The three men pulled up chairs anyway. "We'll just stop for a drink then." Stuart Jones caught Romano's attention. "Azzalin, my good man. A couple of bottles of your finest for my friends if you don't mind."

Romano bowed and signalled for a drinks waiter to see to the request.

"What do you want, Reg?" Milton asked bluntly. He and Edna had known the flamboyant doctor since the days when he was plain Reginald Jones, before he married an heiress and set up his lucrative illegal practice.

Redmond Barry spoke up. "We're racing enthusiasts, real keen... been wanting to show Mr. Sinclair our admiration for his skills. Wombat here wanted an autograph."

Newgate nodded. "Yeah, I wanted you to sign something for me, Sinclair."

Stuart Jones gazed intently at Edna. He placed his hand on his heart as he winked at the sculptress. Rowland remembered vaguely that she had stepped out with the doctor once or twice in the twenties.

"How are you, Eddie?" Jones asked.

"Very well, Dr. Jones."

"By George, there's no need to be so formal, Eddie. I might have married you, darling!"

Rowland bristled immediately.

Edna laughed. "I don't think that's likely, Dr. Jones."

"How are you coping, Sinclair?" Barry asked. "After that appalling accident. Enough to give me the creeping horrors every time I get behind the wheel."

"You mustn't blame yourself, you know," Stuart Jones added. "We all understand that motor racing is a ruthless sport. And the Maroubra Speedway has a hex on it—I reckon the Devil's in more than the name of the cup. You weren't to know that Linklater would lose control when you forced him to go round."

Wombat Newgate nodded emphatically. "You weren't to know."

"Of course, no one would blame you either if you hung back a bit," Barry added. "Before anybody else was killed."

"What the hell do you mean by that?" Clyde demanded.

Milton turned on Stuart Jones. "Just what are you bloody well up to, Reg?"

"Gentlemen, language," Stuart Jones tutted. "We are in the company of a lady after all. One must be considerate of more sensitive dispositions."

Edna had had enough. She grabbed Rowland's hand. "I'm afraid Rowland has promised to dance with me gentlemen, so I'll say goodbye now, since—" her voice was hard and uncharacteristically cold, "—I'm sure you'll have gone by the time we return."

The men rose from their chairs as she stood.

"Good afternoon, gentlemen," Rowland said evenly with a warning glance at Milton who looked ready to take a swing.

"Don't be so hasty, Sinclair," Barry said grabbing Rowland's arm.

"You might want take to your hand off him, Barry," Clyde growled.

Azzalin Romano spotted the impasse from across the room and began to make his way over.

Barry removed his hand slowly. "You'd be well advised to talk to us, Sinclair."

Stuart Jones reached for the sculptress. "You stay and talk, I'll dance with Eddie."

Rowland moved so that he was standing between the doctor and Edna, his fists clenched and his ire undisguised. Reginald Stuart Jones backed off hastily but Wombat Newgate stepped up and the encounter threatened to deteriorate.

"Is there a problem, gentlemen?" Azzalin Romano reached the table.

"Not at all Mr. Romano," Rowland said clearly. "Dr. Stuart Jones and his associates were just taking their leave."

For a few tense seconds it seemed that Barry might refuse, and then finally he nodded, smiling broadly. He shook his finger at Rowland. "Next time, Mr. Sinclair, we shall arrive in time to insist you join us for a meal."

"Indeed. Goodbye, Mr. Barry."

Romano discreetly ushered the three men to a table on the other side of the dining room.

Rowland pulled Clyde aside. "Would you mind settling our account and organising for a motor taxi to be waiting?" He handed him his pocketbook. "Have Romano signal us when it's here. I don't want to give these jokers a chance to follow us out."

Clyde nodded. "What are you going to do?"

"I'm going to dance with Ed."

21

LONDON

---◆---

"Brightest City in Europe"
MR. ROMANO'S IMPRESSIONS

Vienna is no longer the fairy land of fame, according to Mr. A. O. Romano, of Romano's Cafe, who returned last night by the Remo from England and the Continent. London, he says, is now the brightest capital in Europe. Paris, in comparison, is a dead city.

Mr. Romano said he went abroad to learn of the latest novelties in cafe entertainment. London cabarets were employing more and more American artists and were becoming brighter. The latest craze was to have small dancing floors. Australians who attended cabarets were more conservative than Englishmen. The cabaret proprietors in England could more easily cater for the people, who were outspoken and indicated what they wanted.

Mr. Romano said he preferred Australia to any country in the world, and on making purchases abroad he realised that it was not the most expensive country.

The Sydney Morning Herald, 1934

R owland lay back on the couch in his studio with the latest edition of *Smith's Weekly* and every intention of finding Mollie Horseman's drawings and familiarising himself with the journalistic style of the various writers he'd met in Frank Marien's hospital room. Once prone, however, he was reminded that he had been up since four-thirty that morning. He might have dozed off if Lenin had not jumped on top of him, circling and settling despite his master's protests.

The shouting brought Edna from her own studio to investigate.

"Oh Rowly." She pulled the greyhound off. "Are you all right?"

He winced as he sat up. Lenin's bony weight on his already bruised chest had startled him painfully out of languor. "I'm fine, Ed." He scratched the greyhound's single ear to reassure the dog that there were no hard feelings.

Edna sat down beside him. "Rowly, would it be such an awful thing if you did pull out of the race?" she asked quietly.

"Do you want me to?"

"Those men at Romano's…"

"They're bookmakers, Ed. They stand to make a lot of money if Joan Richmond's team is scuttled, which it might be if I pull out now."

"But they said—"

"They're just trying to unnerve me. You mustn't let them worry you."

"Reginald Jones…"

"Yes… I can't believe you ever stepped out with him." Rowland broke his usual rule of never commenting on Edna's loves.

"It was only the once, a long time ago. I felt sorry for him."

"Why?"

"He was very chubby and awkward back then. Everybody called him 'Pudgy Reggie'." Edna shook her head as she recalled. "I came to realise that was the least of his problems."

Rowland laughed. "Still, he would have been excited to have you on his arm."

"Sadly, when Reggie got excited he would take out a revolver and shoot at the ceiling."

Rowland's brow rose. "I see."

Edna rested her head against his shoulder as she confided. "Milt and I used to move with a fairly wild set in those days, Rowly. But Reggie liked to associate with the most dangerous men. He'd seek them out, do anything to be included into their fold."

Rowland sat back, enjoying the easy closeness of her. "I'm glad you only stepped out with him the once."

"Rowly, if these men are Reggie's friends, you can take for granted that they're dangerous, and capable of much more than inviting themselves to lunch."

"I'll have a word with Delaney," Rowland promised in compromise. He frowned as a thought occurred. "We'll have to warn both Joan and Flynn that they may be approached as well, if it's not already too late."

"I don't know about Joan, but I don't think they've tried to influence Errol," Edna said. "I suspect Reggie told them you'd be the most amenable to fixing the race."

"Why would he think that?" Rowland asked sharply.

Edna looked at him archly. "Your reputation is not exactly immaculate, my darling. You were once the proprietor of the 50-50 Club, after all."

"For about five minutes," Rowland muttered. But she was correct. On the face of it, he did seem the least upstanding and perhaps the most corruptible member of Joan Richmond's racing team.

"Rowly, I wouldn't be terribly surprised if Reggie fired that shot through your studio window. He's always been obsessed with guns, and it's just the kind of cowardly, stupid thing he would do."

Rowland heard the barely perceptible tremor in Edna's voice. Realising that she was truly anxious about his safety, he placed an arm firmly about her shoulders and spoke calmly. "Thanks to my dear brother's paranoia, I find myself the most protected man in New South Wales. This place is a fortress! If it were Stuart Jones or one of his associates who took that shot, he won't have another opportunity, Ed."

"That's fine if you never leave *Woodlands*."

"Nonsense… Wil has a band of men following me about." Rowland glanced at his wristwatch. "I expect he'll telephone any moment now to find out exactly what I was doing at Central Police Station, and why I've chosen to wear a red tie on a weekday."

Edna smiled and Rowland felt sure he was impervious to bullets anyway.

Rowland affixed his cufflinks as he made his way down. Milton met him on the staircase. The poet had accessorised his dinner suit with a white silk scarf and a deep red boutonniere.

"It seems a waste to get this dressed up when you've neglected to invite any members of the fairer sex."

"Standards old boy," Rowland replied. "Anyway, there's Ed and Joan."

Milton snorted.

The dinner party would be rather imbalanced in terms of gender, but its purpose was primarily to discuss the race and team strategy. They found Edna and Clyde already entertaining their guests in what had once been the ladies' drawing room. It had been used as a general reception hall since Rowland had claimed the main parlour as his studio.

Noticeably feminine in style, the room was papered rather than panelled and the wainscoting painted a pale blue. The window dressings were soft and the furnishings were chosen for the delicate elegance that appealed to Elisabeth Sinclair.

Elisabeth herself had retired early after a day spent at the Queen's Club with her sister-in-law.

Over pre-dinner drinks, the topic of discussion focussed on motorcars and race strategy. In truth, it was not so much a discussion as an issue and explanation of instructions by Joan Richmond. Flynn contributed nautical translations and Rowland simply listened. Joan drew up a plan of the speedway, grilling both men on which parts were most worn or dangerous and which sections were to be avoided at all costs. The heaviest, most powerful vehicles were scheduled to drive first, so Rowland and the Mercedes would begin the race.

"You need to give Errol at least three laps head start," she said matter-of-factly. "That way I'll have an even chance of holding Hope Bartlett off in the last leg."

Flynn did not, as far as Rowland could tell, seem offended by the bluntness of Joan Richmond's words. Instead, he offered insights into prevailing winds.

Over dinner, Joan told stories of the various race meets in which she'd competed abroad and, more often than not, triumphed.

It was only after they'd eaten that Rowland raised the issue of Reginald Stuart Jones and his compatriots.

"The scoundrels wanted you to throw the race?" Joan gasped. "Why, that's unsporting, simply outrageous! It's not cricket!"

"From what I can gather," Rowland explained, "we are the favourites to win the Lucky Devil II. If we prevail then some of these characters stand to lose a great deal of money."

Flynn laughed. "Serves them right for underestimating us! They should have known from the beginning that this was the winning crew!"

"Yes, but we'd be prudent not to underestimate them," Milton said firmly.

"I wonder why they've only targeted Rowly," Joan murmured.

"Well, you are a lady—they're not animals—and Flynn here is the weakest driver. You and Rowly could probably replace him easily."

Errol Flynn laughed, assuming that Milton was speaking in jest.

"They may just be trying Rowly first," Clyde pointed out.

Flynn seemed unconcerned. "Rest assured, Cap'n," he said, saluting Joan. "I'll be staying with the ship no matter what these pirates want!"

They returned to the drawing room for brandy and Flynn, clearly fed up with conversation about the race, re-enacted his scenes from *The Bounty* with a commentary of amusing anecdotes about his fellow cast members and the occasional seafaring ditty. He demanded Edna stand in as his leading lady though Rowland was sure there hadn't been a woman amongst the Bounty mutineers. Not to be outdone, Milton contributed verses from Coleridge's *Rime of the Ancient Mariner* presented as his own inspiration, and the time passed in an entirely nonsensical but good-humoured manner.

It was Joan Richmond who responsibly declared the evening at an end, reminding the men on her team that they were expected at the track by nine the following morning for another practice run, and instructing them to stop drinking and get some sleep.

Rowland telephoned through to the gatehouse to alert the guard, and they walked their guests to Joan Richmond's Riley, discreetly averting their eyes and discussing the moon as Flynn kissed Edna good night with an extended cinematic passion. Milton laughed as he glanced back. "Actors!" he muttered. "You can see the flaming credits rolling."

"Edna does realise that Flynn's a cad, doesn't she?" Joan whispered.

"Yes, I believe she does," Rowland replied.

"I'm afraid he might break her heart."

"Much more likely to be the other way around, Joan."

Joan looked at him searchingly. "I see."

Clyde scanned the outer perimeter fence of the Maroubra Speedway. "Wombat Newgate's here," he murmured.

Rowland nodded. "I noticed. I believe I saw Stuart Jones skulking about earlier too."

Clyde shook his head in disbelief. "They must have a king's ransom riding on this race."

"I wonder if that's all it is," Rowland said, as he pulled on his driving helmet.

"What do you mean?"

"I've begun to wonder why they haven't approached Joan or Flynn. Perhaps there's more to it than good manners and an indifference to Flynn."

"What exactly?"

"I don't know. But I do wonder if there's something more to it." Rowland pulled down his goggles. There was no time to think about that now.

Clyde moved his head sideways to the infield. Rowland had seen her too. The Honourable Charlotte Linklater with a contingent of gentlemen.

"I'm certain those blokes are New Guardsmen, Rowly," Clyde said. "I recognise the little fellow with the spectacles from Campbell's book launch."

Rowland climbed into the Mercedes.

Clyde forgot about the spectators and gave Rowland instructions. "Don't forget, let her find her place on the bank—the faster you're going the higher that will be. If you get too close to the perimeter, for God's sake slow down. Let me know if you think she's pulling to the right at all—I can adjust that. The tyres will need a couple of laps to warm up so allow for that…"

Rowland listened, not because he hadn't heard it all before, but because Clyde's instructions served as a mental checklist and helped clear his mind of everything but driving. Flynn's Triumph slowed to a stop and pulled off the main track, signalling that it was his turn.

The S-class roared onto the circuit, easing gently up to speed to give the tyres and the engine a chance to warm. Rowland drove precisely, efficiently, but he didn't push the supercharged motor. His driving was tight but it was safe as he and Clyde had decided it would be at the boxing bag that morning. There was no reason for their competitors or the bookmakers to know how fast Rowland Sinclair could take his Mercedes around the bowl, no reason to signal what he would do in the race. The scheme had been soundly endorsed by Joan Richmond.

"Yes, let the wretches believe they've got to you, Rowly. They may call off the dogs and then we'll give them a bit of a shock in the race proper!"

And so Rowland Sinclair resisted the urge to let his motorcar demonstrate her power, and finished his laps in a time that was respectable but sufficiently slow to put them out of serious contention. He glanced up at the spectators on the perimeter as he climbed out of the vehicle. Stuart Jones tipped his hat. It rankled that the nefarious doctor seemed to think they had an agreement, but for now the ruse appeared to be the most sensible solution.

"Good show, Rowly," Clyde whispered as Rowland got out of the car. "That was just slow enough to look like you'd lost your nerve."

Rowland ignored a vague sense of embarrassment that it would seem so. "Let's get out of here before Stuart Jones sees fit to express his admiration once again."

"Give me a couple of minutes to check everything's in order." Clyde used a cloth to protect his hands as he unfolded the bonnet.

Charlotte Linklater and her contingent approached as Clyde peered at the engine.

"Miss Linklater," Rowland said warily. "Allow me to offer my sincere condolences on the tragic passing of your brother."

"I don't accept your apology, Mr. Sinclair," she said fiercely.

"He didn't apologise, Miss Linklater," Clyde said straightening. "I believe he was expressing sorrow for your loss, nothing more."

Charlotte gasped. She shouted at Rowland, "Are you going to let your man address a lady in such an insolent manner?"

The gentlemen by her side also declared displeasure at Clyde's outburst. "Impertinence… how dare you… ill-mannered wretch… a good thrashing by your betters is what you need."

"As Clyde said," Rowland replied slowly and clearly, "I am truly sorry for your loss, Miss Linklater. I understand you must be distraught. If there is anything at all I can do—"

"You can go to hell, Mr. Sinclair!"

Rowland did not respond. It was clear that Charlotte Linklater and the gentlemen with her were spoiling for a fight. How much of it was bereavement as opposed to political belligerence was difficult to glean. He could not help but liken Charlotte to Unity Mitford, the last Fascist Honourable he'd encountered. The acquaintance was not one he'd enjoyed.

The bespectacled New Guardsmen stepped up and poked him in the chest. "What have you got to say for yourself, Sinclair?"

Rowland looked down at the diminutive man and without really meaning to do so, he smiled. A blow may well have produced a less heated response. The guardsman pushed Rowland back against the Mercedes and the other men in Charlotte's entourage closed in.

Clyde leapt into the fray, grabbing Rowland before the jostling escalated to something more. "Is there something you want, gentlemen?" he demanded. "Because if not, I'm afraid we must get on." He raised the tyre lever he held in his hand. The New Guardsmen stepped back.

"I know you!" Spectacles peered at Clyde. "You're the Commie dog that tried to break up the leader's book launch at Town Hall."

"Is there a problem here?" Beejling emerged from wherever he had been lurking.

"Oh, for the love of God!" Rowland said, further irritated by the presence of the bodyguard he'd been forced to tolerate and was trying to ignore. He suspected that in the current circumstances Beejling's officious protection would serve only to exacerbate hostilities.

Hope Bartlett arrived then. He assessed the situation quickly and acted to elegantly dissipate the tension. "Lottie, come along old girl, it's your turn on the track. Sorry gentlemen, the lady is required to drive."

The Guardsmen hesitated, as Charlotte Linklater moved to follow Bartlett.

"Perhaps you'd care to watch from the perimeter fence, gentlemen," Bartlett called over his shoulder. "I hate to be a bore but the infield is restricted to the public."

"Remind me to buy Hope a drink," Rowland murmured as he and Clyde climbed into the Mercedes. "He arrived in the nick of time."

"I don't know." Clyde put the car into gear and released the clutch. "Tyre levers can be very persuasive."

22

THE MECCA OF COUNTRY VISITORS

WHERE TO STAY WHILE IN SYDNEY
Attractions During Easter Holiday
ROYAL SHOW – A.J.C RACES
– BEACH CARNIVALS

...It is because we work so hard that we so thoroughly enjoy our holidays. This is particularly true of the man on the land who, after a year of unremitting toil, reaps his harvest of grain or wool or fruit, and then sets about a holiday.

In New South Wales the harvest season is so arranged by Nature that the farmer is able to take his holiday at a peculiarly apt period of the year—Easter—when all Christendom is celebrating the resurrection of its Lord. The harvest is over, and the man on the land turns his eyes to Sydney, a place of many delights during the Easter season. Everything combines to make the Easter holiday period in Sydney most interesting and enjoyable. Railway fares are reduced and special concessions are offered to attract the country people to the city... The attractions of Sydney at Easter are so varied and so numerous that space permits only the mention of a few in these columns. First and foremost, of course, is the Royal Show, which will be the Mecca of thousands of country people during the holiday period. The chief sporting event is the Easter racing carnival, and there are many other minor events, such as surf carnivals, athletics, motor racing, boxing, tennis, grade cricket, and so on...

> The country people of the State are fortunate in their seasons,
> fortunate in the arrangement of the Easter holiday period, and
> fortunate that they may spend their holiday in the third greatest
> city of the British Empire, which offers attractions and delights
> unsurpassed by any other city in the world.
>
> *Farmer and Settler, 1934*

"I do believe this might be them," Rowland said as they caught sight of the train from the country platform.

Ernest Sinclair held tightly to his uncle's hand and leaned forward as far as he could to see around the press of milling bodies. The housemaster at Tudor House had put him on a train from Moss Vale early that morning so that he could join his uncle and meet his parents' train in the afternoon. The platform was crowded: Sydney-siders meeting country relatives coming to town for the Royal Easter Show, eager faces anticipating reunion. Life-battered men and ragged boys collected discarded cigarette stubs and pounced on fallen change. Tobacconists and flower vendors walked the length of the platform with their wares. Rowland had bought Ernest a bunch of roses for his mother and slipped the change into the calloused hand of an old man competing with brash youths to earn a coin carrying travellers' bags.

Metal ground against metal as the Yass train slowed to a stop in a screeching cloud of steam. Rowland lifted Ernest up so the boy could see over hatted heads and they made their way to the front of the train and the first-class carriages. Ernest caught sight of his mother through the windows and waved and shouted excitedly, "Mater! Mater!"

"Mater?" Rowland looked at his nephew quizzically.

"It's Latin for mother, Uncle Rowly."

"Yes, of course."

"I'm studying Latin."

"Capital."

Wilfred Sinclair was the first to alight onto the platform. At forty-three he was the uncontested patriarch of the Sinclair family. The epitome of dignity and conservative power, Wilfred wore the mantle well, astutely commanding a pastoral empire that now extended beyond Australian shores.

"Daddy!" Ernest shrieked wriggling out of Rowland's arms. He ran to his father and extended his hand. "Welcome to Sydney, Pater."

Wilfred shook his son's hand solemnly. "Why thank you, son. You're looking well."

"I'm taller I think."

Wilfred tousled his son's head affectionately. "I do believe you are." He turned to help Kate Sinclair down the carriage steps. With his mother, Ernest lost all pretence at decorum and Latin, throwing himself into her arms crying, "Mummy, I missed you, Mummy."

Rowland stood back for a while allowing his brother this time alone with his family. As much as Wilfred was one of the wealthiest and most influential men in the country, it had always been clear that he valued his young wife and sons above all else. It was in stark contrast to the priorities of their own late father.

Two nannies, attired in crisp grey uniforms, followed Kate Sinclair from the carriage, each bearing one of Wilfred's younger sons. Though he had grown considerably from the newborn Rowland had last seen, Gilbert was still a babe in arms. Ewan, Rowland's godson was now nearly two and not impressed with the confinement of his nanny's iron grip.

"Rowly, there you are!" Wilfred shook his brother's hand.

"Hello Wil. Good journey?"

"Tolerable." Wilfred signalled the porters he'd already paid to take the luggage as Rowland kissed Kate's cheek.

"Good Lord," Rowland murmured as trunk after trunk bearing the Sinclair crest was unloaded from the luggage carriage.

Wilfred sighed. "How many cars did you bring?"

"Just two, and mine," Rowland said a little concerned. Then a possible solution occurred. "We can put the extra trunks in Beejling's vehicle. He may as well be useful."

"Who's Beejling?"

"He's one of the men you're paying to follow me about."

"I see."

"In fact, if you ride back with him he could probably apprise you of everything I've been up to."

"You're too old to be petulant, Rowland. I acted for your own safety, and the safety of anyone who might be with you, for that matter." He glanced pointedly at Ernest who was reciting Latin roots to his mother.

Rowland stopped. He winced. "Yes, of course," he said sheepishly.

"But since he's here," Wilfred said, signalling the bodyguard, "he might as well take a trunk or two."

And so they arrived in convoy at *Roburvale*. Not quite as large as *Woodlands House*, the Sinclairs' second Woollahra mansion was nevertheless a substantial property. Its gatehouse was already occupied by Wilfred's security. Rowland had deployed Bessie to assist the elderly Mrs. Donnelly in preparing for the arrival of the greater Sinclairs. The more risqué artwork which Rowland's late uncle and namesake had hung throughout his home had been taken down, and a nursery prepared for the children. A cook and a scullery maid had been borrowed from another grand house whose family was abroad to cater for the needs of Wilfred Sinclair's household. Bessie had ensured all the rooms were prepared and fresh flowers set in every vase. The staff were lined up by the portico to meet and greet the family.

Rowland stayed a while to play with his nephews. Young Ewan was a much less contained and more physical child than his elder brother. He demanded to be hung upside down and squealed in delight.

"For pity's sake, Rowly, I thought someone was murdering the children," Wilfred muttered as he entered the room to find Rowland on the floor with both Ernest and Ewan on top of him. Ernest got off his uncle immediately but Ewan simply chanted, "Again, again, again…"

Rowland stood up and swung the two-year-old into the air one more time. "Would you like me to take Ernest back to school?" he asked.

Ernest's face fell, his shoulders slumped but he said nothing. Rowland felt like the worst kind of traitor.

"Do you have the time? I could have my driver take him back?" Wilfred asked. "I'm afraid I have to get straight down to Moore Park to make sure everything's in order for tomorrow when the Show opens."

"I haven't anything pressing to attend to, and long runs are good practice."

"Oh yes, the race." Wilfred put his hand on Ernest's shoulder. "Chin up, Ernie. I'll come and get you Friday evening for the whole weekend."

"But…" The boy's lower lip trembled as he tried valiantly not to cry.

Wilfred took his son's hand. "I must say, I'm looking forward to hearing all the new Latin words you will have learned by then. Still, we'll have to be careful that Ewan isn't jealous that you are allowed to go to school with other boys, while he has to stay here with his strict old nanny!"

"Is she very strict?" Ewan asked quietly.

"Dreadfully. Your Uncle Rowly's positively terrified of her."

"What about you, Daddy?"

"I'm like you, Ernie. I'm not afraid of anything."

Ernest nodded gravely.

"Maybe you ought to escape before Nanny gets back from the kitchen, but run and say goodbye to your mother first. I'll stay with your uncle in case Ewan's nanny gets back early."

Ernest giggled now and set out to find his mother. He paused at the door. "Can we pick up Mr. Isaacs on the way, Uncle Rowly?"

Rowland smiled. It appeared Ernest was turning Milton into quite a lucrative sideshow. "If he's at home, we'll ask," he promised.

"I'll call at *Woodlands* tomorrow morning to see Mother," Wilfred said as he lit a cigarette. "Is there anything for which you might need to prepare me?"

"Prepare you? No, I don't believe so."

"Very well," Wilfred's voice was dubious. He had agreed to allow Elisabeth Sinclair to live with his brother in a moment of weakness and was yet to be convinced that it would not end in disaster. "We do need to speak about this latest trouble in which you've managed to become embroiled, but that can wait till tomorrow."

"Bloody oath, Wil!" Rowland murmured indignantly. "Someone shot at me, not the other way around!"

"I do occasionally wonder, Rowly, what it is about you that makes so many people want to do so."

Milton was more than willing to accompany Rowland and his nephew on the long drive to Tudor House. He paused to collect a red neck scarf and a beret, on to which he had pinned a Communist star badge.

"What are you doing?" Rowland demanded as the poet added a hammer and sickle pin to his lapel.

"Looking the part," Milton said. "Gotta give the people value for money."

Ernest nodded solemnly. "Can you say something Communist, Mr. Isaacs? Digby Cossington Smythe said he'd give me an extra shilling and his pudding on Wednesday, if I could get you to say something Communist."

Milton stroked his goatee thoughtfully. "How about… Come the revolution, the worker shall rise up and crush the capitalist—"

"Steady on, Milt," Rowland said alarmed. "You'll get us killed!"

"They're seven-year-olds."

"I was talking about Wil."

"Oh. I suppose you're right. I could just sing The Red Flag. Would that do, Ernie?"

"Yes please, Mr. Isaacs!"

And so Ernest Sinclair was delivered back to Tudor House by his uncle and an increasingly conspicuous Communist who was belting out the people's song. The housemaster came out to glare at Milton, but the egg-shaped boy whom Rowland assumed was Digby seemed adequately impressed.

Rowland checked the time. The run back to *Woodlands* from Moss Vale would take at least a couple of hours. They'd get back to Sydney well after dark but before eight o'clock. The reporters who had followed him for days seeking comment, seemed finally to have given up.

"Do you have an appointment?" Milton asked.

"I thought I might finally drop in on this chap, Bocquet, who claims White's tiepin was stolen from him. He lives in Lindfield."

"Haven't the police talked to him already?"

"Yes, but I get the impression that it was a very cursory interview."

"Even so, why would he talk to you?"

"Can only ask."

"Fair enough. Let's go."

They spent the time in the car talking about the mystery of White's death, the race, the shooting and the latest machinations of the New Guard. Milton was predisposed to blame Eric Campbell for everything including the murder of Crispin White. "For all we know, Rowly, the Fascist Legion took issue with White. You remember what they did to me… to you."

"I'm not sure the Fascist Legion still exists, Milt, and White wasn't a Communist as far as I know."

"You weren't a Communist either, they still belted you half to death. And whatever he called himself in recent years, White was Jewish."

Rowland's knuckles whitened on the steering wheel. There was that. But the New Guard had not to date followed its European cousins into anti-Semitism—at least not publicly.

Milton pressed on. "How do we know that White wasn't writing a story on Campbell? You know how Campbell feels about the press these days. Anyway the New Guard still might be behind the shot fired at your studio window."

"They might," Rowland conceded. "Though why they'd suddenly want me dead badly enough to do something about it, I don't know."

"What do you reckon about this book of Campbell's?"

Rowland frowned. "I expect it depends upon whether Campbell's Centre Party is successful at the election. If it is, then the book may become a manifesto of some sort. The fact that Campbell seems to be following the Adolf Hitler School of Dictatorship is more concerning than his bloody book."

Milton swore his agreement. "How long do you think it'll be before he takes on Hitler's other tactics?" he asked.

"Against Jews? He hasn't yet, as far as I'm aware."

"But you believe he may?"

"He might if he gets desperate. Or he may decide to vilify the Chinese, or the Irish or some other scapegoat." Rowland shook his head as he thought of Norman Lindsay. "God help me, I'm no longer sure Australians would just laugh at him."

Milton glanced at his friend. He'd always believed Rowland Sinclair naïve—doggedly romantic, conditioned by a privileged upbringing to expect the best from the world. That Rowland was coming to doubt his fellow man was probably inevitable but alarming, nevertheless. "So, we'll have to stop him."

"How exactly?"

"Relax, Rowly. I'm not suggesting we shoot him. Not yet anyway." Rowland smiled. "What then?"

"We let the establishment destroy him." Milton stroked the dark hair on his chin. "The Old Guard sent us to Germany to make sure Campbell didn't make friends with the Nazis. How about we let them finish the colonel's ambitions of becoming Australia's Führer?"

"You're suggesting we should do nothing?" Rowland said uneasily.

"No. I'm saying we should make your brother's lot aware of how dangerous Campbell is. He only got as powerful as he did because the establishment found him useful against Lang. They need to know he's more of a threat to democracy than the Labor Party or the Communists will ever be."

"I don't know, Milt."

"Look, Rowly, I've had a read of Campbell's manifesto."

"You bought his book?" Rowland asked surprised.

"God no. Let's say I borrowed it. I'll throw it back at him when I see him next. Anyway, I can see what he's doing. He's appealing to the middle classes, the petite bourgeoisie. Those who haven't been born to the establishment, but who are privileged enough to feel that they are on merit somehow better than the working stiff. The more the Left rails against Campbell, the more they'll flock to his side. The establishment are tolerating him because they hope in the end to bring his minions across to them, because they are convinced New Guardsmen could be moderated and tamed to become loyal Old

Guardsmen in time. They expect they can bring Campbell to heel the way they brought Hardy to heel."

Senator Charles Hardy had once been the leader of the Riverina Movement, and a self-avowed Fascist. He had roused the rural masses against Communists and Jack Lang, inciting mobs to reach for the tar and feathers. Cromwell of the Riverina, as Hardy had been known, was as revolutionary and charismatic as Eric Campbell. But the Old Guard had won him over with a senate ticket, and the men of the Riverina Movement had been quietly absorbed into the armies of the establishment. Rowland knew all this, but he had not before considered the strategy behind it. He was reminded that Milton Isaacs' understanding of politics far exceeded his, and that as frivolous as his friend often seemed, Milton's intellect and insight were rarely surpassed.

"I reckon," Milton continued, "that Campbell would still love to be welcomed back into the bosom of the landed gentry."

"You're saying we should—"

"I'm saying that your brother and his mates could best neutralise the bastard by throwing him a bone."

"I don't know, Milt, there's a lot of bad blood there."

"I'm not suggesting they do it because they like him."

Rowland could see the sense in Milton's words. "I'll speak to Wilfred," he said. His brother was a political player. Perhaps Wilfred would be able to put aside his personal feelings to ensure Campbell didn't wreak any more havoc than he already had.

"It's worth a try," Milton said. "If it doesn't work, we'll just tell Hartley that Campbell killed Crispin White."

23

SMOKING AN AID TO DOMESTIC BLISS

BENEFIT IN MODERATION

"Most wives know that a smoker lets off his temper on his pipe, rather than on his family—having no hope of the last word, he resolves to vigorous puffing and blowing of smoke," said a well-known Brisbane doctor. He considered there was room for further scientific investigation, and no scientific obstacle to the new theory, as cabled from London, that nicotine stimulates the adrenal glands, which help to regulate the amount of sugar circulating in the blood. It was a rational explanation of why a cigarette relieved fatigue and irritability, which were associated with a low level of sugar in the blood. He smoked so much himself that he had taken it for granted that the effect was that of a sedative on the nervous system. There was much yet to be learned about the glands, and the new theory might have a valuable medicinal incidence. In excess, tobacco first stimulated then paralysed the motor nerves, and the secreting nerves of the glands. In moderation—and that might mean for a healthy man a good deal—smoking was of benefit in relieving exhaustion, calming excited nerves, aiding digestion, and increasing the pleasure of life. Sherlock Holmes smoked extensively in solving his problems. Sir Arthur Conan Doyle, his creator, was a medical man, in direct touch with scientific thought and practice.

The Braidwood Review and District Advocate, 1934

The Bocquet residence was typical of the architecturally pleasing houses of middle-class Lindfield. Not a mansion by any means, but the tidy, well-maintained dwelling of the comfortably well-off with double street frontage and a tennis court. Rowland recalled that Rosaleen Norton, too, lived in Lindfield. It intrigued him that the strange young reporter came from what seemed to be such a picture of suburban respectability. Perhaps Lindfield was not as conventional as it appeared at first glance.

Milton checked the address against the one that Delaney had scrawled. "This is it." He spotted a movement of the curtains. "Someone's home."

A swarthy solid gentleman answered their knock, with a folded newspaper under one arm and a briar pipe in the other.

Rowland introduced both himself and Milton. "I know this is a frightful imposition, Mr. Bocquet, but I hoped we might talk to you about your stolen tiepin."

"My tiepin?" Bocquet said incredulously. "You want to talk about my tiepin!"

"Yes, if you'd be so kind."

"Can you tell me why you're so interested in my tiepin, Mr... Sinclair, was it?"

"Yes. Crispin White was a good friend of mine," Rowland said, exaggerating the case. "As you're probably aware, your tiepin was found on his body. The fact is, Mr. Bocquet, I can't imagine that Crispin was a thief—I certainly don't want him to die as one. I had hoped that by talking to you I might be able to work out how he came to have your property... to clear his name, as it were."

Milton nodded in agreement, impressed by the smooth manner in which Rowland justified their interference.

Bocquet seemed moved by Rowland's claim. "Would that every man had such loyal friends!" he said, inviting them in. He directed them in to a cosy drawing room, insisting they take the armchairs and offering them drinks and seats. Rowland accepted tea and Bocquet called for his wife who had been hovering with some intent in the hallway.

The gentlemen stood as she came into the room. Mrs. Bocquet was a good deal younger than her husband, blonde and plump and dimpled. Rowland apologised for imposing unannounced. She made a point to explain that they were temporarily without staff before excusing herself to make tea. She spoke with an accent more refined than her husband's and, to Rowland, seemed quite embarrassed by the fact that she to do for herself.

"Can you tell us when you first noticed your tiepin was missing, Mr. Bocquet?" Milton opened the questions.

"A couple of weeks ago, but it may have been missing for a good while, to be honest. I don't wear it very often... it's a trifle loud," he said, his gaze lingering on Milton's beret and gold cravat. The poet had fortunately divested himself of the scarf and Communist paraphernalia he had worn to satisfy Digby Cossington Smythe.

"I see. Well, when did you wear it last?"

"About a month ago. I took Beryl out for a meal. It was our anniversary, you see, and she likes me to wear the tiepin seeing as she gave it to me. We got a table at Romano's. Beryl was the most beautiful dame in the room, you know. A man can't help but be proud."

"Are you sure you didn't lose the tiepin that evening, Mr. Bocquet?"

Bocquet hesitated. "I thought I'd put it back in my cufflinks drawer, like I always do... that's why I thought we'd been burgled."

"But you're not sure?"

"Well frankly, I thought it was the girl who comes in to help Beryl with the housework. Things had been going missing for a time—money mainly. I thought the police might get her to confess."

"And did she?"

"No, but they never do, do they, that type? You try to give them the benefit of the doubt and you get robbed for your trouble."

Mrs. Bocquet entered the room with a laden tray.

"Thank you, pet." Les Bocquet said, rushing to help her. She swatted him away.

"You'll only drop them, Les. Remember the Wedgwood!"

"She's right, I'm all thumbs. Broke the Wedgwood," Les explained. He stood back as his wife poured and handed out cups of tea.

"Frances swears she's innocent," she said. "Maybe Les did lose it after all. We let her go, of course."

"We couldn't really keep her on after dobbing her in to the police," Les protested, puffing industriously on his pipe. "Beryl's too tender-hearted. Makes her vulnerable to people taking advantage." He sighed. "But maybe I did just lose it. Perhaps your friend White simply found it. That'd explain it if you say he's not the kind of man to thieve it."

Rowland directed his question to the lady of the house. "Do you think Frances would have stolen from you, Mrs. Bocquet?"

She glanced at her husband before answering. "I suppose she might," she said folding her arms. "We didn't trust her. She was a busy body... always poking through my things."

"And you're sure Crispin White's never been here?" Milton asked.

"No." On this point Beryl was definite. "Never. Not once."

They stayed to finish their tea, though those minutes yielded nothing more by way of information. Rowland left his card as they thanked the Bocquets for their hospitality and took their leave. The couple stood together on the porch, Les waving congenially until the Mercedes had pulled out of their driveway.

"So what did you think of that?" Milton asked.

"He's friendly enough. But I feel jolly sorry for Frances."

"Yes, me too."

"I presume the police have already spoken to her," Rowland mused.

"If the maid did take the pin perhaps she was White's mystery woman. He wouldn't be the first man to fall in love with the help."

"She wasn't his help," Rowland murmured.

"No, that's true. If she was sacked for a tiepin she stole to give White, she'd probably be very angry if he jilted her."

"That's true… if she knew him at all. We're guessing at much of this. We don't even know for certain that White had a lover."

Milton groaned, frustrated. "We should speak with Frances."

Wilfred Sinclair rubbed his chin as he perused the watercolours spread out on the long dining table. Studies of flowers, and paintings of the garden, executed with a discernibly increasing degree of proficiency and confidence.

"Aubrey found me some brushes and paper, and Mr. Watson Jones has been ever so helpful," Elisabeth said, laughing nervously. She pointed to a painting of yellow roses in a vase. The flowers were delicately rendered, a gentle explosion of colour against the crazed porcelain of the vase. "The shading is wrong in this one, I fear."

"They're tremendous, Mother," Wilfred said quietly. "Quite marvellous. I wasn't aware you painted."

"Oh, I don't really… not since I was a girl. But I have been enjoying it."

"That pleases me greatly. Will you allow me to drag you away from your easel to take luncheon at *Roburvale?* Kate and the children would love to see you."

"Children? What children, Wilfred darling?"

A pause cut with fear. "My children, my boys."

"Oh yes, of course. What was I thinking!"

Wilfred smiled. "Why don't you get ready while I have a word with Rowly," he said, refusing to pander to his mother's delusion by calling his brother anything else.

"Well, don't be too long." Elisabeth Sinclair did not seem to notice.

"How long has she been…?" Wilfred began as he accompanied Rowland from their mother's wing.

"Only a few days," Rowland said. "She's quite good, actually."

"I suppose you must get it from somewhere."

Rowland was a little surprised by the vague compliment. For the most part Wilfred regarded his brother's artistic proclivities as a bad habit. "We might use the study," Rowland said, diverting from his studio.

"Why?" Wilfred asked suspiciously. Their father's study was one of the few rooms left untouched since Rowland had become master of *Woodlands*. Wilfred was well aware that the reason was not sentimental.

"I've been working. My studio is a bit of a dog's breakfast at the moment."

"It always is."

"I'm preparing for an exhibition, Wil. It's more of a mess than usual." Rowland opened the study door and allowed his brother to enter ahead of him. As much as he hated this room, Rowland knew Wilfred preferred its traditional gravitas to the informality and idiosyncrasy which had worked its way into the rest of the mansion.

Rowland pulled the copy of Campbell's *The New Road* that Milton had borrowed from his pocket and handed it to Wilfred. "Have you seen this?"

Wilfred nodded. "I've read it, in fact."

Rowland had intended to argue his case reasonably, logically, but quite soon he became aware that he was ranting about the possibility that Campbell would regain the public support he'd once had, the possibility that the anti-Communist hysteria which had gripped New South Wales two years before would return.

Wilfred listened patiently, waiting until his brother was finished before he cautioned, "I'm not sure the fear of a Communist insurgency was, or is, unwarranted, Rowly."

"For God's sake, Wil!"

"Look, Rowly, I'm no more enamoured with Campbell's corporate state than you are, but he's a spent force, old boy. You're wasting your energy fighting him."

"I can't help wondering if perhaps there were people who thought Adolf Hitler was a spent force, too."

"We are not Germany, Rowly."

"Not yet."

"Not ever!" Wilfred said, so sharply that Rowland was reminded that his brother had served. "We live in a democracy. As much as it means your Communist chums can spread their poison, it also means Campbell's free to do the same. There's nothing we can do."

Rowland put Milton's proposal to Wilfred then, without mentioning that it was the poet's idea, of course.

Wilfred regarded his brother incredulously. "You want me to foster relations with Campbell?"

"I want you to absorb him into the fold of the Graziers' Association. Make him feel important, give him a knighthood... I don't care. If Campbell feels appreciated by the status quo, he'll have no reason to follow Hitler's path."

"The king gives knighthoods, Rowly, the Graziers' Association does not."

"You know what I mean." Rowland did not want to argue about honours. "Look Wil, the New Guard, the Fascist Legion, Campbell's attempts to meet Hitler and Mussolini were all about his own ego. You shut Hardy up with a senate seat—why not Campbell?"

"We don't like him."

Rowland was startled by the simple admission. "You're not serious."

"I am. Campbell rubs people the wrong way. He's a self-important, arrogant braggart."

The description seemed to Rowland to be applicable to most of the Graziers' Association but he was diplomatic enough to leave that unspoken. "Which is why what I'm suggesting will work better than decrying him."

Wilfred sat forward in his chair. "Rowly, I'm genuinely worried about you."

Rowland straightened, startled. "Me? Why?"

"I'm concerned that you've developed a tendency to become anxious."

"What? You're the one who's having me followed."

"Calm down Rowly. Hear me out. The trouble you got into in Munich has left you unjustifiably apprehensive about Eric Campbell. It's nothing to be ashamed of—after the war there were many men—"

"Dammit, Wil, I'm not suffering from some kind of shell shock!"

"You've got to let this go, Rowly. You did well. If not for you, Campbell may well have forged dangerous alliances. But it's time to move on, find a real purpose. If its politics you're interested in the United Country Party could use—"

"No!" Rowland stood. "I promise you Wil, the UCP and I have no use for each other."

The exchange deteriorated from there. The Sinclair brothers fell easily into battle, for they were adversaries of old and knew well the art of infuriating each other. In the end, Rowland stormed out of the study more livid with his brother than he had been in years.

"Whoa, Rowly... what the Dickens are you doing?" Clyde grabbed his friend's shoulder and pulled him away from the boxing bag. "At least put on gloves," he said glancing at Rowland's already grazed knuckles.

Rowland stopped, embarrassed. He wasn't sure why he was so angry. He should have anticipated Wilfred's response. But he hadn't. For some reason he thought that Wilfred would understand, even share, his concerns about the Fascists. It seemed he'd temporarily forgotten the nature of his brother's politics. Wilfred had reminded him.

Rowland dragged one hand through his hair and adjusted his tie. "Sorry," he said sheepishly.

"No skin off my nose, Rowly, only your knuckles. What in the blazes is going on?"

Rowland leaned back against the stall, his arms folded. Clyde did the same, and he listened as Rowland recounted his conversation, such as it was, with Wilfred.

"He thinks you're having a nervous breakdown?" Clyde said, aghast.

"I wouldn't go that far, but he does believe I've lost perspective." Rowland glowered at the bag as if it were, in fact, Wilfred Sinclair. "What are you doing out here anyway?" he asked, changing the subject. He had come out to the stables to vent his frustrations alone, and while he did not resent Clyde's intrusion, he was surprised by it.

"I was looking for you, actually," Clyde said awkwardly.

"Oh, why?"

"I just took a telephone call."

"For me?"

"No, he wanted to talk to me. It was Rosie's father."

Rowland turned. "And what did he want?"

"He wants to meet with me. He says we should talk."

"What about?"

"He didn't say." Clyde stared at his calloused hands. "Perhaps he's changed his mind. Perhaps that chap Antonio's done a runner and—" He rubbed his face. "I don't want to build up my hopes, Rowly."

"But it's too late," Rowland murmured. Clyde had said little about Rosalina in the past days but he was aware she rarely left his friend's thoughts. "When does he want to meet you?"

"Now."

"Let's go. You don't mind if Beejling and I tag along, do you?"

Clyde laughed. "It just wouldn't be the same without Beejling."

24

DISAPPOINT THAT
NERVOUS BREAKDOWN

If, by all the signs, you know you're heading for a nervous
breakdown, why not take the matter in hand right now? Put
office problems, household cares, behind you for a couple
of weeks. Give yourself some sunny, happy days and restful
nights at VICTORIA'S LEADING HYDRO, where curative
baths, electrical treatments, massage, correct diet will tone
up your entire system, give you a fresh start. Building heated
throughout. Phone Warburton 5, or write for booklet A,
Victoria's Hydro, Warburton.—[Advt.]

The Argus, 1934

Martinelli had asked, or perhaps directed, Clyde to meet him at a
wine bar in Leichhardt.

"I reckon giving Rosie that painting must have changed her mind,
made her realise I'm willing to put her before my art... or your art at
least," Clyde said happily.

"Well then, it was worth every penny," Rowland said, pleased for
his friend. They were using the Rolls Royce because Clyde had taken
the carburettor out of the Mercedes. Under normal circumstances this
would have meant using Johnston, too, but the chauffeur was driving
for Wilfred and Kate while the family were in Sydney.

The wine bar was a less than salubrious affair, and it was only because it seemed to be a haunt of Italian men that Rowland didn't wonder at it. The proprietor welcomed them quite affably and led them to a private room at the back of the narrow building.

Martinelli was not alone. Rowland held back as he recognised the half dozen younger men who had thrown them out of the hotel restaurant just weeks before. Unsmiling, Martinelli invited them to sit at a long table set with bread and olives and wine. Clyde seemed so hopeful that Rowland ignored his misgivings and took a seat.

The door was closed. Rowland turned to see that four more men had walked into the room before locking the door behind them.

"We have no money," Martinelli announced loudly.

"That's all right, I'm happy to pay for the food," Rowland offered, wondering what they had walked into.

"No, we don't pay your tax!"

"I'm not sure I understand what you mean, Mr. Martinelli," Clyde said, as confused as Rowland, but still clinging to the hope this was some kind of welcome to the family.

"Blackmail. We will not be blackmailed!"

"What exactly are you talking about, sir?" Rowland asked calmly.

"The picture." The old man slammed the table with his fist before pointing at Clyde. "You paint Rosalina's face on a body with no clothes like some… some…" Martinelli lapsed into Italian but his meaning was clear. "My Rosalina, she is like the Madonna! This picture is an insult, it is a threat, a slander, and you demand money or you will ruin her." He pulled the receipt Clyde had secured to the back of *Psyche by the Styx* from his pocket and threw it down.

"No!" Clyde said, horrified. "You've got it all wrong!"

"Why else would you send us a dirty picture?"

Rowland tried to help. "I painted that picture, Mr. Martinelli, not Clyde. I can assure you—"

The eldest of Rosalina's brothers launched himself over the table at Rowland. "You insult my sister, you bastard!" Taken by surprise Rowland was knocked to the ground. Clyde leapt up immediately, but there were others to take him.

"It was a gift!" Rowland shouted as the angry men converged.

"What kind of man imagines a good girl in such a way? What kind of fiend defames the image of a decent girl?"

"I didn't, Miss Martinelli was—" Rowland stopped. Telling the outraged Martinellis that he had not simply imagined Rosalina posing nude, that he'd painted her from life, might indeed ruin her. He glanced at Clyde helplessly.

The first punch was not unexpected. Rowland and Clyde had, by then, both realised they'd been lured to the wine bar to be taught a lesson, that they'd walked into a trap, the only escape from which, it seemed, would be to betray Rosalina's secret. That path was one neither Rowland nor Clyde would consider. So they fought back because it was all that was left, but they were grossly outnumbered and aware from the beginning that it was hopeless. Still, it was satisfying to get in a few blows of their own before they were overpowered.

Rosalina's father sat down at the table, eating stuffed olives as he watched the two men who sought to compromise his daughter's good name being taught that Enrico Martinelli would not be blackmailed.

Robert Beejling had parked his Singer behind the Rolls Royce. The bodyguard no longer bothered to stay out of sight—Rowland Sinclair was well aware of his presence. He remained with the automobiles for the first two hours. In this neighbourhood, he decided, the vehicles probably needed more protection than young Sinclair. Hunger as opposed to the passing hours prompted Beejling to enter the wine bar. When he couldn't see either Rowland or Clyde at the tables inside, he enquired of the proprietor. These places, he knew, often had private rooms or courtyards.

"Yes, sir, we do have a private dining room. It's available if you'd like to—"

"Available? Are you sure it hasn't been hired?"

"No sir, it's available."

Beejling became alarmed. "Two gentlemen came in a couple of hours ago... one was tall, dark hair, striking blue eyes... his friend was rougher looking, stocky and sandy haired."

The proprietor looked at him blankly. "No, no gentlemen like that."

"When did you start your shift? Could you have missed them?"

"No. I've been here since eight o'clock, sir. They didn't come in."

"That's impossible. I saw them come in!"

"Perhaps they went into another shop."

Beejling demanded to see the private room. The proprietor showed him to a room at the back of the building. A single long table set with a checked tablecloth and cutlery. A youth mopped the tiled floor. The water in the bucket was red.

"What happened here?" Beejling snapped at the boy.

He shrugged. "Sauce," he said. "Enrico spilled the sauce."

Beejling swore, turned on his heel and made his way out of the wine bar. He hesitated before climbing into the Singer, debating the advisability of leaving the Rolls Royce unattended. He pulled away from the kerb wondering how he was going to explain having lost Rowland Sinclair.

"No, I'm afraid I don't know where Rowly and Clyde went, Mr. Sinclair," Edna said, wiping the film of clay from her hands with a towel. She'd been working on a bust when Wilfred had tapped on the door of her studio. "I was at the Royal Easter Show this morning when they left. Did you need to see Rowly?"

"Yes."

Edna looked carefully at Wilfred. "Is something the matter, Mr. Sinclair?"

"Rowly and Mr. Watson Jones seem to have vanished."

"Vanished? How do you mean?"

"Mr. Beejling saw them enter some wine bar, out of which they did not re-emerge. The proprietor claims they'd never been there in the first place," Wilfred said testily.

"Well, what happened to them?" Edna asked alarmed.

"That's what I'm trying to ascertain, Miss Higgins." He removed his glasses and polished the lenses with his handkerchief. "It occurred to me that my brother might consider it a great joke to give his bodyguard the slip."

Edna shook her head. "If he were with Milt, perhaps, but not Clyde. How long have they been missing?"

"Beejling last saw them nearly five hours ago. Where is Mr. Isaacs? Might they have joined him somewhere?"

"I suppose… but Milton is not a magician. He can't have caused them to vanish."

"According to Beejling, the establishment backs on to a lane. It's possible they simply walked through the premises."

"But surely they couldn't have done that without being noticed?"

"I expect not, unless the proprietor is complicit."

"Complicit with whom, Mr. Sinclair?" Edna was becoming increasingly distressed.

"If this is Rowly being funny, so help me I'll…" Wilfred muttered.

"Mr. Sinclair, someone tried to shoot Rowly a few days ago!"

"Yes, I am aware of that, Miss Higgins. Would you mind locating Mr. Isaacs while I call the police?"

━━━━━━━━　　　━━━━━━━━

Rowland became aware of the jarring movement beneath him, the rattling shake of a truck's tray. Over him, a heavy tarpaulin. Instinctively, he struggled. A kick to the back and a growled warning not to move. He began to remember more clearly then. Without moving he couldn't tell if he was seriously hurt… whether the pain was a sign of something debilitating.

"Clyde—"

A groan in response and another kick, this time to the stomach.

Rowland gasped, the weight of a man's knee pressed on his spine and a more explicit warning. He wasn't sure how long he'd been unconscious. He couldn't hear any other traffic… they were out of the city. How far and in what direction he had no idea.

He told himself to calm down, to relax and allow himself to recover while he could. When the truck stopped the real danger would begin. They would need to be ready to run or fight.

━━━━━━━━　　　━━━━━━━━

Milton paced as he detailed their encounter with the bookmakers at Romano's. "Newgate's just the village idiot, and Reggie Jones a simpering buffoon, but Redmond Barry is probably dangerous."

Delaney's face was grim as he made notes.

It was nearly dark now and there was still no sign of either Rowland or Clyde.

"Do you suppose Reggie and his friends might have them, Detective Delaney?" Edna asked.

"I hope so, Miss Higgins," Delaney replied. "Stuart Jones and his associates at least have no real reason to kill them. They just need to hold them till the race is over."

The logic of Delaney's argument gave Edna no comfort whatsoever.

"For God's sake sit down, Mr. Isaacs!" Wilfred said irritably.

Milton took the chair beside Delaney's. "It's Campbell," he said. "Campbell abducted them or instructed his latest band of hooded thugs to do so."

"Why would he do that?" Wilfred asked, stiffening.

"Because Rowly is on to him... because Rowly knows how dangerous he could be!"

The conversation he'd had with Rowland that morning played on Wilfred's mind. "Why would they suddenly come after Rowly? All that business is finished. Did Rowly go after Campbell, is that who he was meeting?" he demanded.

"I don't know," Milton said. "He didn't tell me if he was."

"It's only been a few hours," Delaney said, trying to inject some calm into the situation. "We'll speak to all the relevant parties—see what we can find out. May I suggest gentlemen, Miss Higgins, that you also make enquiries of anyone to whom Mr. Sinclair or Mr. Watson Jones might have spoken about what they were up to."

The truck came to a stop. Rowland tensed. The tarpaulin was dragged off. It was dark now, but there was a three-quarter moon. He could make out several men stretching after the long drive, smoking, a prone body on the tray with him who he presumed was Clyde. They were pulled to their feet and thrown off the back of the truck. The ground was hard, bare. Rowland rolled on to his knees and tried to stand. Someone belted him. He could hear Clyde swearing. All the time he listened for the click of a gun, watched for any sign of a weapon. It did occur to him that they'd been brought to some remote place to be shot.

Another beating… less thorough than before. Just a refresher really. Then a warning as they lay on the ground. "Blackmailers die young. If you shame Rosalina, if you make another painting of her or speak ill of her character, we will find you."

Rowland said nothing. Protesting their innocence would be pointless and possibly dangerous now.

The truck was refuelled with the tins of petrol brought with them, and restarted. Men climbed back into the cabin or onto the tray as the old Bedford began to move. Soon the rattling throb of the motor faded and there was only the cut and slice of the wind. Rowland struggled to his feet and moved to the form on the ground a few yards away. "Clyde, are you all right?"

Clyde cursed. "I don't know," he said. "I can't see properly."

"Just hold still." Rowland patted his pockets. His pocketbook had been taken but they'd left his lighter. He used the weak flickering flame to inspect Clyde's face. One eye was swollen shut, the other nearly so. "Bloody hell! Can you stand?"

"I think so."

Rowland helped Clyde to his feet, cursing as his friend's weight told painfully on his own battered body.

"Rowly, I can't see to tell… are you all right?"

"I'll live," Rowland said tightly. "We're both going to be a bit black and blue for a while. I wonder where the devil we are."

"What does it look like?"

"The middle of nowhere. I can't see any sign of civilisation."

"Are we in the bush?"

"Yes. But it's not too heavily wooded. The terrain is steep."

"How long were we in the truck?"

"At least an hour after I came to."

"Do you still have your watch? What's the time?"

Rowland checked. The crystal had been cracked but the watch's movement still seemed to be functioning. "Nearly eight o'clock."

"So we could have been in the back of that truck for five or so hours. God, we could be anywhere!" Clyde took a deep breath. He kept a hand on Rowland's shoulder to steady himself. "Is there a road?"

Rowland squinted. "More a dirt track. Goodness knows how those bastards managed to get the truck down it."

"I'm so sorry, Rowly," Clyde said quietly.

"Returning the painting to Miss Martinelli was my great idea," Rowland said. "In fact, I'm pretty sure I insisted."

"How could those fools think we were trying to blackmail them?" Clyde moaned.

"It was the receipt, I suspect."

"Milt thought I should include it, so Rosie knew I didn't steal the painting."

"Oh… well it sounds like this is all Milt's fault then," Rowland replied.

"Yes, let's agree on that."

Rowland pulled his jacket tighter. The temperature was dropping. "I'm afraid we're going to have to walk, if for nothing else than to keep warm."

"In which direction?" Clyde asked dubiously. "We have no idea where we are."

"If we go back the way the truck came, it'll get us on to a major road eventually. The other direction could lead nowhere. It isn't worth the risk." Rowland studied his friend critically. "We need to get you to a doctor." He'd seen plenty of black eyes in his boxing days and knew the swelling could hide more serious damage. "Are you going to be able to walk?"

Clyde nodded. "I can walk."

25

SHELTER FOR TRAMPS

Practically every town is visited by tramps, who pass along from one town to another, and since the depression the number has increased considerably. Some are very decent fellows, in search of work, but others often make a nuisance of themselves, and it is a difficult problem to know what is best to do about these "birds of passage." One of the first things they naturally do on arrival in a town is to find a place of shelter, and get some wood to make a fire. Sheds on reserves and empty houses are generally sought, and although the unfortunate men need shelter, they are seldom made welcome in any of their locations, and often adjacent wood-heaps suffer, while nearby residents are frequently perturbed by the proximity of so many of whom are of doubtful character.

Morwell Advertiser, 1934

They had been walking for an hour or more. Rowland's eyes had become accustomed to the darkness, but unable to see, Clyde stumbled often on the steep uneven ground and each yard was hard won. Razor sharp, the cold bit through exhaustion and pain. They stopped talking, and concentrated grimly on moving forward.

When Rowland first saw the distant light he said nothing, worried he might be imagining it. The light persisted. He told Clyde—

hoarsely, because he was parched. "It's hard to tell, but there's a light that couldn't be more than half a mile off."

Clyde nodded. "Carry on, Rowly," he wheezed. "I'm fine."

Soon Rowland realised the light was cast by a campfire. He had hoped it would be a more substantial sign of civilisation, but a camp at least meant humans and hopefully ones who were familiar with their bearings.

As they came within earshot, there were voices. Someone was playing a harmonica and perhaps, because of this, they were unnoticed until they walked into the midst of the campers. The man with the harmonica turned and caught sight of them first. He screamed, a high pitched cry of pure terror. He dropped the harmonica and scrambled away. "Sweet mother of God protect us!" The second man grabbed a stick and a third seized rocks.

Rowland pushed Clyde behind him, confused. "I'm sorry... Please don't..."

An Aboriginal man squatting by the fire started to laugh. "Cripes, what's wrong with you blokes?" he roared. He waved his hands above his head and wailed, "Wooooooooo."

"Rowly, what the devil is going on?" Clyde demanded, trying to make out something with the eye that was not completely closed.

"I'm not entirely sure," Rowland replied.

"They're just blokes who's been living rough, you fools," the laughing man told his compatriots. "Gawd that was funny... never seen men so scared. Petey here screaming for his mama... you lot getting ready to pelt these poor fellas with rocks!" He wiped tears from his eyes, and shook out his mirth. "Whoa, haven't laughed like that in ages." He stood and walked up to the bewildered intruders. "Albert Thompson. And who be you two?"

"Rowland Sinclair, Mr. Thompson. This is my friend, Clyde Watson Jones."

246 — SULARI GENTILL

Thompson turned to his companions. "Where are your manners, fellas? Let these gentlemen sit down; they've clearly had a hard day! And introduce yourselves for heaven's sake!"

The men made room beside the fire, sheepishly muttering their names as Petey Holmes, Steve Eather, Mick Green, Bruce McIntyre and Johnny Grady.

"What can we do for you gentlemen?" asked Eather, as he tossed the stick he'd grabbed to fight them off onto the fire.

"If we could trouble you for some water?" Rowland said.

"Oh, we can do better than that." Thompson pulled a billy off the coals and poured tea into tin enamel cups. He instructed his companions to shut up until their guests had drunk. The tea was weak but it was hot and it coated the woolly dryness of their throats.

"So did you fellas fall off that lorry that come past a couple of hours back?" Thompson asked.

"Yes, I suppose we did," Rowland replied.

"You blokes look like hell!" Thompson grinned. "Petey here thought he was looking at some kinda apparition!"

"Leave off, Albert!" Petey Holmes' voice was still a little shrill.

Rowland pulled a handkerchief from his pocket and, with Thompson's permission, moistened it from a water pail by the fire. He put the soaked cloth in Clyde's hand. "Hold this against your eye—one of them anyway. It's not as good as ice but it'll help."

Clyde applied the makeshift compress to his face.

"There'll be plenty of ice later," Eather said. "It's going be a cold night and that old bastard Jack Frost might visit, I reckon."

Rowland noticed how thin and thinly clad the men around the fire were. "What are you gentlemen doing out here?" he asked.

"Travelling," Thompson said. "We're looking for work... heading for Penrith."

"If we don't freeze to death in Leura," Mick Green added.

"Leura?" Rowland murmured. "We're in the Blue Mountains?"

Thompson nodded.

"How far are we out of Leura?" Clyde asked.

"'About ten miles."

Rowland groaned. They'd never make it tonight. Even if Clyde were in better shape, his own limbs were stiffening and heavy now.

"Are you in a hurry, Mr. Sinclair?" Thompson asked cheerily.

"There are a few people who are probably worried about us by now," Rowland said, wincing as he contemplated the reaction to their disappearance.

Thompson looked from him to Clyde. "Looks to me like they had good reason to be worried."

Eather chimed in sombrely. "We've only got one blanket to spare, so you gentlemen will have to share."

"Thank you," Rowland said, in no doubt that the spare blanket probably wasn't particularly surplus to requirements.

"It won't be enough," Thompson warned. He pulled several old newspapers out of a swag and showed Rowland how to line his jacket and Clyde's with the extra insulation. "If you blokes sleep close to the fire, you shouldn't freeze to death," he said optimistically.

Bruce McIntyre, who until that point had said barely a word, set the billy back on the coals. "We'd best clean you fellas up a little or you're going to scare the living Dickens out of Leura."

It was only then that Rowland realised how they must look. He couldn't see his own face of course, and he hadn't taken as many blows there as Clyde obviously had, but he was aware of dried blood on his forehead and in his hair.

Thompson took charge of Clyde, softening encrusted blood with a warm, soaked cloth and cleaning up his face in a manner that was surprisingly gentle. One of Clyde's eyes was starting to open again.

Grady produced a small flask and regretfully handed it over. "Seems like a bloody waste but you should probably clean out those cuts."

Thompson resoaked Rowland's handkerchief with rum and applied it to Clyde's cheek. Clyde swore, blanching as the alcohol burned the open wound.

"Sorry," Thompson murmured, giving the flask to Rowland. "On your forehead above your right eye."

"Here, I'll do it," Holmes volunteered, grabbing the flask and pouring rum directly upon the cut. Rowland pulled back from the sting as rum mixed with blood ran down his face and soaked his collar.

Grady leapt up and snatched back his flask. "Not so much, you bloody fool. This has gotta last me till we find work."

"So what is it that sees you fellas in such a state of dishevelment?" Thompson asked as his comrades bickered.

Clyde told him, more or less.

The campers made more tea as they listened, and when Clyde was finished Eather whistled low. "Where I come from, this kinda intervention is generally only called for when some bastard flatly refuses to marry your sister. So what are you gonna do?"

Clyde shrugged miserably. "I'm going to walk away."

"Because you'll get killed if you don't?"

"No, because Rosie wants it that way. She doesn't want me anymore."

"You won't be the first man to have his heart broken, mate," McIntyre said with obvious compassion. "I was in love once…"

One by one the men about the fire shared their own stories of romantic disaster. McIntyre's wife had run away with his brother; Eather's great love had thrown him over for a stockman from Kalgoorlie; Grady, it appeared, was running from his wife who, he claimed, had a murderous nature; Green had once proposed to a beauty who turned out to be a young man in a frock; and poor Petey Holmes had never even kissed a girl. Rowland wasn't wholly sure how comforting Clyde found the tales of empathetic woe, but they did help pass the time and distract them from the cold and the gnawing hunger of their bellies.

Rowland had no tale of tragic love to offer because he did not see his story that way, was determined it would not end that way. Instead he found his notebook, apparently overlooked by their abductors, and proceeded to draw the company of men from the snatches the flames illuminated. The firelight shaded their faces into stark gaunt planes, but their eyes were bright and unbeaten. Rowland pencilled thin limbs and hollow cheeks, suspecting that they too had gone some time without a meal, holding starvation at bay with weak, warm tea and conversation. He wondered how long they'd been travelling in search of work.

"My brother has a property in Yass," Rowland said quietly. "If you don't mind heading out there, I'm sure he could use some extra men." He had no idea if that were true, but something would be found.

"What, all of us?" Grady asked.

"Yes, of course."

"Must be a bloody big property to take on five extra men!" They laughed at him. They had met delusional men on the track before, raggedy men who believed they were kings and offered knighthoods for a cigarette. And la-di-da accents were not unheard of on the wallaby—the Depression had seen to that.

Edna strode determinedly up to the double doors. Nine in the morning was a strange time to find oneself at the threshold of a nightclub, but she was not there for the usual reasons.

Rowland and Clyde had not returned. There was no sign of them, though an envelope containing Rowland's pocketbook had been delivered to the gatehouse. The police were making enquiries of course, but they could find no one who would admit to having seen the two gentlemen enter the wine bar. Wilfred Sinclair had arranged and attended a meeting with Eric Campbell the previous evening to demand the return of his brother. The gleeful colonel had offered his sympathies and the services of his New Guardsmen in any search. Milton had set off to locate Wombat Newgate with every intention of beating the whereabouts of Clyde and Rowland out of the bookmaker. Edna too was not about to suffer quietly the abduction of her dearest friends. She had slipped out to call on old acquaintances.

The Lido at Bondi Beach was notorious for a disreputable clientele, expensive sly grog and cheap women. Its proprietor and the architect of its flamboyant immorality was Dr. Reginald Stuart Jones.

Jones' wife had informed Edna that her husband would be at the Lido that morning, doing what she did not know or care. Edna had considered waiting for Milton's return, but had decided the precaution was unnecessary. While Stuart Jones liked to attach himself to dangerous men, it was because he himself was a coward. In fact, false bravado would probably make the doctor less likely to cooperate in Milton's presence.

She pounded on the door of the converted dance hall. For a time there was no response, but she persisted. Eventually the door opened a crack and a furtive eye peered out. The eye widened and brightened and the door was swung wide. "Eddie, darlin'. What a simply delicious surprise!"

She pushed past and stepped into the Lido. "I need to speak to you."

Stuart Jones beamed. "I knew it! Your feigned indifference was for Sinclair's benefit, I suppose. But what he doesn't know..." His eyes moved quite deliberately to her waist. "I say, you're not in trouble, are you, gorgeous? Is that why you're here?"

"Don't be an idiot, Reggie. I want to know where you've taken Rowly."

"It's not Sinclair I want to take somewhere, darling." Stuart Jones put his arm about Edna's shoulders. "Unfortunately I'm just a teensy bit busy at the moment—"

"I don't care how busy you are!" Edna said, removing his arm.

"Eddie, angel," Stuart Jones pleaded. "I won't be long." He laughed and grabbed her around the waist. "You always were an irresistible minx. How about a kiss to tide you over?"

Edna hit him with her handbag. "Don't touch me! This is not funny, Reggie. Look, for old times' sake or because I'll kill you otherwise, tell me what you've done with them."

"Them?"

"Rowly and Clyde."

"I haven't done anything with them!"

"But you know who has. Just tell me Reggie—the authorities would probably look kindly on your help."

"It's not the police I would need to worry about, Eddie. But honestly darlin', I didn't even know they were missing till just now."

"Reg!" A man's voice from deep within the club. "Where the hell have you got to?"

Edna turned, as did Stuart Jones. The men who had come out of the offices behind the dance floor remained there for only seconds, but Edna saw them. And she recognised one of their number.

"What is Detective Hartley doing here?" she demanded.

"He's asking questions. The police always have questions."

"What is he asking about?"

"That's none of your business, beautiful."

"Perhaps he should ask you about Rowly and Clyde," Edna snapped. "How about I speak to him?"

"No!" Stuart Jones grabbed her arm before she could move. "Now Eddie, you just leave John Hartley alone. You seem... a little anxious, agitated... I could give you something for that."

"Let go of me!" Edna tried to shake him off but this time his grip was iron, and his face was as hard.

"I might just administer an anaesthetic to help you calm down."

Edna heard a door slam. Hartley and the other men had made an exit. She was alone with Stuart Jones. "I'll scream."

"Go ahead. If anyone hears you they'll understand why I had to give you something to settle your nerves."

"No one will believe that. I'm not one of your unfortunate patients, Reggie!"

"A woman like you? Just the kind to need my discreet professional services."

Edna kicked, connecting with the doctor's shin. She broke for the door. He came after her, catching Edna at the door and clamping a manicured hand over her mouth. The sculptress fought like a wildcat, and Stuart Jones whispered as much in her ear as he dragged her back into the nightclub.

26

WOMAN'S DEATH

Doctor Exonerated

SYDNEY, Wednesday

"Death could have been caused by shock, but it is the most extraordinary death that I have ever seen," declared Dr. Reginald Stuart Jones, of Macquarie Street city, today, giving evidence at the inquest into the death of Mrs. Adeline Amy Jones, 42, wife of a Grenfell farmer, while she was being given an anaesthetic by Dr. Jones to facilitate a medical examination.

The witness said that he had been called in to see Mrs. Jones. She was extremely nervous and agitated, however, and he suggested the anaesthetic to complete the examination. She agreed. She had only taken about twelve breaths when he saw her colour change. When he removed the mask she was barely conscious. He gave her an injection of adrenalin, and asked for someone to call another doctor. He then resorted to artificial respiration until she died.

"I had just finished, and stood up exhausted and dripping with perspiration, when Di Macnamara came in," continued the witness. He said "It is jolly bad luck."

Witnesses said that it was usual to administer an anaesthetic to examine a patient in such circumstances, and even without anyone else being present.

The Coroner returning a finding of death from shock said that he thought the practice of giving anaesthetics in private houses by a doctor who was by himself was not a desirable one. In the evidence disclosed the deceased was a woman of excessive nervous temperament. The state of her nerves was entirely due to her own feelings, and caused the cessation of her heart action. The doctor was entirely absolved.

The Canberra Times, 1935

They set out for Leura at first light, slowly, as the blood frozen in their veins was coaxed to flow again with movement and billy tea. The swelling around one of Clyde's eyes had subsided and he could see to walk. Rowland stayed within reach nevertheless. The dirt track joined a more substantial road within a mile, and seven men trudged two abreast, with Thompson at the lead. Petey Holmes whistled God Save the King in a manner that seemed to have no end. Otherwise they said little.

Rowland's mind settled on the murder of White and he brooded there, wrestling with what had evolved over the past days. The race had muddled his thinking, crowded his perspective so that he was distracted. The miles before him were an opportunity to focus and think clearly.

He tried to picture White, portly with thinning slicked hair, a creased suit and that tiepin—Les Bocquet's tiepin. Bocquet had claimed the pin was an anniversary gift from his wife. Rowland considered the design—two horseshoes in the centre of a bar. Was it intended as a lucky charm or did Bocquet simply like horses? Why would Beryl give her husband a talisman of good fortune, unless fortune was something Les called on regularly? Perhaps he gambled. On reflection, Rowland didn't believe that the Bocquets had been burgled, or that the maid had taken the jewellery. The tiepin had almost certainly left the Bocquet residence through the hands of either Mr. or Mrs. Bocquet. Which, he wasn't sure.

What White had been doing at Magdalene's still perplexed him. Perhaps there'd be some clue in the reporter's notebook. Mollie

Horseman had said White was looking into the occult, and the girl employed to weep at the House of the Macabre had spoken of clandestine meetings. Rowland had never really embraced the current fascination with the supernatural but he was aware that some took the fashion quite seriously. He remembered, fondly, Annie Besant who had passed away the year before. The old theosophist had been his friend. Rowland admired her deeply and though she seemed to believe in the stuff of myth and fancy, he had never dismissed the honesty of that belief. Perhaps it was some exposé of alternative religion or black magic that had incited someone to murder the reporter.

"Rowly," Clyde said quietly. "What are we actually going to do when we get to Leura? We have no money."

"I'll book a call through to Wil, reverse the charges. He'll sort something out—send someone to get us."

"You might ask him to send a few sandwiches as well."

It was nearly mid-morning when they finally walked into the small mountain town of Leura. Rowland cast his eyes up to the Italianate guesthouse which looked over the town from its highest point. The smoke that spilled from its chimneys promised warmth and perhaps a meal. He pointed it out to his companions. "There's bound to be a telephone there."

Thompson and Eather exchanged an amused glance. "You're ambitious Sinclair, I'll give you that."

Clyde squinted at the street through his one good eye. There didn't seem to be a police station that he could see. He was, by virtue of experience, a little more realistic about how men in their current state would be received at a genteel guesthouse. But perhaps the Sinclair name would be recognised even here.

They were stopped at the gatehouse where a gardener informed them that there was no work. He pointed to a sign that prohibited hawkers and beggars.

Politely, but firmly, Rowland asked to see the manager. As firmly, though not at all politely, the gardener told them to clear off.

"Come on, mate, let's go," Thompson said. "You don't need to impress us. We ain't nothing."

A housekeeper came out to investigate the disturbance. Rowland introduced himself and Clyde. "Mr. Watson Jones and I have been involved in… an accident. Could I trouble you, madam, for the use of your telephone?"

The housekeeper inhaled conspicuously and then grimaced in a manner pointed. "It seems to me, Mr. Sinclair—if that is your name—that you and your companions have been consorting with the demon drink. I will not allow you and your kind onto the premises! Now get on your way before I call the police."

Having, like Clyde, ascertained that the town didn't have its own police station, Rowland decided to press his luck. "Madam, if you are making a call perhaps you could telephone Mr. Wilfred Sinclair at *Roburvale* in Woollahra, yourself. I'd be happy to compensate you for the telephone call and for your trouble."

"I don't believe you are in any position to compensate anyone, my good man." She sighed. "It's against my better judgement, but if you go around to the tradesmen's entrance I'll see if Cook has any porridge left over from breakfast."

"That's not necessary—" Rowland began.

"Be quiet, Sinclair," Thompson interrupted, pushing Rowland back. "Thank you, kindly, madam. The trade entrance is this way, is it?"

The housekeeper sniffed. "Wait outside the door and don't let the guests see you, mind. If there's any trouble I'll have Gerry fetch his shotgun!"

The gardener nodded. "Happy to oblige."

"We don't want any trouble, madam," Thompson said with his hands in the air. "But that porridge would be most welcome."

"Go on with you then. I'll have someone come to the back door, and then you'll have to move on."

Thompson thanked her and grabbing Rowland's arm to make sure he didn't talk them out of breakfast, led his derelict band around the property to the door at the back of the kitchen.

Gerry, the gardener, watched every step, a spade at the ready.

"What are we going to do now, Rowly?" Clyde murmured.

"Breakfast, I believe."

"And after that?"

"We might be able to send a telegram at the post office."

"With no money?"

Rowland rubbed the back of his neck. "We'll have to try."

Milton Isaacs guessed immediately that Edna had gone after Reginald Stuart Jones. He cursed. The sculptress had always underestimated how dangerous their old acquaintance could be. To her, he was still "pudgy Reggie"; ineffectual and pitiful. Even now, he elicited her compassion as much as her ire.

But the poet knew full well that Reginald Stuart Jones had changed. He was no longer innocuous and he had learned much from the associations he had made while moving with the criminal classes.

Milton did not need to telephone Stuart Jones' wife to know the doctor would be at the Lido. The nightclub had been Stuart Jones' primary place of business for a couple of years.

As he was leaving *Woodlands* to find Edna, Milton spotted Errol Flynn's Triumph easing to a stop at the gate. He sprinted down the long driveway to meet it and jumped into the passenger seat.

"I say, old chap, what are you doing?" Flynn asked as the wild-eyed poet landed beside him.

"Ed's in a spot of trouble. Turn around. We need to get to Bondi Beach."

"What sort of trouble?"

"The kind that might just get her killed. Now drive!"

Without any further hesitation Flynn turned the car around and applied the skills he'd learned on the Maroubra Speedway.

A maid came to the back door with green and yellow enamel plates of thick porridge. Leftover from earlier in the morning the porridge had become lumpy and congealed, but, to the cold, famished men, it was ambrosia. They ate without speaking, scraping the plates clean as they stood at the back door. When the maid came to the door to collect the plates, Rowland asked if she would call her mistress to speak with him.

"The mistress is very busy," the servant said uncertainly.

"Please," he said. "It's extremely important."

The maid wiped her hands on the crisp white of her apron.

"I'll only need a moment of her time."

"Wait here," the maid said, relenting. "I'll ask."

The housekeeper came to the door clearly irritated by the further imposition. "What is it?" she snapped.

"I hoped, madam, to persuade you to reconsider the use of your telephone." Rowland spoke quickly before she could stop him. "I am Rowland Sinclair of Woollahra. Mr. Watson Jones and I were abducted and robbed. If not for the kindness of strangers, we might have frozen to death last night." He unfastened his wristwatch and handed it to her. "Please take this as a sign of good faith that I will compensate you and this establishment for the kindness you've already shown. We have been missing for over a day now and I must get word to my brother."

The housekeeper looked at the watch he'd pressed into her hand. Despite the cracked crystal it was obviously an expensive piece. Probably stolen. She turned it over. The initials RHFS were engraved on the case.

"Rowland Henry Ffrench Sinclair," Rowland said quietly.

"Ffrench…?"

"My mother's family name."

"With two 'f's?"

"Yes."

"My aunt did for a family called Ffrench…" the housekeeper said almost to herself.

"Mother's people were from Cootamundra."

Perhaps the housekeeper's aunt had worked for the Ffrenches of Cootamundra—Rowland could not tell, but she did ask him for Wilfred's details. He obliged, and she instructed him to wait. Minutes later she returned, and asked him to follow her.

With a hopeful glance at Clyde, Rowland did so. She directed him to a telephone in the office.

"Rowly, what the hell are you doing in Leura?" Wilfred demanded the moment he took the phone. "Are you all right?"

"Yes, I think so," Rowland replied. He told his brother that he and Clyde had been abducted and robbed, that they'd been left in the wilderness a few miles from Leura. But he was deliberately vague as to the details of why.

"Why did these ruffians feel the need to give you a thrashing? Do you need medical attention?" Wilfred asked brusquely.

"Clyde should probably see a doctor, but we'll be fine until we get back to Sydney."

"I'll send a car and driver directly. I've already made arrangements with Mrs. Garrick to provide you with whatever else you need until they arrive."

"Look Wil, the five chaps that helped us... they're looking for work. I don't suppose you could use anyone on *Oaklea*?"

"Are they Communists?"

"I really have no idea."

Wilfred sighed. "Put them on a train to Yass. Tell them to alight at the *Oaklea* siding. I'll have Harry arrange something for them."

Errol Flynn's Triumph approached the Lido just as several motorcars pulled out. "Looks like Reggie's had some friends over," Milton murmured. He knew Stuart Jones' Studebaker and it was not among the departing vehicles. They pulled over on Ramsgate Road and waited until the last car had moved out of sight before driving onto the premises. He recognised Stuart Jones' vehicle parked inconspicuously at the far end of the Beach Court complex.

Milton led Flynn behind the nightclub building. "The door 'round the back will be easier to force," he said.

"Shouldn't we knock first?" Flynn asked uneasily.

"Reggie Jones carries a gun, Errol. All we've got is the element of surprise."

"I see," Flynn said gravely. "Carry on then."

The back door of the dance hall was not particularly secure. The lock was rusted and it had clearly been kicked in and repaired a number of times.

"Right." Milton's voice was grim. "On the count of three."

Flynn licked his lips and stood ready.

The door gave way on the second charge, bursting open into a long dimly lit hallway with several doors on either side.

A woman in a nurse's uniform waiting outside one closed door screamed as they stumbled in. Milton pushed past the woman and threw open the door to reveal Stuart Jones. He wore a white smock over his suit which was possibly what hampered him in pulling the gun out of this pocket. The nurse continued to scream, as Flynn launched himself at the doctor bringing Stuart Jones unceremoniously to the ground. The revolver, which he had just managed to grasp, skittered across the floor and under a bench. Milton left it there, preoccupied with the unconscious form laid out on a makeshift operating table.

A white sheet only partially covered the sculptress. Her dress and stockings had been removed and she was attired in only her cotton slip. A medical mask designed for the administration of ether covered most of her face and she had been strapped down. Milton ripped off the mask and unfastened the restraints. Edna was unnaturally pale and her breathing shallow.

He swore at Stuart Jones. "What the devil have you done to her, you belly-crawling worm?"

"I was examining her," Stuart Jones said calmly. "Miss Higgins suffers from a somewhat nervous disposition and so I administered just a whiff of anaesthetic to keep her calm."

"Examining her? Like hell! Why isn't she waking up, you bastard?"

"Sometimes the anaesthetic can lead to shock. If you'd get your pretty buffoon to unhand me, I could have a look at her—"

"Touch her and you'll answer to me, Jones." Milton slipped his arms under Edna and lifted her from the table. "We need to get her to a doctor—"

"Dear fellow, I am a doctor—" Stuart Jones protested.

"And then we go to the police and have this dingo locked up," Milton finished.

Stuart Jones did not seem the least bit perturbed. "As my nurse will attest, Miss Higgins came in for an examination of a discreet nature. I administered anaesthetic to calm her so I could carry out that examination, which you interrupted. If Miss Higgins' heart stops due to shock, it'll be jolly bad luck exacerbated by the fact that you will not allow me to attend to my patient."

Milton might have swung at the doctor if his arms had not been otherwise occupied carrying Edna out of the Lido. Flynn dragged Stuart Jones out to the Triumph with them, waiting for Milton's instructions on how to deal with the doctor.

Milton placed Edna carefully into the vehicle. "Just hang on old thing," he whispered as he placed his ear to her lips to check she was still breathing.

"What do you want me to do with this scurvy wretch, Mr. Isaacs?" Flynn asked.

"Let him go," Milton said straightening. "The police'll know where to find him."

Somewhat reluctantly Flynn obliged. Stuart Jones rubbed the arm the actor had twisted behind his back, and opened his mouth to speak.

Milton punched him. He watched the doctor stagger and fall before he climbed into the Triumph beside the unconscious sculptress and valiantly resisted instructing Flynn to drive over Stuart Jones on the way out.

27

ABORTION ALLEGED

Following on the admission of a 17-year-old girl to the Women's Hospital last night in a serious condition, police arrested the mother of the girl, a nurse, another woman and a young man on a charge of conspiring to bring about a certain event.

The Braidwood Dispatch and Mining Journal, 1932

While awaiting the arrival of Johnston and the Rolls Royce, Rowland took rooms at *Leura House* for the five men who'd given them refuge the night before. Arrangements were made with the manager and housekeeper to keep them in every comfort. He'd had to press the point with respect to Thompson whom the housekeeper initially refused to accommodate. However, in the face of Rowland's insistence, his obvious offence that she was in any way reluctant to afford hospitality to the gentleman, and the fact that he was turning out to be a very good customer indeed, she relented.

"I've taken the liberty of booking your passages to Central Station and then out to Yass for the day after tomorrow," Rowland said as they were seated in the dining room for a proper breakfast. "If you'd care to work on a sheep property, there's employment at *Oaklea.*"

They regarded him with a mute awe that made Rowland intensely uncomfortable. "Did I misunderstand…?"

"No. Crikey no," Thompson said shaking his head. "It's just we thought you was having us on... a bit of wag trying to save face you know. We figured you was just a bloke down on his luck, like us."

"I am just a bloke," Rowland said. "But I'm more fortunate than most, I suppose. Believe me, happening upon you chaps last night was a tremendous stroke of luck."

"You don't have to do all this Mr. Sinclair," said Petey Holmes. "We woulda let anyone sit at our fire."

"Thank God, bacon!" Rowland murmured as a platter of rashers was placed on the table with eggs and sausages. "You were generous with what you had, Mr. Holmes. Please allow me to express my gratitude and then let us agree to never talk of it again."

"You're a good egg, Sinclair," murmured Grady as he crammed fresh bread spread with pale yellow butter into his mouth.

"How about you, Jones?" Eather said to Clyde. "Are you rich, too?"

"Haven't got two pennies to rub together," Clyde replied, gazing with his one good eye upon a plate piled high with the kind of fare to which he'd become accustomed at Rowland Sinclair's table. He was getting quite disgracefully soft, but at that moment he was too excited about the bacon to care.

By the time Johnston arrived, it was nearly midday and Rowland and Clyde had cleaned themselves up a little with soap and water and iodine. They still smelled vaguely of rum, Clyde's face remained alarming and their suits were in need of a tailor's attention, but they felt much restored by the comforts of *Leura House*.

Wilfred Sinclair was at his brother's house when Flynn's Triumph returned. Percy Armstrong had called from the gate to tell him that Miss Higgins had been injured. Exasperated but concerned nonetheless, he telephoned the surgery of Frederick Maguire and summoned him hence. Why the prominent Sydney surgeon dropped everything to respond was not apparent, but the exact machinations of Wilfred Sinclair's influence were often inscrutable.

Milton carried Edna into the house, laying her on the chaise longue in the ladies' drawing room. He explained to Wilfred what had happened, as he watched anxiously for any sign that her breathing had slowed further. Appalled for many reasons, Wilfred sent servants for blankets, brandy and smelling salts. And he telephoned the police.

"What happened to Miss Higgins' clothes?" Wilfred asked quietly. He needed to know how bad this was.

"That bastard, Stuart Jones, wanted to make it look like he was examining her, I expect," Milton said firmly, determinedly. "If she'd been fully clothed that story would have seemed untenable."

"I see." Wilfred did not voice an alternative, whatever he may have feared. "And what exactly was his purpose, Mr. Isaacs?"

"Clearly, Ed discovered where he'd stowed Rowly and Clyde. He was trying to keep her quiet."

"My brother has been found, Mr. Isaacs—he and Mr. Watson Jones. I came to inform you in person."

"What? Where are they?" Milton demanded.

Wilfred walked to the window to look for Maguire's motorcar. "Leura—I sent Johnston to fetch them. It appears they were abducted from Leichhardt and abandoned in the wilderness some miles out of town."

"Are they all right?"

"Rowly seems to think they'll live, which does beg the question as to why Mr. Stuart Jones would go so far as to attempt to murder Miss Higgins."

Maguire's arrival forestalled further discussion. The gentlemen stood aside as the eminent surgeon examined Edna.

"She's suffering from an overdose of ethyl ether," he concluded, reaching into his bag. "Fortunately Miss. Higgins has not gone into severe shock or stopped breathing, but she will nevertheless require some assistance to come out of the anaesthetic." Maguire filled a hypodermic and injected the sculptress with what he informed them was adrenalin. The results were immediate.

Edna gasped, her eyelids fluttered. "Rowly?" she breathed.

Flynn rushed to her side. "How are you, sailor? It's me, Errol."

Edna retched and Maguire informed them that nausea was a perfectly normal and expected reaction to the anaesthetic. He issued instructions to Mary Brown for Edna's care, prescribing sweet foods, hydration and bed rest.

As she was still disoriented when the police arrived, they spoke to Milton and Flynn first, taking over the study for that purpose. Ordinarily Milton would have been startled by the fact that not only Detectives Delaney and Hartley, but Bill Mackay, the Superintendent of the Metropolitan Police, had been despatched to investigate. But then, it had been Wilfred Sinclair who had called the police. Given that, it was probably more surprising that Commissioner Childs had not come himself.

Milton and Flynn recounted what had happened. Delaney and Hartley asked the questions. Mackay stood back, silently watching his detectives. "How did you know Miss Higgins would seek out Dr. Stuart Jones, Mr. Isaacs?" Hartley began.

"We had assumed Rowly and Clyde had fallen foul of bookmakers, Detective. Edna knew Reginald Stuart Jones had contacts in that world."

"She might simply have been shopping might she not?"

"Not with Rowly and Clyde missing. Anyway it turns out I was right, so what does it matter what she might have been doing?"

Hartley ignored the challenge. "Mr. Sinclair and Mr. Watson Jones have been located, I believe."

"Yes."

"So Dr. Stuart Jones had nothing to do with their disappearance."

"We don't know that yet." Milton glanced at Delaney. The detective looked troubled, but he did not interfere with Hartley's line of questioning.

"Why was Miss Higgins acquainted with Dr. Stuart Jones?"

"We knew him years ago…, when he was still a medical student."

"You and Miss Higgins seem to have a number of unfortunate past acquaintances."

"What do you mean by that, Detective?"

"Didn't you also describe the late Mr. Crispin White as an old acquaintance?"

"What has one thing got to do with the other?" Milton demanded, incensed that Hartley would use this to pursue him for White's murder.

Delaney cleared his throat and pulled Hartley aside. Though Milton could not hear what was said, it was clearly not an amicable conversation. Mackay joined the sidebar briefly and the whispered dispute was curtailed.

"Are you aware that Dr. Stuart Jones has a reputation for being willing to carry out certain illegal procedures on women?" Hartley barked when they returned.

"If that's the case, shouldn't you jolly well arrest him?"

"I don't suppose Miss Higgins visited Dr. Stuart Jones in his professional capacity."

"I beg your bloody pardon!" Milton roared, outraged.

"Dr. Stuart Jones presented at CIB Headquarters just minutes before we received Mr. Sinclair's telephone call," Hartley said steadily, almost smugly. "He states that he was assaulted, and a patient he was examining, abducted. He feared for the patient's wellbeing as she was forcibly removed from his care while under anaesthetic. His account is collaborated by the statement of his nurse, a Miss Macnamara."

For a moment Milton was speechless. "I expect Miss Higgins will confirm why she called on that lowlife grub and it will have nothing to do with his professional capacity."

"I have no doubt," Delaney said glaring at John Hartley.

Hartley would not retreat. "Miss Higgins has every reason to deny Dr. Stuart Jones' account."

"Because it's a pack of lies!" Milton appealed to Delaney. "You can't believe this!"

"What I believe is immaterial," Delaney said with a wary glance at Mackay. "It's a matter of what will stand up in court, Mr. Isaacs. Stuart Jones is a doctor."

"But Flynn was there too," Milton persisted. "Surely that's enough?"

"Unfortunately, nothing Mr. Flynn has said actually contradicts Dr. Stuart Jones' version of events," Hartley said, with no indication that he thought it unfortunate at all.

"This is insane! If we hadn't arrived he might have killed her!" Milton slammed his fist on the table.

"Mr. Isaacs, calm yourself, sir!" the superintendent intervened as the feelings rose dangerously.

Wilfred Sinclair entered the room. The policemen and the poet all fell silent as he glared from one to the other. "Miss Higgins' physician is willing to allow you to speak with her now," he said.

"Very good," Mackay replied. He motioned for Delaney and Hartley to proceed before him, and nodding curtly, followed his detectives into the ladies' drawing room.

Edna now sat upright on the chaise longue holding a cup of sweet honeyed tea. Still wearing only a cotton slip, her modesty was maintained by blankets. She smiled when she saw Delaney, though her voice was hoarse and strained. "Hello, Colin. Did you hear? Rowly and Clyde have been found!"

Professional though he was, Delaney could not help smiling in return. "I'm so glad you weren't hurt, Miss Higgins."

Hartley cleared his throat primly and Edna noticed his presence for the first time. The tea cup clattered into its saucer and her hands shook perceptibly. Delaney moved quickly to take the cup and saucer from her. "Are you unwell, Miss Higgins? Can I get you anything?"

"Of course she's unwell," Maguire growled from his stance by the fire. "Ether is a particularly dangerous chemical in the wrong hands, and Miss Higgins was clearly in the wrong hands."

Mackay exhaled impatiently. "Dr. Maguire—"

"Mr. Maguire," the surgeon corrected.

"Mr. Maguire, then. Would you mind leaving the room while the detectives and I interview Miss Higgins?"

"Actually yes, I would mind. Miss Higgins has only just been brought out of anaesthetic." Maguire met Mackay's cold gaze with one that was equally icy. "I have always been taught to be cautious," he said slowly, "and leaving Miss Higgins now would undoubtedly be an abrogation of my duty of care as her physician."

In the silence that followed Edna struggled to remember why the presence of John Hartley distressed her particularly.

"Very well," Mackay said, irritably. "You may stay." He motioned for Hartley to carry on.

Hartley positioned himself so he was facing Edna, his arms crossed. "Miss Higgins, can you tell us why you called upon Dr. Stuart Jones at his place of work?"

"I thought Reggie's idiot friends had taken Rowly and Clyde to fix this stupid car race," Edna said. "I thought I could get him to tell me where they were."

"Were you not afraid for your own safety, Miss Higgins, if you were as you say convinced Dr. Stuart Jones was involved in the abduction of Mr. Sinclair and Mr. Watson Jones?"

"I've known Reggie Jones since I was fifteen."

"You trusted him?"

"Trust is too strong a word… I didn't think he'd…" She stopped.

"Was there no other reason?"

"What other reason could there be?"

"Dr. Stuart Jones has made a claim that you are his patient and that you came to the premises at Beach Court for an examination."

Shocked, Edna addressed the detective sharply, "I am not his patient, and even if I were, I promise you I would not seek treatment of any sort in a sordid nightclub!"

Hartley's barrel chest seemed to deflate a little. "Yes, well…"

Edna was not finished. "And what's more, I have no need of Reggie's particular specialty!"

Delaney intervened. "Do you have any thoughts as to why he would claim that you were his patient, why he would do what he did?"

"He panicked," Edna said tentatively. So much was still hazy, confused.

"Why do you say that?"

"I'm not sure… I remember we were shouting and then he grabbed me… and then…" she shook her head.

"I believe that's quite enough for today." Maguire intervened, moving to the chaise longue and checking Edna's eyes. "Miss Higgins needs to rest. Perhaps you might conclude this interview tomorrow when her recollections are clearer."

"Of course," Delaney said quickly.

But Hartley was reluctant. "It's important to establish—"

"Superintendent Mackay," Maguire cut Hartley off by addressing his superior. "I'm sure you would not wish to place Miss Higgins' wellbeing at unnecessary risk."

Mackay's nostrils flared and his jaw tensed truculently. "Very well. Tomorrow then."

Johnston delivered Rowland and Clyde to *Woodlands House* just as it was getting dark. Meeting them on the sandstone steps, Wilfred looked hard at both men, grimacing slightly at the sight of Clyde's battered face even in the waning light. "Clearly we have a great deal to discuss," he said, "but perhaps I ought to have Maguire look at you while he's here."

"Why is he here?" Rowland asked. Wilfred had always seemed able to produce the surgeon as if Maguire resided in his back pocket, but surely he would not have summoned the poor man to sit and wait for their return.

Wilfred hesitated. "He was called to treat Miss Higgins."

"Ed?" Both Rowland and Clyde reacted. "Why?"

Wilfred told them what had happened, as he understood it. He was quite honest. "It seems Mr. Isaacs and Mr. Flynn arrived in the nick of time."

"Where is she?" Rowland demanded.

"Maguire has had her confined to bed. Mr. Isaacs is sitting with her, I believe."

Rowland and Clyde were already charging into the entrance hall, taking the grand staircase two and three steps at a time to Edna's bedroom on the second floor. The suite had once been the guest quarters reserved for the Sinclairs' most illustrious and discerning guests. Rowland had given it to the sculptress. Built into one of the corner towers of the gothic-styled mansion, the room boasted a ceiling some thirty feet above its mosaicked floor. The windows were commensurately immense in scale and looked out over the grounds and beyond. It was furnished eclectically with finely crafted pieces, chosen by past generations of Sinclairs, and the battered trunks and gramophone, which Edna herself had added. Behind a folding oriental screen a marble bust in progress sat on a working plinth. There was artwork, of course, paintings by Rowland and Clyde, etchings by Norman Lindsay and the occasional two dimensional work by Edna herself.

Rowland and Clyde paused at the doorway, not wanting to startle Edna. Milton, ensconced in an armchair, looked up from his vigil. Edna was asleep, child-like in too-big pyjamas she'd stolen from Rowland at some point in the past. Lenin had settled on the end of the bed with his long nose burrowed into the covers by Edna's feet. Edna's rescued cat nursed her kittens in a basket near the hearth.

The poet smiled, relieved to see his friends, though he was shocked by the state of them. "Flaming oath, aren't you blokes a sight for sore eyes!"

28

CHARGES OF POLICE CORRUPTION

SYDNEY, Thursday

The Commissioner of Police this morning detailed a senior detective to investigate the charges of corruption in connection with starting price betting made by Mr. McDicken in the Legislative Assembly yesterday.

Northern Star, 1932

Edna heard the deep murmur of men in conversation before she opened her eyes. For a while she didn't interrupt them, until she heard Rowland say quite plainly, "I'm going to kill him!"

"Don't you dare plot murder without me," she said, sitting up.

They rushed to her bedside and she screamed. "Clyde! What happened to your face?"

Lenin leapt off the bed, collecting his master in exuberant mid-flight. Rowland staggered back. "Settle down, Len. I've only been gone a day," he said, trying vainly to calm the dog.

Horrified, Edna reached up to touch Clyde's swollen and blackened eyes. "Oh, does it hurt? I really will kill Reggie for this!"

"This wasn't the doc or any of his mates, Ed," Clyde confessed.

"Perhaps you and Rowly could enlighten us as to what exactly happened to you, Mr. Watson Jones." Wilfred stood at the door unwilling to enter a lady's bedroom without invitation, even in a house that was technically his.

"Mr. Sinclair," Edna said. "Please come in."

Wilfred nodded and stepped into the room. "Thank you, Miss Higgins. I trust you're feeling better?"

"I am, Mr. Sinclair, thanks to Mr. Maguire. Is he still here? Clyde appears to be in pressing need of him and Rowly's really not much better." The sculptress knelt on the bed to scrutinise their faces. "What on earth happened?"

Clyde told them, adding humiliation to all the other injuries of the past days.

"They thought you were trying to blackmail them?" Edna said, aghast.

"It was all a dreadful misunderstanding," Clyde said glumly.

Wilfred walked towards the door, and then changed his mind and came back. He poked his brother in the chest. "How many times have I told you that your insistence on painting these poor women in such a disgraceful state of undress would catch up with you? If she'd been my daughter... For the love of God, Rowly!"

"It really wasn't Rowly's—" Clyde began in defence of his friend, but Wilfred wouldn't hear it.

"I'll tell Maguire to expect you down in a couple of minutes," he said, stalking out of the room in disgust.

For several moments there was silence in Wilfred's wake.

Then Milton laughed. "I'm sorry mate," he said to Clyde. "I feel for you, I really do. But blackmail..."

"I'm sorry about Wilfred, Rowly." Clyde sighed.

Rowland wrinkled his nose. "Don't let it concern you. Wil's happiest when he has something to berate me about."

Edna took his hand and Clyde's in each of hers. "I'd hug you both but I'm afraid I might hurt you," she said biting her lower lip as she considered them. "You go and see Mr. Maguire... get him to patch you up. You mustn't worry about me; I'm well on the mend."

Rowland pressed her hand to his lips. "We won't be long. And then we shall plot that murder." With that promise, they left to deal with their injuries.

The Sinclair brothers argued while Maguire finished examining Clyde to ensure that the artist's eyes had not sustained any permanent damage. Rowland took his brother's displeasure in his stride. He'd grown accustomed to Wilfred's disapprobation, learned to judge its level. Wilfred was more exasperated than truly angry. It was not as if Rowland's interest in painting from life was a recent passion. Wilfred knew what his brother did.

Wilfred wanted to inform the police and have the Martinelli men arrested en masse. Clyde was reluctant, and Rowland indifferent enough to defer to the feelings of his jilted friend.

"They dropped us near a road outside Leura, Wil. I believe they were trying to frighten more than really hurt us."

"I beg to differ," Maguire murmured. "While your face isn't nearly as damaged as Mr. Watson Jones', you're both black and blue." He stepped back and considered Clyde thoughtfully. "It's as if Mr. Watson Jones' face offended them particularly."

"I think it's more to do with the fact that I'm taller." Rowland spoke as a past pugilist. "It's easier to hit me in the body than to leave yourself open reaching for my head. You'd hardly need to raise your arm at all to punch Clyde in the eye."

"Fair go," Clyde muttered, straightening.

But Maguire nodded. "Yes, I can see how that would happen. I take it these hoodlums weren't particularly tall?"

"The police will measure them when they're processed," Wilfred said curtly.

"If this goes to court," Clyde said desperately, "the fact that Rosie modelled for the painting will come out. She'll be humiliated, ruined. I'm not sure her new fiancé even knows I exist."

"I don't know how things are done in Italy, but they can't go about abducting and assaulting innocent citizens here!" Wilfred declared angrily.

"To be fair, they didn't know we were innocent citizens," Rowland offered. "They thought we were blackmailers attempting to destroy the good name of their sister and daughter. Milt tells us they even returned my pocketbook."

"You want to let this matter go?" Wilfred asked, clearly unhappy with the mere idea.

"It might be the gentlemanly thing to do, all things considered." Rowland resorted to what he knew was Wilfred's quite earnest and entrenched sense of chivalry.

Wilfred stared at them both. "They may have been behind the shooting!"

"The timing isn't right," Rowland argued. "Clyde had just left the painting with Miss Martinelli's landlady when the shot was fired. They hadn't had time to want me dead."

"What if this isn't the end of it?"

"It will be," Clyde said. "There was only one painting."

Wilfred closed his eyes. "Lord, give me patience. Very well, we won't involve the police, though I'm sure it won't be long before you give them cause to call again!"

They gathered that night in Edna's bedroom, dragging their chairs around her bed as she sat cross-legged amongst the rumpled bedclothes. In lieu of supper, and on Rowland's request, Mary Brown had sent up a tray of bread, a dish of butter, a silver pot of some new hot chocolate drink and a decanter of brandy, which Milton insisted upon for its medicinal properties.

"I'll telephone Joan tomorrow and tell her I'm pulling out of the race," Rowland said determinedly.

"What?" Edna gasped. "Why on earth would you do that?"

"I'm not putting you in any further danger, Ed."

"Don't be daft, Rowly. I'm not in any danger."

"That blasted coward tried to kill you! God, if he'd succeeded, I would never have—"

Edna reached out and placed her hand on his. "He didn't Rowly. And even if he had, it wouldn't have been because you were driving in some silly charity race."

"How do you surmise that?" Milton asked.

"There were men meeting with him at the Lido when I arrived. I interrupted them. I think that was what panicked him."

"And who were these gentlemen?" Rowland asked.

"I think one of them was Detective Hartley."

"The bloke in charge of the investigation into White's murder?" Clyde asked incredulously.

"Yes, I'm almost certain of it."

"Almost?"

"It's all still a little confused… but I remember now that Reggie and I argued about Detective Hartley… Reggie didn't want me to talk to him."

Milton poured himself a cup of frothing milky chocolate from the silver pot and took a sip. "What is this stuff?"

"It's called Milo," Edna said. "It came in my sample bag. They launched it at the show this year."

Milton tilted his head as he considered the taste, and then added a liberal splash of brandy to what was remaining in his cup. "It's a bit odd that Mackay came to interview Edna himself, don't you think? One would have thought he had superintendent-type activities to occupy his time… and why was that fool Hartley here?"

"Perhaps he wanted to be on hand if Ed revealed he was at the Lido." Rowland loosened his tie.

"What about Mackay?" Clyde placed the plate of bread he'd just toasted in the fireplace on the bed in front of Edna.

"I got the distinct impression that he was there to referee between Hartley and Delaney," Milton said on reflection.

Edna buttered a slice for Lenin who was watching the proceedings with liquid-brown begging eyes. "Since Reggie didn't abduct you two," she said thoughtfully, "there must have been some other reason he panicked like that. Perhaps it was to do with Hartley."

Rowland took the thick toast that Edna handed him. He met her eye sternly. "Ed, please don't do anything like that again."

"Like what?" she asked innocently, allocating toast to Milton and Clyde and handing a loaded toasting fork to the latter.

"Like setting out to confront a dangerous criminal on your own."

She smiled. "I would have taken you along, Rowly, but you had very carelessly got yourself abducted!"

"I'm serious, Ed."

"Well don't be, it doesn't suit you." Edna pulled her knees up and clasped her hands around them.

"Ed, please…" Rowland shook his head. "You should have waited for Milt."

Edna's face softened but there was an edge to her words. "I made a mistake with Reggie, I admit it. But I'm not made of glass and I'm not nearly as reckless as you and Milt, or even Clyde."

Rowland hesitated. He'd caught the warning in the sculptress' voice. Edna would not be told what to do, however well the direction was meant. She would not tolerate any attempt to contain her. But his instinct was to protect her.

"Well you were bloody lucky that Flynn and I turned up when we did." Milton was less circumspect about Edna's independence. "The police seem inclined to believe Stuart Jones' cock and bull story even with you around to deny it. He'd have had no trouble getting away with this if you'd died of an overdose of ether." Milton swigged his brandy bitterly. "He may yet get away with it." The poet recounted his interview with the police—Hartley's apparent reluctance to believe that Edna had not gone to see Stuart Jones as a patient. "It all makes sense if the bastard is trying to cover up something."

"Reggie's cleverer than I thought," Edna said quietly.

Rowland was silent now, angry and unnerved. He considered Delaney his friend.

Edna saw. "Rowly, I wasn't—"

"God, I know that, Ed," he said quickly. "I just want to kill Stuart Jones for even touching you. Whatever he was trying to do, he might have killed you, sweetheart."

"Yes, I know." The sculptress' face lost its bravado only fleetingly before she straightened her shoulders again. "I'm sick of talking about Reggie. The police have it in hand. I want to know exactly what happened to the two of you."

They told her.

"And you've decided to do nothing and let them get away with nearly killing you?" Edna demanded, aghast.

"They didn't nearly kill us," Rowland protested. "Just roughed us up somewhat."

"Look at Clyde's face!" Edna said.

"There's no permanent damage, Ed," Clyde said, blowing on a piece of toast that had caught alight. "And what's more, I was never a handsome man." He pulled the burnt slice off the fork and dropped it onto the plate. "Better butter that one for Len."

"I think you're handsome!" Edna said with such fierce protective conviction that Clyde blushed, Milton laughed and Rowland loved her all the more.

"The Martinellis did nothing to Clyde and Rowly that we aren't going to do to bloody Reginald Stuart Jones," Milton promised quietly.

———

Colin Delaney arrived so early that Rowland alone was awake and about.

He'd been painting while brooding on what might have happened had Milton and Flynn not arrived when they did. Edna seemed determined to treat Stuart Jones' handling as a miscalculated attempt to restrain her. Perhaps it was. But that didn't stop Rowland wanting to tear the doctor limb from miserable limb. Edna had forbidden murder, of course.

And so the detective found him in a less than sunny disposition.

"How is Miss Higgins?" Delaney asked.

"She's alive."

Delaney sighed. "Rowly, I did not for a moment believe a word Dr. Stuart Jones said."

"That's not the impression you gave Milt."

"I'm a police detective. I'm under obligation to at least appear impartial." Delaney blanched and continued to explain himself. "The problem is that Stuart Jones' nurse is adamant that Miss Higgins had an appointment for a medical examination, and Miss Higgins doesn't remember a great deal."

"She remembers why she went to the Lido and it had nothing to do with a medical examination, Colin."

"Yes, I know. I'm glad you and Clyde are back, by the way. Where the hell were you?"

"We thought we might give Beejling the slip—I was rather fed up with being shadowed," Rowland followed his lie with the truth in the hope that the result would be vaguely believable.

It wasn't. Not to Delaney anyway, but he didn't press Rowland on that count. He handed Rowland an old leather-bound notebook. "White's," he said. "You wanted to have a look, I recall. Consider it a peace offering."

Rowland relented. "I'm sorry, Colin. I know you're simply doing your job. It's just the thought of that bastard touching Ed..." He dragged a hand through his hair and smiled apologetically. "Have you had breakfast?"

Relieved, Delaney accepted the invitation. He had no wish to fall out with Rowland Sinclair. He liked the man for one thing.

The breakfast room had been set. Steaming silver warming trays graced the sideboard. On request, a maid disappeared and returned a short while later with a bowl of porridge, which she placed before Rowland.

"Is that...?" Delaney began.

Rowland drizzled honey over the cooked oats. "Yes, I seem to have developed a taste for it." He waited until Delaney's plate was piled high. "Detective Hartley was at the Lido, you know."

"When?"

"Ed saw him just before Stuart Jones attacked her. She wonders if that might be the reason he panicked and tried to silence her."

Delaney pulled at the knot of his tie. "Hartley has his own way of doing things, Rowly."

"By consorting with criminals?"

"Sometimes. It's only the low-level crims that won't speak to the police. Honour among thieves is negotiable when you're dealing with the likes of Stuart Jones. It may well be that Hartley is on some undercover operation. He's Superintendent Mackay's golden-haired boy at the moment."

"Or involved in something untoward."

Delaney exhaled loudly. "I'd be mighty careful about making allegations like that."

"He's a police detective associating with Stuart Jones and then turning up to personally question the witnesses to that association. What does that look like to you?"

Detective Delaney chewed and swallowed before speaking. "Being a good copper isn't always about following every rule, Rowly. We all bend the rules. It's just a matter of how much and for what reason. I've allowed you to see evidence—in fact, I've borrowed evidence from case files to which I'm not assigned—I've shared information and intervened on your behalf often enough. And here I am enjoying your fine bacon and drinking your coffee. Would you say I'm on the take?"

"No… of course not, but—"

"All I'm saying is that if Hartley was there, as Miss Higgins believes, it may not be without good reason. If he is meeting with Stuart Jones, it may not be because he's in league with the bastard. Sometimes you have to deal with the devil for the greater good." Delaney put down his knife and fork. "Look, Rowly, I'll keep an eye on Hartley, but we can't be making loose accusations."

"Are you going to arrest Reginald Stuart Jones or not?" Rowland asked, angry despite being able to see Delaney's point, or perhaps because of it.

"At the moment we've only got Miss Higgins' word against his that she was not there for medical reasons."

"That's ridiculous, Colin. Ed had no reason to seek his dubious medical expertise."

Delaney paused. "Are you sure, Rowly? Would Miss Higgins necessarily tell you if she were in trouble? Now hear me out before you lose your temper—I've seen girls move heaven and earth to ensure their families never find out about this sort of thing." Delaney looked at his plate and kept talking. "I mean, what would you do if Miss Higgins told you she was in trouble? Could she go on living here, would you still feel the same way? These are the kinds of things Stuart Jones' lawyers are going to put to the court to make it look like she had every reason to lie."

They ate in silence for a while, as Delaney gave Rowland a chance to calm down, to resist the impulse to deck a police officer. The detective knew that Edna Higgins was the soft underbelly of Rowland Sinclair and that he'd probably tested their friendship with his words, but the man had to know what was ahead.

Rowland eventually spoke. His voice was tight, barely controlled. "Ed does not lie. She doesn't pretend she's anyone but who she is. And yes, I think she would tell me, and no, I doubt it would change how I feel. But more to the point, Colin, you know Edna Higgins! Do you really believe she would accuse an innocent man of attacking her, even scum like Stuart Jones, simply to protect her reputation?"

"No, I don't. I believe that Stuart Jones, at the very least, tried to keep her quiet for a while by putting her forcibly under anaesthetic. But my faith in Miss Higgins' good character is not evidence, Rowly. I just want you to understand why we haven't rushed out and hanged the bastard, and to caution you against undertaking such a course yourself."

"Oh, I wasn't thinking about hanging him," Rowland muttered.

29

NSW FREEMASONS

Grand Master Installed

SYDNEY, Tuesday

Before a brilliant assemblage in the Town Hull to night, Most
Wor. Bro. Dr. F.A. Maguire was installed as Grand Master of the
United Grand Lodge of New South Wales of Ancient Free and
Accepted Masons. The installation ceremony was performed by
the retiring Grand Master (Most Worshipful Bro. A. Halloran).
Among the visitors were R. Wor. Bro. E.A. Jones, Grand
Master of Queensland; M. Wor. Bro. L.J. Abra, Grand Master
of Tasmania; M. Wor. Bro. W. Warren Kerr, Grand Master of
Victoria; R.W. Bro Sir William Brunton. Deputy Grand Master
of Victoria; and H.W. Bro. A.D. Young, Deputy Grand Master
of South Australia. Greetings were received from England and
other parts of the Empire. In the afternoon the visiting delegates
were given a reception at the Masonic Club.

The Argus, 1933

Rowland leafed through Crispin White's notebook, noticing as he
did so white chalk dust on his fingertips. "Your chaps don't dust
for fingerprints with chalk dust, do they?" he asked Delaney, a little
perplexed by the presence of the stuff.

"Of course not." Delaney was finishing a second helping of

breakfast. "I assume the dust came from *Smith's Weekly*. Don't they use powder to blot ink when they're drafting?"

Rowland nodded. "That makes sense."

The last entries in the notebook were of course about Rowland Sinclair—abbreviated notes from the interview and dinner. The earlier entries concerned a wide range of stories: the cricket, Campbell's launch of the Centre Party, a house fire in Wollstonecraft, a stabbing in Darlinghurst and a single reference to the Kings Cross coven.

"Do you have any idea what these numbers might signify?"

"They're odds," Milton said peering over Rowland's shoulder as he took a seat at the table. Clyde and Edna had also come down. "Bookmakers' odds."

"They're on every page."

"I'd say White was a seasoned punter then." Milton pointed to a note written on the perpendicular. "That's a horse and race number."

"Perhaps White owed the bookmakers money. They can be a tough bunch," Delaney said standing to see the notebook.

Milton raised a brow. "We seem to be encountering rather a lot of bookies lately."

Rowland nodded. "Perhaps they're behind more than White's demise."

"Like the shooting," Edna suggested, spooning sugar into her tea.

"I dunno." Milton was sceptical. "Dead men can be replaced, as we saw with Linklater. If the bookies wanted to make sure that Joan Richmond's team doesn't win, it'd be more effective to simply convince Rowly to throw the race. They hadn't even tried when the shot was fired."

"Perhaps that's what that shot was meant to do," Delaney pointed out.

"You'd have to be a crack shot to shoot the painting and still miss me," Rowland said.

"Perhaps he was just lucky."

"Reggie is a very good target shooter," Edna said quietly. "Do you remember, Milt? He was forever shooting out light bulbs to show off."

Delaney took out his notebook and wrote the possibility down. "We'll certainly look into his whereabouts when the shooting occurred. If we can put him at *Woodlands* that morning it could go towards his credibility, or lack thereof, on other matters."

Edna moved to sit next to Delaney. "I expect Rowly's already growled at you this morning, Colin. I want you to know that I don't hold what happened yesterday against you."

Delaney stuttered, flustered and clearly embarrassed. "I am sorry if it seemed—"

"I'm glad you were there," she said. "Detective Hartley and Superintendent Mackay seemed determined to 'crack' me."

"I'm sure that wasn't their intention, but I must admit, I'm happy Maguire was able to remind the superintendent of the importance of being cautious, considering what you'd been through."

Rowland looked up sharply, but said nothing.

"You're licensed to carry a pistol, aren't you, Rowly?" Delaney asked.

"Yes," Rowland said carefully.

"Do you have a weapon?"

"Wil's old service revolver is in a box somewhere."

"It mightn't be a bad idea to carry it, just until this flaming race is over at least."

Rowland shook his head. "I think I might be safer if it stays in the box."

"You're not in the least bit amusing, Rowly," Edna said, assuming he was making some tangential reference to the fact that she'd shot him with that gun.

He hadn't been, but now they were all reminded. Rowland laughed.

Delaney stood. "I'd best get on." He glanced at Edna awkwardly. "Would you mind coming in to the station to finish your statement, Miss Higgins?"

"Not at all, Detective Delaney," Edna replied.

"You might be able to help us on another matter, Colin," Rowland began, glancing at Milton. "This chap Bocquet who claims to have had his tiepin stolen, employed a young woman called Frances as a housemaid. I don't suppose you could find out if someone's recorded her details?"

"Do you have a surname?"

"No."

"The case is John Hartley's, but I'll see what I can do."

Edna and Rowland walked Delaney out as the others were still eating.

As soon as the detective had left, Edna quizzed Rowland on his peculiar reaction when Delaney made reference to Maguire's words on her behalf. "I know you, Rowly. What were you thinking?"

"It wasn't anything... I just realised that Bill Mackay must be a Mason."

"What do you mean?"

"Fredrick Maguire is a member of the Grand Lodge. He reminded Mackay of the fact that they are brothers... and that he's the bigger brother. It's probably why Mackay agreed to postpone the interview."

"I didn't hear him say anything about—"

"It's a code, a particular turn of phrase."

"Oh," Edna said intrigued. "What turn of phrase?"

"I can't tell you that."

Edna's hands sat indignantly upon her hips. "Why not?"

"I'm a Mason."

"You're also a grown man."

288 - **SULARI GENTILL**

Rowland's face was grave though there was an unmistakable smile in his eyes. "If I tell you my throat will be cut and my name forever decried as that of a miserable cowan."

"What? By the Freemasons?"

"No, just Wil—goodness knows what the brotherhood would do."

Edna laughed. She linked her arm with his. "So, just because he's a higher ranking Freemason, Frederick Maguire can order Superintendent Mackay about?"

"It doesn't quite work that way, but his rank does carry influence."

"Well that's hardly fair."

"Possibly not."

Elisabeth Sinclair returned to *Woodlands House* late that morning. Wilfred had thought it best she stay at *Roburvale* while Rowland was missing, though he kept that fact from her. Elisabeth was a little put out. "As much as I love spending time with you and the children, Wilfred, I am a busy woman. You cannot simply abduct me and refuse to allow me to come home!" she said as he walked her in the door.

Rowland met them in the vestibule. "Hello Mother," he said unable to keep the grin off his face as he watched Elisabeth scold her eldest son.

She looked in consternation at Rowland's face. "Good heavens! What on earth have you been up to, Aubrey? Did you have another accident in that automobile? You'd best learn to drive that contraption properly before the race. The Red Cross is relying on you! I did not raise you boys to be so careless about your social obligations and responsibilities!"

Rowland glanced at his brother enquiringly. Their mother seemed unusually spirited this morning.

"She gets like this when she feels her routine's been disrupted," Wilfred whispered wearily.

"Oh dear," Elisabeth lamented with equal measures of irritation and sadness. "Miss Higgins promised to teach me all about papier-mâché yesterday, but of course Wilfred would not let me come home for some ridiculous reason!"

"I'm afraid Ed was not very well yesterday, in any case. But I'm sure she'd be delighted to show you today, Mother," Rowland said soothingly. "I'll take you to her studio now if you like."

"No, I couldn't. I set aside today to catch up with correspondence. I do wish you'd stop calling that poor girl, Ed. It's very confusing. Oh, I'm all at sixes and sevens!"

"Perhaps a nice cup of tea," Wilfred suggested.

Milton came in whistling Waltzing Matilda. "Oh, hello Mr. Sinclair. Welcome back, Mrs. Sinclair!"

Elisabeth's face lit noticeably. "Thank you, Mr. Isaacs, though I'm sure none of you even noticed I was gone."

"Au contraire," Milton insisted. "I was bereft. This place is unbearably dull without you. I nearly packed my bags as well."

Wilfred muttered his scepticism that such an event would ever occur, but Elisabeth was mollified.

"Perhaps you could join us for tea, Mr. Isaacs?"

Milton bowed. "A pleasure." He offered Elisabeth his arm and escorted her into the ladies' drawing room while Rowland rang for tea.

Wilfred Sinclair did not stay long, departing for some business to do with the Graziers' Association's displays in the main pavilion at the Royal Easter Show. Rowland and Milton took tea with Elisabeth and by the second pot she seemed to have forgotten she was cross. Rowland suspected that his mother was a little besotted with Milton Isaacs, which was probably not as outrageous as it sounded since she'd decided just that morning that she was thirty-six years old.

In time, Elisabeth retired to her own part of the house under the supervision of Sister O'Hara to see to her correspondence, and Rowland and Milton made plans for that afternoon. They'd decided to visit Magdalene's House of the Macabre again, with the express intent of seeing what was upstairs. Clyde would come this time to stage a diversion if necessary, or for numbers if there was trouble. The fact that the artist's face was a rainbow of bruises would probably serve to camouflage him among the exhibits. Indeed if one eye had not been still partially closed, he would have been the ideal choice to infiltrate.

Of course Edna was furious when she discovered they intended to go without her.

"You're not coming, Ed." Rowland was adamant. "Do I need to remind you that you nearly died yesterday?"

"Don't be melodramatic, Rowly."

"You're not invited, dear girl." Milton was equally resolute. "Just try and be gracious about it."

"I'm coming."

"You're just not." Clyde, too, was immovable.

Edna put up a good fight. Rowland had nearly been worn down into relenting, when she stormed off vowing all manner of vengeance, and denouncing the condescending, patriarchal arrogance of the men with whom she lived.

Milton winced. "We're never going to hear the end of this," he warned.

Rowland was a little surprised that the sculptress had given up, but perhaps she did not yet feel as well as she purported. Anyway, it would be easier to placate Edna than to live with himself for putting her in danger again.

Milton had made enquiries among the less respectable citizens who inhabited the streets of Kings Cross after dark, confirming that a coven did in fact meet at Magdalene's House of the Macabre. Gossip told of figures in robes and masks seen arriving and departing the building at all hours. Most people were afraid to even approach the building after dark.

"Perhaps Rosaleen Norton's story was more accurate than we thought," the poet said uneasily.

"More likely she was inspired by Magdalene's in the first place," Rowland suggested.

Clyde crossed himself just in case. "What exactly are we doing, Rowly?"

"If we could find out what the coven is hiding, perhaps we'll find a link to White. I thought if I got myself locked in there after closing, I might be able to have a look at what's upstairs."

"Locked in? Like the character in Miss Norton's story?"

"Yes... if you like."

"That's insanely risky, Rowly."

"Not really," Rowland replied. "They're not actually witches... probably just some occult club if anything. I wouldn't be surprised if they're all Miss Norton's age, gathering in secret to drink cheap sherry, smoke and recite bad poetry."

"Steady on!" Milton protested. "Slandering poets is uncalled for."

"You may want to remember that someone cut White's throat," Clyde pointed out.

Rowland conceded that fact. "You chaps wait for me outside. I'll hold up my lighter in a window facing Macleay Street every half hour. If you don't see it," he grinned, "or you hear screaming, fetch the police."

"I dunno, Rowly." Clyde rubbed the back of his neck. "I have a bad feeling. And why does it have to be you? Milt or I could—"

"While you look a bit like an exhibit at the moment, old mate, you still can't see properly, and we can't risk Milt being arrested for any reason. I came out of our encounter with the Martinellis rather better than you and I'm not currently the major suspect in a murder."

"Yes, but—"

"It'll be all right," Rowland assured him. "If I get caught, I'll just say that I was so engrossed in their wonderful displays that I failed to hear the closing bell and got locked in. Don't worry."

And so they bought tickets about half an hour before closing time.

"Oh hello, what are you chaps doing aboard?" Errol Flynn spotted them amongst the milling crowd. He had his arms around Edna. The couple made their way over, hand in hand. "Fancy running into you gentlemen. Edna said she'd heard this place was a very romantic venue," he winked at Milton, "so we thought it would do nicely."

Edna looked at them all innocently, swinging Flynn's hand in hers.

The actor glanced around. "So, where are your young ladies?"

"We didn't bring any guests," Rowland said curtly.

"Oh I say, really?" Flynn said, apparently surprised that they would spend time at Magdalene's for any purpose other than seduction.

"We were having a drink nearby, and we thought we'd come in… just for a lark," Milton said quickly. "They'll be closing soon… perhaps I could suggest a restaurant I know in Milson's Point? Also very romantic."

"Oh no, I like it here," Edna said. "It's quite fun to be frightened when I have Errol to protect me."

"This is not funny, Ed," Rowland said quietly.

"Of course it's not funny, it's a House of the Macabre."

It was Milton who eventually made the decision to bring them into the plan as it became clear that Edna would not leave. He checked first to see they would not be overheard before he whispered. "Right, Rowly's going to have himself locked in here. Don't argue or ask why—I'll explain later. We have to locate somewhere he can hide, and then create a diversion so he can do so. You two may actually be useful."

"What?" Edna whispered back, appalled.

"You insisted on joining us Ed, so don't make a scene. We've thought this caper out—we won't let anything happen to Rowly. Now are you in?"

"Ready to heave to, mate," Flynn said, saluting.

Edna thought for a moment. She poked Rowland. "You be careful."

30

Staggering Revelations by 'High Priest' of
BLACK MAGIC

VETERAN JUDGE DENOUNCES "BEAST 666"
Tales of Mystic Rites

SINISTER and appalling secrets of so called magic—black and white—were revealed during the hearing of a case that has stirred the British public, the jury and even the judge himself in the King's Bench. As the case unfolded there were told strange stories of weird ceremonies and mystic rites, of blood sacrifices and exotic ceremonies, of a mysterious 'Beast 666' and of a 'poet magician' Aleister Crowley, who 'made a sonnet of unspeakable things.' "I have been engaged for forty years in the administration of the law in one capacity or another," said the veteran judge, Mr. Justice Swift, "and I thought that I knew every conceivable form of wickedness. I have learned in this case that you can always learn something more if you live long enough. Never have I heard such dreadful, horrible, blasphemous, abominable stuff as that which has been produced by this man (Crowley), who describes himself as the greatest living poet."

THE case was brought by Mr. Edward Alexander (Aleister) Crowley of Carlos Place, Grosvenor Square, against Miss Nina Hamnett, the writer of a book called 'Laughing Torso,' in which Mr. Crowley alleged he had been libelled. Miss Hamnett, a well-known artist and a popular figure in Bohemian London, put forward as her defence a denial that the words complained of were defamatory and further stated that they were true in substance and in fact. According to Mr. J. P. Eddy, who appeared for Mr. Crowley, this book, 'Laughing Torso,' purported to be an account of Miss Hamnett's own life with a number of intimate sketches of friends and acquaintances introduced. It was stated in one passage that Mr. Crowley had a temple called the Temple of Thelema at Cefalu (in Sicily) where he was supposed to practice black magic.

FRIGHTENED

"One day a baby was said to have disappeared mysteriously. There was also a goat there. This all pointed to black magic, so people said, and the inhabitants of the village were frightened of him."

...He admitted that he had made a sonnet of unspeakable things, but he had not advocated unrestricted sexual freedom, though he had protested against the sexual oppression that existed in England... Then came a dramatic passage of cross-examination. "As a part of your magic you do believe in a practice of blood sacrifice?" asked counsel. "I believe in its efficacy," was the reply. "If you believe in its efficacy, you would believe in it being practised, and you would say it could be practised without impropriety?" "I do not approve of it at all."

"You say in your book of magic for nearly all purposes human sacrifice is best?" "Yes, it is."...

Truth, 1934

An ideal hiding spot for Rowland was found behind the guillotine display where he would be entirely hidden by a pile of decapitated waxen heads. And then Edna went to work.

She chose the werewolf exhibit at the other end of the gallery, and pointing to the largest figure she screamed, "It moved, my God it moved. It's real... it's come to life!"

Then Milton cried, "By George, I think you're right madam. The evil fiend moved! What's going on here?"

Then Edna collapsed into hysteria while Flynn put up his fists to the wax werewolf.

Clyde crossed himself and began muttering the Lord's Prayer, though it was debatable whether that was an act.

Not unexpectedly there was mayhem as customers surged for either the werewolf or the exit. Rowland slipped quietly into the space they'd identified, and waited.

A staff member emerged to verify and demonstrate that the wax werewolf had not come to life and calm was duly restored, though the air was charged with the extra thrill of possibility. Many patrons left, whether it was because the waxworks was closing or because of residual concern that other exhibits would animate, was difficult to determine. Edna departed on Errol Flynn's arm and Clyde and Milton followed soon after. The House of the Macabre was cleared, the lights switched off and the doors secured.

When he'd heard nothing for a minute or two, Rowland used his lighter to check his watch making a vague mental note to have the cracked crystal replaced. He had half an hour from now to signal, or Clyde would summon the police, which would be embarrassing if the only felony was his.

He waited where he was for a further ten minutes and then stepped out, wishing he'd thought to bring a torch. Fumbling his way to a window he made the first signal, again checking the time as he did so. As his eyes adjusted, the wax figures became an ominous presence, unnerving though he knew they were lifeless. Rowland resolutely ignored the grotesques and monstrous manifestations, looking instead for the arched exit that led into the area in which he'd encountered the weeping Daisy Forster. He made his way through the arch, picking out the denser darkness of the prohibited stairwell, occasionally groping some monster or other in his stumbling progress. He thought briefly about trying to find the Greek Room but decided against it. Better to see what was upstairs.

Rowland headed up the narrow stairwell using the feeble illumination from his cigarette lighter to gauge the steps. It was probably fortunate he didn't smoke—at least the lighter was full. He emerged into the hallway of the second floor. Two doors. The first led to what was a small office as far as he could tell: filing cabinets, a roll-top desk, a coat rack on which were hung what appeared to be long black gowns and pointed hoods. Rowland stiffened. The Fascist Legion had worn similar costumes when they'd dealt the New Guard's justice to Communists and other opponents of the movement. Could Milton be right, after all? Was Campbell behind all this?

Though it had only been twenty-five minutes since he last signalled, he did so again via the office's window, before he crossed the corridor and opened the other door. The room was pitch black. He couldn't even make out the outline of windows. He used his lighter to find the ceiling light cord and risked pulling it on. Rowland breathed, relieved when he saw that all the windows had been blacked out. He closed the door behind him. Though smaller than he expected, considering there seemed to be only two rooms on this upper floor, the chamber was still a reasonable size. The floor and the ceiling were painted with pentagrams and other symbols, and an imposing altar occupied the centre of the space.

Rowland knew he had roughly twenty-eight minutes before he'd have to return to the office and signal again. He examined the marble-topped altar—a curious piece of furniture indeed. Its base was carved with demonic figures which declared absolutely that this was a place where black magic was practised. Conspicuously placed atop the altar was a copy of Aleister Crowley's *Magick in Theory and Practice*. Rowland didn't know the title but had heard of the notorious occultist and recalled that Inky Stephensen had mentioned publishing his work at one time.

It struck Rowland that the room was unexpectedly neat, no cobwebs or bloodstains, that sort of thing. Perhaps witches were naturally tidy, he reasoned, countering the tension with idle flippancy—they carried brooms, after all.

The walls around him were panelled with cedar. It was unusual for the age and style of the building, though the room might well have been refurbished. Rowland paced the perimeter. It was then he noticed the scrap of fabric caught between two panels on the far wall. Pulling out his pocketknife, he slid the blade into the barely discernible join. It met no resistance—there was no wall behind the panelling. He pushed on the opposite side of the panel and it gave, revolving around a pivot to reveal a hidden adjunct to the room. Large enough to accommodate six cubicles each housing telephones. Rowland applied the same principle to other panels along the same wall, discovering behind them blackboards, more telephones and totes. And he realised he was standing in an illicit SP bookmakers' den. He laughed. It was a quite brilliant disguise. A coven seemed at home in a House of the Macabre. It explained the afterhours comings and goings which most people would be too frightened to investigate. Though he was pretty sure witchcraft was illegal, it was unlikely it would interest the police as much as an illicit bookmaker. The discovery also explained what White might have been doing here.

Rowland closed up the panels. He was not due to signal again for at least thirteen minutes, but there was no point lingering. It was not until he stepped into the corridor that he realised the lights on the floor below had been turned on, and there were voices and movement on the stairs. There was no time for anything but to retreat into the room from which he had just emerged. He shut the door, pulled the light cord and crouched behind the satanic altar.

The voices became louder, interspersed with drunken laughter. All

Rowland could do was hope they would go directly into the office…
but that hope proved in vain.

The door was pushed open and Rowland heard a number of people
enter. He knew then that discovery was inevitable. He braced himself.

The light was switched on. The first figure to walk around the
altar was wearing women's shoes. Beyond that, she wore full-length
black robes and an owl-like facemask complete with beak. The lips
beneath the beak twisted in horror and screamed.

Rowland had no time to ponder the irony of someone dressed as
a ghoul being frightened by a man in a three-piece suit. He broke for
the door. Intercepted, he was tackled to the ground and then dragged
to his feet under restraint.

Someone wearing a Horus mask pushed the point of a straight
dagger against his throat.

"What the hell are you doing here?" snarled a man whose mask
resembled the face of a goat.

Rowland said nothing.

"Who sent you?" the goat demanded.

"No one."

"What were you looking for?"

The owl whispered in the goat's ear. He nodded. "Well, you are in
a great deal of trouble boy. Your soul is in peril."

A second voice, from behind a cat mask. "Do you know how we
punish interlopers who dare to trespass into our magic circle?"

Despite the dagger poised at his throat, Rowland fought the
impulse to laugh. Bookmakers invoking magic circles… it was absurd.
But he did know his chances were better if they didn't realise he'd
seen behind the panelling. So he didn't laugh and he tried to look
concerned by the threat of black magic.

"What are you doing here?" the cat asked.

A right hook to the jaw and Rowland reeled.

"You better answer darling," the owl advised.

Rowland wiped the blood from his lip. He met the cat's eyes through the holes in its mask. "I want to join."

"Join what?"

"Your coven."

"What?"

Rowland scrambled through his paltry knowledge of the occult. "There only appears to be nine of you," he said making a quick headcount. "A coven requires thirteen. It seems to me that you need members to complete your... circle."

The cat hit him again. "We have all the members we need."

Rowland shook his head to settle the ringing in his ears. Clyde would go for the police soon if he hadn't already. "Oh, I say. Terribly sorry—how embarrassing. I'll just be on my way then."

A third blow, to the stomach this time. "You have a smart mouth. I ask again, for the last time, what the hell are you doing here?"

Rowland staggered as old bruises were impacted by the punch. Gasping he tried another tack. "A wager. There are rumours about this place with that chap being killed and all." He paused to cough, to catch his breath and think swiftly. "One of the fellows at my club wagered that I wouldn't have the courage to spend the night. A gentleman can't be called a coward, after all..."

Anonymous eyes behind the masks all stared at him. Fleetingly Rowland wondered if this was what White last saw. They whispered among themselves. Rowland strained to catch any stray word, but he could pick up nothing.

The figure in the bear mask spoke to him. The voice was male, angry and Rowland had heard it before. "You're bloody Rowland Sinclair."

"Yes." Rowland's voice did not betray his growing panic. He struggled to place the voice.

"What do you want, Sinclair?"

"What I said at the outset. I have an interest in the occult," Rowland maintained the lie steadily, his eyes fixed on the slits in the bear mask. He was a poker player—he knew how to bluff and he wanted the bear to speak again. "I met Aleister Crowley when I was in England. We got on rather famously. I had heard a coven operated from here. It's not as if I could apply for membership through conventional channels, so I thought I'd come along and observe. You are a real coven, aren't you?"

Perhaps the bear realised that his voice had been recognised because he didn't reply.

Horus raised his arms. "We are servants of Satan! We are the children of Hell!"

Rowland nodded slowly wondering where the ludicrous pantomime would lead.

"You should never have come here Sinclair," said the wolf. "Now we're going to have to make sure you don't betray us."

"I say we kill him, offer him as a sacrifice," crooned the owl. "Like we did that reporter."

"Shut up!" the bear snarled. "He's a friend of the mongrel."

Rowland stiffened. "You killed White?"

31

THE GREATER EVIL

To the Editor, Sir—

The great outcry against Sunday sport by some of the ministers of religion seems amazing when no voice is raised against the two greatest evils and enemies of the working man and his family—afterhours drinking and public-house betting. It seems incredible that the Ministerial Association has remained silent and let this huge cancer sap the morals of our young men and girls on the one hand, and steel the money from the workers' women and children and deprive them of the necessaries of life…

There is a bookmaker in practically every hotel and club in Broken Hill to get the cash that should go to feed and clothe the children (in lots of cases) of the workers, and non-workers trying to pick winners with the endowment money. The bookmakers flaunt around in their expensive cars, exhibiting their ill-gotten gains, procured at the expense of the women and children…

The reverend gentlemen have, in my humble opinion, worried about the "fly" and permitted the human blood-sucking spiders to have a free go.

Yours, etc.,
"DECEMBER."

Barrier Miner, 1934

The wolf grabbed Rowland by the throat. "The devil requires his tribute."

Rowland began to reconsider his assumption that these men, and at least one woman, were playing at the occult.

The wolf motioned the owl. "Sinclair wants to join the coven. Let's give him our highest honour."

The dagger was held again to Rowland's throat, his protests silenced with a blow to the ribs. He was confused now. This was all happening too quickly and too inconsistently with what he'd seen behind the panel... but some part of him knew instinctively that it would be more dangerous to reveal what he'd discovered. A rubber mask was thrust over his face and tied tightly at the back. Through the restriction of inadequate eye slits, everything he saw became all the more surreal—altered and threatening. Black and white images of White in death came too easily to mind.

"Look here..." Rowland tried feebly to negotiate.

"Speak again and we'll cut out your tongue," the cat warned.

They forced him on to the altar and the wolf cursed him, calling on Satan to accept Rowland Sinclair as an offering from his servants. The razor was raised.

"No... stop..."

The wail of sirens seemed to precede the crash below by only seconds. And then the shouts of police. The owl, the bear, the goat and a couple of bird-like creatures opened the windows and climbed out. The wolf pushed Rowland back. "Right, Sinclair, you give the name Alan Smith and it'll all work out fine. You say nothing, and neither will we."

Rowland was disoriented. One moment he was about to be murdered as a ritual sacrifice and the next, the coven was offering to protect his identity and reputation.

The police found the altar room soon enough, bursting through the door in numbers. The officer in charge of the constables seemed young and, to be honest, mildly terrified. The wolf pulled off his mask to reveal a soft smiling face as he explained that they were members of a secret society carrying out an ancient rite. "We're not unlike the Freemasons, the Druids or the Oddfellows," he said affably. "I know it must look a little peculiar, but there's really nothing to be alarmed about."

"They were planning to kill me!" Rowland protested, struggling to remove his mask.

The coven laughed. "Nonsense!" the unmasked wolf declared. "It's all part of the ritual, that's all. The young fella's just taken it all too seriously."

"Who are you?" the constable demanded.

"Thaddeus Magdalene. I'm the proprietor of this establishment. This young man," he nodded at Rowland, "is Alan Smith, the newest initiate to our little... club."

"The panels in this room are false," Rowland said, finally yanking loose the mask. "This is a bookmakers' den."

The silence was stunned and momentary. Then the cat lunged for Rowland. "Why you lying bastard!" Free to defend himself this time, Rowland punched the hooded man.

A scramble and two constables pulled both men apart.

Delaney appeared at the doorway. "Rowly?" he said staring. "What on earth's going on here?" He didn't wait for Rowland to reply, assuming control of the scene. "Take Mr. Sinclair downstairs while I speak with Mr. Magdalene and inspect these premises a little more thoroughly," Delaney ordered. "I'll interview Sinclair once we ascertain what exactly is in this room."

"They killed White," Rowland told Delaney quietly as he was escorted past. "They told me."

In the first exhibit room Rowland was reunited with his friends. Edna threw her arms around him and embraced him tightly. "Thank goodness you're all right."

"We went to the police as soon as we spotted the flaming menagerie go in. They thought we were drunk," Clyde said as he shook Rowland's hand. "Milton made a scene and they telephoned Delaney at home in the end."

"Where's Flynn?" Rowland asked, looking for the actor.

"He's gone back to the car to release Beejling. We had to tie the poor man up to prevent him going to the police as soon as you didn't come out of Magdalene's."

Rowland grimaced. He'd completely forgotten about Beejling.

"What happened?" Edna asked noting the blood on his lip. "What did they do to you?"

Rowland filled them in.

"I'm confused," Milton said. "Are they bookies or occultists?"

"I'm rather confused myself, but I think they're probably bookmakers pretending to be Satanists to scare people into staying clear."

"But they killed White."

"That's what they said."

"But why?"

"Perhaps he discovered they were running a bookmakers' operation."

They waited over an hour before Delaney came down. The coven members who had not escaped via the windows were escorted through in handcuffs first, some still clad in masks. They shouted abuse and threats at Rowland Sinclair as they were led past.

Delaney shook his head as he lit a cigarette. "More enemies, Rowly?" He sighed. "Come on, I'd best take your statement."

They used the upstairs office rather than go back to the station where the coven was being processed. Rowland gave his account of what happened.

"Once they knew the jig was up, they confessed that the occult business was a ruse to disguise the bookmakers' shop," Delaney said. "Apparently they scared the last chap who accidentally discovered them into taking holy orders, so they thought they could do the same with you, or alternatively make you think you'd been initiated into the coven to procure your silence. They claim to use the daggers for opening letters and deny any intention of murdering you."

"That's not the impression I got. What about White?"

"They say they took credit for that to scare you."

"How did they recognise me?"

"They've been taking bets on the race—that Red Cross motor marathon. Your picture's been in the papers. Magdalene wants you charged with breaking and entering."

"I didn't break and enter. I got locked in."

Delaney tapped the side of his nose. "And that's the story I'm sticking to."

"Do they know anything at all about White's murder?"

"They say not."

"It seems an awful coincidence."

"You think White's death was some kind of ritual sacrifice?" Delaney asked.

Rowland considered it. "No," he said in the end. "There was nothing ritualistic about White's murder—no mask, he was fully dressed and he was in the wrong room, unless the Greek Room has an altar?"

"It doesn't," Delaney confirmed. He consulted his watch. "I don't suppose you want to have a look at it?"

Rowland shrugged. "That would be easier than getting myself locked in again I suppose."

The Greek Room was much smaller than it appeared in the crime scene photographs but the exhibits were the same: Spartan warriors, the Minotaur, Medusa, an Egyptian pharaoh and Pan. They were as Daisy Forster had described them: nothing particularly spectacular. And of course the pharaoh wasn't Greek, but that point was probably irrelevant to the fact that Crispin White was murdered here.

Rowland's eyes fell once again on the wiring Edna had noticed in the photographs. He knew exactly what they were now: telephone cables. The Greek Room was directly below the altar room where he'd found the illicit bookmakers' shop. Perhaps White too had realised what the wires were and sniffed out the bookmakers like the newshound he was. There had been a reference to the Kings Cross coven in his notebook.

Delaney nodded his agreement. "I think it was an astute move to conceal that you knew what they were up to."

"Look Colin, I didn't really get a look at all those jokers. Were any of them…?"

"Wombat Newgate."

Rowland tensed. "So Stuart Jones might be involved with this lot, too?"

"He wasn't here, Rowly, but rest assured we will question Newgate vigorously. We'll find out if this is connected to what happened to Miss Higgins."

"Which mask was he wearing?"

"I beg your pardon?"

"Which mask was Wombat wearing? Which one was he?"

"The clown. Why?"

"The bear's voice was familiar."

"Are you sure it wasn't a clown?"

"No, definitely a bear. I didn't notice the clown. I might have been a good deal more unnerved if I had."

"We didn't apprehend a bear."

308 — **SULARI GENTILL**

Rowland swore. "He must have been one of the chaps who jumped out the window."

Delaney tapped a cigarette out of its case. "I'll have the boys keep an eye out for a bear in Kings Cross."

Rowland smiled. "Also an owl and a couple of things that looked like parrots."

Delaney groaned. "They'll think I've been drinking." He checked his notebook as he recalled a promise, and found the relevant information. "The Bocquets' maid is called Frances Webb," he said. "She lived in so we haven't got a current address."

"Terrific," Rowland replied, frustrated.

"I have a number of statements to take tonight so I'd best get back to the station. You go home, Rowly. I'll be in touch once I've sorted this mess out."

Rowland offered the detective his hand. "Thank you, Colin."

Delaney accepted the handshake. "You won't leave town, will you, old boy?"

―――――――――――   ―――――――――――

When Rowland and his friends finally left the waxworks most of the police had already gone. Two constables had been left to guard the premises while the door the police had forced was insecure. They walked across the street to where the cars were parked near a streetlight and it was only then they noticed that three men awaited them.

Flynn and Beejling had, it seemed, joined forces to restrain a thin, ragged man against the bonnet of the Rolls Royce.

"What's going on here?" Rowland demanded.

Beejling replied, "This gentleman was interfering with your car, sir."

"I weren't!" the man protested.

"You were crouched next to the wheels!" Flynn barked. "Getting ready to slash the tyres, no doubt. The bloody cheek!"

"I weren't!" the man said again.

"He doesn't have a knife," Rowland pointed out.

"Empty your pockets," Beejling instructed his prisoner.

Plunging his hands into his trousers, the man pulled out four thick sticks of chalk. "See, this is all I got."

"What were you doing crouched next to the car, sir?" Edna asked gently.

The man looked frightened, trapped. His face seemed, at the moment, to be only startled eyes.

Rowland opened the trunk on the back of the Rolls Royce and found the torch Johnston always kept in there. He turned it on to inspect the front tyre beside which the man had reportedly been crouched. The beam caught a word chalked in meticulous copperplate on the footpath: "Eturnity."

Rowland turned back to the man in the custody of Beejling and Flynn. "I'm Rowland Sinclair," he said proffering his hand. "Pleased to meet you Mr...?"

"Stace," the man said, warily shaking Rowland's hand. "Arthur Stace."

"Did you write this, Mr. Stace?"

Stace said nothing.

"Why eternity?" Edna asked. "I've seen it written on footpaths and walls before around Kings Cross. Was it always you, Mr. Stace?"

Stace still appeared to be looking for an opportunity to run. "I like it. It's a good word. Folks need to think about God and how they're gonna spend eternity."

Rowland was reminded then of Frank Marien's account of the man who returned White's notebook. "Do you always carry chalk in your pockets, Mr. Stace?"

"Most times."

"Did you return a notebook to Frank Marien of *Smith's Weekly?*"

"I didn't steal it! That man threw it away."

"Which man?"

Stace shook his head. "Dunno… a man."

"Where was this, Mr. Stace?"

"He was coming out of Magdalene's. Had a key—locked the door."

"What was he wearing?"

Stace looked at him blankly. "Clothes."

"Nothing unusual?"

"No, just clothes."

"And where exactly did this man throw the notebook?"

Stace shifted his weight, agitated. "He didn't 'xactly throw it. He was reading it as he walked out and he stumbled on the gutter and dropped it through the grate of the stormwater drain. Couldn't get it out. He swore a bit and left it. But I got it out."

"Was there anyone with him?"

"Nope."

Rowland reached into his jacket for his pocketbook. "I'm afraid we've detained and accused you unfairly Mr. Stace." He pressed two pound notes into Stace's calloused hand. "Please accept this as some small compensation for the inconvenience and the affront."

Stace put the notes in his pocket. "That'll purchase me a lot of chalk, Mr. Sinclair."

"I hope it helps, Mr. Stace."

"Do you write anything other than this word 'eternity'?" Milton asked curiously.

"I don't know many other words. It's the only perfect word I know."

Beejling who had quite obviously been restraining himself, broke, and said stiffly, "My good man, you do realise it's usually spelled E-T-E-R-N-I-T-Y?"

Stace's face fell. "I thought I'd written it right."

"It's poetic licence," Milton said. "I, for one, like the way you spelled it better."

"No," Stace said, distressed. "It's got to be right."

Rowland found his notebook and pencil, and while his first impulse was to draw the furtive Arthur Stace—the wide anxious eyes, the startled stance, muscles tensed to flee—he instead wrote the word out in clear letters and tore out the page. "I like the way you spelled it, too, but if it's got to be correct…"

Stace accepted the page as gratefully as he had the two pounds. He turned to go and then paused. "You won't tell anybody 'bout me, will you? 'Bout me writing the word? It's not vandalism or nothin', I only use chalk."

"Of course we'd never tell anyone, Mr. Stace," Edna assured him, earnestly. "We promise."

Stace tipped his battered hat. "Thank you, miss. I'm sorry if I startled you folks." With that he departed, leaving them to contemplate the beautifully rendered misspelled word which seemed to illuminate the concrete footpath.

32

BRIEFLY

New Zealand Women

To welcome their new president, Miss Edith Stout, members of the New Zealand Women's Association Younger Set met last night at the club rooms, Bank of New Zealand Chambers, for bridge and dancing. This was the first of a series of entertainments which the younger set members will arrange throughout the year. Those present included the Misses Doris Clarke (hon. secretary), Betty Bannerman, Rosaleen Norton, Marie Cook, Eileen Graham, Marjorie Coburn, Cecilie Webb.

The Sydney Morning Herald, 1935

"If Stuart Jones is involved in what went on at Magdalene's, Wombat Newgate isn't saying," Rowland reported as he returned the receiver to its cradle. "Delaney wants me to pull out of the race and leave the country for a while."

"It's not that bad, surely?" Edna said.

"I wouldn't count on it," Milton said grimly. "I fear you may have upset some ruthless people, my friend."

"So what's new?" Clyde muttered. "What are you going to do, Rowly? It's been a tough few days—it's a wonder you're still standing."

Rowland shrugged. "I don't have to stand to drive… I plan to carry on. Delaney's overreacting. I'm willing to wager Bill Mackay's hauled the poor chap over the coals a bit."

Milton snorted. "Wombat could probably give you odds on that."

"Are they going to charge you over Magdalene's?" Edna asked.

"For getting accidentally locked in? I wouldn't think so. In fact, I expect I could take action for deprivation of liberty."

Milton poured drinks for everyone but Rowland, who Clyde had now banned from indulging until after the race. Grateful for the innumerable hours Clyde had spent ensuring the Mercedes was race ready, it seemed churlish for Rowland to do anything but comply, however excessively puritanical his friend's notions seemed to be.

"The doc is one heck of a slippery bastard," Milton said bitterly.

Rowland nodded. Edna had attended Central Police Station in the company of the Sinclair family solicitors that morning, to make a full statement and be interviewed by Delaney and Hartley. She had returned unusually quiet and retreated to her studio with barely a word.

Rowland had followed, standing by silently as she pummelled clay until the very concept of an air bubble was beaten out of existence. And then she had cried like a child in his arms.

He hadn't asked why. Just held her until his shirt front was soaked and she was spent.

She'd told him eventually. It seemed the word of Edna Higgins was not enough to refute that of Dr. Stuart Jones and his nurse. Delaney had been kind but Hartley's questions were offensive. The detective had neither denied nor confirmed that he'd been at the Lido, treating Edna's claims as irrelevant and hysterical. It had made her feel so. She didn't quite know why she was so upset…It was silly—perhaps it was the aftereffects of the ether.

Edna had pulled herself together, and told Rowland to go change his shirt which was not only wet but smeared with clay from her hands. He'd done so, but not before he'd telephoned John Hartley and made his displeasure known in such strident terms that the detective had threatened to have him arrested. Somehow Wilfred had come to know of the exchange, and by the afternoon had duly called at *Woodlands* to reason with his brother.

"What happened to Miss Higgins was an outrage, and I know you feel it keenly for many reasons. But Rowly, getting yourself arrested will only play into Stuart Jones' claims that she is an immoral woman who keeps questionable company and was therefore in need of his services!"

"Why is it, Wil, that the bloody New South Wales Police Force can't seem to touch men like Stuart Jones? Why is it they seem to be protected?"

Wilfred either had no answer or chose not to share it with his brother. "We all do what we can. How is Miss Higgins? Shall I ask Maguire to call in?"

Rowland shook his head. Edna was physically recovered.

Wilfred sighed. "I could not be more sorry for what has happened to Miss Higgins, Rowly, but as I have said before, the way you and your friends live has consequences. Perhaps it's time you all became a little more circumspect." Wilfred went on to say a few words about the fact that his brother had apparently been discovered participating in a satanic ritual, but Rowland had expected that. He promised to attend church with the family that Sunday to placate Wilfred and God.

And so the day had been one of conflict and frustration and guilt. It was Edna herself who had called an end to it. She'd asked Rowland to carry the gramophone into the *Woodlands* ballroom and dragged Clyde up to dance with her. Possibly she knew Clyde's struggle with steps and rhythm would take their minds to inconsequential things and they would be themselves. Elisabeth Sinclair heard the music and came out to dance with Milton. They'd made something of a party of it until Elisabeth had retired exhausted.

Delaney telephoned and spoke first with Edna. Rowland was, of course, unable to hear the detective's part in the conversation, but Edna responded quite warmly. "Don't be silly, Colin," she said. "I know you believe me. This is not your fault. Reggie's so despicable I sometimes forget how clever he is."

When Rowland took the receiver, he was as a result of Edna's response to Delaney, more reasonable than he might otherwise have been. He told the detective of their conversation with Arthur Stace. "It seems the chap who had White's notebook also had a key to Magdalene's," Rowland said. "It's probably how he let White into the building in the first place."

"Magdalene appears to have issued keys to almost the entire coven," Delaney replied. "Only two blokes, both apparently named Smith, didn't have keys on them. They'd come in most nights and take bets confident that any activity would be attributed to witchcraft. It all seems to fit, Rowly. We just have to work out which one of them killed White."

"What about Hartley?"

"He still likes Milton for it. Pointed out that Wombat Newgate was known to Milt and could well have given him the key."

Rowland found himself unexpectedly uneasy about the conclusion that White had been murdered by one of the bookmakers in order to keep their operation secret. As much as the arrest of the bookmakers' coven presented alternatives to Milton, there seemed something more personal about the way White had been slaughtered. The reporter hadn't been bound, so the attack was unexpected and carried out face to face. The tiepin was taken and the body left to be found the next day. Surely it wasn't in the interests of illicit bookmakers to have a body found on premises they were trying to keep from the notice of the constabulary.

"We didn't find White's tiepin on any of the suspects," Delaney confirmed. "Magdalene and his fellow bookies are denying anything to do with White's murder, but you would expect that." The receiver crackled a little as Delaney paused. "Look Rowly, I am genuinely sorry about how hard Hartley was on Miss Higgins. But Stuart Jones' solicitors will be much harder in court."

Milton was right. Stuart Jones was a slippery bastard.

To keep their minds clear of bookmakers and the Lido, they focussed instead on the murder of Crispin White, discussing what had come out of Rowland's encounter with the coven and the account of Arthur Stace.

"They said they killed him," Clyde said.

"I think they suspected I wasn't taking them seriously," Rowland replied. "They were trying to scare me off."

"You don't know that they wouldn't have cut your throat if the police hadn't arrived."

Rowland pondered the idea. "No, but I don't think they would have. We know they're not really a coven. If they'd planned to kill me surely they would just have done it without all the theatrics."

Edna smiled. "It was all mildly ridiculous, come to think of it."

"It mightn't have been such a lark if they knew Rowly had discovered what they were really up to," Clyde said. "But I reckon Rowly's right. They didn't kill White. Not as a coven anyway."

"What do you mean?"

"It might have been one of them acting on his own, for his own reasons. It would explain why the murder took place at Magdalene's."

Rowland shared his conversation with the detective and the fact that most of the coven members had keys. "I could ask Delaney for the names, though, by the sounds of it, everyone except Magdalene is a Mr. Smith or Jones," Rowland mused. "But perhaps one of them had a link of some sort with White."

"What do the police think?" Clyde asked.

"Hartley is still convinced Milt killed Crispin." Rowland winced. "Wombat Newgate was in the coven, so now Milt is connected with someone who had a key."

"Well, that was well done," Milton said, letting his head fall back against the armchair.

"Arthur Stace seems to think the man who dropped the notebook was reading it," Rowland said. "That he was upset when he lost it. I wonder what in it interested him."

"One of the news stories Mr. White was working on, perhaps," Edna suggested. "Was he investigating something that would offend someone?"

"Other than Rowly?"

"Yes, other than Rowly."

"He was a punter," Milton reminded them. "Perhaps he owed money to one of those jokers in the masks."

"Surely killing him would be counterproductive to collecting a debt," Rowland argued.

"They might have been threatening White and got carried away. Maybe the killer took the tiepin as compensation."

Rowland groaned. "I don't suppose the person who took the tiepin would be stupid enough to wear it."

Edna laughed. "I don't think so, Rowly." She moved to sit on the arm of the couch beside him.

"White was also reporting on the Centre Party and Campbell," Milton said recollecting suddenly. "And didn't he ask you about Campbell that first night, Rowly? Wanted to know if you were ever a member of the New Guard?"

Rowland rolled his eyes. "Eric Campbell did not kill Crispin White, Milt."

"No—not him personally but one of his minions. You can't tell me Campbell no longer has a Fascist Legion of some sort at his beck and call."

"Campbell's right thinking men favour pick axe handles and guns. A razor seems a less... bourgeois sort of weapon."

"I wouldn't be too quick to assume the criminal underclasses don't have an interest in politics," Milton warned.

"No, Rowly's right." Clyde came back into the discussion. "The New Guard is much more likely to use guns or Queensbury rules." He sighed. "The fact that White's throat was slashed is what makes it look like the bookies were behind it."

"I thought we'd already decided they didn't do it," Milton said wearily.

They may well have argued in circles for some time if Mary Brown had not come in to announce a late caller. "A Miss Rosaleen Norton for you, Master Rowly. I've asked her to wait in the anteroom."

"Oh," Rowland glanced at the clock on the mantle, surprised the young reporter would be calling so late. "Please show her in, Mary." They were in Rowland's studio, but most of the paintings for the exhibition had been packed and transported to the gallery for hanging.

"Miss Norton." Rowland met her at the door. He introduced Clyde and Edna, and reminded her of Milton Isaacs whom she had already met.

Rosaleen Norton was wearing another figure-embracing garment, made up of artfully secured scarves, and a red camellia in her hair. She smiled and nodded politely through the introductions like a shy debutante. Rowland found himself glancing at her shoes. They were very like the ones worn by the woman in the coven, but not being an expert on women's shoes he could not be sure. He did wonder though.

"And what can I do for you, Miss Norton?"

"I came to thank you for showing Norman Lindsay my work. He's asked me to model for him."

"He did? My congratulations."

"I'm very grateful for your intervention on my behalf, Mr. Sinclair."

"Believe me when I say I did very little, Miss Norton."

"I thought I might pay you a visit and see how you were on the count of... you know."

"I'm sorry?"

"My premonition. Did you finish that painting?"

"Indeed, I did."

"Did something evil come out of it?"

Rowland hesitated. He did not wish to lie but surely the bullet didn't count. That had come through the painting rather than out of it, after all.

"I mean metaphorically, " Rosaleen said while he vacillated. "The story is about the compulsion of artists to examine the darkest parts of their souls, to lay bare the most dangerous ideas and how, in the end, we are all doomed to be consumed by the very thing we have created."

Rowland blinked. In the periphery of his vision he could see Milton smirking. "As you can see, I haven't been consumed," he said carefully.

"Haven't you, Mr. Sinclair?" she said, rising on her toes to gaze searchingly into his eyes. "Haven't you?"

Rowland shot Milton a silent plea for help.

"The only thing Rowly's been consumed by is the Maroubra Invitational!" Milton stepped ably into the breach. "Are you still covering that story, Miss Norton?"

"Oh that. No, Ken Slessor's taken over. Frank wants me to write another story for him," she said, taking the chair Rowland offered her. The gentlemen resumed their own seats.

"What's this one about?" Edna asked enthusiastically.

Rosaleen straightened her shoulders. "Actually that's the other reason I've come—there's a full moon tonight."

"I beg your pardon?" Rowland asked. Rosaleen Norton had a very cryptic way of communicating.

"I've been thinking of the statue of Pan in your garden, Mr. Sinclair. I wondered what it would look like in the moonlight."

Edna regarded the girl curiously. "Why don't we have a look now?" she suggested.

"Oh, I was hoping you'd say that!" Rosaleen jumped to her feet.

Edna stood too and the men rose less enthusiastically. Milton grabbed the decanter of sherry as they walked out.

There was indeed a full moon that night, so bright that the garden was rendered in stark colourless clarity. The air was cold. Perhaps that was what chilled them into a kind of acute awareness. It seemed to Rowland that he heard every footfall and crackle, every night bird and frog. He saw the faint glow of a cigarette near the gatehouse and the black silhouettes of each leaf. Of course, he'd walked the grounds in the moonlight before, but on those occasions he might have been somewhat distracted by the company and purpose of taking the night air. Certainly it was the first time he'd stepped out at this time to inspect a statue.

Edna's sculptures, bathed in moonsilver and shadow, were ethereal, and strangely threatening. Rosaleen Norton's eyes were large and bright. They fell upon the statue of Pan with a kind of reverent lust.

"He's really quite alive under this Pagan moon," she whispered. "Marvellously beautiful." She touched the statue's lips. "His face is exquisite… exotic and soulless."

Clyde guffawed.

"It's Milt's—Mr. Isaacs' face," Edna said, shoving Clyde. "I used him as my model. See, his nose is distinctly crooked, just like Milt's."

"I believe the word Miss Norton used was exquisite," Milton said, adopting the pose of the statue. He winked at Rosaleen. "Perhaps your next story could be about a particularly handsome statue that comes to life and becomes the toast of society."

"It'll be your most frightening tale yet," Clyde added.

"I must say, being a statue rather suits you, Mr. Isaacs," Rosaleen said running her hands over Pan's shoulders. "He's quite wonderful—makes me want to dance wantonly in the moonlight like some ancient priestess."

Milton offered the young reporter his hand. "If you'll allow me to stand in for my statue?"

"But there is no music."

"Oh, I'll sing!" the poet said, undeterred.

The Red Flag was possibly an unusual song by which to dance the foxtrot, and probably not what Rosaleen had meant by "wanton", but they danced nonetheless. Rowland, Clyde and Edna watched, amused. Beejling and Armstrong wandered up from the gatehouse to investigate the disturbance and stayed to watch, disapproval declared in their tightly crossed arms. Rowland grimaced. The episode would probably be reported to Wilfred soon. He was accustomed to Milton's idiotic notions, but his brother was likely to be less understanding.

33

MOON MADNESS
by Rosaleen Norton

———————◆———————

...His face was marvellously beautiful and sad with all the sadness of the ages—sad yet utterly, soullessly evil. His was a detached wickedness of something beyond humanity, like an archangel of evil. It might in fact have been a mask of Lucifer at the time of his fall—still young, yet incredibly ancient in the knowledge of ghastly secrets and fearful rites that were old when mankind lived like apes in the trees...

Smith's Weekly, 1934

The Australian Red Cross' refreshment tent at the back of the horticultural pavilion at the Royal Easter Show was enjoying a surge in popularity. The Maroubra Invitational Race was generating considerable interest and a static display model of the speedway complete with racing cars added a certain excitement to tea and biscuits.

Rowland lifted his godson onto his shoulders. Ewan promptly knocked the hat off his uncle's head. Ernest retrieved it.

"Thank you, Ernie." Rowland held on to the hat as he could feel that Ewan's small hands were entwined in his hair.

Wilfred and Kate were viewing the roses in the pavilion. Young Gilbert had remained with his nanny at *Roburvale*, but Ernest and Ewan had accompanied their parents to the show. Inevitably the boys had become bored, and Rowland and Milton had volunteered to take them for ice-cream. Of course, Beejling was presumably also nearby.

They were not actually heading for, but past the Red Cross tent in search of an ice-cream vendor. Indeed, Rowland was trying to give the tent as wide a berth as possible to ensure he didn't find himself being endlessly introduced to the venerable patrons and matrons of the charity.

Even so they passed close enough to notice Redmond Barry and Reginald Stuart Jones in conversation outside the tent.

If not for his nephews, Rowland might have responded in a manner that was at the very least rash.

"What the blazes are they doing here?"

"I expect some of the gentlemen coming out of that tent may be placing bets on the outcome of the Maroubra Invitational." Milton pointed out the spotters walking in and out of the tent in the company of men eager to part with their pounds and pennies. "There'll be a bookie nearby to take wagers."

"Clearly the police didn't see fit to hold Stuart Jones," Rowland said angrily.

"Is something wrong, Uncle Rowly?" Ernest asked, looking up. "Are you cross?"

"Of course not, Ernie," Rowland said quickly.

"Are you nervous, Uncle Rowly?"

"Nervous? About what?"

"The race. Digby Cossington Smythe says that it's bewitched. He says you'll be driving on a killer track. He says the track gets everyone eventually."

Rowland pulled a face. "It appears Digby Cossington Smythe is rather an oracle of doom."

"What's an ora... cul?"

Rowland handed Ewan to Milton and bent down to speak to Ernest. "Never mind, Ernie. And never you mind about the racetrack. It's just a track and it doesn't have anything against me or the other racers."

"Daddy says you're safer on the track than you are anywhere else. He told Mummy that you're determined to get yourself killed. You're not are you, Uncle Rowly?" Ernest's face was both fearful and stern; a little boy trying to emulate his father, but with real dread that his uncle would in fact die.

Rowland smiled. "I'm sure your father didn't know you were listening. If he had, he would have told you he was speaking in jest. I quite like being alive."

"Daddy says you have a talent for making enemies."

"Nonsense, I'm thoroughly charming!"

"Then you won't get killed?"

Rowland was tempted to assure his nephew that absolutely, he would not. But the question was familiar. He'd asked it himself when he was not much older than Ernest, as his brothers prepared to go to war—a momentary panic amongst the celebration of impending adventure. He had believed them when they'd said they wouldn't die, that they'd be back before Christmas. Then Aubrey had been killed in France, and mixed into the overwhelming grief, the destruction of life as it had been, was the feeling that he'd been tricked. "Look at it this way, Ernie," he said in the end. "I've had quite a lot of practice at not being killed. I'm getting quite good at it now."

Ernest thought about it. The logic seemed to appeal to him.

"Very well, Uncle Rowly. I really do wish you'd settle down though. Daddy believes you ought to stand for parl'ment. He says you're tall enough to be Premier."

Milton laughed for a number of reasons.

"Your father told you that?" Rowland asked, bemused.

"He told Mummy. I was listening."

Rowland wasn't sure what exactly his brother might have said, but he was pretty sure Wilfred didn't believe height was the deciding factor in the race for public office. However, it was not something he could ever clarify without revealing his nephew had been eavesdropping. So he let it be.

Ewan's demands for "scream" had in any case now become quite vociferous and immediate appeasement seemed the most advisable strategy.

The much-anticipated Royal Easter Show Ball was being held on the evening before the race. Joan Richmond was unhappy with the timing of the lavish affair. The racers were all expected to attend, though Joan was adamant her team should be home and tucked up in bed by half past ten. That, in addition to Clyde's insistence he not drink, meant Rowland was anticipating a very wholesome evening.

He collected Joan from her hotel. Clyde had declined the evening's invitation to sit with the Mercedes, lest an intruder get past Wilfred's security to interfere with the vehicle. Rowland suspected that, in truth, Clyde couldn't bring himself to attend a ball to which he might once have taken Rosalina Martinelli. He understood—in fact he would happily have kept his friend company in the stables if the Red Cross' organising committee had not insisted he make an appearance. Instead, Milton had decided to guard the Mercedes with Clyde, much to Elisabeth Sinclair's disappointment.

Errol Flynn had invited Edna, leaving Rowland to escort "the cap'n" as Flynn insisted upon calling Joan Richmond.

"He makes me feel like I ought to have an eye-patch and a wooden leg," Joan complained as she took Rowland's arm into the Town Hall.

Rowland glanced down at the racer's crimson gown. "I like what you're wearing better," he said.

Joan laughed. "Well let's get this over with then."

The Town Hall had been bedecked with bunting and festoons of blue hydrangea. Supper had been laid out on linen-draped tables and an orchestra played from the stage. The gentlemen presented a consistent elegance in white tie and tails whilst the ladies were given the privilege and responsibility of appropriate individuality. Even amongst the competitive spectacle of gowns and jewellery and poise, Rowland's eyes found Edna immediately, and rested there a while. The sculptress seemed to sense his gaze and turned towards him to smile and wave. She grabbed Flynn's hand and pulled him through the crowd towards Joan and Rowland.

"Hello you two. Isn't the hall just lovely?"

"It is terribly swish," Joan agreed. "Have you been here long?"

"No, we just arrived."

"Sinclair! I'm glad to see Wilfred found you in the end. Last I heard you were absent without leave!"

Rowland turned stiffly towards the greeting. "Colonel Campbell, Mrs. Campbell," he said with painstakingly conscious civility. "May I introduce Miss Joan Richmond and Mr. Errol Flynn? I believe you know Miss Higgins."

"Oh yes," the leader of the New Guard said, glancing at his wife. "You remember, my dear. This is the young lady who purported to be Mr. Sinclair's fiancée and then shot him in my study. Ruined the Axminster." Campbell laughed loudly.

Mrs. Campbell looked mortified. "It was such an ugly carpet, Eric. I was glad of the excuse to replace it," she said nervously.

Rowland met Campbell's eye, wondering what the man was up to. "Then we are both glad of Miss Higgins' actions, Mrs. Campbell. You were able to replace the carpet and I was able to avoid being beaten to death."

"Yes, well I'm afraid the chaps can be a little zealous when they feel I'm in danger. They're a jolly decent and loyal bunch."

"I hear you've become a politician, Colonel Campbell," Rowland said with a smile that did not reach his eyes. "I'm so glad to see democracy has finally won you over."

"Sometimes it's necessary to effect change from within," Campbell replied smoothly. "And what are you doing with your time these days, Sinclair? By the time I was your age, I'd fought a war, progressed in business, married and founded a thriving legal firm."

"Not to mention a militia," Rowland said brightly. "Actually, I'm thinking about standing for parliament myself, since it seems to be the thing to do these days."

Edna beamed and rubbed Rowland's arm in a show of pride. "I don't believe Lane Cove will have ever had so handsome a member." If she had exhibited the slightest surprise, Campbell might have realised that Rowland Sinclair was fabricating his intended candidacy, that his interest in the seat of Lane Cove was being feigned to irritate the man who hoped to win it. But Edna Higgins was a convincing actress, and having been offended by his reference to the shooting incident she carried on. "The publicity surrounding the race has been just wonderful for raising Rowly's public profile!"

Campbell was noticeably shaken. "You haven't announced…"

"Well, I didn't want to take attention away from the race—the car race, that is," Rowland said unfazed. "It's for charity, after all. Time and place, you know."

Campbell's smile looked more like a barring of teeth. "If you'll excuse us, I've promised Nancy a turn on the dance floor."

Edna giggled as the Campbells flounced away. "Now we've done it," she said, delighted.

"I didn't realise you were standing for parliament, Rowly," Joan ventured.

"I'm not," Rowland whispered. "Ed and I were just playing the fool, to be honest."

"I sense you may have upset Colonel Campbell," Joan observed.

"Yes, it's a terrible pity," Edna said blithely.

A pause in the music signalled that the formalities were about to begin. Various dignitaries took the stage to acknowledge other dignitaries and to deliver words of welcome and thanks. When the music started again, Rowland danced with Joan, discussing race strategy through the slides of a Gypsy Tap and two waltzes. Then he took Edna on to the floor while Joan gave the same instructions to Errol.

Rowland saw that Campbell had abandoned any pretence of dancing, spending the evening instead in earnest conversations with various gentlemen and the Honourable Charlotte Linklater who'd attended the ball wearing a black gown in remembrance of her brother.

"Are you all right, Rowly?" Edna asked as she sensed him become distant and tense.

"Yes," he replied. "I just wish Miss Linklater would allow me to—"

"The accident wasn't your fault."

"I know. But it seems callous that we're all just carrying on as if nothing happened."

"That wasn't your decision, darling. Miss Linklater wanted to race in her brother's place." Edna glanced over her shoulder at the bereaved motorist. Charlotte Linklater was watching them from beside the punch bowl. She looked more wistful than anything else. "Why don't you try speaking to her again? Put all this nonsense to rest before tomorrow's race."

"Would you mind?"

"Of course not." Edna squeezed his hand. "Just so long as you remember you don't need absolution."

He brought her gloved hand to his lips and kissed it. "Thank you."

Rowland relinquished the sculptress to one of the many admirers circling hopefully for a chance to cut in, and made his way to Charlotte Linklater.

"Miss Linklater?"

"Yes?"

Suddenly Rowland was unsure what exactly he wanted to say and so he asked her for that dance. She accepted without any sign of enthusiasm whatsoever. He led her onto the floor and for a while they waltzed without exchanging words. Rowland's height meant that by keeping her eyes straight ahead she could avoid looking at his face. Even so, the fact that Charlotte had accepted gave Rowland some hope. Finally he broke the silence between them.

"Miss Linklater, I know our dealings have been difficult to date, but I hope you'll believe me when I say I do not wish for us to be enemies."

She said nothing.

Rowland continued. "I know that you're racing in your late brother's memory and if there's anything I can do to help you honour that memory—"

"Yes, there is," she said, raising her eyes. Rowland pulled back, startled by the seething hostility in them. "Stay out of my way," Charlotte hissed. "Because on the track I shall drive as ruthlessly as you did when you forced Charles into the fence. Dear Charles had only toured before, but I've raced in bowls. I understand the peculiarities of speedways and I will show you no measure of mercy. I suggest you withdraw Mr. Sinclair and retreat behind that red easel of yours because I have not forgiven you!"

Rowland stayed in step. "It's regrettable that you feel that way and whether you believe me or not, I am sorry for what happened to your brother."

"Have you ever lost a brother, Mr. Sinclair?"

"Yes. Aubrey was killed in the war."

"And how do you feel about the people who killed him? Mr. Campbell told me about your ongoing animosity against the German government."

"That has nothing to do with Aubrey."

"Are you sure? How else do you explain your opposition to a government that has returned Germany to its former greatness?"

The bracket finished. Rowland thanked Charlotte Linklater for the dance and abandoned his attempts at a pre-race reconciliation. But he wished her luck, quite sincerely, as she turned her back on him.

Wilfred found him before he could re-join Joan and Flynn. Kate Sinclair was on her husband's arm. The pale blue sheath suited her porcelain complexion. She was, as always, a picture of understated elegance.

"Rowly. Best of British for tomorrow, old boy." Wilfred shook his brother's hand. "Don't get carried away. The Red Cross will make plenty of money whether or not you win."

"Thank you, Wil. Are you bringing the boys?"

Wilfred nodded. "Ernie and Ewan, anyway. Gilbert's a bit young to enjoy the finer points of motor racing. I understand the organisers are expecting quite a crowd, so let's hope that Fritz jalopy of yours lives up to expectations."

Kate turned to her husband. "For heaven's sake, Wil. You're not going to quarrel about Rowly's motorcar now!"

Rowland laughed. "No we're not." Joan Richmond caught his eye from across the room and tapped her watch. He sighed. "I'm afraid I must be going. Joan's imposed a strict curfew." His kissed Kate's cheek. "I'll see you tomorrow. I'll be the one in the Fritz jalopy at the front."

34

MOTOR SPORT

Popularity Increasing

Judging by the record number of visitors to Cowes for the 100-mile race on New Year's Day motor racing is at last becoming as popular in Australia as it has been for many years overseas. The 6 ½ miles rectangular course on Phillip Island is very suitable for motor racing, and it can be closed to ordinary traffic while races are being decided. It is hoped that later other good roads on the island will be used to form a much longer course, making a complete circuit of the island. By facilitating the holding of races the shire council and residents have materially increased the popularity of the island as a holiday resort, and have greatly assisted the motoring clubs. This year promises to be a record one for motor sport. It is hoped that several overseas drivers will compete in a special Centenary programme of racing.

The Argus, 1934

The residents of *Woodlands House* set out for the Maroubra Speedway at dawn. Despite all the drama and mayhem leading up to the event they embarked with a spirit that was both festive and adventurous. Clyde had ensured the Mercedes was ready, Rowland knew his motorcar and had become well acquainted with the idiosyncrasies of the speedway; Joan Richmond was a racing veteran and her Riley, top shelf; Errol Flynn was enthusiastic and his Triumph at least sea-worthy. Surely a good time would be had by all.

They were among the first to arrive at the track. Speedway officials with brooms, shovels and bags were clearing the bowl of debris as well as the snakes, lizards and the occasional cat that had come to enjoy the morning sun on warm concrete. Each team had been given a makeshift bay into which their cars could pull off for refuelling, minor repairs or wheel changes if necessary. The Red Cross marquee in the centre of the bowl served the racers breakfast to the strains of a bombastic brass band. After months of preparation, setbacks and anxiety, the day of the race had broken clear of clouds and the atmosphere was buoyant and infectious.

With wishes of good luck and exhortations to be careful, Edna and Milton set off to find seats among the burgeoning throng of spectators. There was still a while till flag fall, but the venue was filling fast. Clyde hummed tunelessly as he checked the Mercedes once again, and Rowland mentally paced out his part of the race, until familiar figures caught their attention.

It was the doctor's ostentatious sense of style—reminiscent of Milton's—that attracted their notice. Stuart Jones stood in the infield talking to Redmond Barry and another. For a moment the second man merely sparked a sense of vague recognition and then Rowland placed him: Les Bocquet. What was Les Bocquet doing with Stuart Jones?

Rowland glanced at his watch—recently repaired and synchronised with Clyde's. They still had nearly an hour. He signalled Clyde. "I'm just going to have a brief word with Stuart Jones."

"Rowly, the race—"

"It won't be a long conversation. I'll be back in time."

"Well then, I'll come with you," Clyde said, wiping his hands on his overalls. "Ed reckons Stuart Jones carries a revolver, remember."

Rowland nodded. "Best bring the tyre lever."

They intercepted the doctor near the underpass which afforded public entry from outside the bowl through a culvert that ran under the track. Redmond Barry and Les Bocquet might have seen them coming—they were gone by the time Rowland grabbed Stuart Jones by the collar. He dragged the protesting gynaecologist into the tunnel opening and slammed him against the poster-plastered wall. Clyde stood back, keeping an eye out for anyone who might come to Stuart Jones' aid.

"Rowly, look, I fully understand you're upset but you must let me explain…"

"Explain what, you cretin?"

"That misunderstanding with Eddie. You see Eddie and I go back a long way, it's only natural that she come to me when—"

Rowland punched him. "If you ever lay your filthy hands on her again, so help me—"

"Is everything all right here?" The first good Samaritan.

"Just move on, sir," Clyde growled. It seemed to work.

Rowland seized Stuart Jones' arm as the doctor reached for his pocket, pinning it to the wall. "You're not carrying a loaded gun are you, Reggie? Do you know how many people accidentally shoot themselves with their own firearm?"

"What do you want, Sinclair?" Stuart Jones was discernibly nervous now.

"How do you know Les Bocquet?"

"Bocquet?" Stuart Jones was clearly perplexed. "He places a couple of bets for me."

"He's a bookmaker?"

"What's it to you?"

Rowland hit him again. "Is he a bookmaker?"

"Yes. How else would he afford that grand residence in Lindfield and that pretty little wife of his? Bocquet's a street rat!"

A second and third Samaritan approached. "Is there some kind of problem here?" To Stuart Jones: "Do you need some assistance, mate? Should we get the police?"

At this Stuart Jones became tense. "No, no… just a bit of horseplay… We're old friends, aren't we, Rowland?" Rowland looked anything but friendly, but, keen to find seats, the Samaritans took the doctor at his word and moved on.

Rowland relaxed his fist, and spoke to Stuart Jones with quiet and chilling certainty. "If you venture near Miss Higgins again, I'll find you, Jones, and even the devil won't be able to help you then."

Stuart Jones reacted to the mention of Edna. "I'm a doctor, Rowland. I've taken an oath. If Eddie comes to me for help, I can't refuse, and nothing you say—"

"Right." Rowland grabbed him by the scruff of his jacket and dragged him with them. Once they were out of the tunnel, Stuart Jones regained some confidence. There was not much Sinclair could do with thousands of people watching.

By the time they reached the improvised pits, Stuart Jones was chatting about the race like they were old friends. Rowland was calmly livid. Clyde did not ask what his friend had planned.

Joan Richmond was waiting for them. She barely glanced at Stuart Jones. "Clyde, quickly, you must conduct a thorough check of Rowly's vehicle."

"Why?" Clyde asked, already unfolding the bonnet.

"Saboteurs. I just chased off some chap fiddling around beneath it. The race begins in twenty minutes."

"What did this fellow look like?" Rowland asked, glancing at Stuart Jones, who shrugged innocently.

"Shifty," Joan replied. "I would normally have assumed he was simply retrieving a dropped penny or something, but with everything that's happened…"

"I can't see anything," Clyde said from under the bonnet. "Rowly, start her up will you?"

Rowland did so and Clyde checked and tested. Joan left them to it and checked her Riley as well.

"What did you do?" Rowland demanded of Stuart Jones.

"Nothing, I know nothing about this." The doctor smiled broadly. "Still, it's rather troubling."

Clyde closed the bonnet, his face creased with undisguised worry.

"Did you find a problem?" Rowland asked.

"No. I can't find any tampering."

"Well, that's good, isn't it?"

Clyde sighed. "I dunno. If I'd found something then we'd know what he'd been doing and I'd fix it. Now, we just don't know what this bloke was up to … whether I've missed something."

Stuart Jones slipped into the passenger seat of the Mercedes. "Perhaps you ought to check it over again, my good man. You'll be late to start, of course, but we can't put too high a value on Rowland's safety."

"Get the hell out of my car," Rowland snarled.

"Don't be like that, Rowly," Stuart Jones said, clearly enjoying himself. "This is rather a spiffing automobile." He sat back. "Do you generally have a chauffeur? I prefer to be driven myself." For a moment Rowland considered pulling the doctor bodily and none too gently from the vehicle, but he stopped. "I'll take the chance that if you can't find something, it's because there isn't anything," he told Clyde.

Clyde cursed. "You be careful, Rowly," he said. "If the Mercedes feels strange in any way, you stop immediately. You bring her in."

"You have my word," Rowland promised. "Perhaps the poor chap Joan saw was just chasing a runaway penny after all."

"I hope so," Clyde said. "I'm not happy sending you out when I'm not sure."

"You are sure," Rowland said. "We're just all a little jumpy." He nodded at Stuart Jones. "That buffoon doesn't help."

"Maybe he arranged for one of his mates to—"

"You couldn't find anything wrong. I suspect the good doctor's trying to unnerve us enough to ensure we lose before the start."

A siren summoned the contestants to their starting positions. "Let's get that blasted fool out of your car," Clyde said. "It's time to go."

"Leave it to me." Rowland fastened the leather helmet and pulled on his goggles.

Clyde slapped his shoulder. "Good luck, mate. Remember, if anything feels wrong, pull off."

Rowland nodded. He opened the door and gave his unwanted passenger one last chance. "Right, get out!"

Stuart Jones smirked. "Oh dear, my foot seems to be stuck. I do hope I'm not delaying you."

Without another word, Rowland slipped behind the wheel and started the car. Stuart Jones folded his arms ready to call what he assumed was a bluff. Joan and Flynn ran over to wave the Mercedes away.

"Don't forget, we need at least three laps," Joan said, running beside the Mercedes as Rowland took his starting position. "If you lose count of the laps, look for Clyde—he'll hold up a number. Rowly, there's some chap in your vehicle!"

Rowland nodded as he gunned the motor. Only then did Stuart Jones panic. The Mercedes took off into the bowl with the doctor screaming from the passenger seat.

The first five laps were designated to allow the drivers to warm their tyres, at which point they would line up at the start once more. But Stuart Jones didn't know that, and even at a relatively gentle speed, the prospect of the bowl clearly terrified him. He wailed like a banshee and wept, clinging white-knuckled to the dash and promising Rowland anything and everything if only he'd stop the car. Rowland kept his eyes on the track.

Clyde pulled the hysterical doctor out when Rowland took his position for the beginning of the race proper. Rowland waved at his friend, hoping Stuart Jones' reaction was not connected to any actual knowledge that the motorcar had been compromised. The flag came down and they were away, this time in earnest.

The rest seemed a dream, the sequence of events he'd practised for weeks, with the addition of a cheering, thirty-thousand strong crowd to make it more surreal. It was no longer just him and his car. For the first ten laps, Rowland was tense, painfully alert to any malfunction, a slight wobble, a miniscule rattle, any sign of interference. But there was nothing. He settled into a rhythm, a pattern by which he avoided the most deteriorated sections of the track.

The Mercedes was responsive, building up to speed and finding her position high on the bowl, but not so high that he was at risk of going over the edge of the "Killer Track". Rowland focussed his mind and shut out everything else. The crowd disappeared into the blurred mass of everything but the track. Though it had been publicised as an endurance event, he had only to complete two hundred laps. His part of the race would be over in about two hours. The Honourable Charlotte Linklater's Bentley Speed Six stuck stubbornly with him, pulling in to refuel and change tyres when he did. He engaged the supercharger and pulled away, climbing higher on the bowl as he accelerated. By seventy laps he was one ahead of Charlotte, with at least two laps on every other contestant. Charlotte Linklater was clearly a better racer than her late brother had been. At one hundred laps, she'd clawed back Rowland's lead. Rowland knew the Mercedes had more in her, though to unleash the extra power he'd have to risk the highest point of the bowl. But he was confident now.

Clyde watched from the infield as the Mercedes climbed to the very rim of the speedway. Under his breath, he prayed. The 1927 S-Class was a fine machine, but he was not sure she was built for this. Clyde's eyes stayed fixed on the yellow saloon, watching for any sign of trouble. He'd driven the bowl with Rowland. He knew what seemed precarious and downright foolhardy from the infield would seem less so from behind the wheel. He could only guess that was why Rowland was tempting disaster.

With her hands over her eyes, Edna watched through the small spaces between her fingers, turning her face into Milton's shoulder when it became unbearable. The Mercedes seemed to be clinging to an almost vertical plane as spiralled up to the very top of the bowl. "It's all right, Ed," Milton whispered. "Rowly knows and loves that car. He won't risk scratching it."

The absurd reminder was strangely comforting. Edna had often accused Rowland of being in thrall to a gaudy German mistress. He'd been most offended by the word "gaudy".

Ernest Sinclair rotated in his seat, determined not to take his eyes off his uncle's car. He was consequently becoming quite dizzy. Wilfred was tempted to demand the boy sit still, but the excitement on his son's face stayed any censure. He remembered that same expression on Rowland's face years ago, when the Sinclairs had acquired their very first automobile. Wilfred glanced at the position of the Mercedes, telling himself that men of his brother's age had grown up tearing about in motorcars—it was second nature to them and not as dangerous as it seemed to those whose youth had been spent on horseback. Still, the reputation of the track had not escaped him and Wilfred wondered if he ought to have forbidden Rowland's participation, at the same time realising that doing so would probably only have cemented his brother's determination to race.

Rowland had extended his lead to four laps when Charlotte Linklater made her move. She climbed higher onto the bowl until the Mercedes and the Bentley were virtually abreast. He remembered her words, her warning to stay out of her way and he realised she would pull in front of him regardless of whether or not she had the speed to complete the manoeuvre. He made the decision to slow down, sure he had more than the three laps lead he needed, though he'd lost count of how many he'd completed. Charlotte reefed the Bentley to the left in front of the Mercedes. Rowland swore, his car fishtailing wildly as he was forced to take what evasive action he could.

Thirty thousand spectators gasped with a collective horror. Many stood, bracing to witness the killer track take yet another life.

"Come on darling. Settle." Rowland spoke to his motorcar like she was a skittish horse as he tried to bring her under control. Avoiding a collision with the Bentley had forced him onto a deteriorated patch of the track. He could hear loose concrete peppering the mudguards and scraping against the undercarriage. The wheels skidded violently. A front tyre blew and there was no longer any control to be had. Orange sparks, the gouging screech of metal on concrete. The top of the bowl and then the sky as the yellow Mercedes hurtled over the edge. One of the towering light poles just outside the track stopped her progress, and parts of Rowland Sinclair's beloved motorcar were flung back onto the speedway.

For a moment the bowl seemed to fall silent of everything but the roar of vehicles still in the race. And then screams. Wilfred Sinclair stared, struggling to comprehend what he had just witnessed. There were sirens now, and more screeching as vehicles swerved to avoid the debris of Rowland's car. Kate Sinclair started to cry.

"I don't understand," Elisabeth Sinclair said. "What's happened? I didn't see."

Numbly Wilfred signalled the nurses who sat discreetly in the row behind the family. He hugged his wife, too tightly. "Katie, I must—"

"Go," she whispered. "I'll take the children and Mother home."

"Daddy, that was Uncle Rowly's car," Ernest sobbed.

Wilfred paused to embrace his son. "Yes, I know Ernie."

The other racers were called into the infield. People spilled on to the track, trying to run up the steep embankment to reach the Mercedes, or what was left of it.

"That didn't happen," Edna said quietly. "No." But she wanted to scream. That stupid car. Why did it do that?

Milton grabbed her hand. He looked strange, she thought... green. "Ed?"

"No," she said.

"I've got to go find him."

"Who?" she said vaguely.

"Rowly."

She nodded. That was right. They should find Rowly.

Clyde was on his knees. He'd missed something. My God, he'd missed something. It was Joan Richmond who reached him first. She grabbed him by the shoulders, looked into his eyes and spoke slowly. "Come on, old bean. We'll go around the outside."

He wasn't sure what she meant, but he went with her. She drove him out of the bowl. The particular section of the speedway where the Mercedes had gone over was built up by a sand dune. Though most of the spectators had been seated in the infield several hundred had chosen to avoid admission and picnic on the dune instead. Clyde felt sick. The worst thing suddenly became even worse. They ran up to the light pole, to the smashed hulk of the yellow Mercedes that Rowland had so cherished.

There was a crowd gathered there already. Joan asked. No spectators had been hurt. The light pole in question had claimed the life of the great Phil Garlick in a similar accident years ago—it was given a wide berth out of respect and superstition.

Clyde steeled himself to the task of retrieving his friend's body. He needed desperately to get Rowland out of the twisted chassis. The Mercedes had clipped the pole and wrapped around it. The passenger side of the cabin was crushed, the driver's side empty.

"Where the bloody hell is Rowly?" Clyde demanded, forgetting himself in his horror and grief.

"His body must have been thrown out," Joan's voice caught.

The search began. By then thousands of spectators had climbed up to the accident site as well as officials with megaphones, the inevitable media and an ambulance. The sheer number of people hampered rather than helped the hunt for Rowland Sinclair, with false sightings and hysteria.

It was a child who found him, at least forty feet away in the scrub that dotted the dune. Of course everybody surged to see. Someone began to sing The Lord is my Shepherd and soon other well-meaning voices joined the impromptu requiem.

"Why the hell are they singing hymns?" Milton muttered angrily as he and Edna fought to get through the crowd. "He'll be all right. There's no call for hymns."

Edna said nothing. She was pale with fury and fear. Of all the things that Rowland stood for, of all the people and noble causes for which he was willing to fight, for which he had fought, he could not die in a stupid car race. The sculptress' heart clenched, resisting the knowledge that would break it. He could not be dead.

Officials with megaphones instructed the crowds to stay back. But they allowed Wilfred Sinclair through. Clyde and Joan were already bent over the crumpled body. Wilfred dropped to his knees beside his brother trying to ignore the resurgent familiarity that threatened to engulf him. The Great War was over and Rowland was not Aubrey, however much they looked alike... bloodied and so very still. This grief had its own ache, this loss its own abyss.

When Clyde declared that Rowland Sinclair was not dead, they thought that it was the grief which spoke and they tried to calm him, to comfort him.

"No!" Clyde turned to Wilfred for help. "I can feel a pulse, I'm sure it's a pulse."

Wilfred had no hope when he took Rowland's wrist from Clyde. Silently, he removed his glasses and placed the lens on Rowland's lips. Mist.

He roared for a doctor, for the ambulance, for help.

35

HEALTH IN THE HOME
By Dr. E. U. STANG.

Public Health Department, Perth (W.A.)

CONVALESCENCE

It is important that a cheerful attitude be maintained, as convalescent patients are apt to feel very depressed, and this feeling reacts against them. This, however, does not mean that the sickroom should be noisy, with a large number of friends and relatives. On the contrary, friends should be admitted with caution, and should never be allowed to stay longer than from 15 to 20 minutes, and only two friends at the most on one day, because it cannot be stressed too strongly that a person recovering from an illness has but feeble strength, and noise and excitement as well as depression steal it away. Everything surrounding the patient should be restful, happy, and cheerful. All worries and irritations should be kept away, and the room made attractive with bright flowers—sunny and fresh-looking—not overburdened with furniture and knick knacks.

The Australasian, 1934

Rowland Sinclair did not regain consciousness for two days. In that time it was widely reported that he had died. Certainly it did not seem possible that he could survive so terrible an accident. In their haste to secure the scoop, perhaps the reporters had not bothered to check the ultimate accuracy of their stories on the latest speedway tragedy. Whatever the case, Rowland was quite movingly eulogised as a talented, if sometimes controversial artist, cut down in his prime.

Strangely, however, while Rowland's injuries were not trivial, they were not catastrophic. A dislocated shoulder, some fractured ribs, a collapsed lung and severe grazing. Painful, certainly, but considering what had happened, he had escaped lightly. He should have been dead. The newspapers all said he was, and his doctors were at a loss to explain why he wasn't. They speculated that the sand dune had cushioned the impact after he was thrown from the motorcar. It seemed the only explanation.

After regaining consciousness it was another day before Rowland could clearly comprehend what his brother and friends were able to tell him. After an initial panicked agitation, Clyde had reassured him that no one else had been injured or killed despite the fact that the Mercedes had flown off the edge into the crowd. Later they would tell him that the race was continued once he'd been taken to hospital. Indeed, Joan Richmond's team had won in a result that was popular with the crowds and disastrous for bookmakers.

Edna hadn't said a great deal in those first days though he was aware of her presence. Her rose perfume had been the first familiar thing to penetrate the fog, and then, the pressure of her hand in his. And when pain swamped his senses, her hand had still been there.

Wilfred Sinclair had made arrangements with the hospital to allow the sculptress to stay with his brother, irrespective of visiting hours. It was irregular and highly improper, but in this instance Wilfred was willing to sacrifice propriety. While Rowland was in danger, Edna rarely left his bedside.

In the time before Rowland revived, Milton Isaacs was arrested for the murder of Crispin White. At Wilfred's insistence that fact was kept from Rowland until the poet's release on bail had been secured.

Even so, the news, as Wilfred had anticipated, was not conducive to Rowland's state of mind, nor to the bed rest which had been prescribed.

"Rowly! What on earth are you doing out of bed?" Edna demanded as she came into the hospital room. Rowland was on his feet though he leaned heavily on the iron foot of the cot. Milton stood beside him, Clyde by the door.

The poet shook his head. "Maybe you can talk some sense into him, Ed."

"I'm going home," Rowland said, smiling determinedly.

"Rowly, the doctor said you were to stay in bed."

"I can do that at *Woodlands*." Milton grabbed him as he released the bed.

"I'll call Johnston to bring the car," he gasped. A cold sweat was beaded on his forehead and it was only Milton who kept him upright.

"We'll talk to your doctors." Edna slipped under his arm and gave him her shoulder for support. "But you can't just walk out of here in your pyjamas."

"I was going to get dressed first." Rowland inhaled sharply, trying not to lean too heavily on Edna.

"Into what?" she asked. "We haven't brought you in any clothes, so unless you were planning to steal a nurse's uniform…"

Milton grinned. "Now that would be worth seeing."

With help, Rowland made it back into the bed. "I forgot about that," he admitted, wincing. God, how could a few steps be so exhausting?

Edna pulled up the bedclothes and adjusted the pillows. Clyde poured him a glass of water from the jug on the bedside table. "How do you feel, mate?"

"Like a motorcar fell on me." He glanced at Clyde. "I don't suppose…" he began hopefully. He'd been avoiding asking about the state of the Mercedes because he feared the answer. And nobody had raised the subject to date.

His friends glanced at one another and said nothing.

He groaned. "How bad is it?"

"I'm sorry, mate," Clyde said. "I don't think even the good Lord himself could fix her now. The fact that you survived is miracle enough."

"Are you sure we couldn't—"

"Not a chance, Rowly. She's gone, I'm afraid." Clyde delivered this blow honestly but with compassion. "I'm sorry, mate. I know she meant a lot to you."

"Oh." Rowland took the glass of water Clyde had poured, as the fact settled. "Damn." He drank a silent toast to his automobile, chastising himself even as he did so for feeling the loss so acutely when there were more important things to worry about. But he did feel it. "Hartley is not going to be looking for anybody else now that he's arrested Milt," he said forcing his thoughts away. "If he ever did."

"You don't need to worry about that now, Rowly," Milton said firmly. "We're still getting used to the fact that you're not dead."

Rowland shook his head, slowly, because sudden movements hurt. "I remembered something just now... before the accident..." His memory from the day of the accident was fragmented and so he hesitated. "I think Stuart Jones said Lesley Bocquet was a bookmaker."

Clyde nodded. "You're right. He did say something to you about a chap called Bocquet. Who is he?"

"Bocquet claims to be the rightful owner of White's horseshoe tiepin." Rowland rubbed his shoulder. The bones had been put back into place while he was still unconscious, but the traumatised joint ached like the blazes. "He and his wife have a place in Lindfield. They both deny knowing Crispin White."

"But you don't believe them?"

"No, I don't."

"So he's a bookie, living respectably?" Clyde asked.

"Well, appearing to do so anyway."

"And you think he might have killed White?"

"Stuart Jones called him a street rat. A razor's probably his weapon of choice," Rowland replied.

"But how would he have got into Magdalene's and lured White there?"

"Perhaps we should try to talk to Mrs. Bocquet—on her own." Milton suggested. "There was something about the way she reacted when we asked about Crispin White. Perhaps he'd been up to his old tricks again. And it's possible that she borrowed her husband's razor."

"Frances," Rowland said suddenly. "The maid. If they knew she didn't steal the tiepin, why did they sack her? Perhaps she knows something."

"You're right," Milton said thoughtfully. "But how are we going to find her? What did Delaney say her name was?"

"Frances Webb, I believe."

"Well, that's a start." Edna adjusted the pillows on the bed. "We'll find Frances. You need to rest, Rowly." She placed her hand on his forehead. "You're a little warm, my darling."

"If I just discharge myself, I could—"

"You'll do nothing of the sort!" Edna's tone was firm, her lips soft as she kissed his brow. "We do miss you, Rowly. But we've all made deals with the devil for your life. Let's not tempt him to renege."

Three days later, Rowland's doctors came to the conclusion that he was out of any danger and strong enough to recuperate perfectly well at home. The decision may or may not have been encouraged by the patient's campaign to that end, and the fact that he had taken to sketching nurses in a manner that the matron feared would turn their heads.

While the enforced bed rest, imposed by the hospital, had tested Rowland's patience, it had done much to restore his strength. When he walked out to the waiting Rolls Royce, he moved a little more slowly than usual, but without assistance.

On a whim, Clyde had Johnston drive them out to the Maroubra Speedway before returning to *Woodlands*. "You might take doctor's orders more seriously if you see what happened," he said. They took him to the sand dune first, and the light pole upon which the Mercedes had met her end. The remains of Rowland's motorcar had been removed, of course, and signs warned that the light pole was no longer safe.

Rowland stared at the shattered fragments of windscreen at the base of the pole, yellow paint embedded in the damage inflicted yards above the ground. There were flowers laid at the spot where he'd been found, and someone had even made a rough cross out of driftwood to which they'd attached a mangled Mercedes mascot. Rowland removed the mascot and slipped it into his pocket. He could remember nothing about the actual accident, and seeing this, it seemed inconceivable, even to him, that he'd survived.

Edna took his hand. "Are you all right, Rowly? Do you need to rest?"

He shook his head. "No, I'm glad you brought me. I don't remember much of the race." He looked back at the buckled pole. "God, the poor old girl. She deserved better."

Edna pressed Rowland's hand sympathetically as she searched for the appropriate words. "She had a wonderfully adventurous life for a motorcar, Rowly, and we'll always remember her."

"She was a beautiful machine, comrade," Milton said squinting up at the point where the Mercedes had met the pole. "But for a while there, we thought she'd taken you with her." He considered the distance between the pole and where Rowland had been found. "You must have been thrown out before impact... you couldn't have survived otherwise."

They drove into the bowl next. The speedway was empty and eerily quiet though the concrete bowl seemed to hold a faint echo of the ripping scream of supercharged engines. The odd newspaper blew across the deserted infield and seagulls picked over stale food scraps. Johnston took them to the pit they'd used. Clyde checked with Milton and Edna. "It hasn't rained since the race, has it?"

"No, I don't think so."

"Good, it might still be there. Come on, Rowly, I want to show you something."

He took Rowland to the bay in which the Mercedes had been parked awaiting the race's start. "Do you remember the shifty bloke Joan saw under your car?"

Rowland nodded. "We were concerned he'd sabotaged the engine."

Clyde pointed to the cement.

The word "Eternity" in blue and white chalk... a little scuffed but still plainly visible.

"I only saw it when you pulled out," Clyde said, grinning. "I reckon it must have been Stace under the car writing his damn word. He's even spelled it correctly."

"What was he doing here?" Edna asked.

"He probably came to the races, saw Rowly and decided to bless his motorcar with the correct spelling this time." Clyde squatted down to touch the epigraph in a manner that was quite reverent. "To be honest, when you went over the top I thought he might have hexed you with his flaming word, but perhaps it was just the opposite."

Rowland smiled. "It seems that way."

Milton groaned. "For pity's sake, it's 1934. Rowly was not saved by some magician with a stick of chalk!"

Clyde called Milton a godless Communist who believed in nothing, and Milton began a speech on science over superstition. But Rowland wasn't so sure.

There was a familial reception committee gathered at *Woodlands* when Rowland finally got home. Ewan, who'd not been allowed to go to the hospital, greeted his uncle with all the boisterous exuberance of childish joy.

Wilfred took his middle son from Rowland's arms. "Your uncle Rowly is not really up to being bounced on just yet, sport." He shook his brother's hand. "Welcome home, Rowly. Are you sure you're—"

"Quite well, Wil. I could even go another round with Ewan, here."

Ernest Sinclair did not greet his uncle with the same high spirits. Indeed, he said nothing, simply taking Rowland's hand and holding on. Rowland made no attempt to escape the boy's grasp. Elisabeth Sinclair wept and, though she still called him Aubrey, Rowland was moved by his mother's rare show of emotion. They had simple luncheon in the breakfast room with the children—finger sandwiches, sausage rolls and jam tarts, and for Rowland, stout, prescribed as a restorative of some sort.

"Do you remember what happened, Uncle Rowly?" Ernest whispered.

"I'm afraid not, Ernie."

"I saw it. You drove off the racing track and hit a pole."

"I see. That'd explain what happened to the car, I suppose."

"Nobody could wake you up."

Rowland glanced briefly at the Lucky Devil II which, at Joan

Richmond's insistence, graced his mantel with all its dubious glory. "I'm awake now."

"I don't like motor racing."

"I'm not so keen on it myself anymore."

"Do you miss your motorcar, Uncle Rowly?"

"Yes, I do rather."

"She was a capital vehicle."

"I always thought so."

"Will you get another one?"

"Another car?" Rowland faltered. "I expect I will, eventually." The idea seemed indecent.

Ernest appeared to understand. He selected a tart with the hand that was not firmly in his uncle's.

After lunch Wilfred took his young family home insisting as he left that Rowland should rest. "Maguire will call by at about five o'clock."

Rowland didn't protest, though he thought the house call unnecessary, accustomed to the fact that Wilfred expressed concern through the attendance of Maguire.

Edna waited till they were just themselves before she told Rowland that she had found Frances Webb.

"Really? How?"

"I asked the maid at the house next door. I thought they might be friends. I mentioned I was looking to hire, and that Mrs. Bocquet had told me she needed to let Frances go." Edna's smile was triumphant. "She's living with her mother in Woolloomooloo."

"Well, let's go talk to her," Rowland said, pushing himself up from the chair.

"Tomorrow," Milton said. "You look done in, comrade."

"I'm—"

"Going to listen to the doctors, just for today," Edna finished for him. "Tomorrow we'll regroup."

36

---◆---

Domestic Servants' Wages

Sir,—

   May I say a word in defence of Australian domestic servants?
Like "Common Sense," I have lived in other countries and
other States, and can say, from my own experience, that the
average Australian domestic worker is a very fine type of girl,
hard-working, capable, trust-worthy, and obliging. Of course,
there are exceptions. I have seldom found that any training or
enlightenment is received with scornful resentment by the maid.
As a rule she is eager to learn and is grateful to a mistress who
can instruct her. Any young girl likes amusements and dancing.
If she works an honest eight hours a day, has she not a right
to so many hours of liberty every day, as well as her six half-
days and one full day a month? Let mistresses treat these fine
young Australians as we would like our own young daughters
to be treated, and there will be less of this dissatisfaction with
domestics and with domestic service.

   Yours, &c,

FRANCIA
The Argus, 1936

Frances Webb was more than willing to talk about her time in the
employ of Les and Beryl Bocquet. She had been sacked unfairly,
she believed, with no notice and barely a week's pay. The strength

of her resentment was such that she did not even ask why the posh gentlemen and his friends wanted to know.

"They thought they was so good, they did, living in Lindfield like Lord and Lady Muck. But that Beryl Bocquet was no lady. I knew there was something going on… that Dr. Something Jones calling, and their nibs suddenly giving me the afternoon off."

"Do you mean Dr. Stuart Jones?" Edna asked.

"Yes. And I know why people call him too, and it ain't for a cold."

"And they sacked you after that?" Milton asked.

"They knew that I knew and that I weren't of a mind to approve. It were murder, plain and simple, and Mrs. Bocquet will be answering to the good Lord for it!"

"What about the tiepin?" Clyde asked, flinching as he heard his own position come so harshly out of Frances Webb's mouth. "The one they accused you of stealing."

"Why I never and they never!" Frances put her sturdy arms indignantly upon her hips. "Nobody said nothing about any tiepin!"

"You said Mrs. Bocquet wasn't a lady," Rowland ventured. "May I ask what you meant by that?"

"She were stepping out on him. Waiting till he were at the track and then she'd powder herself up and go out. A couple of times he got back before her and then it were on… not so lord and lady then! But it didn't stop her. Alley cat that one!"

"When Dr. Stuart Jones called," Rowland asked, "did Mr. Bocquet know?"

"Of course—he called him, told him to come."

Rowland thanked Frances Webb for her assistance, slipping her a couple of pounds to help until she found work.

"That's real decent of you, sir," she said. "I'm a good worker, and I didn't say nothing the whole time I were with the Bocquets. It weren't right them sacking me."

"What do you think?" Clyde asked as they made their way back to the Rolls Royce.

"I think I'd better stay on the good side of Mary Brown," Rowland replied.

"Bloody oath! For all our sakes," Milton muttered.

"I was talking about Stuart Jones' visit," Clyde chuckled. "Why would a married couple need his services?"

"Well clearly Lesley Bocquet was not the father," Edna said.

"How could they be sure of that?" Rowland asked.

"Perhaps Mr. Bocquet knows he can't father children. Perhaps he's just sure he didn't father this one, or perhaps knowing that someone else may have was enough."

"Crispin White was Mrs. Bocquet's lover." Milton opened the door for Edna. "Lesley Bocquet was cuckolded and took his revenge by killing White."

Rowland agreed. "But how on earth do we prove it? Delaney can't do anything officially and Hartley isn't going to listen to our theories on the crime."

"Mrs. Bocquet," Edna suggested as she climbed into the vehicle. "She loved Crispin White. Perhaps she'll turn on her husband."

Milton shrugged. "If she didn't kill White herself. It's worth a shot."

And so it was decided. Clyde slipped behind the wheel of the Rolls Royce, which they'd taken out that day without its chauffeur. Rowland's conscience smarted a little on that account. Johnston had been deeply offended by the unintended slight. It occurred to Rowland that he would have to either acquire another car or become accustomed to being chauffeured. The thought of replacing the Mercedes, however, was not one he was yet able to face. Clyde drove them to Lindfield and parked a street away from the Bocquet residence.

"What if Les Bocquet is home?" Milton asked, frowning.

"I could knock on the door and ask for the gentleman of the house first," Clyde suggested. "If he's home, I tell him I want to place a bet and if he isn't there, then we'll be free to speak to his wife."

"That's not a bad idea," Rowland said. "Neither of them has met Clyde."

"Perhaps I ought to go in to speak to Mrs. Bocquet," Edna proposed. "If what we think happened, did in fact happen, then it's all terribly personal. She mightn't be keen to talk of it to three gentlemen she's barely met."

Rowland objected immediately. "It's too dangerous."

"Why?"

"There is a possibility that Mrs. Bocquet and not her husband is the murderer, Ed, or that they were in it together. We're not going to let you invite yourself to tea and cakes with a woman who might have cut Crispin White's throat."

Edna took Rowland's hand. She found his gallantry quaint— archaic, excessive and entirely unnecessary, but sweet in its way. Even so, the sculptress might have spoken less gently if Rowland had not only days ago been so close to death. That knowledge tempered her response. "I'm not an idiot, Rowly. I'll speak to her about Mr. White on her threshold. I won't go into the house. That way, if she does produce a shotgun or a knife or a bottle of arsenic, the three of you can rush in and save the day!"

Rowland was not convinced. He tried to persuade her to stay in the car.

"Don't be ridiculous, Rowly. If anyone should stay in the car, it's you. You probably shouldn't be out of bed!"

Rowland's argument faltered under her offensive. He looked to Clyde and Milton for support, but he found little.

"She has a point, mate," Clyde said regretfully.

"When has Ed ever stayed in the car, Rowly?" Milton said laughing. "This is not a fight you can win."

"We'll be nearby," Clyde added more sympathetically. "She'll be safe this time."

Beryl Bocquet had obviously been cooking when she answered the door. Her hair was tied up in a scarf and she wore a brown pinafore apron over a floral printed dress and still held a kitchen knife in one hand. Before Clyde could say a word she apologised for the dishevelled state in which she had answered the door, explaining that she was temporarily without staff.

Clyde stood on the portico with his hat in his hand. When she'd finished telling him that she wasn't ordinarily expected to cook, he told her he'd like to see Mr. Bocquet about a financial matter. He tapped his finger to his nose.

"I'm afraid Lesley isn't here," she said wearily. "He's out of town for a couple of days. If you're here for winnings you'll need to come back next week for your money."

Clyde thanked her and returned to his friends. "I reckon he's taken losses on the Red Cross Invitational and skedaddled."

It was Edna's turn. The men waited at a distance beyond likely notice.

"Mrs. Bocquet?" Edna asked putting out her hand. "Beryl Bocquet? I hoped I might talk to you. I'm Edna Higgins... Crispin White was a friend of mine."

"What kind of friend..." Beryl Bocquet's voice was almost

inaudible. She moved the kitchen knife to her left hand so she could shake Edna's.

"A good friend. I must say you're just as beautiful as Crispin said you were."

"He said that?" Beryl's face crumpled. "That wretched man! Why would he say that? It's too late now..."

Edna stuttered, confused. She took a guess. "He was sorry—that's what he wanted to tell you."

"Oh god, he didn't have a chance." Beryl's hand tightened on the handle of the knife until her knuckles were white. "What have I done?"

Edna stepped back her eyes on the knife. Could it have been used to slay a man? "Perhaps I should come back some other time..."

Beryl Bocquet glanced behind her. She started to cry. "Please..."

"Did I hear you say you were a chum of Crispy White's?" The voice was congenial and male. Lesley Bocquet came to the door and stood behind his young wife. "We knew your Crispin very well, didn't we, Beryl?"

"Mr. Bocquet? I thought you were out of town."

Beryl looked up sharply. "I didn't tell you that. Who are you?"

Edna turned to go. Lesley Bocquet reached out suddenly and grabbed her elbow, dragging her into the generous foyer.

"Get your bloody hands off her!" Milton roared.

Rowland, Clyde and Milton had run for the house the moment they realised that Bocquet was at home. Clyde pushed his foot into the doorway as the bookmaker tried to slam shut the door. Edna screamed and fought to escape his grasp. Milton added his shoulder to Clyde's and they forced the door.

Clyde pulled Edna behind him as Bocquet flicked out his razor. Beryl Bocquet held up the knife sobbing hysterically. Rowland stepped between them, unsure now on which Bocquet he could turn his back.

Then Beryl let the knife fall and moved behind Rowland screaming, "No Les, don't!"

"Beryl…" Lesley Bocquet looked wounded. "What the hell are you playing at, Sinclair? That's my bloody missus!"

"Put down the razor, Bocquet."

"That'd be right!" He shouted at his wife. "You've been whoring around with Sinclair as well! There'll be hell to pay if you have! You know I won't be made a fool of! I won't have it! My God, Beryl, haven't you learned? He won't stand by you."

Beryl huddled behind Rowland, sobbing and terrified. "No, Les, we never…"

Rowland jerked back as the razor slashed wildly at his throat, following instinctively with a right hook which found its mark.

For a second, Bocquet was stunned. Milton used that moment to rush the man, locking his hand around Bocquet's wrist as he brought him to the ground. Clyde lodged his knee against the bookmaker's back as Milton forced the blade out of his hand.

Pinned and disarmed, Bocquet could only respond with profanity and threats, and he did so with volume and vigour. And then he appealed to his wife. "I did it for you, Beryl. After what that bastard did to us… What would you have had me do?"

Edna took the distraught lady of the house into the drawing room, calming her as best she could and telephoning the police on one of the lines Bocquet used to take bets. It took only a few minutes for the local constables to attend. Rowland was trying his best to explain their presence, when both Hartley and Delaney arrived. The detectives began to argue over who would take charge of the scene.

"I think this is more about Detective Hartley's murder investigation than your SP bookmaker, Detective Delaney," Rowland said apologetically.

Delaney looked him up and down, grinning openly. "The papers said you were dead."

"I may have to sue them." Rowland shook the detective's hand.

Between them, Rowland, Milton and Clyde clarified how they had found themselves forced to subdue Lesley Bocquet in his own house.

"One of the Bocquets killed White," Rowland said. "I'm not sure which."

"My money's on Les," Milton said. "Stace saw a man drop the notebook, remember."

"So this Lesley Bocquet killed White over gambling debts?" Hartley asked jostling in front of Delaney.

"No. From what I can gather, Mrs. Bocquet was having an affair with White," Rowland said. "I expect she gave him the horseshoe tiepin."

"Bocquet reported it stolen."

"He might have believed that initially. Talk to Mrs. Bocquet. I'm not really sure who did what, to be honest."

Edna came in from the drawing room where she'd been sitting with Beryl under the watchful eye of a constable.

"Miss Higgins. What are you doing here?" Hartley demanded.

"Talking to Mrs. Bocquet," Edna said frostily. "When you interview her, Detective Hartley, you will discover that Mr. Bocquet was Crispin White's bookmaker. That's how Beryl and Crispin met. Apparently they fell in love, as one does. It was their custom to meet at Magdalene's at midnight. Unfortunately, Mr. Bocquet found out about the affair, but only after Mr. White had ended it. On the night in question, Mr. Bocquet had his wife summon Mr. White to Magdalene's. He met Mr. White instead, and returned with the tiepin."

Rowland noticed that she'd left out the intervention of Reginald Stuart Jones in the sordid affair. It was not relevant—they could leave that to the poor woman to reveal herself if she so chose. "Did Mrs. Bocquet know that her husband killed White to get the tiepin?" he asked.

"Beryl swears she only realised when she read about Crispin's death in the paper. She's been living in terror that her husband would kill her, too."

Hartley blustered for a moment before he could speak clearly. "This is all nonsense. How would Lesley or Beryl Bocquet get into Magdalene's?"

Rowland paused to listen to Bocquet who was making threats and demanding his rights without pause. Of course. The bear. "I suspect he had a key. I'm fairly certain Mr. Bocquet was one of the gentlemen in masks. You might find his bear disguise on the premises somewhere. Perhaps Mrs. Bocquet was there too," he added, remembering the woman's shoes.

As it was, a search proved unnecessary. Desperate to demonstrate somehow that she had not been involved in the murder, Beryl handed over her husband's mask and robes as well as the tiepin he had taken from Crispin White's body. She denied any part in the bookmakers' coven. Lesley was so visibly shocked and crushed by her betrayal that Rowland felt almost sorry for him. Bocquet did not deny his wife's account, begging her to remember that he loved her, that he'd taken care of White for her.

"So I suppose Bocquet's the chap who took a shot at you, Rowly," Delaney said, grinning broadly. He was enjoying Hartley's humiliation and looking forward to the detective explaining it all to Superintendent Mackay.

"No. I think that might have been the Honourable Charlotte Linklater."

"What? Why?"

"Something she said about me hiding behind my red easel... I had thought she was just calling me a Communist, but I realise now she was talking about the actual colour."

"It's not a great leap to assume an artist has an easel, Rowly."

"They're not often red though. Mine only is because I knocked over a pot of vermillion and then inadvertently rubbed the pigment into the wood when I tried to stop it dripping... Anyway, I can't imagine how she'd know my easel was red unless she saw it, and from what I understand she's a champion shot."

Delaney sighed and scribbled the facts down in his notebook. "I don't disbelieve you, mate, but it might be hard to prove... and charging the daughter of a peer will be one hell of a job. I'm afraid she might already be on a ship back to England."

"That's the third woman who's tried to shoot you and escaped, Rowly," Milton observed.

"I wasn't *trying* to shoot Rowly!" Edna clarified haughtily.

Delaney shook his head. "You know, Sinclair, I still can't work out if you're the unluckiest or the luckiest man alive."

"I suspect the fact that I am still alive argues for the latter."

37

IMPORTANCE OF ART

———————◆———————

MR. LYONS' OBSERVATIONS

SYDNEY, April 8

"The cultural side of a nation is extremely important. If there
is no art, there is no culture; if there is no culture, there is no
nation," said the Prime Minister, Mr. Lyons, to-day...

Western Argus, 1938

There was no doubt that the exhibition opening at Frasier's
gallery was one of considerable import. The street outside the
building was congested with Rolls Royces and the occasional Cadillac.
Chauffeurs congregated between vehicles to smoke and chat as they
waited to be summoned for the journey home. Dark-suited security
men were a visible presence at the entrance to the gallery. Gentlemen
in evening dress and ladies in fur stoles filed in, collecting programs
from the reception and murmuring appreciatively at the glorious
landscapes scattered along the corridors to the main hall like a
tempting trail of crumbs that promised a journey's end of exquisite
and ample cake.

The main gallery hall was, for the moment, still closed pending the
arrival of the prime minister, who would officially open the exhibition.

It was there that Rowland stood alone, with a large glass of gin. The hall had come up as he intended. It was uncomfortable to be in.

Copies of the books banned and burned by the Nazis—which they had mostly sourced from the bookshelves at *Woodlands House*—had been used in an extraordinary display. Edna had created life-size figures out of papier-mâché and trapped them, with the books, in a cage of barbed wire. Once more, Rowland read over the explanatory plaques beside each painting, which spoke bluntly of what he'd seen in Germany. He was, here, nailing his colours publicly and quite literally to the wall. Still, it surprised him that he was quite so anxious. Rowland suspected the critics would be brutal, that many would be offended and he might never again hold such an eminently attended exhibition. What he was doing was probably professional and social suicide.

Edna came to fetch him. "The prime minister is here, Rowly. Wilfred says you have to come and meet him." She slipped her hand into his and looked searchingly into his face. "Are you having second thoughts?"

He shook his head. "No. I'm just a trifle nervous, Ed. I hope this works."

Edna's eyes softened. Rowland always seemed so quietly self-assured. Moved by his sudden uncertainty, she embraced him. "It may not work, Rowly, but at least we will have not said nothing while the world went mad. We will have tried to make them see."

"And if they won't see?"

She reached up and clasped his face between her hands. "We're still young," she said. "If this doesn't work, we'll simply try something else. We have years before we're too old to fight."

He smiled. He could easily have remained forever with the sculptress in his arms—God, he wanted to.

"Come along," Edna said, smoothing down his lapel. "There are some rather important people waiting for you."

To a glittering assembly, Prime Minister Joseph Lyons spoke warmly of the place of art in bringing the world to Australia, in allowing those unable to travel and experience the wonders and beauty of Europe to understand the landscape of countries like Germany. He apologised that the opening was three weeks later than originally planned, delayed because the artist had, by all accounts, been killed in a car race. The gathering chuckled politely, tittering at the folly of the newspapers. Buoyed by the laughter, the prime minister continued, pointing out that most artists were lauded only after their deaths. "It seems that Rowland Sinclair was not inclined to wait!" he finished, looking around for confirmation that he was indeed a man of rare and extraordinary jest. He was the prime minister, so he got just that.

When invited to say a few words, Rowland thanked everybody for their attendance, and mentioned with grateful admiration the friends who had helped him put the exhibition together. "It is my fervent hope," he said in conclusion, "that on these walls you might see what we saw in Germany. And that you will respond accordingly." Most people put the simplicity of his ambition down to the charming humility one would expect from a well-bred young man.

Then Lyons launched the exhibition with a toast to the artist, and the main gallery was opened.

A strange silence fell over the invited guests as the stark uncompromising depictions of a rising oppression were viewed. Rowland's paintings were sobering and unequivocally confronting. And they were not what the social art-lovers had expected.

Wilfred Sinclair pulled his brother aside, clearly livid. "What is the meaning of this, Rowly? You didn't tell me this so-called exhibition was some kind of propaganda campaign for the Communists."

"You know this isn't propaganda, Wilfred. It's what I saw."

Wilfred gritted his teeth. "You're losing perspective, Rowly."

The exchange was interrupted by a raised voice from among the guests. "Why, this is outrageous! Preposterous! I was in Germany last year and can assure you that this is not what I saw. Clearly Sinclair is a disturbed young man, being influenced by his Bolshevik connections no doubt."

Rowland turned. Campbell stood before the painting of the book burning. Other guests, who had been unsure how to respond to the confronting images, took Campbell's lead, tittering.

"What the hell is he doing here?"

"I invited him!" Wilfred replied fiercely. "You wanted me to offer an olive branch. I thought this would be a good forum to do it in. Of course I had no bloody idea what you were really doing."

"It's quite worrying that Mr. Sinclair intends on standing for parliament." Campbell's voice was loud, his intent clear. "Corrupt as the party politic machine is, he may succeed."

But Milton Isaacs had also invited guests, who had been until now, quiet, a little uncomfortable in the elite surroundings. It was they who spoke in Rowland's defence, deriding Campbell as an apologist for the Nazis.

Wilfred cursed as hostility caught and spread. "I must get the prime minister out of here, not to mention Kate and Mother!" He turned on his brother fiercely. "Congratulations Rowly, you've succeeded in not only humiliating me and Kate, but have publicly demonstrated that you have lost all sense of proportion. You're a bloody fool!"

Rowland didn't try to defend himself. There would be time to reason with Wilfred later. For now there was Campbell and his cohorts to sort out.

A further disturbance at the entrance as more of Campbell's supporters tried to enter the gallery. There was panic now, fear that the elegant opening would become a riot. Gallery staff opened up the back doors to let people out. Dignitaries were ushered discreetly to their cars.

Campbell had embarked on a speech, decrying what he considered the "defamation of the German government by a servant of Bolshevik interests". He wasn't without sympathy.

"There are many good men in New South Wales who would consider that subversives who cloak themselves in the mantle of high art ought to be dragged out and taught a lesson," he declared. "I venture that those good men would be applauded!"

"Sod off, you Fascist mongrel!" Milton shouted. Someone swung at the poet. A scream. Then several. A painting was pulled off the wall and smashed underfoot. The opening to Rowland Sinclair's exhibition deteriorated rapidly. The artist himself might have been in serious danger if it were not for the fact there were many members of Sydney's artistic community in the gathering, who had attended for the sake of art, and who stayed to defend their colleague and their beliefs. Even so, the police presence which came with the prime minister was possibly all that saved the gallery being damaged and the exhibition completely destroyed.

It was in the early hours of the next morning that Rowland and his companions returned to *Woodlands House* after cleaning up what they could. The mansion was quiet, the servants all long since retired to their beds. Milton poured drinks as they sat a little stunned in Rowland's studio. Lenin, who'd been asleep by the hearth beside his cats, yawned in greeting and closed his eyes again. The one ginger kitten, that Edna had named Mercedes in memory of Rowland's late automobile, peered out from beneath the greyhound's long muzzle.

Edna curled up on the couch beside Rowland. "I'm sorry it all went so wrong, Rowly," she said, stifling a yawn.

Rowland slipped his arm around the sculptress as she closed her eyes and relaxed against him. They were all tired. The exhibition had not gone as expected, but he wasn't sure what he'd expected in the first place. Rowland tried not to catastrophise. "They saw what I wanted them to see," he said. "And they'll probably not forget this evening in a hurry."

"They will certainly not," Clyde agreed.

"It's lucky we're still young," Edna murmured.

Rowland pulled his arm tighter, reminded.

"I expect you might get a bit of a thrashing in the papers, Rowly," Milton sighed.

"Wilfred was cross," Edna said softly.

"Yes," Rowland said. He suspected that it would take some time for Wilfred to forgive him for this transgression. He hadn't thought through how the exhibition might embarrass his brother, and although he regretted that, he couldn't spend his life politely ignoring what he believed.

"Perhaps tonight was the monster Miss Norton predicted you'd release with that painting, Rowly." Milton handed him a glass of sherry. "Some of those blokes looked like they wanted to tear you limb from limb."

Rowland laughed. "Let's not make Rosaleen Norton a prophet, Milt."

"One dance in the moonlight and he's joined the devil," Clyde muttered.

"Hell is empty and all the devils are here," Milton declared quite sadly.

"Shakespeare," Rowland said. "I'm afraid he might be right."

Epilogue

Lesley Bocquet was charged with illegal bookmaking and the murder of Crispin White. The charges against Milton Isaacs were dropped.

———◆———

As Milton Isaacs predicted, the conservative newspapers were scathing of Rowland Sinclair's exhibition. *The Sydney Morning Herald*, *Truth*, *Telegraph* and *Canberra Times* all lamented the gullibility of the artistic community which seemed to be so easily swayed by the propaganda of Bolshevik interests. The dignitaries who had attended were at pains to distance themselves from the renegade artist and his fanciful paintings. Arts editors dismissed the exhibition as sensationalist nonsense. *Smith's Weekly* was a notable exception. It concentrated its criticism on Eric Campbell and the violent thugs who seemed at his beck and call, and commended Rowland Sinclair for his dogged pursuit of the truth. Perhaps it did so in memory of Crispin White.

———◆———

While the Red Cross raised significant funds through staging the Maroubra Invitational, the bookmakers did not. The ultimate victory of the favourites was quite the financial blow. The Maroubra Speedway continued to claim lives through the 1930s and was eventually demolished in 1947.

———◆———

Errol Flynn departed Australia for England shortly after the Maroubra Invitational. Flynn was cast as the lead in *Murder at Monte Carlo*, during the filming of which he was offered a contract with Warner Bros. Studios. He emigrated to America and, quickly thereafter, became a Hollywood sensation. Edna Higgins genuinely wished him the best, and wrote him a letter of introduction to Archibald Leach whom she believed had done quite well for himself since last she'd seen him.

Rosaleen Norton's short story, *Moon Madness*, was published in July 1934. She left the employ of *Smith's Weekly* at the end of that year, determined to pursue a career as an artist. Her increasingly bizarre, sexually charged pictures would provoke controversy throughout her career, as would her connection with early European witchcraft and the occult. In time the press would brand her the "Witch of Kings Cross".

Percy Reginald "Inky" Stephensen shifted his allegiances from the left to the far right sometime in the mid 1930s. In 1936, he wrote and published *The Foundations of Culture in Australia*, which was credited with influencing the formation of the Jindyworobak poetry movement. That same year, he launched the monthly *Publicist* which had a strongly anti-British, anti-Semitic and anti-democratic flavour. In 1941, he founded the Australia First Movement, a political pressure group based on the program advocated by the *Publicist*.

Joan Richmond returned to Europe in time for the 1934 Munich Alpine Rally, after which she was selected to meet the German Chancellor at an entirely different kind of rally. Later, despite not liking what she'd seen of the Nazis, she would recount a strange irresistible urge to cheer Adolf Hitler, along with all masses in attendance.

———————•———————

Dr. Reginald Stuart Jones was never charged over the incident involving Edna Higgins, though it was an episode that Rowland Sinclair would, in time, give him cause to regret. His relationship with John Hartley, while never officially investigated, would eventually end the detective's career.

———————•———————

Wilfred Sinclair was for some time quite furious with his brother. Indeed, he may have insisted their mother cease residence at *Woodlands House* with "Rowly's band of godless Communists" if it weren't for the fact that Elisabeth Sinclair would not hear of it. She quite liked living in Sydney with Aubrey and his friends, and was adamant that at thirty-five she was quite old enough to choose where she lived.

———————•———————

For over thirty years after he met Rowland Sinclair, Arthur Stace would write the word "Eternity" in copperplate style on footpaths and walls all over Sydney, where he became something of a legend. Rowland would see the epigraph, freshly drawn from time to time, and wonder if it might have had anything to do with the fact that he survived the Maroubra Invitational.

Acknowledgments

I find myself preparing to thank a number of people for the tenth time. It seems those who were instrumental in my first book remain so in my tenth. For the sake of not repeating myself, I'm tempted to truncate this acknowledgment with the words "to all those who I've mentioned before and will mention again", but that seems a poor way to honour the extraordinary individuals who have travelled with me as navigators, mechanics and passengers on this continuing road trip, and without whose company and skill, I would have long ago been stopped by the side of the road with my bonnet up. I hope you'll indulge me then while I repeat myself and forgive me for the rather trite motoring theme I've used to do so. I am deeply grateful to:

My husband, Michael, who first suggested this route and kept me from getting lost. My boys, Edmund and Atticus, who shout advice from the backseat.

My Dad, who refuels my car from time to time, and who will still drive out to get me when I break down.

My sister Devini who comes along for every ride in the very latest designer racing-gear.

My mother, for whom I can think of no appropriate car-related analogy, but who, at the very beginning, taught me to read.

The Greens and the wonderful team at Pantera Press who are my talented and generous pit crew.

My brilliant agent, Jo Butler, who keeps me headed in the right direction.

Glenda Downing, my editor, who serviced this novel and ensured it was roadworthy. Sofya Karmazina, my cover designer whose genius gives my work a showroom finish; Desanka Vukelich and Graeme Jones who made sure the interior was perfectly detailed.

Leith Henry who knows Rowly so well she could take the wheel at any time... if something happens to me, she'll tell you how it all ends.

Sarah Kynaston who creates detours with ludicrous projects because she knows that I write best when I'm also trying to sculpt a life-size cow out of granny smith apples. Lesley Bocquet (whose name I misappropriated for this novel) and Cheryl Bousfield, who have both worn my team colours since the very first book.

My comrades in the writing community who have always been generous with their knowledge of the road ahead.

The reviewers, bloggers, booksellers and readers whose support has allowed me to be in the position of repeating myself. Thank you for riding with me.

If you liked *Give the Devil His Due*
then look out for the next book in the
Award-Winning Rowland Sinclair Mysteries

A Dangerous Language

When a Communist agent is murdered on the steps of Parliament House, Rowland Sinclair finds himself drawn into a dangerous world of politics and assassination.

Volunteering his services as a pilot to fly renowned international peace advocate Egon Kisch between Fremantle and Melbourne, Rowland is unaware how hard Australia's new attorney-general will fight to keep the "raging reporter" off Australian soil.

In this, it seems, the government is not alone, as clandestine right-wing militias reconstitute into deadly strike forces.

A disgraced minister, an unidentified corpse and an old flame all bring their own special bedlam. Once again Rowland Sinclair stands against the unthinkable, with an artist, a poet and a brazen sculptress by his side.

PanteraPress
great storytelling

For more information, please visit:
www.PanteraPress.com

Please Enjoy this Excerpt from

A Dangerous Language

1

PREVIEWS OF SHOW EXHIBITS

Outstanding features of the Motor Show
described by Table Talk's
Motoring Correspondent

CHRYSLER SHOWS AIRFLOW

INTRODUCED to Melbourne by Lanes Motors and with Miss Judy Price and Mary Guy Smith as official hostesses, Chrysler for 1934 springs one of the most complete Show surprises by co-ordinating aeroplane and car design and construction in the production of a truly amazing car.

Claimed to be two years ahead in design and performance, the Airflow Chrysler Eight is being featured at the Show in a way that makes impossible a display of the Morris and M.G. cars, also marketed by this firm.

The Airflows shown are the model CU Eight—a 33.8 h.p. car developing 122 h.p., and the larger Imperial Eight, of the same rating but at 128 h.p. development. Both cars possess a speed of 90 m.p.h. and a completeness and originality of streamlining and body-plus-chassis unit engineering that leaves one gasping.

Fundamentally, Chrysler in these cars has set out to remedy inherent defects in normal cars by new methods. He has built body and chassis on the plan of a cantilever truss—an amazingly strong yet light structure—then has dispositioned the weight and placings of engine, luggage, and passengers in such a way, relative to the axles, that an ideal of suspension is provided. By adding an improved springing and new type steering, a car has been produced in which it is possible to "read, write, and sleep" in comfort on any road at 60 m.p.h.

The astonishing interior carries three passengers with comfort on each seat, the seats in turn being of a new armchair type, wholly isolated from the body walls and made very modern by the provision of chromium-plated arm rests, which incorporate ash trays and match the predominating body motif.

Perfected draftless ventilation and floating power engine mountings, to eliminate the transmission of vibrations to passengers or body, are other comfort features and added control is provided by the novel steering, improved hydraulic braking, coincidental starting, all silent transmission, cam and roller free wheeling and extra large low pressure tyres.

A remarkable innovation, an automatic over drive transmission is optional on the C-U- and standard or the Imperial model and reduces engine speed by 30 per cent at speeds above 45 m.p.h.

The aerodynamically streamlined body cannot be described. It must be seen to be appreciated, and for its advantages to be understood.

Table Talk, 24 May 1934

She never knew that she was found by a man leading a footsore bull. She didn't see him tether the beast and clamber down to where she lay, and so she felt no embarrassment for the nakedness of her body where the clothes had been burnt away. It was not the burlap sack covering her face that kept her in darkness. The world would always be dark now. And she would keep the secret of how she came to lie alone in a country ditch.

The 1934 Melbourne International Motor Show was in its final day. Several thousand people had passed through its doors to view the latest in engineering and innovation and marvel at advances in technology.

The great British names of Austin, Vauxhall and Hillman vied for attention with the brash American houses of Studebaker, Pontiac, Oldsmobile and Chevrolet. The Rolls Royce Phantom II stood with as much decorum and dignity as possible, among the miles of bunting, balloons and roving brass bands. The show sensation was, however, undisputed. Elevated on a rotating stage it seemed to reign over the other displays. Even surrounded by the world's best machines its revolutionary shape caught the eye. Motoring enthusiasts jostled the popular press for the best vantage from which to view the ultramodern lines and avant-garde design of the Chrysler Airflow.

The gentlemen from Sydney stood back from the main crowd, observing the Chrysler exhibit at a distance. They stood shoulder to shoulder: a flamboyantly dressed Bohemian with a Leninist goatee; a solid, sturdy man whose weathered face aged him beyond his thirty-two years; and between them, the tallest of the three, whose immaculately tailored suit was offset by dark hair that refused to stay in place.

"What do you think?" Rowland Sinclair pushed his hair back, trying to ignore an absurd feeling of disloyalty.

His companions showed no such reluctance.

"She might just be the most beautiful thing I've ever seen." Clyde Watson Jones was determined to encourage Rowland to finally bury the 1927 S-Class Mercedes he'd lost in the racing accident that had nearly taken his life. To Clyde's mind it was time Rowland got over his first love and allowed another to take her place.

"I wouldn't go that far," Rowland murmured, distracted for a moment by a thought of Edna. She'd refused to come to Melbourne with them on the grounds that she preferred not to witness "grown men reduced to simpering lovesick boys by shiny machines". Edna was ever direct. He missed her.

"Aesthetically she's a little unusual," Rowland offered as both praise and concession. The automobile was yellow, as the Mercedes had been, but the similarities stopped there. The Chrysler was sleek and low with a chrome grille that cascaded over its curved hood like a waterfall. The rear wheels were encased in fender skirts and the full metal body rested between the wheels rather than upon them. She was like no other car on the road. Rowland thought her a work of art.

"There is no exquisite beauty... without some strangeness in the proportion." Milton Isaacs nudged Rowland companionably.

Rowland smiled. "Poe," he said, acknowledging the author whom Milton had clearly no intention of crediting. Some years before, Milton Isaacs had been introduced to Rowland as a poet, a title he embraced in every way but by actually writing verse. Instead he maintained his erudite literary reputation by randomly quoting the work of the great romantic bards without the tedious formality of attribution.

"She'd cost a small fortune, I expect," Clyde said half-heartedly. What did small fortunes matter to a man who had such a large one? The Sinclairs' holdings had begun as pastoral enterprises but under the astute control of Rowland's elder brother they had become an empire that seemed to Clyde to know no bounds.

"Johnston's getting old," Rowland replied.

Clyde nodded. Johnston, Rowland's chauffeur, had begun in the service of the Sinclairs in the days of horse and carriage. He had come with *Woodlands House*, the Sinclairs' grand home in exclusive Woollahra of which Rowland was now master. Use of the Rolls Royce which also came with *Woodlands* necessitated the use of Johnston, who took any attempt to use the vehicle without him very personally. It was the nature of Rowland Sinclair that he would buy a new motorcar rather than risk offending his chauffeur.

"Are you going to buy her then, Rowly?"

"Yes. Actually, I already have. I thought we could drive her back up to Sydney."

"Well that's cause for celebration. Good show, comrade!" Milton responded as though Rowland was a new father, clapping his shoulder and shaking his hand in congratulations. "This calls for a drink. Bloody oath, won't Ed be surprised when we pick her up in that jalopy?"

"If she even notices," Rowland said, laughing. Edna was determinedly disinterested in automobiles. Particularly since his accident. They were to meet her train in Albury early the following day then travel together to a house party at the Yackandandah abode of a fellow artist.

"Mr. Sinclair, sir! I trust you're enjoying the show." The gentleman who approached was almost as tall as Rowland. Sporting a luxuriant waxed moustache and top hat, he looked rather like a ringmaster.

Rowland shook his hand. "I am indeed, Mr. Carter." He introduced his companions to the automobile dealer. "I was just informing Mr. Isaacs and Mr. Watson Jones that we will be driving the Airflow back to Sydney."

Carter addressed Milton and Clyde. "Your friend is a man of singular good taste, gentlemen. There are few men in this room who are worthy of a vehicle as fine and progressive as the Chrysler Airflow."

"I don't know, old boy…" Milton airily adopted what he called the inflection of the capitalist establishment. "I rather liked the look of the Rolls Royce, myself. Mother would approve, I think. Tell me, my good man, has the one on display been spoken for yet?"

Clyde groaned audibly but Carter was already baited. "Not at all, Mr. Isaacs. I had no idea you were looking to… Why don't I personally show you the motorcar? It would be a truly excellent and discerning choice, I assure you."

Clyde and Rowland watched as Carter escorted Milton towards the Rolls Royce display.

"Poor bloke's salivating," Clyde observed. "Perhaps we should tell him."

Though he so easily adopted the airs and graces of a well-heeled aristocrat, Milton was as penniless as Clyde, a status only belied by their association with Rowland Sinclair, who kept his friends in the same manner to which he was accustomed.

"I wouldn't worry about Carter," Rowland replied. "He's already made at least one very healthy commission today."

"Then perhaps we should leave him to it and go find that drink Milt suggested."

"Capital idea."

The Mitre in Bank Place was a comfortable stroll from the Royal Exhibition Building in which the International Motor Show was being held. En route Rowland and Clyde discussed the engine specifications, shock absorbers and capacity of the Chrysler Airflow. Clyde muttered about oil and valves and pressure. Rowland's Mercedes had not often been welcome in the mechanics' garages of post-war Sydney, and so Clyde had taken to servicing and repairing her himself. At first by necessity, and then because he'd come to see it as one small way in which he could repay his friend's generosity in all things. Naturally he assumed the maintenance of the new Airflow would also fall to him.

Rowland had never expected anything from the beneficiaries of his largesse beyond their company, but it was easier to allow Clyde to tinker with his car if that was what he needed to do.

They found a table by the window of the small gothic drinking house and Rowland signalled the publican. Having already patronised the tavern a number of times in the week they'd been in Melbourne, they were welcomed with the kind of friendly presumption reserved for locals—a pint of beer and a tall glass of gin and tonic duly placed before them. Rowland and Clyde were still removing their coats when they were joined by a contingent of the many artists who frequented the Mitre. The conversation turned to painting—a robust discussion of technique and motif.

Justus Jörgensen sat at their table and invited them once again to join his scheme to found an artistic community. Rowland had known the Victorian artist for years and painted with him on occasion. Earlier that week, he had taken Rowland out to view the acreage he'd purchased in Eltham, outlining his plans for a grand hall constructed of mud brick and stone to be built by his students and fellow artists. Rowland liked Jörgensen but he thought him a little mad.

"Creative communities inspire creative lives, gentlemen." Jörgensen pounded the table, making the glasses jump. Rowland's hand shot out to save his gin. "We will build a lifestyle surrounded by art, break bread each day with men and women who are like us in passion and vision, unfettered by the constraints of middle-class monogamy and social convention."

Clyde laughed. Their lives at *Woodlands* were not far removed from the utopia Jörgensen envisaged. Over the years many artists, writers and actors had lived for a time in the Woollahra mansion. Three had never moved out.

"We're not bricklayers, Jorgie." Rowland downed his drink before the artist decided to pound the table again.

But Jörgensen would not have it. "Affluence stagnates the creative spirit." He pointed at Clyde. "You cannot compare a community of artists, working for a common good with Rowland's domestic arrangements. Middle-class comfort makes for fat commercial artists whose creative life is dictated by the profit-driven, critic-enslaved demands of exhibitionism!"

"Just who are you calling fat?" Clyde demanded.

"You! You are fat! Fat and complacent!"

And so the debate warmed. Jörgensen waxed lyrical and loud, Clyde stood his ground. After all, he exhibited, so did Rowland. The publican, and a number of other patrons at varying degrees of sobriety contributed from time to time, but Rowland refused to be drawn. He liked Justus Jörgensen but the man seemed to take his daily exercise by shouting, and Rowland had learned long ago that anything remotely resembling a defence of the wealth for which he'd done nothing beyond being born, was a fool's errand. Instead, he extracted a notebook from his breast pocket and sketched the battle in the tavern—capturing the movement and urgency of men at philosophical combat, in what he considered a more worthwhile use of the time.

The afternoon was passed, not unpleasantly, in this way. It was dark when Milton Isaacs walked into the fray.

"What are they arguing about?" he asked Rowland, glancing towards Clyde and Jörgensen.

"I'm not sure anymore," Rowland replied.

"Look, Rowly, I just ran into a comrade from Melbourne. There's a meeting tomorrow which I think we should attend."

"We?" While he moved with Communists, Rowland was not a member of the faithful. Milton knew that.

"It's not a Party meeting, old mate. MAWF is gathering to discuss Egon's visit. They have a problem I reckon you could help with. I think we should go."

Rowland frowned. The World Movement Against War and Fascism, while having a natural affinity with the Communist cause, did not belong to the Party. Rowland's experience of German Fascism had seen him join the Australian branch of MAWF, though to date his support had been purely financial. He expected the problem Milton mentioned was also financial in nature. MAWF had invited Egon Kisch—a journalist and speaker of international renown—to speak at its National Congress against War and Fascism in Melbourne.

Rowland knew Kisch personally, indeed, he owed the activist a great debt, and he looked forward to seeing him again.

"Ed's train gets in early tomorrow morning." Rowland glanced at his watch. "She's probably already left for Central."

"We could send word to the station master… let Ed know to take a room at the Albury Terminus and wait for us. She won't mind… she can go to the cinema or shop for a new hat or something."

"Or something, more likely," Rowland said ruefully.

"I really think we should be at this meeting."

Rowland nodded slowly. He trusted Milton's instincts on matters such as this. Though Rowland Sinclair was not a Communist, he and the poet had, at heart, always been on the same side.

"Ed will understand," Milton prodded further.

"Of course. I'll book a call through to the Albury station tonight."

2

WAR AND FASCISM

HENRI BARBUSSE SUMS UP
(TO THE EDITOR)

Sir,— While all capitalist countries are in one stage or another
of fascisation; in the process of being led, or of having been led,
back to the barbarism of middle ages; while ideas and schemes
of a fascist character are being flaunted abroad as Socialistic,
e.g., the Roosevelt plan, claimed by the N.S.W. Labor Party
Leadership as being synonymous with the 'Lang Plan'—as a
'socialistic road to prosperity'; while the fascist flame spreads
in Australia with the proposed Disloyalty Bill, and a great class
conscious movement gathers its forces in active opposition,
your readers will be interested in the following from the pen of
Henri Barbusse, eminent French writer, and noted leader of the
world-wide movement against war.

"It is desirable that we draw up a balance sheet for 1933.
Those who have been labouring under illusions, those who
have been hoping that things would improve, those who have
remained outside of our great world-wide movement, would do
well to pause before this balance, and—reflect. The ten months
of Hitler's rule has been sufficient to convince everybody of the
dangers that fascism brings in its train. His promises of better
conditions have proved false one after another. Only the terror
has proved real. In January, 1933, the eyes of the workers of the
whole world were turned upon events in Germany. Everywhere
the question was raised: Would the revolutionary unity
necessary to smash fascism be at last set up? Tens of thousands
of socialist and non-Party workers grouped themselves during
that month around the revolutionary front. But they weren't

> sufficient. To smash fascism more were necessary—the
> majority of the working class... We are headed again for a new
> world war..."
>
> *The Cessnock Eagle and*
> *South Maitland Recorder, 19 March 1934*

The offices of MAWF were conveniently located on Bourke Street near Unity Hall which housed the offices of the Australian Railways Union, the Tramways Union and the Storemen and Packers Union. The premises were utilitarian: the furniture patched and hodgepodge—possibly scrounged from the homes of members. The space was cluttered with boxes and stacks of propaganda leaflets and paraphernalia. There were three desks, two with typewriters and what looked like an old rotary stencil duplicator. The bright colours of the political posters which adorned the walls were muted by what seemed to be a permanent haze of pipe and cigarette smoke. In one section of the office was a large wooden table which bore a history of past campaigns in smears of paint and ink. About this were gathered some of the nation's most eminent writers, poets and journalists—the newly convened Kisch Reception Committee.

Milton facilitated the necessary introductions. Arthur Howells insisted they call him "Bluey" and explained that he, as a member of the MAWF executive, had been tasked with organising the Reception Committee. Among the gathering's intellectual luminaries were novelist Vance Palmer and his wife Nettie, an established literary critic of considerable influence; the internationally lauded writer Katharine Prichard who it seemed had travelled from her home in Western Australia to be present; journalists Gavin Greenlees, Edgar Holt and John Fisher, son of Australia's fifth prime minister; Percy Beckett and Antonio Falcioni who called themselves philosophers; and the artist Max Meldrum whom Rowland had met before.

In this assembly Rowland began to feel a little out of place. Clearly the intention was to receive Egon Kisch with a dazzling show of literary and artistic distinction. While the name of Rowland Sinclair was not entirely obscure, it was more commonly associated with scandal than anything else.

Milton did not seem burdened with any such awkwardness, but perhaps that in itself was the secret to being a poet without ever writing a line of original verse. He chatted easily to Katharine Prichard about socialist realism in literature and advised Vance Palmer on iambic pentameter.

Arthur Howells called the meeting to order, announcing somewhat unnecessarily that Egon Kisch had accepted an invitation to be the keynote speaker at the inaugural National Congress against War and Fascism. There was applause—heartfelt—and excitement.

For some time the discussion focused on how Egon Kisch would be publicised and promoted. John Fisher, who was currently on the staff of the *Melbourne Herald*, was given primary responsibility for press coverage. He accepted the role enthusiastically, vowing to pull whatever journalistic strings were necessary to ensure the Kisch campaign was afforded adequate publicity.

They spoke also of how Kisch would be entertained while he was in the country, to whom he would be introduced, at which venues he would speak and what sights he would be shown.

Through all of this Rowland said very little. He knew nothing about promotion and he didn't really feel in a position to suggest how best to occupy the great man. In fact, he was beginning to wonder why Milton had insisted they attend the meeting. Rowland would happily have written a cheque for the cause without being privy to the deliberations.

It was only after these other matters had been thoroughly discussed that Arthur Howells raised a logistical problem. It appeared that Kisch's ship would not reach port in Melbourne until the twelfth of November, thereby missing the National Congress. "As you can imagine, having the keynote speaker arrive after the congress is something of a difficulty."

Many voices concurred that it was indeed a difficulty.

"We'll simply have to change the date of the congress," Katharine Prichard declared.

"And lose the impact of Armistice Day?" Fisher groaned.

"When does the ship actually reach Fremantle?" Vance Palmer asked.

Howells nodded. He was thinking along similar lines. "If Mr. Kisch disembarks at Fremantle and catches a train, we could get him here on time. It'll be a close-run thing, but possible."

Milton leant over to Rowland and whispered, "Rowly, what if—"

Rowland was ahead of him. "I could fly him," he said.

"Fly him? Whatever do you mean, Comrade Sinclair?" Katharine Prichard spoke over the murmur of voices.

"In an aeroplane. I could fly across to Fremantle, meet his ship, and fly him directly to Melbourne."

"May I enquire what manner of aeroplane you own, Mr. Sinclair?" Nettie Palmer said.

Rowland laughed. "My plane's a Gipsy Moth. But I don't propose to use her—she wouldn't be much faster than the train."

"Then what do you propose, Mr. Sinclair?"

"A twin-engine craft. It won't be as comfortable as the liner but it will be a jolly sight quicker."

"And you have such a craft?"

"I'll get one."

"An aeroplane… we can't expect a man like Egon Kisch to come to Melbourne in an aeroplane!"

"I'm sure he'd prefer it to not arriving in time," Fisher mused. "Under the circumstances, we can't risk him missing the congress. It might also circumvent any visa issues."

"Yes, of course!" Katharine Prichard leant forward enthusiastically. "Collecting Egon from Fremantle will mean he's in the country before the government has a chance to ban him. They'll think they have till he arrives in Melbourne to trump up some charge."

"It's too dangerous," Palmer persisted.

"Rowly was taught to fly by Kingsford Smith," Milton offered by way of assurance. "Egon will be in good hands."

Both Vance and Nettie Palmer raised a number of further objections which were countered at first by Katharine Prichard and then Fisher. Howells joined the case for flying Kisch from Fremantle and, eventually, Rowland Sinclair's offer was accepted.

"Success depends on utmost secrecy," Katharine warned. "No one must suspect Herr Kisch will disembark in Fremantle."

A general murmur of agreement served as a pledge of silence on the matter.

The meeting adjourned to the Swanston Family Hotel where they spent the evening in increasingly high spirits. There was a definite air of celebration—it was an optimistic party. After months of trying to make his countrymen understand the threat of German Fascism, Rowland was hopeful that Egon Kisch would meet with greater success.

Clyde joined them after having spent the afternoon checking over Rowland's new car for himself. His eyes were bright as he described the automobile's performance and for a time he and Rowland were immersed in praise of the Airflow.

"She's built like a battleship, Rowly... an elegant battleship," Clyde said. "I know you miss the Mercedes, mate, but she's a worthy replacement."

"I'm looking forward to seeing what she can do," Rowland admitted.

"We'll have to do that before we pick up Ed," Milton warned. "Ever since the accident she wants you to drive like you're bringing up the rear of an ANZAC parade!"

Rowland grimaced. Edna had become irrationally nervous about his ability to keep a car on the road. In fact, he'd purchased the Airflow with that in mind. He hoped the motorcar's radical safety features—the all-metal body, the shatter-proof windscreens—would allay her fears to some extent.

They drank with the Kisch Reception Committee until the early hours of the next morning before finally taking their leave. The short walk in the bracing cold to their accommodation had a conveniently sobering effect, though it was hardly long enough to mitigate the effects of the evening entirely. Perhaps for this reason Rowland did not wonder overmuch about the message, awaiting him at the reception desk, that a Detective Delaney from the Sydney Criminal Investigation Bureau had telephoned.

Have you downloaded

The Prodigal Son?

A novella written as a gift for fans of the
Rowland Sinclair Mysteries.

The free e-book is available for download from
www.RowlandSinclairNovella.com

Sulari Gentill

Award-winning author Sulari Gentill set out to study astrophysics, ended up graduating in law, and later abandoned her legal career to write books instead of contracts. When the mood takes her, she paints, although she maintains that she does so only well enough to know that she should write.

She grows French black truffles on a farm in the foothills of the Snowy Mountains of NSW, which she shares with her young family and several animals.

Sulari is the author of the award-winning Rowland Sinclair Mysteries, a series of historical crime novels set in the 1930s about Rowland Sinclair, the gentleman artist-cum-amateur detective.

The first in the series, *A Few Right Thinking Men*, was shortlisted for the Commonwealth Writers' Prize for Best First Book. *A Decline in Prophets*, the second in the series, won the Davitt Award for Best Adult Crime Fiction. *Miles Off Course* was released in early 2012, *Paving the New Road* was released later that year and was shortlisted for the Davitt Award for Best Crime Fiction 2013. *Gentlemen Formerly Dressed* was released in November 2013. The sixth book in the series, *A Murder Unmentioned*, was Highly Commended for the Davitt Award for Best Adult Crime Fiction 2015, and was shortlisted for the ABIA Small Publisher Adult Book of the Year 2015, and the Ned Kelly Award 2015. *A Murder Unmentioned* also received the 2015 APPA Platinum Award for Excellence. *Give the Devil His Due*, the seventh book in the series, was also shortlisted for the Davitt Award for Best Adult Crime Fiction and the ABIA Small Publisher Adult Book of the Year 2016. In November 2016 Sulari released the novella, *The Prodigal Son*, a free prequel to the series written as a gift for her Rowland Sinclair fans. The latest book in the series, *A Dangerous Language* is the eighth novel in the series.

Under the name S.D. Gentill, Sulari also writes fantasy adventure, including The Hero Trilogy. All three books in the trilogy, *Chasing Odysseus*, *Trying War* and *The Blood of Wolves*, are out now, and available in paperback, in a trilogy pack, and eBook. *Crossing the Lines* is Sulari's first stand-alone novel, and will be released internationally in August 2017.